THE TURN OF THE KEY

ALSO BY RUTH WARE

In a Dark, Dark Wood
The Woman in Cabin 10
The Lying Game
The Death of Mrs Westaway

THE TURN OF THE KEY

RUTH WARE

Harvill *Secker*

LONDON

1 3 5 7 9 10 8 6 4 2

Harvill Secker, an imprint of Vintage,
20 Vauxhall Bridge Road,
London SW1V 2SA

Harvill Secker is part of the Penguin Random House group of companies
whose addresses can be found at global.penguinrandomhouse.com

Penguin
Random House
UK

First published by Harvill Secker in 2019

A CIP catalogue record for this book is available from the British Library

penguin.co.uk/vintage

ISBN 9781787300439 (hardback)
ISBN 9781787300446 (trade paperback)

Typeset in 10.75/15.75 pt Scala Pro
by Integra Software Services Pvt. Ltd, Pondicherry

Printed and bound in Great Britain by Clays Ltd, Elcograf S.p.A.

Penguin Random House is committed to a sustainable future for
our business, our readers and our planet. This book is made from
Forest Stewardship Council® certified paper.

For Ian, with more love than I know how to put into words.

THE TURN OF THE KEY

3 September 2017

Dear Mr Wrexham,

I know you don't know me but please, please, please you have
to help me

3 September 2017
HMP Charnworth

Dear Mr Wrexham,

You don't know me, but you may have seen coverage of my case in the newspapers. The reason I am writing to you is to ask you please

4 September 2017
HMP Charnworth

Dear Mr Wrexham,

I hope that's the right way to address you. I have never written
to a barrister before.

The first thing I have to say is that I know this is unconventional. I know I should have gone via my solicitor, but he's

5 September 2017

Dear Mr Wrexham,

Are you a father? An uncle? If so, let me appeal

Dear Mr Wrexham,

Please help me. I *didn't* kill anyone.

7 September 2017
HMP Charnworth

Dear Mr Wrexham,

You have no idea how many times I've started this letter and
screwed up the resulting mess, but I've realised there is no
magic formula here. There is no way I can MAKE you listen to
my case. So I'm just going to have to do my best to set things
out. However long it takes, however much I mess this up, I'm
just going to keep going, and tell the truth.

My name is … And here I stop, wanting to tear up the page
again.

Because if I tell you my name, you will know why I am writing
to you. My case has been all over the papers, my name in every
headline, my agonised face staring out of every front page – and
every single article insinuating my guilt in a way that falls only
just short of contempt of court. If I tell you my name, I have
a horrible feeling you might write me off as a lost cause, and
throw my letter away. I wouldn't entirely blame you, but please
– before you do that, hear me out.

I am a young woman, twenty-seven years old, and as you'll
have seen from the return address above, I am currently at the
Scottish women's prison HMP Charnworth. I've never received

a letter from anyone in prison, so I don't know what they look like when they come through the door, but I imagine my current living arrangements were pretty obvious even before you opened the envelope.

What you probably don't know is that I'm on remand.

And what you cannot know is that I'm innocent.

I know, I know. They all say that. Every single person I've met here is innocent – according to them, anyway. But in my case it's true.

You may have guessed what's coming next. I'm writing to ask you to represent me as my solicitor advocate at my trial.

I realise that this is unconventional, and not how defendants are supposed to approach advocates. (I accidentally called you a barrister in an earlier draft of this letter – I know nothing about the law, and even less about the Scottish system. Everything I do know I have picked up from the women I'm in prison with, including your name.)

I have a solicitor already – Mr Gates – and from what I understand, he is the person who should be appointing an advocate for the actual trial. But he is also the person who landed me here in the first place. I didn't choose him – the police picked him for me when I began to get scared and finally had the sense to shut up and refuse to answer questions until they found me a lawyer.

I thought that he would straighten everything out – help me to make my case. But when he arrived – I don't know, I can't explain it. He just made everything worse. He didn't let me *speak*. Everything I tried to say he was cutting in with 'my client has no comment at this time' and it just made me look so much more guilty. I feel like if only I could have explained properly, it would never have got this far. But somehow the facts kept twisting in my mouth, and the police, they made everything sound so bad, so incriminating.

It's not that Mr Gates hasn't heard my side of the story, exactly. He has of course – but somehow – oh God, this is so hard to explain in writing. He's sat down and talked to me but he doesn't *listen*. Or if he does, he doesn't believe me. Every time I try to tell him what happened, starting from the beginning, he cuts in with these questions that muddle me up and my story gets all tangled and I want to scream at him to just *shut the fuck up*.

And he keeps talking to me about what I said in the transcripts from that awful first night at the police station when they grilled me and grilled me and I said – God, I don't know what I said. I'm sorry, I'm crying now. I'm sorry – I'm so sorry for the stains on the paper. I hope you can read my writing through the blotches.

What I said, what I said then, there's no undoing that. I know that. They have all that on tape. And it's bad – it's really bad. But it came out wrong, I feel like if only I could be given a chance to get my case across, to someone who would really listen ... do you see what I'm saying?

Oh God, maybe you don't. You've never been here after all. You've never sat across a desk feeling so exhausted you want to drop and so scared you want to vomit, with the police asking and asking and asking until you don't know what you're saying any more.

I guess it comes down to this in the end.

I am the nanny in the Elincourt case, Mr Wrexham.

And I *didn't* kill that child.

I started writing to you last night, Mr Wrexham, and when I woke up this morning and looked at the crumpled pages covered with my pleading scrawl, my first instinct was to rip them up and start again just like I had a dozen times before. I had meant to be so cool, so calm and collected – I had meant to set everything out so clearly and *make* you see. And instead I ended up crying onto the page in a mess of recrimination.

But then I reread what I'd written and I thought, no. I can't start again. I just have to keep going.

All this time I have been telling myself that if only someone would let me clear my head and get my side of the story straight, without interrupting, maybe this whole awful mess would get sorted out.

And here I am. This is my chance, right?

140 days they can hold you in Scotland before a trial. Though there's a woman here who has been waiting almost ten months. Ten months! Do you know how long that is, Mr Wrexham? You probably think you do, but let me tell you. In her case that's 297 days. She's missed Christmas with her kids. She's missed all their birthdays. She's missed Mother's Day and Easter and first days at school.

297 days. And they still keep pushing back the date of her trial.

Mr Gates says he doesn't think mine will take that long because of all the publicity, but I don't see how he can be sure.

Either way, 100 days, 140 days, 297 days … that's a lot of writing time, Mr Wrexham. A lot of time to think, and remember, and try to work out what really happened. Because there's so much I don't understand, but there's one thing I know. I did not kill that little girl. I *didn't*. However hard the police try to twist the facts and trip me up, they can't change that.

I didn't kill her. Which means someone else did. And they are out there.

While I am in here, rotting.

I will finish now, because I know I can't make this letter too long – you're a busy man, you'll just stop reading.

But please, you have to believe me. You're the only person who can help.

Please, come and see me, Mr Wrexham. Let me explain the situation to you, and how I got tangled into this nightmare. If anyone can make the jury understand, it's you.

I have put your name down for a visitor's pass – or you can write to me here if you have more questions. It's not like I'm going anywhere. Ha.

Sorry, I didn't mean to end on a joke. It's not a laughing matter, I know that. If I'm convicted, I'm facing –

But no. I can't think about that. Not right now. I won't be. I won't be convicted because I'm innocent. I just have to make everyone understand that. Starting with you.

Please, Mr Wrexham, please say you'll help. Please write back. I don't want to be melodramatic about this but I feel like you're my only hope.

Mr Gates doesn't believe me, I see it in his eyes.

But I think that you might.

12 September 2017
HMP Charnworth

Dear Mr Wrexham,

It's been three days since I wrote to you, and I'm not going to lie, I've been waiting for a reply with my heart in my mouth. Every day the post comes round and I feel my pulse speed up, with a kind of painful hope, and every day (so far) you've let me down.

I'm sorry. That sounds like emotional blackmail. I don't mean it like that. I get it. You're a busy man, and it's only three days since I sent my letter but ... I guess I half hoped that if the publicity surrounding the case had done nothing else, it would have given me a certain twisted celebrity – made you pick out my letter from among all the others you presumably get from clients and would-be clients and nutters.

Don't you want to know what happened, Mr Wrexham? I would.

Anyway, it's three days now (did I mention that already?) and ... well, I'm beginning to worry. There's not much to do in here, and there's a lot of time to think and fret and start to build up catastrophes inside your head.

I've spent the last few days and nights doing that. Worrying that you didn't get the letter. Worrying that the prison authorities didn't pass it on (can they do that without telling me? I honestly don't know). Worrying that I didn't *explain* right.

It's the last one that has been keeping me awake. Because if it's that, then it's my fault.

I was trying to keep it short and snappy, but now I'm thinking, I shouldn't have stopped so quickly. I should have put in more of the facts, tried to show you WHY I'm innocent. Because you can't just take my word for it – I get that.

When I came here the other women – I can be honest with you, Mr Wrexham – they felt like another species. It's not that I think I'm better than them. But they all seemed ... they all seemed to fit in here. Even the frightened ones, the self-harmers and the ones who screamed and banged their heads against their cell walls and cried at night, even the girls barely out of school. They looked ... I don't know. They looked like they belonged here, with their pale, gaunt faces and their pulled-back hair and their blurred tattoos. They looked ... well, they looked *guilty*.

But I was different.

I'm English for a start, of course, which didn't help. I couldn't understand them when they got angry and started shouting and all up in my face. I had no idea what half the slang meant. And I was visibly middle class, in a way that I can't put my finger on, but which might as well have been written across my forehead as far as the other women were concerned.

But the main thing was, I had never been in prison. I don't think I'd ever even met someone who had, before I came here. There were secret codes I couldn't decipher, and currents I had no way of navigating. I didn't understand what was going on when one woman passed something to another in the corridor and all of a sudden the wardens came barrelling out shouting. I didn't see the fights coming, I didn't know who was off her meds, or who was coming down from a high and might lash out. I didn't know the ones to avoid or the ones with permanent PMT. I didn't know what to wear or what to do, or what would get you spat on or punched by the other inmates, or provoke the wardens to come down hard on you.

I sounded different. I looked different. I *felt* different.

And then one day I went into the bathroom and I caught a glimpse of a woman walking towards me from the far corner. She had her hair scraped back like all the others, her eyes were like chips of granite, and her face was set, hard and white. My first thought was, oh God, she looks pissed off, I wonder what she's in for.

My second thought was, maybe I'd better use the other bathroom.

And then I realised.

It was a mirror on the far wall. The woman was me.

It should have been a shock – the realisation that I wasn't different at all, but just another woman sucked into this soulless system. But in a strange way it helped.

I still don't fit in completely. I'm still the English girl – and they all know what I'm in for. In prison, they don't like people who harm children, you probably know that. I've told them it's not true of course – what I'm accused of. But they look at me and I know what they're thinking – *they all say that*.

And I know – I know that's what you'll be thinking too. That's what I wanted to say. I understand if you're sceptical. I didn't manage to convince the police, after all. I'm here. Without bail. I must be guilty.

But it's not true.

I have 140 days to convince you. All I have to do is tell the truth, right? I just have to start at the beginning, and set it all out, clearly and calmly, until I get to the end.

And the beginning was the advert.

WANTED: Large family seeks experienced live-in nanny

ABOUT US: We are a busy family of four children, living in a beautiful (but remote!) house in the Highlands. Mum and Dad co-run the family architecture practice.

ABOUT YOU: We are seeking an experienced nanny, used to working with children of all ages, from babyhood to teens. You must be practical, unflappable, and comfortable looking after children on your own. Excellent references, DBS check, first-aid certificate and clean driving licence are a must.

ABOUT THE POST: Mum and Dad work mainly from home and during those periods you will have a simple 8–5 post, with one night a week babysitting, and weekends off. As far as possible we arrange our schedule so that one parent is always around. However, there are times when we may both need to be away (very occasionally for up to a fortnight), and when this occurs, you will be *in loco parentis*.

In return we can offer a highly competitive remuneration package totalling £55,000 per annum (gross, including bonus), use of a car, and eight weeks' holiday a year.

Applications to Sandra and Bill Elincourt, Heatherbrae House, Carn Bridge.

I remember it nearly word for word. The funny thing was, I wasn't even looking for a job when it came up on my Google results – I was searching for ... well, it doesn't really matter what I was looking for. But something completely different. And then there it was – like a gift thrown into my hands so unexpectedly I almost didn't catch it.

I read it through once, and then again, my heart beating faster the second time, because it was *perfect*. It was almost too perfect.

When I read it a third time I was scared to look at the closing date for applications – convinced I would have missed it.

But it was that very evening.

It was unbelievable. Not just the salary – though God knows, that was a pretty startling sum. Not just the post. But the luck of it. The whole package – just falling in my lap, right when I was in the perfect position to apply.

You see, my flatmate was away, travelling. We'd met at the Little Nippers nursery in Peckham, working side by side in the baby room, laughing about our terrible boss and the pushy, faddy parents, with their fucking fabric nappies and their home-made –

Sorry. I shouldn't have sworn. I've scribbled it out but you can probably see the word through the paper and, God knows, maybe you've got kids, maybe you even put them in Little Plushy Bottoms or whatever the fashionable brand was at the time.

And I get it, I do. They're your babies. Nothing is too much trouble. I understand that. It's just that when you're the one having to stockpile a whole day's worth of pissy, shitty bits of cloth and hand them back to the parent at collection time with your eyes watering from the ammonia ... it's not that I *mind* exactly, you know? It's part of the job. I get that. But we all deserve a moan, don't we? We all need to let off steam, or we'd explode with frustration.

Sorry. I'm rambling. Maybe this is why Mr Gates is always trying to shut me up. Because I dig myself a hole with my words, and instead of knowing when to stop, I keep digging. You're probably adding two and two together right now. *Doesn't seem to like kids much. Freely admits to frustration with role. What would happen when she was cooped up with four kids and no adults to 'let off steam' with?*

That's exactly what the police did. All those little throwaway remarks – all those unedifying facts. I could see the triumph on their faces every time I dropped one, and I watched them picking them up like breadcrumbs, adding them to the weight of arguments against me.

But that's the thing, Mr Wrexham. I could spin you a web of bullshit about what a perfect, caring, saintly person I am – but it would be just that. Bullshit. And I am not here to bullshit you. I want you to believe that – I want it more than anything in the world.

I am telling you the *truth*. The unvarnished, ugly truth. And it is all that. It *is* unpolished and unpleasant and I don't pretend I acted like an angel. But *I didn't kill anyone*. I just fucking didn't.

I'm sorry. I didn't mean to swear again.

God, I am messing this up so badly. I have to keep a clear head – get this all straight in my head. It's like Mr Gates says – I should stick to the facts.

OK then. Fact. The advert. The advert is a fact, right?

The advert ... with its amazing, dizzying, fabulous salary.

That should have been my first warning signal, you know. The salary. Because it was *stupidly* generous. I mean it would have been generous even for London, even for a live-out nanny. But for a nanny in someone's house, with free accommodation provided, and all bills paid, even down to the car, it was ridiculous.

It was so ridiculous in fact that I half wondered if there had been a typo. Or something that they weren't saying – a child with significant behavioural needs maybe? But wouldn't they have mentioned that in the ad?

Six months ago, I probably would have paused, frowned a little, and then passed on without thinking too much more about it. But then, six months ago I wouldn't have been looking at that web page in the first place. Six months ago I had a flatmate and a job I liked, and even the prospect of promotion. Six months ago I was in a pretty good place. But now ... well, things were a bit different now.

My friend, the girl I mentioned at Little Nippers, had left to go travelling a couple of months ago. It hadn't seemed like the end of the world when she told me – to be honest, I found her quite annoying, her habit of loading the dishwasher but never actually switching it on, her endless Europop disco hits, hissing through my bedroom wall when I was trying to sleep. I mean, I knew I'd miss her, but I didn't realise how much.

She had left her stuff in her room and we'd agreed she'd pay half rent and I'd keep the room open for her. It seemed like a good compromise – I'd had a series of terrible flatmates before we found each other, and I wasn't keen to return to posting on Facebook Local and trying to weed out weirdos by text message and email, and it felt, in some small way, like an anchor – like a guarantee that she would come back.

But when the first flush of freedom wore off, and the novelty of having the whole place to myself and watching whatever I liked on the shared TV in the living room had started to fade a little, I found I was lonely. I missed the way she'd say 'wine o'clock, darling?' when we rolled in together from work. I missed sounding off to her about Val, the owner of Little Nippers, and sharing anecdotes about the worst of the parents. When I applied for a promotion and didn't get it, I went to the pub alone to drown my sorrows and ended up crying into my beer, thinking how different it would have been if she had still been here. We could have laughed about it together, she would have flicked Val the vees behind her back at work, and given her earthy belly laugh when Val turned round to almost catch her in the act.

I am not very good at failing, Mr Wrexham, that's the thing. Exams. Dating. Jobs. Any kind of test, really. My instinct is always to aim low, save myself some pain. Or, in the case of dating, just don't aim at all, rather than risk being rejected. It's why I didn't go to university in the end. I had the grades but I couldn't bear the idea of being turned down, the thought of them reading my application with a scornful snigger. 'Who does she think she is?'

Better to achieve perfect marks in an easy test than flunk a hard one, that was my motto. I've always known that about myself. But what I didn't know, until my flatmate left, was that I am also not very good at being alone. And I think it was that, more than anything, that pushed me out of my comfort zone, and made me scroll down that advert, holding my breath, imagining what lay at the other end of it.

The police made a lot out of the salary, when they first questioned me. But the truth is, the money wasn't the reason I applied for the post. It wasn't even really about my flatmate, though I can't deny, if she hadn't left, none of it would have happened. No, the real reason ... well, you probably know what the real reason was. It was all over the papers, after all.

I called in sick to Little Nippers and spent the entire day working on a CV and getting together everything that I knew I would need to convince the Elincourts that I was the person they were looking for. DBS – check. First-aid certificate – check. Spotless references – check, check and check.

The only problem was the driving licence. But I pushed the issue aside for the moment. I could cross that bridge when I came to it – if I got that far. Right now, I wasn't thinking past the interview.

I added a note to the covering letter asking the Elincourts not to contact Little Nippers for a reference – I told them that I didn't want my current employers knowing that I was casting about for another job, which was true – and then I emailed it off to the address provided and held my breath and waited.

I had given myself the best possible chance of meeting them face-to-face. There was nothing else I could do now.

Those next few days were hard, Mr Wrexham. Not as hard as the time I've spent in here, but hard enough. Because God, I wanted that interview *so much*. I was only just beginning to realise how much. With every day that passed my hopes ebbed a little more, and I had to fight off the urge to contact them again and beg for an answer. The only thing that stopped me was the knowledge that looking so desperate would certainly not help my case if they were still deciding.

But six days later it came, pinging into my email inbox.

To: supernanny1990@ymail.com
From: sandra.elincourt@elincourtandelincourt.com
Subject: Nanny position

Elincourt. The surname alone was enough to make my stomach start churning like a washing machine. My fingers were shaking almost too much to open it, and my heart was hammering in my throat. Surely, surely they didn't often contact unsuccessful applicants. Surely an email must mean …?

I clicked.

Hi Rowan!

Thank you so much for your application, and apologies for taking so long to get back to you. I have to admit, we were slightly taken by surprise at the volume of applications. Your CV was very impressive, and we would like to invite you to interview. Our house is rather remote, so we are happy to pay your train fare, and can offer you a room in our house overnight, as you will not be able to make the trip from London in one day.

However, there is one thing I must make you aware of up front, in case it affects your enthusiasm for the post.

Since we bought Heatherbrae, we have become aware of various superstitions surrounding the house's history. It is an old building, and has had no more than the usual number of deaths and tragedies in its past, but for some reason these have resulted in some local tales of hauntings etc. Unfortunately, this fact has upset some of our recent nannies, to the extent that four have resigned in the past 14 months.

As you can imagine this has been very disruptive for the children, not to mention extremely awkward for myself and my husband professionally.

For that reason we wanted to be completely honest about our predicament, and we are offering a generous salary in the hopes of attracting someone who can really commit to staying with our family for the long term – at least a year.

If you do not feel that is you, or if you feel at all concerned about the history of the house, please say so now as we are very keen to minimise further disruption to the children. With that in mind, the salary will be made up of a basic stipend, paid monthly, and then a generous year-end bonus on the anniversary of employment.

If you are still keen to attend interview, please let me know your availability for the forthcoming week.

Best wishes, and I look forward to meeting you,
Sandra Elincourt

I closed down the email and for a moment just sat there staring at the screen. Then I got up and did a little silent scream, punching the air in jubilation.

I had done it. I had *done* it.

I should have known it was too good to be true.

I had done it, Mr Wrexham. I had cleared the first hurdle. But it *was* only the first hurdle. I had to get through the interview next – and without slipping up.

Almost exactly one week after I had opened the email from Sandra Elincourt, I was on a train up to Scotland, doing my very best impression of Rowan the Perfect Nanny. My normally bushy hair was brushed to a shine and tamed into a neat, jaunty pony-tail, my nails were buffed and my make-up unobtrusively on point, and I was wearing my best 'approachable yet responsible, fun yet hard-working, professional yet not too proud to get down on my knees and clear up sick' outfit – a neat tweed skirt and a white cotton fitted shirt with a cashmere cardigan over the top. Not quite Norland Nanny, but definitely a nod in that direction.

My stomach was flipping with butterflies. I had never done anything like this before. Not the nannying, I mean. Obviously. I had done that for nearly ten years, though mostly in nurseries, rather than private homes.

But … *this*. Putting myself on the line. Setting myself up for rejection like this.

I wanted this *so* much. So much that I was almost scared of what I was going to find.

Much to my annoyance, the train was delayed, so that it took nearly six hours to get to Edinburgh instead of the timetabled four and a half, and when I got off the train at Waverley, stiffly flexing my legs, I found it was gone five o'clock, and I had missed my connection by a good hour. Fortunately there was another train due, and while I waited, I texted Mrs Elincourt, apologising profusely, and warning her that I would be late into Carn Bridge.

At last the train arrived – much smaller than the big Intercity, and older too. I settled myself in a window seat, and as the train headed north, I watched the countryside change from rolling green fields to the smoke-blue and purples of heathered moors, mountains rising behind, darker and bleaker with every station we passed. It was so beautiful it made me forget my irritation at being late. The sight of the huge hills rising inexorably around us somehow put everything else into perspective. I felt the hard lump of trepidation lodged in my gut start to soften. And something inside me began … I don't know, Mr Wrexham. It was like I began to *hope*. To hope that this could truly be real.

I felt, in some twisted kind of way, like I was coming home.

We passed through stations with half-familiar names, Perth, Pitlochry, Aviemore, the sky growing darker all the time. At last I heard 'Carn Bridge, next stop Carn Bridge' and the train pulled into a little Victorian station and I got out. I stood on the platform, jumpy with nerves, wondering what to do.

Someone will meet you, Mrs Elincourt's email had said. What did that mean? A taxi? Someone holding up a sign with my name?

I followed the small straggle of travellers to the exit and stood, awkwardly, while the other passengers dispersed to cars and waiting friends and relatives. My case was heavy, and I set it down by my feet as I looked up and down the dusky platform. The shadows were lengthening into evening, and the fleeting optimism I had felt on the train was starting to fade. What if Mrs Elincourt hadn't got my text? She hadn't replied. Perhaps a pre-booked taxi had come and gone hours ago, and I'd been marked up as a no-show.

Suddenly the butterflies were back – and badly.

It was early June, but we were pretty far north, and the night air was surprisingly cold after the fuggy summer warmth of London. I found I was shivering as I pulled my coat around me, a cool wind whipping down from the hills. The platform had emptied, and I was all alone.

I felt a strong urge for a cigarette, but I knew from experience that turning up to an interview stinking of fags was not a great start. Instead, I looked at my phone. The train had arrived exactly on time – at least, exactly at the revised time I had told Mrs Elincourt in my text. I would give it five minutes, and then call her.

Five minutes passed, but I told myself I'd give it just five minutes more. I didn't want to start off on the wrong foot, badgering them if they were stuck in traffic.

Five more minutes ticked away, and I was just digging in my bag, looking for the printout of Mrs Elincourt's email, when I saw a man walking down the platform, hands in pockets.

For a moment something seemed to stutter in my chest, but then he got closer and looked up, his eyes meeting mine, and I realised, it couldn't possibly be *him*. He was much too young. Thirty, thirty-five at the outside. He was also – and even in my nervousness I couldn't help but clock it – extremely good-looking, in a scrubby unshaven kind of way, with tangled dark hair and a tall, lean frame.

He was wearing overalls and as he came up to me he took his hands out of his pockets, and I saw they were grained with something – soil, or engine oil, though he'd made an attempt to clean them. For a moment I thought perhaps he was an employee of the railway, but as he drew level with me he spoke.

'Rowan Caine?'

I nodded.

'I'm Jack Grant.' He grinned, his mouth curling disarmingly at the edges, as though appreciating a private joke. His accent was Scottish, but softer and more distinct than the Glaswegian girl I'd worked with after school. He pronounced his surname with a lilt, to rhyme with ant, not the longer English aunt. 'I work up at Heatherbrae House. Sandra asked me to pick you up. Sorry I'm late.'

'Hi,' I said, suddenly shy for no reason I could pin down. I coughed, trying to think of something to say. 'Um, it's fine. No problem.'

'It's why I'm in such a state.' He looked ruefully down at his hands. She didn't tell me you'd be wanting a lift until half an hour ago. I was halfway through fixing the mower, but I was worried I'd miss your train, so I just set out, dirt and all. Can I take your case?'

'Honestly, it's fine.' I picked up my case. 'It's not heavy. Thank you for coming out.'

He shrugged.

'No need to thank me, it's my job.'

'You work for the Elincourts?'

'For Bill and Sandra, aye. I'm ... well, I don't know quite what my job title would be. I think Bill's got me on his company pay-roll as a driver, but odd-job man would cover it better. I do the gardening, fix the cars, run them in and out of Carn Bridge. You'll be the nanny?'

'Not yet,' I said nervously, but he grinned sideways at me, and I smiled in spite of myself. There was something infectious about his expression. 'I mean, that's the position I'm going for, yes. Have they had many other interviewees?'

'Two or three. You're doing better than the first one. She didn't speak much English – I don't know who she got to write her application, but from what Sandra said it wasnae her.'

'Oh.' Somehow his words made me feel better. I'd been im-agining a parade of starched and fiercely competent Mary Pop-pins types. I stood straighter, smoothing the wrinkles out of my tweed skirt. 'Good. I mean, not good for her, I suppose. Good for me.'

We were outside the station now, walking across the little sparsely populated car park, towards a long black car on the opposite side of the road. Jack clicked something on a fob in his pocket and the lights flashed and the doors opened, shooting up like bat wings, making my jaw drop involuntarily. I thought of my stepfather's bland grey Volvo, his pride and joy, and gave a short laugh. Jack grinned again.

'It's a bit conspicuous, isn't it? It's a Tesla. Electric. I don't know if it would have been my choice of vehicle, but Bill ... well, you'll see. He's into technology.'

'Is he?' The words were meaningless as a response, but somehow ... just the knowledge of this small thing was a little nugget, a connection to this faceless man.

Jack stood back as I put my case into the rear of the car.

'Do you want to ride in the back, or up front?' he asked, and I felt my face colour up.

'Oh, in front, please!'

The thought of sitting regally in the back, treating him like a chauffeur, was enough to make me squirm.

'The views are better anyway,' was all he said, but he clicked something that made the bat-wing doors at the rear of the car swing closed, and then held open the front passenger door.

'After you, Rowan.'

For a moment I didn't move, almost forgetting who he was speaking to. Then, with a start, I pulled myself together and climbed into the car.

I had known, on some level, I suppose, that the Elincourts were rich. I mean, they had a driver slash odd-job man, and they were offering fifty-five grand for a nanny position, so they must have had cash to spare, but it wasn't until we reached Heatherbrae House that I began to realise quite *how* rich they were.

The knowledge gave me a strange feeling.

I don't care about the money I wanted to tell Jack as we stopped at a high steel gate, which swung slowly inwards, clearly sensing some sort of transmitter in the car. But it wasn't completely true.

How much do Sandra and Bill make? I found myself wondering.

The Tesla was eerily silent as we drove up the long, winding drive, the sound of the gravel beneath the wheels louder by far than the hushed electric engine.

'Jesus,' I muttered under my breath as we rounded yet another bend, and still no house was in sight. Jack shot me a sideways look.

'Big place, isn't it?'

'Just a bit.'

Land must be cheaper round here than down south of course, but it couldn't be *that* cheap. We bumped across a bridge over a quick-running burn, the waters dark with peat, and then drove through a cluster of pines. I thought I saw a flash of something scarlet through the trees and craned to look, but it was getting dark, and I wasn't completely sure if I had imagined the movement.

At last we came out of the shelter of the trees and into a clearing, and I saw Heatherbrae House for the first time.

I had been expecting something ostentatious, a McMansion, maybe, or a sprawling log-built ranch. But that wasn't what greeted me at all. The house in front of me was a modest Victorian lodge, four-square, like a child's drawing of a house, with a glossy black door in the centre and windows on each side. It was not big, but solidly built of granite blocks, with lush Virginia creeper rambling up one side of it, and I could not have put my finger on exactly why, but it exuded warmth and luxury and *comfort*.

Dusk had fallen, and as Jack turned off the engine of the Tesla and extinguished the headlights, the only illumination from all around was the stars, and the lamps from inside the house itself, shining out across the gravel. It looked like something from a sentimental illustration, those nostalgia-soaked twinkly photographs on the front of the jigsaws that my grandmother had loved.

Soft grey stone, lichened and weathered, golden lamps shining out through the clean rippled glass of the windows, overblown roses scattering their petals in the dusk – it was almost too perfect, unbearably perfect, in some strange way.

As I stepped out of the car and the cool evening air settled around me, pine-scented and sharp and clear as mineral water, I felt suddenly choked with longing for this life and all that it represented. The contrast with my own upbringing, the cheerless boxy suburbia of my parents' 1950s identikit bungalow, every room except my own neat as a pin, yet all utterly devoid of any character or comfort, was almost too bitter to bear, and it was more to banish the thought than because I was ready to meet Sandra that I stepped forward into the shelter of the covered porch.

Instantly, something felt off-kilter. But what was it? The door in front of me was traditional enough, panelled wood painted a rich glossy black, but something seemed wrong, *missing*, even. It took me a second to notice what it was. There was no keyhole.

The realisation was somehow unsettling. Such a small detail, and yet without it I was left wondering – was the door a fake? Should I go round the other side of the house?

There was no knocker either, and I looked over my shoulder, seeking Jack's guidance as to how I should announce myself. But he was still inside the car, checking something on the big illuminated touchscreen that served as the dashboard controls.

I turned back and put out my hand, ready to rap on the wood with my knuckles, but as I did so, something embedded in the wall to the left of the door caught my eye. A ghostly illuminated icon in the shape of a bell had appeared from nowhere, shining out of what had seemed to be solid stone, and I saw that what I had taken for simply part of the wall was actually a cleverly inlaid panel. I went to press it, but it must have been motion-sensitive, for I had not even made contact when a chime sounded from inside the house.

I blinked, suddenly thinking of Jack's comment in the car. *Bill … well, you'll see. He's into technology.* Was this what he had meant?

'Rowan! Hello!' The female voice seemed to come out of no-where, and I jumped, looking around for a camera, a micro-phone, a grille to speak into. There was none. Or none that I could see.

'Um … y-yes,' I said, speaking to the air in general, feeling like a complete fool. 'Hi. Is that … Sandra?'

'Yes! I'm just getting changed. I'll be down in ten seconds. Sorry to keep you standing around.'

There was no 'click' to tell me that a receiver had been replaced, or any other indication that the conversation was over, but the panel faded back to blank and I stood waiting, feeling curiously both watched and ignored.

Finally, after what felt like a long time, but was probably less than thirty seconds, there was a sudden cacophony of barking and the front door opened. Two black Labradors shot out, followed by a slim honey-blonde woman of perhaps forty, laughing and snatching ineffectually at their collars as they ran rings around her, yelping joyfully.

'Hero! Claude! Get back here!'

But the dogs paid no attention, leaping up at me as I took a couple of steps backwards. One of them shoved its nose into my crotch, painfully hard, and I found myself laughing nervously, trying to push its muzzle away, thinking of my one spare pair of tights in my bag, and gritting my teeth in case the dog ripped the ones I was wearing. It jumped up at me again and I sneezed, feeling an itching begin in the back of my skull. Shit. Had I brought my inhaler?

'Hero!' the woman said again. 'Hero, *stop* it.' She stepped out of the shelter of the porch towards me, holding out her hand. 'You must be Rowan. Calm *down*, Hero, honestly!' She managed to clip the lead she was holding onto the dog's collar and dragged it back beside her. 'Sorry, sorry, she's so friendly. Do you mind dogs?'

'Not at all,' I said, though it was only partly true. I didn't mind dogs exactly, but they triggered my asthma if I didn't take my antihistamines. Besides, asthma or no asthma, I didn't want their noses shoved between my legs in a professional situation. I felt my chest tighten, though out here it couldn't be anything other than psychosomatic. 'Good boy,' I said, with all the enthusiasm I could muster, patting it on the head.

'Good girl, actually. Hero's a bitch, Claude is the boy. They're brother and sister.'

'Good girl,' I amended half-heartedly. Hero licked my hand enthusiastically and I stifled the impulse to wipe my palm on my skirt. Behind me I heard a door slam, followed by Jack's feet

37

crunching across the gravel, and it was with some relief that I watched the dogs turn their attention to him, woofing happily as he retrieved my case from the back of the car.

'Here's your case, Rowan. Pleasure meeting you,' he said as he set it down beside me, and then, turning to Mrs Elincourt, 'I'll be getting back to fixing the mower, if it's all right, Sandra. Unless you need me for anything else?'

'What's that?' Mrs Elincourt said distractedly, and then she nodded. 'Oh, the mower. Yes, please do. Can you get it working again?'

'I hope so. If not, I'll call Aleckie Brown in the morning.'

'Thank you, Jack,' Sandra said, and shook her head as he walked away round the side of the building, his silhouette tall and square-shouldered against the evening sky. 'Honestly, that man is *such* a treasure. I don't know what we'd do without him. He and Jean have been absolute rocks – it's what makes the whole nanny business all the more inexplicable.'

The whole nanny business. There it was then. The first reference to the odd fact that had been at the back of my mind all the way up here: four women had already walked out of this post.

In the initial flush of exultation, I hadn't really worried very much about that part of Sandra's letter. In the context of getting an interview, it hadn't seemed very important, but as I reread the emails and travel instructions on the way up to Carn Bridge, I had stumbled over it again, and this time the remark had stuck out – its strangeness and faint absurdity. I had spent some time thinking about it during the long, boring hours on the train, turning her words over in my mind, torn between a desire to laugh, and something more puzzled and uneasy.

I *didn't* believe in the supernatural – I should say that up front, Mr Wrexham. And so the legends of the house didn't bother me at all, in fact the whole idea of nannies and servants driven out by mysterious spooky happenings seemed more than a little ridiculous – almost Victorian.

But the fact was that four women had left the Elincourts' employment in the last year. Having the bad luck to engage one nervous, superstitious employee seemed quite likely. Getting four in a row seemed ... less so.

Which meant that there was a strong chance that something else was going on, and all sorts of possibilities had run through my mind on the long journey up to Scotland. I had been half expecting to find that Heatherbrae was a draughty ruin of a house, or that Mrs Elincourt was a very difficult employer. So far, at least, that didn't seem to be the case. But I was reserving judgement.

Inside Heatherbrae the dogs were, if anything, more boisterous and excited to find a stranger admitted into the house, and at last Mrs Elincourt gave up trying to control them and dragged them both by their collars through to a room at the back, to shut them up.

As she disappeared, I hastily fumbled my inhaler out of my pocket and took a surreptitious puff, then waited for her just inside the front door, feeling the atmosphere of the house settle around me.

It wasn't a big house, just a family home. And the furnishings weren't ostentatious, just incredibly comfortable and well built. But there was a sense of . . . of *money*. That's the only way I can put it. From the polished wooden bannister and deep peat-coloured carpet runner that curved around the long, elegant flight, to the squashy bronze velvet armchair squeezed beneath the stairs and the frayed Persian rug spread across the worn flagstones in the hall. From the slow sure tick of a beautiful grandfather clock standing beside the long window, to the deep patina of age on the refectory table against the wall, everything conspired into an almost overwhelming sense of luxury. It wasn't that it was neat exactly – there were piles of newspapers scattered by the sofa, and a child's wellington boot left abandoned by the front door – but there was not a single thing that felt wrong. The sofa cushions were plump with feathers, there were no drifts of dog hairs in the corners of the room, or muddy scuffs on the stairs.

Even the *smell* was right – not a trace of wet dog or stale cooking, just beeswax polish, woodsmoke, and the faintest hint of dried rose petals.

It was … it was *perfect*, Mr Wrexham. It was the house I would have made for myself if I had the money and the taste and the time to create something so deeply, infinitely welcoming and warm.

I was just thinking all this, when I heard a door shut and saw Sandra coming back from the far side of the hallway, shaking her heavy, honey-coloured hair out of her face and smiling.

'Oh dear, sorry, they don't see many strangers so they do get terribly excited when new faces appear. They aren't like this all the time, I do assure you. Let's start again. Hello, Rowan, I'm Sandra.'

She held out her hand for the second time, slim and strong and tanned, and studded with three or four expensive-looking rings. I shook it, feeling her fingers grip mine with unusual firmness, and returned her smile.

'Right, well, you must be famished and rather tired after such a long trip. You came up from London, is that right?'

I nodded.

'Let me show you to your room and then when you've changed and made yourself comfortable, come down and we'll have something to eat. I can't believe it's so late. Gone nine already. Was your journey awful?'

'Not awful, no,' I said. 'Just slow. There was some kind of points failure at York, so I missed my connection. I'm really sorry, I'm usually very punctual.'

That at least was true. Whatever my other flaws and failings, I'm very rarely late.

'I got your text. So sorry I didn't reply, I didn't see it at first, I was up to my elbows in the kids' bathtime when it came through, and I only just managed to rush out and tell Jack to collect you. I hope you weren't waiting at the station for ages.'

It wasn't a question exactly – more of a remark, but I answered anyway.

'Not too long. Are the children in bed then?'

'The three youngest, yes. Maddie is eight, Ellie is five, and the baby, Petra, is just eighteen months, so they're all in bed.'

'And your other child?' I asked, thinking of the flash of red I'd seen between the trees on the drive up. 'You said in the advert you had four?'

'Rhiannon is fourteen going on twenty-four. She's at boarding school – not really our choice, I'd prefer to have her at home, but there's no secondary close enough. The nearest day school is more than an hour's drive and it would just be too much every day. So she boards over near Inverness and comes home most weekends. It breaks my heart a little bit every time she goes, but she seems to enjoy it.'

If you want her at home that badly, why don't you move? I thought.

'So I won't meet her?' I asked. Sandra shook her head.

'No, unfortunately not, but to be honest your time would be spent mostly with the little ones. Anyway – it means we can have a lovely chat now, and you can get to know the kids tomorrow. Oh, and I'm afraid my husband – Bill – can't be here either.'

'Oh?' It was a surprise – a shock even. I wasn't going to meet him, then. I had been so sure that someone would want to meet the person they were considering hiring to look after their children … but I tried to keep my face neutral. Non-judgemental. 'Oh, that's a shame.'

'Yes, he's away, working. It's been a pretty horrendous struggle, I have to say, with so many nannies leaving this year. The children are understandably very destabilised and the business has really suffered. We're both architects in a two-man firm. Well, one man, one woman!' She flashed a smile, showing very white, perfectly even teeth. 'It's just me and him, and it means that in busy periods when we've got more than one project going on, we can get terribly stretched. We try to juggle it so that there's always one of us around but with Katya leaving – she was our last nanny – it's just been chaos. I've had to pick up all the slack here, and Bill's been trying to hold the business together – I need to be completely honest and say that whoever does get the post isn't going to get a very smooth introductory period. Normally I try to work from home for the first month or so to make sure everything is going OK, but that just won't be possible this time. Bill can't be in two places at once and we have projects that desperately need me to be there and on the ground. We need someone very experienced who isn't going to be fazed by being left with the kids early on, and they need to be able to start asap.' She looked at me, a little anxiously, a furrow between her strongly marked brows. 'Do you think that describes you?'

I swallowed. Time to shed my doubts and step into the role of Rowan the Perfect Nanny.

'Definitely,' I said, and the confidence in my voice almost convinced myself. 'I mean, you've seen my CV –'

'We were very impressed with your CV,' Sandra said, and I gave a little blushing nod of acknowledgement. 'Quite frankly, it's one of the most impressive ones we've had. You tick all the boxes we need in terms of experience with the various age groups. But what's your notice period like? I mean obviously –' she was talking quickly now, as if slightly uncomfortable – 'obviously getting the right nanny is the most important thing, that goes without saying. But actually we do need someone who can start pretty much … well, pretty much now, if I'm being completely honest. So it would be disingenuous of me to pretend that's not a factor.'

'My notice period is four weeks.' I saw Sandra's mouth twist in a little worried moue, and added hastily, 'But I think I could probably negotiate an earlier finish. I have quite a bit of annual leave left, and I'd have to sit down with a calendar and do the sums, but I think there's a good chance I could get it down to two weeks. Maybe less.'

If Little Nippers were prepared to be flexible, that was. God knows, they hadn't given me much reason for loyalty.

I didn't miss the flash of hope and relief that crossed Sandra's face. But then she seemed to realise where we were.

'Look at me, keeping you talking in the hallway. It's hardly fair for me to be interviewing you before you've even got your coat off! Let me show you to your room, and then we can retreat to the kitchen and have a proper talk while you get some food inside you.'

She turned, and began to make her way up the long curving flight of stairs, her feet silent on the thick, velvet-soft carpet. At the landing she stopped and put her finger to her lips. I paused, taking in the wide sweep of space, the little table with a vase of blush peonies just beginning to shed their petals. A corridor disappeared off into semi-darkness, lit only by a rose-tinted night light plugged into a wall socket. Half a dozen doors led off from it. The one at the far end had wonky wooden letters stuck on it, and as my eyes got used to the low lighting, I made out the words. *Princess Ellie* and *Queen Maddie*. The door closest to the stairwell was slightly open, a night light shining dimly in the recesses of the room. I could hear a baby's soft snorting breath coming through.

'The kids are asleep,' Sandra whispered. 'At least, I hope so. I heard some pattering earlier but it all seems to be quiet now! Maddie in particular is a very light sleeper so I do have to tiptoe around a bit. Bill and I sleep on this floor, but Rhi sleeps upstairs. This way.'

At the top of the second flight, three further doors led off a slightly smaller landing. The middle one was open, and inside

I saw a small cupboard housing a jumble of mops and brooms, and a cordless Hoover charging on the wall. Sandra shut it hastily.

The door to the left of it was closed and had *FUCK OFF, KEEP OUT OR YOU DIE* written across the panelled wood in what looked like smeared red lipstick.

'That's Rhiannon's room,' Sandra said with a slight lift of her eyebrows that might have indicated anything from amusement to resignation. 'This one –' she put her hand on the knob of the door to the far right of the stairs – 'is yours. Well, I mean –' She stopped, looking a little flustered. 'I mean, it's where we always put the nanny, and it's where you'll be sleeping tonight. Sorry, don't want to be too presumptuous!'

I gave a slightly nervous attempt at a laugh, as she opened the door. It was dark inside, but instead of groping for a switch Sandra pulled out her phone. I was expecting her to turn on the torch, but instead she pressed something, and the lights inside the room flickered into life.

It wasn't just the main overhead light – in fact that was turned down very low, giving off nothing but a kind of faint golden glow – the reading light by the bed had come on too, as well as a standing lamp by the window next to a little table and some fairy lights twined around the bedhead.

My surprise must have shown on my face, because Sandra gave a delighted laugh.

'Pretty cool, isn't it? We do have switches, obviously – well, panels – but this is a smart house. All the heating and lights and so on can be controlled from our phones.' She swiped at something and the main light grew suddenly much brighter, and then dimmer again, and across the room a light turned on in the en suite bathroom and then flicked off again.

'It's not just lighting ... ' Sandra said, and she pulled across another screen and tapped an icon, and music started playing softly out of an invisible speaker. Miles Davis, I thought, though I wasn't very well up on jazz.

'There's also a voice option, but I find that a bit creepy so I don't often use it. Still, I can show you.' She coughed, and then said in a slightly artificial raised tone, 'Music off!'

There was a pause, and then the Miles Davis shut abruptly off.

'Obviously you can also control the settings from the panel.' She pressed something on the wall to demonstrate, and a white panel lit up briefly as the curtains on the window opposite swished closed, and then opened again.

'Wow,' I said. I really wasn't sure what to say. On the one hand it was impressive. On the other hand ... I found myself coming back to Sandra's word. Creepy.

'I know,' Sandra said with a little laugh. 'It's a bit ridiculous, I do realise. But being architects it's a professional duty to try out all the cool gadgets. Anyway –' she looked at her phone again, checking the clock this time – 'I *must* stop talking and get the supper out of the oven, and you must take off your coat and un-pack. Shall I see you downstairs in ... fifteen minutes?'

'Sounds good,' I said, a little faintly, and she gave me a grin, and disappeared, closing the door behind her.

After she'd gone I set my case on the floor and crossed the room to the window. Outside it was completely dark, but by press-ing my face to the glass and cupping my hands to my temples I could just make out a star-spattered sky and the dark shapes of mountains against the horizon. There were almost no lights.

The realisation of how isolated this place really was made me shiver, just for a moment, and I turned my back on the window and set about surveying the room.

What struck me instantly was that it was an odd mixture of traditional and modern. The window was pure Victorian, right down to the brass latch and the slightly rippled glass panes. But the lights were twenty-first century – no boring bulb in the centre of the ceiling. Instead there was a plethora of spotlights, lamps and uplighters, each focused on a different part of the room, and tuned to a different warmth and brightness. There were no radiators either, in fact I couldn't see where the heat was coming from, but clearly there must be some source – the night was cool enough for my breath to have left white mist on the windowpane. Underfloor heating? Some kind of concealed vent?

The furniture was more conservative, with a strong air of an expensive country-house hotel. Opposite me, facing the window, was a king-size bed covered with the ubiquitous array of brocade cushions, and beneath the window was a small plumply stuffed sofa, with a little table beside it – the perfect space for entertaining a friend, or having a drink. There were chests of drawers, a desk, two upright chairs, and an upholstered blanket chest at the foot of the bed that could have done duty either as storage or additional seating. Doors led off to either side, and opening one at random I found a walk-in closet filled with empty racks and shelves, spotlights flickering into life above the bare shelves automatically as I pulled open the door. I tried the second one, but it seemed to be locked.

The third was ajar, and I remembered it was the one that Sandra had lit up to show the bathroom inside. Venturing in, I saw there was a panel on the wall, like the one Sandra had pressed by the main door to the room. I touched it, not entirely expecting it to work, but it glowed into life displaying a confusing configuration of icons and squares. I pressed one at random, not completely sure what was going to happen, and the lights became slowly brighter, revealing a state-of-the-art wet room with a huge rainwater shower and a concrete vanity unit the size of my kitchen counter. There was nothing faux-Victorian about this room at all. It was space age in its complexity, sleek and modern in its styling, and had more glamour in one metro tile than most bathrooms possessed in their entirety.

I thought of my bathroom at home – hair in the rusting plughole, dirty towels kicked into the corner, make-up stains on the mirror.

God, I wanted this.

Before ... I don't know what I had wanted before. I had focused on nothing except getting here and meeting the Elincourts and finding out what was at the end of this advert. That was it. I honestly hadn't even thought about actually getting the job.

Now ... now I *wanted* it. Not just the fifty-five thousand a year, but everything. I wanted this beautiful house and this gorgeous room, right down to the sumptuous, marble-tiled shower, with its sparkling limescale-free glass and polished chrome fittings.

More than that, I wanted to be part of this family.

If I had had any doubts about what I was doing here, this room had crushed them.

For a long, long moment, I just stood at the vanity unit, my hands splayed on the counter, staring at myself in the mirror. The face that stared back at me was somehow unsettling. Not the expression, exactly, but something in my eyes. There was something there – a kind of hunger. I must not look too desperate in front of Sandra. Keen, yes. But desperation – the kind of hungry desperation I saw staring back at me now – that was nothing but off-putting.

Slowly, I smoothed down my hair, licked a finger, wetted an unruly brow back into place. Then my hand went to my necklace.

I wore it every day – had done ever since I had left school, and jewellery was no longer banned by uniform codes. Even as a child I'd worn it at weekends and whenever I could get away with it, ignoring my mother's sighs and her comments about cheap nasty tat that turned your skin green. It had been a present for my first birthday and now, after more than two decades, it felt like part of myself, something I barely even noticed, even when I reached to play with it in moments of stress or boredom.

Now I noticed it.

An ornate silver R on the end of a dangling chain. Or rather, as my mother had so frequently reminded me, not silver, but silver plate, something that was becoming more and more apparent, as the brassy metal beneath shone through where I had rubbed the pendant absent-mindedly with my fingers.

There was no reason to take it off. It wasn't inappropriate. The chances of anyone even noticing it were very low. And yet ...

Slowly, I reached round to the back of my neck and undid the clasp.

Then I put on a slick of lip gloss, straightened my skirt, tightened my ponytail, and prepared to go back downstairs to Sandra Elincourt and give the interview of my life.

When I got downstairs, Sandra was nowhere to be seen, but I could smell some kind of delicious, savoury scent coming from the far side of the hallway. Remembering that that was where Sandra had ushered the dogs, I moved forward, cautiously. But when I pushed open the door I found I had stepped into another world.

It was like the back of the house had been sliced brutally off, and grafted onto a startling modernist box, almost aggressively twenty-first century. Soaring metal beams went up to a glass roof, and beneath my feet the Victorian encaustic tiles of the hall had abruptly stopped, replaced by a poured concrete floor, polished to a dull sheen. It looked like a combination of a brutalist cathedral and an industrial kitchen. In the centre was a shiny metal breakfast bar, surrounded by chrome stools, dividing the room into the bright kitchen area, and beyond it the dimly lit dining space, where a long concrete-topped table ran the length of the room.

In the middle was Sandra, standing in front of a monstrous free-standing stove, the largest I had ever seen, and ladling some kind of casserole into two bowls. She looked up as I came in.

'Rowan! Listen, I'm so sorry but I forgot to ask, you're not veggie, are you?'

'No,' I said. 'No, I eat pretty much anything.'

'Oh phew, that's a relief, because we've got beef casserole and not a lot else! I was just frantically wondering if I had time to do a baked potato. Which reminds me.' She walked across to the huge steel fridge, tapped an invisible button on the fridge door with the knuckle of one hand, and said, enunciating her words clearly, 'Happy, order potatoes please.'

'Adding potatoes to your shopping list,' replied a robotic voice, and a screen lit up, showing a typed list of groceries. 'Eat happy, Sandra!'

The shock of it made me want to laugh, but I pushed down the urge, and instead watched as Sandra put both bowls onto the long table along with a crusty loaf on a board, and a little dish of something like sour cream. The bowls were bone china and looked as if they were probably Victorian, hand-painted with delicate little flowers and embellished with gold-leaf details. Somehow the contrast between the mathematically severe modernist lines of the glass room and the fragile antique bowls was almost absurd, and I felt slightly off-balance. It was like the rest of the house in reverse – Victorian stuffiness punctuated by splashes of space-age modernity. Here, the modernism had taken over, but the bowls and the heavy floral whirls of the silver cutlery were a reminder of what lay behind the closed door.

'There we go,' Sandra said unnecessarily as she sat down and waved me to the seat opposite her. 'Beef stew. Help yourself to bread to soak up the juices, and that's horseradish crème fraiche which is very nice stirred in.'

'It smells amazing,' I said, truthfully, and Sandra shook back her hair and gave a little smile that tried to look modest, but really said *I know.*

'Well, it's the stove, you know. A La Cornue. It's almost im-possible to screw up – you just pop the ingredients in and forget about it! I do miss a gas hob sometimes, but we're not on the mains here, so it's all electric. The hobs are induction.'

'I've never used an induction hob,' I said, eyeing it rather doubtfully. It was a beast of a thing, six feet of metal doors, knobs, drawers and handles, and on top a smooth cooking surface that seemed to be zoned in ways I couldn't even begin to guess at.

'They take a bit of getting used to,' Sandra said. 'But I promise you, they're really very intuitive to use. The flat plate in the middle is a teppanyaki. I was rather sceptical about the cost, but Bill was insistent, and I have to admit, it was worth every penny and then some.'

'Oh,' I said. 'I see,' though I didn't really. What on earth was a teppanyaki? I took a mouthful of the stew, which was thick and rich and delicious, the kind of meal I never had the time or organisation to cook for myself at home, and let Sandra plop a blob of crème fraiche on top, and ply me with a crusty chunk of bread. There was a bottle of red wine already open on the table and she poured us out two glasses in beautifully etched Victorian goblets, and pushed one across to me.

'Now, would you rather eat first and then talk, or shall we get started?'

'I ... ' I looked down at my plate, and then gave a mental shrug. No point in putting it off. I tugged my skirt down and sat up a little straighter on the metal stool. 'Get started, I suppose. What would you like to know?'

'Well, your CV was very comprehensive, and *very* impressive. I already contacted your previous employer – what was her name? Grace Devonshire?'

'Er ... yes, that's right,' I said.

'And she couldn't say enough good things about you. I hope you don't mind me taking up references before the interview, but I've been bitten a few times with unsuitable candidates and I think there's no point in wasting everyone's time dragging you up here only to fail at the last fence. But Grace was positively gushing about you. The Harcourts seem to have moved, but I also spoke to Mrs Grainger, and she was very complimentary as well.'

'You didn't contact Little Nippers, did you?' I said slightly uneasily, but she shook her head.

'No, I completely understand, it's not always easy job hunting in an existing post. But perhaps you could tell me about your employment there?'

'Well, it's pretty much like I explained on the CV really – I've been there for two years, in charge of the baby room. I wanted a change from one-family nannying and a nursery seemed like a good option. It's been excellent experience having a bit more managerial responsibility, and having to organise staff rotas and stuff, but quite honestly I've found I miss the family feel of nannying. I love the children, but you don't get to spend as much one-on-one time with them as you do with a private position. What was stopping me making a change was the idea of taking a step backwards in terms of pay and responsibility, but your post seems like it might be the challenge I'm looking for.'

I had rehearsed the speech inside my head on the train on the way, and now the words rattled out with a practised authenticity. I had been to enough interviews to know that this was the key – to explain why you wanted to leave your current post, without running down your existing employer and looking like a disloyal employee. But my – slightly massaged – version of events seemed to have done the trick, for Mrs Elincourt was nodding sympathetically.

'I can quite imagine.'

'Plus of course,' I added, this on the spur of the moment, for I had not thought this particular line through, 'I'm keen to get out of London. It's so busy and polluted, I guess I'm just looking for a change of scenery.'

'That I can *quite* understand,' Mrs Elincourt said with a smile. 'Bill and I had the same long night of the soul a few years back. Rhiannon was about eight or nine and we were beginning to think about secondaries. Maddie was a toddler, and I was so sick of pushing her around dirty parks and having to check for needles in the sandpit before I let her play. This just seemed like the perfect chance to break away completely – build a new life, find a really super independent for Rhi.'

'And are you glad you made the move?'

'Oh, totally. It was tough on the children at the time of course, but it was definitely the right thing. We adore Scotland – and we never wanted to be that kind of family who buys a second home and then puts it on Airbnb for nine months of the year. We wanted to really *live* here, become part of the community, you know?'

I nodded, as though second-home dilemmas were part of my everyday existence.

'Heatherbrae House was a real project,' Sandra continued. 'It had been totally neglected for decades, lived in by a very eccentric old man who went into a care home, and then allowed to fall into disrepair until his death. Dry rot everywhere, burst pipes, dodgy electrics – it was a case of really stripping it back to the bones and completely revamping it. Two years of absolute grind, reconfiguring the rooms and doing everything from rewiring through to putting in a new cesspit. But it was worth it – and of course it made a wonderful case study for the business. We have a whole folder of before and after, and it really shows that good architecture can be as much about bringing out the spirit of an existing house, as creating a new one from scratch. Though we do that too of course. Our speciality is vernacular architecture.'

I nodded as though I had a clue what this meant, and took a gulp of wine.

'But that's enough about me and the house – what about yourself?' Sandra said, with the air of getting down to business. 'Tell me a bit about what attracted you to nannying?'

Wow. That was a big question. About a dozen images flashed through my mind, all at once. My parents, shouting at me for getting Play-Doh in the kitchen carpet tiles age six. Age nine, my mother shaking her head over my report card, not bothering to hide her disappointment. At twelve, the school play no one bothered to come to. Age sixteen, 'what a shame you didn't revise more for history' instead of congratulations on the As I got in maths, English and science. Eighteen years of not being good enough, not being the daughter I was supposed to be. Eighteen years of not measuring up.

'Well ... ' I felt myself flounder. This was not part of the story I had practised, and now I cursed myself for it. It was an obvious question, one I should have prepared. 'Well, I suppose ... I mean ... I just like kids.' It was lame. Very lame. And also not completely true. But as the words left my mouth, I realised something else. Sandra was still smiling, but there was a certain neutrality in her expression that had not been there before, and suddenly I understood why. A woman on the cusp of her thirties, going on about how much she likes kids ...

I hurried to repair my mistake.

'But I have to say, I'm in awe of anyone who wants to be a parent. I'm definitely not ready for that yet!'

Bingo. I could not miss the flash of relief that crossed Sandra's face, though it was quickly suppressed.

'Not that it's an option right now anyway,' I said, feeling confident enough for a little joke, 'since I'm firmly single.'

'So ... no ties to London then?'

'Not really. I have friends of course, but my parents retired abroad a few years back. In fact, once I've sorted things out with Little Nippers there's really nothing keeping me in London. I could take up a new post almost straight away.'

I carefully avoided saying *your post*, not wanting to seem like I was making assumptions that I would get the job, but Sandra was smiling and nodding enthusiastically.

'Yes, as you can probably tell from our talk earlier, I'd be lying if I said that wasn't a significant factor. We're coming up to the summer holidays and we absolutely *must* get someone in the position before the schools break up or I'll be sunk. Plus there's a really, *really* important trade fair in a few weeks and both Bill and I really need to be there.'

'What's your deadline?'

'Rhi breaks up towards the end of June which is what – about three or four weeks? But the trade fair begins the weekend before she breaks up. The truth is, the sooner the better. Two weeks is doable. Three weeks is … well, just about OK. Four weeks would be starting to get into disaster zone. You said your notice period is four weeks?'

I nodded.

'Yes, but I was figuring it out while I unpacked and I have at least eight days' holiday owing, so I can definitely get it down to just over two weeks, if I factor in my leave, and maybe even less. I think they'll be prepared to negotiate.'

In actual fact, I had no idea how helpful they would be, and my suspicion was, not very. Janine, my boss, and current head of the baby room, wasn't my biggest fan. I didn't think she'd be particularly sorry to see me go, but I didn't think she'd bend over backwards to help me. However, there were ways and means – nursery workers weren't allowed to come into work for forty-eight hours after a vomiting bug. I was prepared to have a lot of vomiting bugs around the middle of June. Again, though, I didn't say that to Sandra. For some reason, no one wants a nanny with a flexible moral code, even when she's flexing it to help them out.

As we ate, Sandra ran through a few more interviewing-by-numbers questions of the kind I had come to expect – outline your strengths and weaknesses, give me an example of a difficult situation and how you handled it … all the usual suspects. I had answered these before in a dozen other interviews, so my responses were practised, just slightly tweaked for what I thought Sandra in particular would want to hear. My standard answer to the question about a difficult situation concerned a little boy who had come to his settling-in day at Little Nippers covered in bruises, and the way I had dealt with the parents over the subsequent safeguarding concerns. It went down well with nurseries, but I didn't think Sandra would want to hear about me shopping parents to the authorities. Instead I gave a different story, about a little bullying four-year-old at a previous post, and the way I had managed to trace it back to her own fears over starting primary school.

As I talked she looked through the papers I had brought with me, the DBS check, the first-aid certificates. They were all in order of course, I knew that, but I still felt a little flutter of nerves beneath my ribs as she reviewed them. My chest tightened, though whether that was down to nerves or the dogs, I couldn't quite tell, and I pushed down the urge to pull out my inhaler and take a puff.

'And the driving licence?' she asked as I finished my anecdote about the four-year-old. I put down my fork onto the smooth polished concrete top of the table and took a deep breath.

'Ah, right, yes. I'm afraid that's a problem. I do have a full UK driving licence and it's clean, but the actual card was stolen last month when I lost my purse. I've ordered a new one but they wanted an updated photo and it's taking an age to come through. But I promise you, I *can* drive.'

That last part was true after all. I crossed my fingers, and to my relief she nodded, and moved on to something about my professional ambitions. Did I want to get any additional qualifications. Where did I see myself in a year's time. It was the second question that really mattered, I could tell that from the way Sandra set down her wine glass and actually looked at me as I answered.

'In a year's time?' I said slowly, frantically trying to figure out what she wanted to hear from me. Did she want ambition?

Commitment? Personal development? A year was a funny length of time to choose, most interviewers said five years, and the question had thrown me. What was she testing?

At last I made up my mind.

'Well ... you know I want this job, Sandra, and to be honest, in a year's time I would hope to be here. If you were to offer me this position, I wouldn't want to uproot myself from London and all my friends just for a short-term post. When I work for a family, I want to think it's a long-term relationship, both for me and the kids. I want to really get to know them, see them grow up a little bit. If you'd asked me where I saw myself in five years ... well, that's a different question. And I'd probably give you a different answer. I'm ambitious – I'd like to do a master's in childcare or child psychology at some point. But a year – any post I took now, I would definitely want to think of it lasting longer than a year, for all our sakes.'

Sandra's face broke into a huge grin, and I knew – I just *knew* that I had given the right answer, the one she had been hoping for. But was it enough to get me the post? I didn't honestly know.

We chatted for about another hour or so, Sandra refilling my glass along with her own, though at some point after the second or third top-up I had the sense to put my hand over the goblet and shake my head.

'Better not. I'm not really much of a drinker – wine goes straight to my head.'

It wasn't completely true. I could hold my wine as well as most of my friends, but I knew that another glass would probably see me throw caution to the wind, and then it would be harder to keep my answers diplomatic and on-message. Stories would get tangled, I'd get names and dates in a muddle, and I'd wake up tomorrow with my head in my hands wondering what truths I'd let slip and what terrible faux pas I had made.

As it was, Sandra looked at the clock as she topped up her own glass, and gave a little gulp of shock.

'Heavens, ten past eleven! I had no idea it was so late. You must be shattered, Rowan.'

'I am a bit,' I said truthfully. I'd been travelling all day, and the fact was starting to catch up with me.

'Well, look, I think we've covered everything I wanted to ask, but I was hoping you could meet the little ones tomorrow, see if you click, and then Jack will drive you back to Carn Bridge to catch your train, if that's OK? What time does it leave?'

'11.25, so that works fine for me.'

'Great.' She stood up, and swept all the crockery into a stack, which she put beside the sink. 'Let's leave that for Jean, and call it a night.'

I nodded, wondering again who this mysterious Jean was, but not quite wanting to ask.

'I'll just go and let the dogs out. Goodnight, Rowan.'

'Goodnight,' I said back. 'Thank you so much for a delicious supper, Sandra.'

'My pleasure. Sleep well. The children are usually up at six but there's no need for you to get up that early – unless you want to!'

She gave a little tinkly laugh, and I made a mental note to set my alarm for six, even while my eyes felt heavy at the thought.

As Sandra shooed the dogs into the garden, I made my way back into the old part of the house, with the same strange sense of jolting dislocation I had felt before, going the other way. The soaring glass ceiling abruptly lowered to wedding-cake-style frosting. The echoing sound of my kitten heels on the concrete floor changed to the soft click of parquet, and then the hush of carpet as I began to make my way up the staircase. At the first landing I stopped. The door closest to me, the baby's room, was still ajar, and I couldn't resist, I pushed it open and stepped inside, smelling the good, warm smells of clean, contented baby.

Petra was lying on her back, her arms and legs thrown out froggy style. She had kicked off her blanket and, very gently, I drew it back over her, feeling her soft breath stirring the fine hairs on the back of my hand.

As I tucked it around her, she started, flinging up one arm, and for a moment I froze, thinking that she was about to wake and cry. But she only sighed, and settled back down, and I padded quietly from the room and up to my luxurious, waiting bedroom.

I tiptoed around cautiously as I washed and brushed my teeth, listening to the floorboards beneath my feet quietly creaking, and not wanting to disturb Sandra below. But at last I was ready for bed, my alarm set, my clothes for tomorrow neatly set out on the plump little sofa.

Then I realised, I had not drawn the curtains.

Wrapping my dressing gown around myself, I walked across the room and tugged gently at their fabric. They didn't move.

Puzzled, I tried harder, then stopped, peering behind them in case they were somehow fake, ornamental drapes, and I was really supposed to use a blind. But no, they were real curtains, they had real runners. Then I remembered – Sandra pressing something on the wall, and the curtains swishing closed then open again. They were automatic.

Shit. I walked across to the panel beside the door and waved a hand in front of it. Instantly it lit up with that confusing configuration of squares and icons. None looked like curtains. There was one that might have been a window, but when I pressed it, cautiously, a blast of jazz trumpet split the silence, and I hastily stabbed it with a finger.

Thank God it cut off immediately, and I stood for a moment, waiting, poised for a wail from Petra, or for Sandra to come pounding up the stairs demanding to know why I was waking the children, but nothing happened.

I returned to studying the panel, but this time I didn't press anything. I tried to remember what Sandra had done earlier. The big square in the centre was the main light, I was fairly sure of that. And the mishmash of squares to the right presumably controlled the other lights in the room. But what was that spiral thing, and the slider to the left? Music volume? Heat?

Then I remembered Sandra's comment about the voice settings.

'Shut curtains,' I said in a low voice, and somewhat to my shock, the curtains whisked across with a barely audible swoosh.

Great. OK. That only left the lights to figure out.

The bedside light had a switch, so I knew I'd be able to handle that one, and the others I managed to figure out by trial and error, but there was one lamp by the armchair that I could not manage to extinguish.

'Turn off lights,' I tried, but nothing happened. 'Turn off lamp.'

The bedside lamp extinguished.

'Turn off armchair lamp.' Nothing happened. Bloody hell.

In the end I traced the cord back to an oddly shaped plug socket on the wall, not like a normal appliance socket, and pulled it out. The room was plunged instantly into darkness so thick, I could almost feel it.

Slowly, I groped my way back across the room to the foot of the bed, and crawled into it. I was just snuggling down when I remembered, with a sigh, that I hadn't plugged my phone into charge. Shit.

I couldn't face contending with the lights again, so instead I switched on the torch on my phone, got out of bed, and began to rummage through my case.

The charger wasn't there. Had I taken it out already? I was sure I'd packed it.

I tipped the bag upside down, letting my possessions tumble out onto the thick carpet, but no electrical wire came snaking out with the other belongings. Shit. *Shit*. If I couldn't charge my phone, I'd have the world's most boring journey tomorrow. I hadn't even brought a book – all my reading matter was on the Kindle app. Had I forgotten it? Left it on the train? Either way, it clearly wasn't in my case. I stood there for a moment, chewing my lip, and then opened up one of the drawers in the bedside table, hoping against expectation that a previous guest might have left a charger behind with them.

And ... bingo. Not a charger, but a charging lead. That was all I needed – there was a USB port built into the socket.

With a sigh of relief I untangled the lead from the leaflets and papers in the drawer, plugged it in, and attached my phone. The little charging icon illuminated, and I got thankfully back into bed. I was about to turn off the torch and lie back down, when I noticed that something had fallen out of the drawer onto my pillow. It was a piece of paper, and I was about to screw it up and throw it onto the floor, but before I did, I glanced at it, just to check it was nothing important.

It wasn't. Just a child's drawing. At least ...

I picked up the phone again, angling the torch at the page, looking more closely at the picture.

It was hardly a work of art, just stick figures and thick cray-oned lines. It showed a house, with four windows and a shiny black front door, not unlike Heatherbrae. The windows were coloured in black, all except for one, which showed a tiny pale face peeping out of the darkness.

It was oddly disconcerting, but there was no name signed to it, and no way of knowing why it was in the bedside drawer. I turned it over, looking for clues. There was writing on the other side. It wasn't a child's, but an adult's – sloped and looping and somehow non-English in a way I couldn't quite define.

To the new nanny, it read in neat, regular italics. *My name is Katya. I am writing you this note because I wanted to tell you to please be –*

And then it stopped.

I frowned. Who was Katya? The name rang a bell, and then I remembered Sandra's voice at dinner saying *but with Katya leaving – she was our last nanny ...*

So Katya had lived here. Slept here even. But what had she wanted to say to her successor? And had she run out of time, or thought better of what she was about to say?

Please be … kind to the children? Please be … happy here? Please be … sure to tell Sandra you like dogs?

It could have been anything. So why was the phrase that kept hovering on the tip of my tongue *please be careful*?

The two taken together, the eerie little drawing, and the unfinished note, gave me a strange feeling that I could not put my finger on. Something like uneasiness, though I could not have said why.

Well, whatever it was she had wanted to say, it was too late now.

I folded the drawing and slipped it back into the drawer. Then I switched off my phone, pulled the covers up to my chin, and tried to forget everything that hung in the balance and sleep.

When I woke, it was to the insistent shrill beep of my alarm, and for a moment I could not think where I was, or why I was so tired. Then I remembered. I was in Scotland. And it was 6 a.m. – a full hour and a half earlier than I was accustomed to waking up.

I sat up, smoothing my rumpled hair and rubbing the sleep from my eyes. Downstairs I could hear thumps, and shrill sounds of excitement. It sounded as though the children were probably up ...

The curtains were blackout, but the sunshine was already streaming through the gaps around the edges, and forcing my legs out of bed I walked across and tried to pull them open, before remembering the previous night.

'Curtains open,' I said aloud, feeling more than slightly stupid, and they swooshed apart like a magician's trick. I don't know what I was expecting, but whatever it was, I was not prepared for the reality.

The beauty of the scene in front of me took my breath away.

The house had been perfectly sited by some long-dead Victorian architect to gaze out across an uninterrupted vista of blue hills, green valleys and deep verdant pine forests. On and on it stretched, the rolling foothills punctuated by little dark burns that rambled here and there, and the corrugated roofs of faraway crofts, and a few miles away a loch, reflecting the morning sun so brightly it looked like a patch of snow. In the distance, presiding above it all, were the Cairngorms – Gaelic for the Blue Mountains, according to Google.

When I had looked up the origin of their name, the translation had seemed faintly absurd. The photos online showed all the colours you might expect – green grass, brown bracken, reddish earth with the occasional purple splotch of heather, and in winter a covering of crisp white. The idea that they were blue seemed fanciful in the extreme.

But here, with the mist rising from their slopes in the morning sun, and the dawn pink still tingeing the sky behind them, they *did* look blue. Not the brackeny foothills, but the unforgiving granite slopes themselves, all jagged crags and peaks, far above the tree line. The highest peak looked like it was tipped with snow, even in June.

I felt my heart lift, and then I heard a noise in the garden below and looked down.

It was Jack Grant. He was walking across from a huddle of outbuildings tucked just around the corner of the house. His hair was wet, as if he had just showered, and he was holding a bag of tools in his hand. For a minute I watched him, staring down at the top of his dark head, before it began to feel more than a little voyeuristic, and I turned away from the window to head to the bathroom for my own shower.

Inside it was dark and I automatically felt around for a switch, before I remembered the damn panel. At my touch it leapt into life, presenting me again with that confusing mosaic of squares, sliders and dots. I pressed one at random, hoping I wasn't going to get more Miles Davis. I had been aiming for the same one I'd pressed yesterday, but evidently I'd missed my mark, because low blue lights suddenly illuminated the skirting. Some sort of night setting, for if you wanted to go to the loo while your partner was asleep? Not bright enough to shower by, at all events.

The next button I tried made the blue lights disappear, and two low, golden lamps came on over the bath, suffusing my skin with a warm, flattering glow. It was exactly what I would have wanted if I was soaking in a long bubble bath, but the shower enclosure was still dark, and I needed something brighter and more ... well, more morning-ish.

I found it on the fourth or fifth try – a setting that was bright, but not agonisingly so, with an illuminated rim around the mirror perfect for doing my make-up. With a sigh of relief I dropped my robe to the floor and stepped into the shower, only to be faced with a different challenge. There was a dazzling array of different nozzles, spouts and shower heads. The question was, how did you operate them? The answer seemed to be yet another panel, a waterproof one this time, set in among the shower tiles. When I touched it, letters appeared. *Good morning, Katya.*

The name gave me a funny little jolt, and I remembered again that unfinished note on the child's drawing, from the night before. There was a smiley face, and a little down button. Well, I wasn't Katya. I pressed the down button, and the letters changed. *Good morning, Jo.* I pressed again. *Good morning, Lauren. Good morning, Holly. Good morning, guest.*

There were no more options. Guest it was, then. I pressed the smiley face. Nothing happened. Instead the display changed to those cryptic dots, squares and sliders. I pressed one at random and screeched when about twenty forceful jets of ice-cold water blasted my stomach and thighs. Hastily I mashed the off switch to the left of the panel and the jets turned off, leaving me panting and shivering, and more than a little annoyed.

OK. Fine. Maybe I should try a preset option, until I had figured out how to work this thing. I touched the panel and *Good morning, Katya* flashed up again. This time with a feeling of slight trepidation, I pressed the smiley face, and the message *We're preparing your favourite shower. Wash Happy!* appeared on the screen. As the message faded away, to my astonishment, one of the shower heads slid smoothly upwards to a preprogrammed height, tilted to an angle, and a jet of warm water began to gush out. I stood for a moment, gaping, and then tested the water with one hand. Whoever Katya was, she had been very tall, and she liked her showers a little bit hotter than I did. I could have put up with the heat, but unfortunately she was so tall that the jet missed the top of my head completely and bounced off the glass screen opposite, which was going to make washing my hair very tricky.

I pressed the off button, and tried again. This time I selected *Good morning, Holly* at random and waited, teeth gritted, for the result.

Bingo. Holly's setting turned out to be set to a kind of hot drenching rain from the grid overhead, which was … well, it was glorious. There was no other word for it. The water gushed out with an almost absurd abundance, soaking me with warmth. I felt the hot water drumming on the top of my skull, driving out the last remnants of my sleepiness and last night's red wine. Holly, whoever she was, had clearly been a woman after my own heart. I shampooed my hair, conditioned, and then rinsed, and then stood, my eyes closed, simply enjoying the feel of the water on my naked skin.

The temptation to stay there, revelling in the luxury, was very strong, but it had taken me probably ten minutes to even figure out the bathroom. If I wasted any more time, I would render that early alarm pointless. There was no point in forcing myself out of bed at the crack of dawn if I didn't make an appearance and ram my enthusiasm home to Sandra.

With a sense of resignation, I pressed the off button on the panel, reached out for the fluffy white towel warming on the heated rail, and reminded myself that if I pulled this off, it wouldn't be the last time I got to enjoy that shower. Very far from it.

*

Venturing downstairs, the first thing that greeted me was the smell of toast, and the sound of children laughing. When I rounded the corner of the bottom of the stairs, I was met by a very small tartan dressing gown abandoned on the bottom step, and a single slipper in the middle of the hall. Picking both up, I made my way through to the kitchen, where Sandra was standing in front of a huge gleaming chrome toaster, holding a piece of brown bread, and waving it at the two little girls in bright red pyjamas sitting at the metal breakfast bar. Their curly heads, one dark, the other white-blonde, were tousled with sleep, and they were both giggling helplessly.

'Don't encourage her! She'll only do it again.'

'Do what again?' I said, and Sandra turned.

'Oh, Rowan! Gosh, you're up early. I hope the girls didn't wake you. We're still trying to train certain members of the family to stay in bed past 6 a.m.' She nodded pointedly at the younger of the two girls, the one with white-blonde hair.

'It's fine,' I said truthfully, adding, slightly less accurately, 'I'm a naturally early riser.'

'Well, that's certainly a good talent to have in this house,' Sandra said with a sigh. She was wearing a dressing gown and looked more than a little harassed.

'Petra threw her porridge,' said the girl, with a gurgling laugh, pointing at the pink-cheeked baby sitting in the high chair at the corner, and I saw that she was right. There was a dollop of porridge the size of an egg sliding down the front of the stove to plop onto the concrete floor, and Petra was crowing with delight, and scooping up another spoonful, ready to throw it again.

'Peta frow!' she said and took aim.

'Uh-uh,' I said with a smile, and held out my hand for the spoon. 'Petra, give it here, please!'

The baby looked at me uncertainly for a moment, sizing me up, her faint blonde brows drawn into an adorable frown, and then her chubby face split in a grin and she repeated, 'Peta frow!' and launched the porridge towards me.

I dodged, but not quick enough, and it hit me full in the chest.

For a minute I just gasped, and then a wave of absolute fury rose up inside me when I realised what she had done. Stupidly I hadn't brought a spare outfit and yesterday's top was crumpled and had a red wine stain on the top that I didn't remember making, but must have done.

I had literally no clean clothes left. I was going to be covered in porridge for the rest of the day. The little *shit*.

It was the younger of the two girls who saved me. She burst out giggling, and then clapped her hands over her mouth, as if horrified.

I remembered who I was, where I was, why I was here.

I forced a smile.

'It's OK,' I said to the little girl. 'Ellie, isn't it? You can laugh. It *is* pretty funny.'

She took her hands away, and gave a cautious grin.

'Oh my God,' Sandra said with a kind of weary resignation. 'Rowan, I am *so* sorry. They talk about the terrible twos but I swear, Petra's been auditioning for them for six months. Is your top OK?'

'Sandra, don't give it a second thought,' I said. The top was not going to be OK, at least not until I could wash it, and possibly not even then. It was a silk blouse, dry-clean only, a stupid choice for a nannying interview, but I hadn't thought about the fact that I would be interacting with the kids. Maybe I could get a small moral advantage from the situation. 'Honestly, these things happen when you have kids, right? It's only porridge! However –' I leaned over and took the bowl of porridge away from Petra before she realised what was happening and put it out of her reach. 'I think you've had enough, little Miss Petra, so maybe I'll take charge of that while I clean up. Where's your mop, Sandra, and I'll clean up that blob on the floor before one of the girls slips on it?'

'It's in the utility room, that door there,' Sandra said with a grateful smile. 'Thank you so much, Rowan. I honestly wasn't expecting you to start pitching in unpaid – this is beyond the call of duty.'

'I'm glad to help,' I said firmly. I ruffled Petra's hair as I passed with an affection I didn't entirely feel, and gave Ellie a little wink. Maddie was not looking at me, she was staring down at her plate as though the whole thing had passed her by. Maybe she was ashamed at her earlier role, egging Petra on.

The utility room turned out to be in the older part of the house – probably the original scullery judging by the Victorian sink and stone-flagged floor – but I wasn't in the mood to appreciate architectural details. Instead, I shut the door behind me and took a couple of deep breaths, trying to rid myself of the last of my irritation, and then set to work trying to rescue my top. The worst of the porridge flicked off into the sink, but I was going to have to sponge the rest. After several tries that only succeeded in getting porridgy water onto my skirt, I pushed a mop against the handle of the kitchen door and peeled off my top.

I was standing there in my bra and skirt, dabbing at the porridgy patch under the tap and trying not to get the rest of the shirt wetter than necessary, when I heard a sound from the other side of the utility room and turned to see the door to the yard open and Jack Grant come in, wiping his hands on his overall trousers.

'Mower's going, San—' he called, and then broke off, his eyes widening in shock. A vivid blush spread across his broad cheekbones.

I gave a yelp of surprise and clutched my wet top to my breasts, trying my best to preserve my modesty.

'Oh my God, I'm so sorry,' Jack said. He was covering his eyes, looking at the ceiling, the floor, anywhere but me. His cheeks were flaming. 'I'll – I'll be – so sorry –'

And then he turned and fled, slamming the yard door behind himself, leaving me gasping and not sure whether to laugh or cry.

There was not much point in either, so I hastily dried my wet top with a towel hanging over the radiator, filled up the mop bucket, and then made my way back to the kitchen with my cheeks almost as pink as Jack's.

'Shirt fixed?' Sandra said over her shoulder as I came in. 'Let me get you a coffee.'

'Yes.' I was not sure whether to tell her what had just happened. Had she heard my squeak of surprise? Would Jack say something? 'Sandra, I –'

But then my nerve failed me. I couldn't think of a way of saying, *Sandra, I just boob-flashed your handyman*, without sounding hopelessly unprofessional. I felt the blush on my face deepen in shame at just the thought of it. I could *not* bring it up. I would just have to hope that Jack was enough of a gentleman not to refer to it himself.

'Milk and sugar?' Sandra said absently, over her shoulder, and I set the conversation aside.

'Milk, thanks,' I said, and put the mop bucket down, and began clearing up Petra's missiles from the stove and floor, feeling my cheeks cool as I worked.

At last, when the coffee had come through and I was seated at the table, eating a piece of excellent toast and marmalade, I was almost able to pretend it had never happened.

'So,' Sandra said, wiping her hands on a cloth. 'Girls. I didn't get a chance to introduce you to Rowan. She's come to have a look around our house and meet you. Say hello.'

'Hi,' Maddie muttered, though she said it more to her plate than me. She looked younger than her eight years, with dark hair and a sallow little face. Beneath the countertop I could see two skinny knees, covered in scabs.

'Hello, Maddie,' I said, with what I hoped was a winning smile, but she kept her eyes firmly down. Ellie was easier, she was looking at me with frank curiosity from beneath a white-blonde fringe. 'Hello, Ellie. How old are you?'

'I'm five,' Ellie said. Her blue eyes were round as buttons. 'Are you going to be our new nanny?'

'I –' I stopped short, not sure what to say. Would I *hope so* come across as too nakedly pleading?

'Maybe,' Sandra cut in firmly. 'Rowan hasn't decided yet whether she wants to work here so we must be very well be-haved to impress her!'

She gave me a little sideways wink.

'I tell you what, run upstairs and get dressed, and then we can show Rowan around.'

'What about Petra?' Ellie asked.

'I'll sort her out. Go on – chop-chop.'

The two girls slid obediently off the tall stools and pattered away across the hallway and up the stairs. Sandra watched them go, fondly.

'Gosh, they're very good!' I said, genuinely impressed. I had nannied enough children to know that five-year-olds getting dressed on command definitely wasn't a given. Even eight-year-olds tended to need supervision. Sandra rolled her eyes.

'They know not to play up in front of visitors. But let's see if they're actually doing as they're told . . . '

She pressed a button on an iPad lying on the counter and a picture flickered into view. It was a children's bedroom, the camera obviously sited up near the ceiling, pointing downwards at two little beds. There was no sound, but the noise of a door slamming was loud enough to filter down the stairs, and a teddy bear on the mantelpiece rocked and fell. As we watched, Maddie stamped angrily into view at the bottom of the screen and sat crossly on the left-hand bed, her arms folded. Sandra pressed something else and the camera zoomed in on Maddie's face, or rather the top of her head, for she was looking down at her lap. There was a faint crackle coming from the iPad now, as if a microphone had been switched on.

'Maddie,' Sandra said, 'what have I told you about slamming doors?'

'I didn't.' The voice came small and tinny from the iPad speaker.

'You did, and I saw you. You could have hurt Ellie. Now get your clothes on and you can watch some TV. They're all laid out on your chair, I put them out this morning.'

Maddie said nothing, but she got up and pulled off her pyjama top, and Sandra shut the screen down.

'Wow,' I said, slightly taken aback. 'Impressive!'

It was not the word I was thinking. *Stalkerish* was closer to the mark, though I wasn't sure why. Plenty of places I'd worked had nanny cams, or baby monitors with inbuilt speakers and cameras. Perhaps it was the fact that I hadn't known about it until now. I hadn't noticed any cameras last night, so wherever they were, they must be well hidden. Had Sandra watched me go up to bed last night? Had she seen me look into Petra's bedroom? The thought made my cheeks flame.

'The whole house is wired up,' Sandra said casually, dropping the iPad back onto the counter. 'It's very handy, especially in a place with several floors. It means I don't have to always be running up and down to check on the girls.'

'Very handy,' I echoed faintly, suppressing my unease. The *whole* house? What did that mean? The children's rooms, clearly. But the reception rooms? The bedrooms? The *bath*rooms? But no, that was beyond possibility. And illegal, surely. I put the remaining bit of toast back on the plate, my appetite suddenly gone.

'Finished?' Sandra said brightly, and when I nodded she swept the bit of toast into a waste-disposal unit and put the plate with the girls' porridge bowls by the sink. The ones from last night had disappeared, I noticed. Had the mysterious Jean come and gone already?

'Well, if you've had enough, let me give you the grand tour while the girls get dressed.' She scooped Petra out of her high chair, scrubbed her face with a damp flannel, hitched her onto her hip, and together we re-entered the old part of the house and crossed the stone-flagged entrance hall to the two doors either side of the front door.

'Right, so just to give you the layout – the hall is the centre of the house – out the back is the kitchen, and leading off that is the utility room, which you've already seen of course. That was part of the old servants' quarters, the only bit that survived, actually. The rest we had to pull down. At the front of the house we have the grander rooms – that's the old dining room.' Sandra waved a hand at an opening to the right of the front door. 'But we found we were always eating in the kitchen, so we've converted it into a study slash library. Have a peek.'

I put my head around the door, and saw a smallish room with panelled walls painted a beautiful rich teal colour. Ranged at one end were bookshelves from floor to ceiling covered in a mix of fiction paperbacks and hardback books on architecture. It could have been a small but perfectly formed library in a National Trust historic property – except that in the middle of the room was an enormous glass desk with a huge double-screen iMac sprawling across it, and a kind of aeronautical ergonomic chair facing the screens.

I blinked. There was something disconcerting about the way the old and new combined in this house. It wasn't like most homes, where modern additions rubbed up alongside original features and somehow combined into a friendly, eclectic whole. Here there was a strange impression of oil and water – everything was either self-consciously original, or glaringly modern, with no attempt to integrate the two.

'What a beautiful room,' I said at last, since Sandra seemed to be waiting for some kind of response. 'The colours are just ... they're fabulous.' Sandra smiled, jiggling Petra on her hip in a pleased sort of way.

'Thank you! Bill does all the technical layout stuff, but the interior design is mostly me. I do love that shade of teal. This particular room is really Bill's domain so I reined myself in, but you'll see I've gone a bit to town on it in the living room. I figure, it's my house, I don't have to please anyone else! Come through and have a look.'

The room she led me into next was the living room she had mentioned, a cluster of deep button-backed sofas arranged in a square around a beautiful tiled fireplace. The ceiling and wood-work were the same shade of teal as the panelling in the study, but the walls themselves were startling – covered in a rich, intri-cate wallpaper with a design almost too convoluted to make out in deep blues, emeralds and aquamarines. As I peered closer I saw that it was a mix of brambles and peacocks – both stylised and intertwined to the point of being practically unrecognisable. The brambles were dark green and indigo black, the peacocks iridescent blue and amethyst, their tails curling and spreading and tangling with the brambles into a kind of nightmarish laby-rinth – half aviary, half briar thicket.

The design echoed the tiles around the fireplace, which had two peacocks standing tall either side of the grate, their bodies on the bottom-most tile, their tails spreading upwards. The fire itself was dead, but the room was not cold, far from it. Wrought-iron Victorian radiators around the walls gave it a cosy warmth, and the sun slanted across another of the artfully faded Persian rugs. More books were strewn across a brass coffee table, along with another vase of peonies, these ones drooping in a dry vase, but Sandra ignored them, and led the way to a door on the left of the fireplace, leading back in the direction of the kitchen.

Behind it was a much smaller oak-panelled room with a scuffed leather sofa and a TV on the far wall. It was easy to see what this room was used for – the floor was covered with discarded toys, scattered Duplo, decapitated Barbie dolls, and a partly collapsed play tent slumped in one corner. The rather dark panelled walls had been decorated with stickers, and children's drawings, even the odd crayoned scribble on the panelling itself.

'This was the old breakfast room,' Sandra said, 'and it was rather gloomy as it faces north and that pine tree blocks out a lot of the light, so we made it into a media room, but obviously the children ended up completely taking over!'

She gave a laugh and picked up a stuffed yellow banana, handing it to Petra.

'And now, to complete the circuit . . . '

She led the way through towards a second door concealed in the panelling – and again I had the feeling of tripping, and finding myself in a different house entirely. We were back in the glass vault at the back of the house, but we had entered it from the opposite side. Without the big stove and the cupboards and appliances blocking the view, there was literally nothing in front of us but glass – and beyond that the landscape falling away, patched with forest and the faraway glimmer of lochs and burns. It was like there was nothing between us and the wilderness beyond. I felt that at any moment an osprey could have swooped down into our midst.

In one corner was a playpen, carpeted with jigsaw-shaped rubber mats, and I watched as Sandra plopped Petra inside with her banana and waved her hand around the walls. 'This side was the old servants' hall, back in the day, but it was riddled with dry rot and the views were much too good to be confined to narrow little sash windows, so we made the decision to just –' She made a slitting gesture at her throat, and then laughed. 'I think some people are a bit shocked, but trust me, if you'd seen it before, you'd understand.'

I thought of my tiny flat in London, the way it could have fitted into even just this one room.

Something inside me seemed to twist and break, just a little, and suddenly I was not sure if I should have come here after all. But I knew one thing. I could not go back. Not now.

You're probably wondering why I'm telling you all this, Mr Wrexham. Because I know you're busy, and I know that on the surface at least, it seems as if this is nothing to do with my case. And yet ... it's everything. I need you to *see* Heatherbrae House, to feel the warmth from the heating striking up through the floor, the sun on your face. I need you to be able to reach out and stroke the soft cat's-tongue roughness of the velvet sofas, and the silky smoothness of the polished concrete surfaces.

I need you to understand why I did what I did.

The rest of the morning seemed to pass in a blur. I spent the time making home-made Play-Doh with the children, and then helping them fashion it into a variety of lumpy, lopsided creations, most of which Petra mashed into shapelessness again with crows of laughter and howls of annoyance from Ellie. Maddie was the one who puzzled me most – she was stiff and unyielding, as if determined not to smile for me, but I persisted, finding little ways of praising her, and at last, in spite of herself, she seemed to unbend a little, even going as far as laughing, a little unwillingly, when Petra unwisely shoved a handful of the pink dough into her mouth and spat it out, retching and gagging at the salty taste, with a comical expression of disgust on her chubby little face.

At last, Sandra tapped me on the shoulder and told me that Jack was waiting to take me to the station, if I was ready, and I stood up and washed my hands, and gave Petra a little chuck under the chin.

My bag was beside the door. I had packed before I came downstairs for breakfast, knowing that I might not have much time later, but I had no idea who had brought it down from the spare room. Not the unseen Jean, I fervently hoped, though I did not know why the thought made me uncomfortable.

Jack was waiting outside with the silently idling car, his hands in his pockets, the sunshine finding specks of deep auburn and red in his dark hair.

'Well, it was a *total* pleasure to meet you,' Sandra said, and there was a genuine warmth in her eyes as she held out her hand. 'I'll need to discuss things with Bill but I think I can say ... well, let's just say, you'll be hearing from us very soon with a final decision. *Very* soon. Thank you, Rowan, you were fabulous.'

'It was lovely to meet you too, Sandra,' I said. 'Your girls are lovely.' Ugh, stop saying lovely. 'I hope I get the chance to meet Rhiannon sometime.' *I hope I get the job*, that meant, in code. 'Goodbye, Ellie.' I stuck out my hand, and she shook it gravely, like a five-year-old businesswoman. 'Goodbye, Maddie.'

But Maddie, to my dismay, did not take my hand. Instead she turned and buried her face in her mother's midriff, refusing to meet my eyes. It was a curiously childish gesture, one that made her seem much younger than her age. Over the top of her head, Sandra gave a little shrug as if to say, *what can you do?*

I shrugged back, ruffled the back of Maddie's hair, and turned towards the car.

I had stowed my luggage in the back seat, and was just walking around the opposite side of the car to climb into the front passenger seat, when something hit me like a small, dark hurricane. Arms wrapped around my waist, a hard little skull digging into my lower ribs.

Wriggling round in the fierce embrace I saw, to my surprise, that it was Maddie. Maybe I had won her over after all?

'Maddie!' I said, but she did not answer. I was unsure of what to do, but in the end I bent down to give her a little hug back. 'Thank you for showing me your lovely house. Goodbye.'

I hoped that the last word might make her let go, but she only tightened her grip, squeezing me uncomfortably tight, making my breath come short.

'Don't –' I heard her whimper into my still-damp top, though I couldn't make out the second word. Don't go?

'I have to,' I whispered back. 'But I hope I'll be able to come back very soon.'

That was the truth, all right. God, I hoped so.

But Maddie was shaking her head, her dark hair swishing against her knobbly spine. I felt the heat of her breath through my top. There was something strangely intimate and uncomfortable about the whole thing, something I could not put my finger on, and all of a sudden I very much wanted her to let go, but, mindful of Sandra's presence, I did not prise Maddie's fingers away. Instead I smiled, and tightened my arms around her momentarily, returning her hug. As I did, she made a little sound, almost a whimper.

'Maddie? Is something wrong?'

'Don't come here,' she whispered, still refusing to look at me. 'It's not safe.'

'It's not safe?' I gave a little laugh. 'Maddie, what do you mean?'

'It's not *safe*,' she repeated, with a little angry sob, shaking her head harder, so that her words were almost lost. 'They wouldn't like it.'

'Who wouldn't like it?'

But with that, she tore herself away, and then she was running, barefoot across the grass, shouting something over her shoulder.

'Maddie!' I called after her. 'Maddie, wait!'

'Don't worry,' Sandra said with a laugh. She came round to my side of the car. It was plain that she had not seen anything apart from Maddie's sudden hug, and her subsequent flight. 'That's Maddie, I'm afraid. Just let her go, she'll be back for lunch. But she must have liked you – I'm not sure she's ever voluntarily hugged a stranger before!'

'Thank you,' I said, rather unsettled, and I let Sandra see me into the car and slam the door shut.

It was only as we began to wind slowly down the drive, keeping one eye out for a fleeting child among the trees, that I found myself replaying Maddie's final remark, wondering if she had really said what I thought I'd heard.

For the thing she had called over her shoulder seemed almost too preposterous to be true – and yet the more I brooded over it, the more I was sure of what I'd heard.

The ghosts, she had sobbed. *The ghosts wouldn't like it.*

'Well, seems it's goodbye for now,' Jack said. He stood at the barrier to the station, holding my bag in one hand, his other outstretched. I took it and shook it. There was oil deeply ground in around the nails from yesterday, but his skin was clean and warm, and the odd intimacy of the contact gave me a little shiver I couldn't explain.

'Nice to meet you,' I said a little awkwardly, and then, with a feeling that I might as well because I'd regret it if I didn't, I added, a little rashly, 'Sorry I didn't get to meet Bill. Or ... or Jean.'

'Jean?' Jack said, looking a little puzzled. 'She's not about much in the day. Goes home to her dad.'

'Is she ... is she young, then?'

'No!' He gave that grin again, the sides of his mouth curving into an expression of such beguiling amusement that I felt my own mouth curve in helpless sympathy, even though I didn't really understand the joke. 'She's fifty if she's a day, maybe more, though I'd never dare ask her age. No, she's a – what's the word? A carer. Her father lives down in the village, he has Alzheimer's, I think. He can't be left alone for more than an hour or two. She comes up in the morning before he's awake and then again first thing in the afternoon. Does the dishes and that.'

'Oh!' I felt my face flush, and I smiled, absurdly, and gave a little laugh. 'Oh, I see. I thought ... never mind. It doesn't matter.'

I did not have time to analyse the relief I felt, but it gave me a strange sense of being off balance, struck by something I had not expected to encounter.

'Well, good to meet you, Rowan.'

'Good to meet you too – Jack.' The name came off my tongue a little awkwardly, and I blushed again. Up the valley I heard the sound of the approaching train. 'Goodbye.'

'Goodbye.' He held out the case, and I took it, still echoing his curving, beguiling smile, and began to walk to the platform, giving myself a stern injunction *not* to look back. When at last the train had drawn in and I had climbed aboard and settled myself in a carriage, I did risk one last glance out of the window, to where he had been standing. But he was gone. And so, as the train pulled out of the station, my last glimpse of Carn Bridge was of an empty platform, crisply clean and sun-soaked, awaiting my return.

Back in London, I prepared myself for an agonising wait. *Very soon*, Sandra had said. But what did that mean? She'd clearly liked me – unless I was deluding myself. But I'd done enough interviews to be able to pinpoint the feeling in the air as I left. In recent months I'd experienced both the triumph of having done myself justice and the furious disappointment of having let myself down. I'd felt much closer to the first one on the train back down to London.

Did they have other people to interview? She had seemed so very desperate to have someone start soon, and she must know that every day that ticked past without me giving notice was a day I couldn't work for her. But what if one of the other candidates could start immediately?

Given Sandra's emphasis on *very soon*, I had dared to hope for something on my phone by the time I got home, but there was nothing that evening, nor the next day when I left for work. We had to leave our phones turned off in our lockers at Little Nippers, so I resigned myself to a long morning, listening to Janine rattling on about her boring boyfriend and bossing Hayley and me about, while all the time my head was elsewhere.

My lunch shift wasn't until 1 p.m., but when the clock ticked over I hastily finished the nappy I was changing and stood up, handing the baby to Hayley.

'Sorry, Hales, can you take him? I've got an emergency I need to sort out.'

I pulled off the plastic disposable apron and virtually ran to the staffroom. There, I grabbed my bag from my locker, and escaped out the back entrance into the little concrete yard, far away from the gaze of the children and parents, that we used for smoking, phone calls and other activities that we weren't supposed to do on clock. It seemed to take an age for the phone to switch on and go through the endless start-up screen – but at last the lock screen came up, and I typed in my passcode with shaking fingers and pressed refresh on my emails, reaching as I did for my necklace, my fingers tracing the loops and ridges as the messages downloaded.

One ... two ... . three came through ... all either spam or completely unimportant, and I felt my heart sink – until I noticed the little icon in the corner of the screen. I had an answerphone message.

My stomach was turning over and over, and I felt a kind of fluttering nausea as I dialled into voicemail and waited impatiently through the automated prompts. If this didn't work out ... if this didn't work out ...

The truth was, I didn't know what I'd do if it didn't work out. And before I could finish the thought there was a beep and I heard Sandra's clipped plummy accent, sounding tinny through the little speaker.

'Oh, hello, Rowan. Sorry not to speak to you in person – I expect you're at work. Well, I'm delighted to say that I've discussed it with Bill and we'd be happy to offer you the job *if* you can start on 17 June at the absolute latest, earlier if you can. I realise that we didn't discuss the exact terms and the bonus I mentioned in the letter. The plan would be for us to issue you with an allowance of a thousand pounds a month, with the remainder of the salary to come at year end in the form of a completion bonus. I hope that's acceptable – I realise it's a little unconventional, but given you'll be living with us you won't have many day-to-day expenses. If you could let me know as soon as possible if you'd like to accept, and oh, yes, lovely to meet you the other day. I was very impressed with how the children warmed to you, particularly Maddie. She's not always the easiest child and – well, I'm rambling so I'd better cut this short, but we'd be happy to have you on board. Looking forward to hearing back from you.'

There was a click, and the message ended.

For a minute I couldn't move. I just stood there, the phone in my hand, gaping at the screen. And then a huge rush of exhilaration raced through me, and I found I was dancing, hopping in circles, punching the air and grinning like a lunatic.

'Bloody hell, what's got into you?' a smoke-roughened voice said over my shoulder, and I turned, still grinning, to see Janine leaning against the door, a cigarette in one hand, lighter in the other.

'What's got into me?' I said, hugging myself, full of a glee I couldn't even try to suppress. 'I'll tell you what's got into me, Janine. I've got a new job.'

'Well –' Janine's expression as she flicked open the lighter was a little sour – 'you needn't look so triumphant about it.'

'Oh, come on, you're as fed up with Val as I am. She's screwing us all and you know it. Ten per cent she put up fees last year,

85

and us assistants are barely getting minimum wage. She can't keep blaming the recession forever.'

'You're just pissed off that I got made head of the baby room,' Janine said. She took a drag of her cigarette, and then offered me the packet. I was trying to give up to improve my asthma (well, officially I *had* given up) but her words had hit home, and so I took one and lit it slowly, more as a way of giving myself time to rearrange my expression than because I actually wanted to smoke. I *had* been pissed off that she'd got promoted, when honestly I thought I had the better shot. I'd applied thinking I was a shoo-in – and the shock when the position had gone to Janine had been like a punch to the gut. But as Val had said at the time, there were two candidates and only one job. There was nothing she could do about that. Still, it had rankled, particularly when Janine had begun throwing her weight around and issuing orders in that grating drawl.

'Well, it doesn't matter now,' I said, handing the lighter back with a sweet smile and exhaling the smoke. 'Onwards and upwards, eh?' The slightly patronising smile she gave made me add, a little maliciously, 'Very much upwards, in fact.'

'What do you mean?' Janine said. She narrowed her eyes. 'Are we talking more than thirty K?'

I made a rising movement with my hand and her eyes widened.

'Forty? *Fifty grand?*'

'*And* it's residential,' I said smugly, watching her jaw drop. She shook her head.

'You're having me on.'

'I'm not.' Suddenly I didn't need the cigarette any more. I took a final drag, then dropped it to join the mush of dead butts in the yard, and ground it out under my heel. 'Thanks for the fag. And now, if you'll excuse me, I need to phone up and accept a job.'

I dialled Sandra's number, listening as it rang and then clicked through to answerphone. In a way I was relieved, I didn't want to get grilled about my start date in front of Janine. If she knew it was a make-or-break condition, she might well tell Val, who could deliberately make life difficult for me.

'Oh, hi, Sandra,' I said, when the beep had sounded. 'Thanks so much for your message, I'm thrilled, and I'd be delighted to accept. I need to sort a few things out this end but I'll email you about the start date. I'm sure it won't be a problem. And … well, thanks, I guess! I'll be in touch. Let me know if there's anything you need from me to get the ball rolling.'

And then I hung up.

I handed in my notice to Val that same day. She tried to act pleased for me, but in truth, she looked mostly pissed off, particularly when I informed her that the amount of leave I had stacked up meant that I would be finishing on 16 June, rather than 1 July as she had assumed. She tried to tell me that I needed to work my notice and take the leave as pay, but when I more or less invited her to see me in court, she caved.

The next few days passed in a whirl of activity and practicalities. Sandra did all her payroll remotely through a company in Manchester, and wanted me to contact them direct with payment details and ID rather than sending all the paperwork up to Scotland. I had expected the process to be a major stumbling block, maybe even requiring me to travel to Manchester for an interview in person, but in the event it was surprisingly, almost disconcertingly, simple – I forwarded them Sandra's email with a reference number, and then when they replied, I sent the passport scan, utility bills and bank details they requested. It went through without a hitch. Like it was meant to be.

The ghosts wouldn't like it.

The phrase floated through my head, spoken in Maddie's reedy little voice, its childlike quaver lending the words an eeriness I would normally have shrugged off.

But that was bollocks. Utter bollocks. I hadn't seen a whiff of the supernatural the whole time I was in Carn Bridge. More likely it was just a cover story seized on by homesick au pairs, girls barely out of their teens with poor English, unable to cope with the isolation and remote location. I'd seen enough of them working at places in London to know the drill – I'd even picked up some emergency work when they scarpered in the night with the return half of their plane ticket, leaving the parents to pick up the pieces. It wasn't uncommon.

I was considerably older and wiser than that, and I had very good reasons for wanting to make this work. No amount of alleged 'haunting' was going to make me turn this chance down.

I look back, and I want to shake that smug young woman, sitting in her London flat, thinking she knew it all, had seen it all.

I want to slap her face and tell her she doesn't know what she's talking about.

Because I was wrong, Mr Wrexham. I was very, very wrong.

Less than three weeks later, I was standing on Carn Bridge station platform, surrounded by more cases and boxes than it seemed possible for one person to carry.

When Jack came striding up the platform, car keys jangling in his hand, he actually broke into a laugh.

'Christ, how did you get all that across London?'

'Slowly,' I said honestly. 'And painfully. I took a taxi but it was a bloody nightmare.'

'Aye, well, you're here now,' he said, and took my largest two cases, giving me a friendly shove when I tried to take the smaller one back off him. 'No, no, you take those others.'

'*Please* be careful,' I said anxiously. 'They're really heavy. I don't want you to put your back out.'

He grinned, as if the possibility was so remote as to be laughable.

'Come on, car's this way.'

It had been another glorious day – hot and sunny – and although the sun was beginning to sink towards the horizon and the shadows were growing longer, the gorse was still popping audibly as we drove silently through the wooded lanes and moorland roads towards Heatherbrae. The house, as we drove up the drive, was even more beautiful than I had remembered, basking in evening sunshine, the doors flung open and the dogs running everywhere, barking their heads off. It suddenly occurred to me, with a little jolt, that I would presumably be in charge of the dogs as well as the kids when Sandra and Bill were away. Or maybe that was Jack's job too? I would have to find out. Two children and a baby were in my comfort zone. A teen as well, I could just about manage. At least, I hoped I could. But add in two boisterous dogs, and I was starting to feel a little overwhelmed.

'Rowan!' Sandra came running out of the front door, her arms outstretched, and before I was fully out of the car she had enveloped me in a maternal hug. Then, she stood back, and waved her hand at a figure standing in the shadows of the porch – a tall man, balding slightly, with close-shaven dark hair.

'Rowan, this is my husband, Bill. Bill – meet Rowan Caine.'

So this – *this* was Bill Elincourt. For a moment I couldn't think of what to say, I just stood there, awkwardly conscious of Sandra's arm around me, not sure of whether I should break away from her grip to go and greet him or –

I was still frozen in indecision when he solved the issue by striding towards me, sticking out his hand, and giving me a quick, businesslike smile.

'Rowan. Good to meet you at last. Sandra's told me all about you. You have a very impressive résumé.'

You don't know the half of it, Bill, I thought, as he picked up one of the cases from the boot and made his way back to the house. I took a deep breath and prepared to follow, and as I did, my hand went nervously to my necklace. But this time, instead of tracing its familiar grooves, I slipped the pendant inside the neck of my shirt, and hurried after them.

Inside the kitchen we had coffee, and I sat nervously on the edge of one of the metal breakfast stools while Bill quizzed me about my qualifications, feeling on edge in a way that I never had when Sandra had interviewed me. I wanted ... I don't know. I wanted to impress him, I suppose. But at the same time, as he droned on about his punishing schedule and the difficulties of recruiting staff in the Highlands, and the inadequacies of his previous nannies, I increasingly wanted to shake him.

I don't know what I had imagined. Someone successful, I guess. I had known that from the advert and the house. Someone fortunate – with his beautiful kids and accomplished wife and interesting job. All that I had taken for granted. But he was so ... so *comfortable*. He was padded – every inch of him. I don't mean he was fat, but he was cushioned, physically, emotionally, financially, in a way that he just didn't seem to grasp, and it was his very ignorance of the fact that made it even more infuriating.

Do you know what it's like? I wanted to shout at him, as he complained about their gardener who had left to take up a full-time teaching job in Edinburgh, and the home help who had broken the £800 waste-disposal unit in the sink, and then run away because she couldn't face telling them what she'd done. *Do you understand what it's like for people who don't have your money, and your protection, and your privilege?*

As he sat there, holding forth as if there was nothing in the world so important as his inconsequential problems, Sandra gazing adoringly into his face like she was happy to listen to him drone on forever, the realisation came to me, painfully. He was *selfish*. A selfish, self-centred man who had barely asked me a single personal question – not even how my journey had been. He just didn't care.

I don't know what I had expected to feel when I met him – this man who hadn't bothered to interview a woman he was planning to leave his children with for weeks at a time – but I hadn't expected to feel this level of hostility. I knew I had to get a grip on myself, or it would show in my face.

Perhaps Sandra saw something of my discomfort, for she gave a little laugh, and broke in.

'Darling, Rowan doesn't want to hear about our domestic travails. Just make sure you don't go putting cutlery down the grinder, Rowan! Anyway, quite seriously, all the instructions are here.' She patted a fat red binder at her elbow. 'It's a physical copy of the document I emailed you last week, and if you've not had a chance to sit down and read it yet, it's got everything from how to work the washing machine, right through to the children's bedtimes and what they do and don't like to eat. If you've got any concerns at all, you'll find the answers here, although of course you can always ring me. Did you download Happy?'

'I'm sorry?'

'Happy – the home management app. I emailed you the authorisation code?'

'Oh, I'm sorry, the app, yes, I downloaded it.'

She looked relieved.

'Well, that's the main thing. I've set up your Happy profile with all the permissions you'll need, and of course it stands in as a baby monitor, though we've got a regular one for Petra's room as well. Belt and braces, you know, but the app is very good. What else … ? Oh, food! I've done you a menu planner here –' she pulled out a loose sheet from a plastic wallet on the first page of the binder – 'which is full of stuff they'll eat fairly reliably, and bought all the ingredients so you're absolutely set for the first week. Plus all the passwords are in there for Waitrose online and so on, and here is a credit card for any household expenses. The statement comes direct to me and Bill, but obviously do keep receipts – a quick snap on your phone is fine, you don't need to keep the physical bit of paper. Um … what else … ? I expect you're full of questions?'

She said the last in a slightly hopeful tone, though I wasn't completely certain whether she was hoping I would prompt her, or hoping I'd say no.

'I did read the email,' I said, though in truth, since the document was about fifty dense pages, I'd only skimmed through the pages. 'But it'll be brilliantly helpful to have a printout of course – it's always so much easier to flick through a physical copy. It was impressively comprehensive. I think I've got a handle on everything – Petra's routine, Ellie's allergies, Maddie's – um –' I stopped, unsure how to phrase what Sandra had called her daughter's *explosive personality*. It sounded as though Maddie was quite the handful, or could be.

Sandra caught my eye and saw my predicament, and gave a little rueful smile that said, yup.

'Well, yes, Maddie really! Rhiannon is staying at school this weekend for end-of-term celebrations. She'll be coming home next week and I've sorted out her lift and everything so you've nothing to worry about there. What else … what else … ?'

'I don't think we completely sorted out when you're leaving,' I said tentatively. 'I know you said in your email that you had the trade show coming up next week –when does it start exactly? Is it next Saturday?'

'Oh.' Sandra looked taken aback. 'Did I not say? Gosh, that was a bit of an oversight. That's the … um … well, that's the only issue really. It is Saturday, but not next Saturday, this one. We leave tomorrow.'

'What?' For a moment I thought I hadn't heard properly. 'Did you say you're leaving *tomorrow*?'

'Yeess … ' Sandra said, her face suddenly uncertain. 'We're on the 12.30 train so we'll be leaving just before lunch. I … is that a problem? If you're not confident about coping straight out of the box, I can try to reschedule my early meetings … '

She trailed off, and I swallowed.

'It's fine,' I said, with a confidence I didn't completely feel. 'I mean, I'd have to hit the ground sometime, I really don't think it'll make much difference whether it's this weekend or next.'

Are you mad? a voice was screaming inside my head. *Are you crazy? You barely know these children.*

But another part of me was whispering something very different – *good*. Because in a way, this made things considerably easier.

'We can play it by ear,' Sandra was saying. 'I'll keep in touch by phone – if the children are too unsettled then I can fly back midweek perhaps? You'll only have the little ones for the first few days, so hopefully that'll make the transition a little bit easier ...'

She stopped again, a little awkwardly this time, but I was nodding. I was actually nodding, my face stiff with the effort of holding in my real feelings.

'Well,' Sandra said at last. She put down her coffee cup. 'Petra's already in bed, but the girls are through in the TV room watching *Peppa Pig*. I don't want to delegate my last bedtime with them to you completely, but shall we do it together, so you can get a feel for their routine?'

I nodded, and followed her as she led the way through the darkened glass cathedral towards the concealed door to the TV room.

Inside the blinds were drawn, the floor was still carpeted with scattered Duplo and battered dolls, and two little girls were curled up together on the sofa, wearing flannel pyjamas and clutching soft, worn teddy bears. Maddie was sucking her thumb, though she took it swiftly out of her mouth as her mother came in, with a slightly guilty jump. I resolved to look that one up in the binder.

We perched on the arms of the sofa, Sandra fondly ruffling her fingers through Ellie's silky curls, while the episode wound its way to the close, and then she picked up the remote control and shut down the screen.

'Oh, Mummeeeee!' The chorus was immediate, though slightly half-hearted, as if they didn't really expect Sandra to acquiesce. 'Just one more!'

'No, darlings,' Sandra said. She scooped up Ellie, who wrapped her legs around her waist and buried her face in her mother's shoulder. 'It's super late. Come on, let's go up. If you're *very* lucky, Rowan will read you a story tonight!'

'I don't want Rowan,' Ellie whispered into the crook of her mother's neck. 'I want you.'

'Well … we'll see when we get up there,' Sandra said. She hitched Ellie into a more comfortable position, and held out her hand to Maddie. 'Come on, sweetie. Up we go.'

'I want *you*,' Ellie said doggedly as Sandra began to climb the stairs, me trailing after her. Sandra gave me a little eye roll and a smile over her shoulder.

'I tell you what,' she whispered to Ellie, though deliberately loud enough for me to hear. 'Maybe you'll get a story from me *and* a story from Rowan. How does that sound?'

Ellie made no reply to this, only dug her face further into Sandra's shoulder.

Upstairs the curtains on the landing were drawn, and I could see the dim pink light of Petra's night light filtering across the carpet. Sandra supervised tooth brushing and the loo while I made my way down the softly carpeted hallway to Maddie and Ellie's doorway.

There they were – two little beds, each bathed in the soft glow of a bedside light, one pink, the other a kind of dusky peach. Above each one was a collection of framed prints – a baby footprint, a scribble, just recognisable as a cat, a butterfly made out of two chubby handprints – and tangled around the frames were strings of fairy lights, giving out their gentle illumination.

It was picture-perfect – like an illustration from a nursery catalogue.

I sat gingerly on the foot of one of the little beds, and at last I heard feet and whining voices, swiftly hushed by Sandra.

'Shh, Maddie, you'll wake Petra. Come on now, dressing gowns off, and into bed.'

Ellie jumped into hers, but Maddie stood stonily for a moment, regarding me, and I realised it must be her bed I was sitting on.

'Do you want me to move?' I asked, but she said nothing, only folded her arms mutinously, got into bed, and turned her face towards the wall, as if pretending I wasn't there.

'Shall I sit on the bean bag?' I asked Sandra, who gave a laugh and shook her head.

'You're fine. Stay there. Maddie takes a bit of time to warm up to people sometimes, don't you, sweetie?'

Maddie said nothing, and I wasn't sure I blamed her. It must be uncomfortable hearing herself discussed with a stranger like this.

Sandra began to read a Winnie-the-Pooh story, her voice low and soporific, and when at last she finished the final sentence, she leaned over, checking Ellie's face. Her eyes were closed, and she was snoring very gently. Sandra kissed her cheek, clicked off the light, and then stood and came across to me.

'Maddie,' she said very quietly. 'Maddie, do you want a story from Rowan?'

Maddie said nothing, and Sandra leaned over and peered at her face, still turned to the wall. Her eyes were shut tight.

'Out like a light!' Sandra whispered, a touch of triumph in her voice. 'Oh well, your rendition will have to wait until tomorrow. I'm sorry I didn't hear it.'

She kissed Maddie's cheek too, drew her covers up a little and tucked some kind of soft toy under her chin – I couldn't see what exactly – and then clicked off her light as well, leaving just the glow of the night light. Then she gave a last glance back at her sleeping daughters and made her way to the door, with me following behind.

'Can you close the door after you?' she said, and I turned, ready to do so, glancing back at the little white beds and their occupants, both in shadow now.

The night light was very soft, and too close to the floor to show much except for shadows around the girls' beds, but for a moment, deep in the blackness, I thought I saw the glint of two little eyes, glaring at me.

Then they snapped shut, and I pulled the door to behind me.

I couldn't sleep that night. It wasn't the bed, which was as sumptuously comfortable as before. It wasn't the heat. The room had been oppressively warm when I first entered, but I had managed to persuade the system to switch to cooling mode and now the air was pleasantly temperate. It wasn't even my worries over being left alone with the children the next day. If anything I was feeling relieved at the thought of getting rid of Bill and Sandra. Well ... not Sandra ... mostly Bill if truth were told.

The uncomfortable end to the evening flashed through my head once more. We had been sitting in the kitchen, talking and chatting, and then at last Sandra had stretched and yawned and announced her intention to make an early night of it.

She'd kissed Bill and headed for the stairs, and just as I was thinking about following her, Bill had refilled both our glasses without asking me.

'Oh,' I said half-heartedly. 'I was ... I mean I shouldn't ... '

'Come on.' He pushed the glass towards me. 'Just one more. This is my only chance to get to know you before I entrust my kids to your care, after all! You could be anyone for all I know.'

He gave me a grin, his tanned cheeks wrinkling, and I wondered how old he was. He could have been anything from forty to sixty, it was hard to tell. He wore rimless glasses, and had one of those tanned, slightly weather-beaten faces, and his cropped hair gave him an almost ageless quality, slightly Bruce Willis-esque.

I was very tired – the long journey and the stress of packing had finally hit me like a ton of bricks. But there was enough truth in his remark for me to sigh inwardly and draw the glass towards me. He was right after all. This was our one chance to get to know each other before he left. It would seem strange and evasive to refuse him that.

He rested his chin on one hand and watched, as I picked up the glass and put it to my lips, his head tilted, his eyes following the movement of the wine to my lips, and staying there.

'So, who are you, Rowan Caine?' he asked. His voice was a little slurred, and I wondered how much he'd had to drink.

Something, something in his tone, in the directness of the question, in the uncomfortably intense intimacy of his gaze, made my stomach shift uneasily.

'What do you want to know?' I said, with an attempt at light-ness.

'You remind me of someone ... but I can't think who. A film star, maybe. You don't have any famous relatives, do you? A sister in Hollywood?'

I gave a smile at this rather tired line.

'No, definitely not. I'm an only child, and anyway, my family's about as ordinary as you can get.'

'Maybe it's work ... anyone in the family work in architec-ture?'

I thought of my stepfather's insurance sales business and only just stopped myself from rolling my eyes. Instead, I shook my head firmly, and he looked at me over his wine glass, frowning so that a deep furrow appeared at the bridge of his nose.

'Maybe it's that ... what's-her-name. That *Devil Wears Prada* woman.'

'What, Meryl Streep?' I said, startled out of my nervousness enough to give a short laugh. He shook his head impatiently.

'No, the other one. The young one. Anne Hathaway – that's it. You've got a look of her.'

'Anne Hathaway?' I tried not to look as sceptical as I felt. Anne Hathaway maybe if she gained three or four stone and had acne scars and a hair cut by the salon trainee. 'I have to say, Bill, you're very kind, but that's the first time I've ever heard that comparison.'

'It's not that, though.' He got up and came around the breakfast bar to my side of it, sitting on the gleaming chrome stool facing me, his legs spread wide so that I couldn't easily move without rubbing his thigh. 'No, it's not that. I definitely feel like we've met. Who did you say you worked for before this?'

I rattled off the list again and he shook his head, dissatisfied.

'I don't know any of them. Maybe I'm imagining it. I feel like I'd remember a face ... well, a face like yours.'

Fuck. Something twisted in the pit of my stomach. I had been in this situation too often not to recognise where this was heading. My first job out of school, a young waitress with a boss who dangled a pay rise and complimented me on my fuchsia-pink bra. Countless creeps on countless nights out, putting themselves between me and the door. Randy dads at the nursery, angling for sympathy about their postpartum wives who didn't understand them ...

Bill was one of *them*.

He was my employer. He was my boss's husband. And worst of all he was ...

Jesus. I can't bring myself to say it.

My hands had begun to shake, and I clenched my fingers more tightly around the stem of my wine glass to try to hide it.

I cleared my throat and tried to push my stool back, but it was wedged against the edge of the breakfast bar. Bill's meaty denim-clad thighs blocked my way, effectively preventing me from getting down.

'Well, I'd better be heading up.' My voice fluted slightly with nerves. 'Early start tomorrow, right?'

'There's no hurry,' he said, and he reached out and took the wine glass from my fingers, filled it up, and then put out his hand towards my face. 'You've just ... you've got a little bit ... '

His smooth, slightly sweaty thumb stroked the corner of my bottom lip, and I felt one knee nudge, very gently, between mine.

For a second I froze, and a fluttering panicked nausea rose up, choking me. Then something inside me seemed to snap, and I slid abruptly down off the stool, barging past him so fast that the wine slopped and spilled onto the concrete.

'Sorry,' I stammered. 'So sorry, let me, I'll get a cloth –'

'It's fine,' he said. He was not one iota discomfited, only amused at my reaction. He stayed in place, half sitting, half leaning comfortably against the bar stool, as I grabbed a dishcloth and mopped at the floor between his legs.

For one second I looked up at him, and he looked down, and the quip I'd heard a thousand times, always accompanied by ribald laughter, flashed through the back of my mind. *While you're down there, love ...*

I stood up, my face burning, and dumped the wine-stained cloth in the sink.

'Goodnight, Bill,' I said abruptly, and I turned on my heel.

'Goodnight, Rowan.'

And I walked up the two flights of stairs to bed, not looking back.

As I shut the door of my new room behind me, I felt a sense of overwhelming relief. I'd unpacked earlier, and even though the room didn't feel like home yet, it did have a sense of being a little corner of the house that was my own territory, somewhere I could spread out, stop acting a part, stop being Rowan the Perfect Nanny and just be ... me.

I pulled the elastic band out of my tight, perky ponytail and felt my thick wiry hair spring out into a crown around my head, and the polite, people-pleasing smile that I'd had plastered on my face since I'd arrived relax into a weary neutrality. As I stripped off the buttoned-up cardigan, blouse and tweed skirt I felt like I was shedding layers of pretence, back to the girl I was behind the facade – the one who wore pyjamas until bedtime at the weekends, who lay on the sofa not reading an improving book, but mainlining *Judge Judy*. The one who would have called Bill a fucking pig, instead of standing there, paralysed into politeness, before offering to wipe up after herself.

The intricacies of the control panels were a welcome distraction from having to think about that part of things, and by the time I'd wrested control of the temperature down to something more reasonable, and remembered how to work the shower, my heart was thumping less and I was talking myself round into an acceptance of the situation.

OK, so Bill was a creep. He wasn't the first I'd encountered. Why was I so disappointed to find him here?

I knew the answer of course. But it wasn't just who he was. It was everything he represented – all the hard work and careful planning that had brought me here, all the hopes and dreams bound up with my decision to apply. That feeling that for once in my life something was going *right*, falling into place. The whole situation had seemed perfect – too perfect perhaps. There had to be a fly in the ointment, and maybe Bill was it.

Suddenly the supernatural stuff didn't seem so mysterious after all. Not a poltergeist. Just your average fifty-something man who couldn't keep his dick in his pants. The same old, boring, depressing story.

Still, it felt like a kick in the guts.

It wasn't until I had finished showering and had done my teeth, and was lying in bed, that I looked up at the ceiling. At the recessed light fittings, and the little blinking smoke alarm by the door, and ... something else in the corner over there. What *was* that? A burglar alarm sensor? A second smoke detector?

Or was it ...

I thought of Sandra's remark at my interview ... *the whole house is wired up* ...

It *couldn't* be a camera ... could it?

But no. That would be more than creepy. That would be illegal surveillance. I was an employee – and I had a reasonable expectation of privacy, or whatever the legal terminology was.

All the same, I got up, wrapped my dressing gown around myself and dragged a chair over to the carpet beneath the egg-shaped thing in the corner. One of my socks was lying on the floor where I'd stripped it off before getting in the shower, and I picked it up, climbed onto the chair, and stood on tiptoes to fit it over the sensor. I could *just* reach. It fitted perfectly and the empty toe of the sock hung there, flaccid and slightly disconsolate.

Only then, comforted, though with a feeling of slight ridiculousness, did I get back into bed and finally let myself fall asleep.

I awoke in the night with a start, and the vague feeling of something wrong – without being able to put my finger on it. I lay there, my heart pounding, wondering what it was that had woken me. I had no memory of having been dreaming – only a sudden jerk into consciousness.

It took a minute, and then it came again – a noise. Footsteps. *Creak ... creak ... creak ...* slow and measured, as though someone was pacing on a wooden floor, which made no sense at all, since all the floors up here were thickly carpeted.

Creak ... creak ... creeeeak ... The sound was hollow, heavy, resonant ... a slow tread like a man's, not the scamper of a child. It sounded as though it was coming from above, which was ridiculous as I was on the top floor.

Slowly, I sat up and groped for the light, but when I turned the switch, nothing happened. I flicked it again, and then realised with a curse that I must have overridden the lamp at the main panel. I couldn't face grappling with the control panel in the middle of the night, and risking turning on the sound system or something, so I grabbed my phone from where it was charging and switched on the torch.

My chest was tight, and as I took a pull at my inhaler I realised suddenly that the room was extremely cold. No doubt when I had changed the temperature settings I had overdone it. Now, outside of the warm cocoon of bedclothes, the chill was uncomfortable. But my dressing gown was on the foot of the bed, so I pulled it on and stood there, trying not to let my teeth chatter, the thin beam of torchlight illuminating a narrow sliver of wheat-coloured carpet and not much else.

The footsteps had stopped, and I hesitated for a moment, holding my breath, listening, wondering if they would start up again. Nothing. I took another puff at my inhaler, waiting, considering. Still nothing.

The bed was warm, and it was tempting to crawl back under the duvet and pretend I hadn't heard anything, but I knew that I wouldn't sleep well unless I at least *tried* to check out the source. Pulling my dressing-gown belt tighter, I opened the door of my room a crack.

There was no one outside, but nevertheless I peered into the broom cupboard. It was, of course, empty except for the brushes, and the winking charge light of the Hoover. No possibility of anything bigger than a mouse hiding in here.

I shut the cupboard and then, feeling a little like a trespasser, I tried Rhiannon's door, resolutely ignoring the scrawled *KEEP OUT OR YOU DIE*. I had thought it might be locked, but the handle turned without resistance and the heavy door swung wide, shushing across the thick carpet.

Inside it was pitch-black, the blackout curtains firmly drawn, but it had the indefinable feel of an empty room. Still, I held up my phone and swung the narrow torch beam from wall to wall. There was no one there.

That was it. There were no other rooms on this floor. And the ceiling above was smooth and unbroken by so much as an attic hatch. For although my memory of the sounds was fading fast, my impression had been that the sounds were coming from above. Something on the roof maybe? A bird? It wasn't a person prowling around at any rate, that much was clear.

Shivering again, I returned to my own room, where I stood for a moment, irresolute, in the middle of the carpet, listening and waiting for the sound to come again, but it did not.

I turned off the torch, climbed back into bed and drew the covers up. But it was a long time before I slept.

'Mummy!'

The Tesla wound its way along the driveway towards the main road, with Ellie running in its wake, the tears streaming down her face as Jack's driving speed outpaced her short legs.

'Mummy, come back!'

'Bye, darlings!' Sandra's head leaned out the rear window, her honey-coloured hair whipping in the breeze as the car picked up speed. There was a cheerful smile on her face, but I could see the distress in her eyes, and I knew that she was keeping up a happy facade for the sake of the children. Bill did not turn round. He was bent over his phone in the back seat beside her.

'Mummy!' Ellie shouted, desperation in her voice. 'Mummy, please don't go!'

'Bye, sweeties! You'll have a wonderful time with Rowan and I'll be back very soon. Goodbye! I love you all!'

And then the car rounded the bend in the drive and disappeared from sight among the trees.

Ellie's legs slowed, and she stumbled to a halt, letting out a wail of grief before she threw herself dramatically to the ground.

'Oh, Ellie!' I hitched Petra higher on my hip and jogged down the drive to where Ellie lay, face first, on the gravel. 'Ellie, darling, come on, let's go and get some ice cream.'

I knew from Sandra's instructions that this was a big treat, something not allowed every day, because it made both girls rather hyper, but Ellie only shook her head and wailed louder.

'Come on, sweetheart.' I bent down, with some difficulty as I was holding Petra, and took her wrist, trying to pull her up, but she only let out a scream and wrenched her arm out of my hand, slamming her little fist onto the gravel.

'Ow!' she screamed, redoubling her sobs, and looking up at me with angry, red, tear-filled eyes. 'You *hurt* me!'

'I was just trying –'

'Go *away*, you *hurt* me, I'm going to tell my mummy!'

I stood for a moment, irresolute over her angry, prone form, unsure what to do.

'Go *away*!' she screamed again.

At last, I gave a sigh and began to walk back up the drive towards the house. It felt wrong leaving her there, in the middle of what was, basically, a road, but the gate at the foot of the drive was shut and it would be at least half an hour before Jack returned. Hopefully she would have calmed down long before then, and I could coax her back into the house.

On my hip Petra had begun grousing, and I suppressed a sigh. Please, not a meltdown from her as well. And where the hell was Maddie? She had disappeared before her parents left, flitting off into the woods to the east of the house, refusing to say goodbye.

'Oh, let her go,' Bill had said, as Sandra flapped around trying to find her to kiss her goodbye. 'You know what she's like, she prefers to lick her wounds in private.'

Lick her wounds. Just a silly cliché, right? At the time I hadn't dwelt on it, but now I wondered. Was Maddie wounded? If so, how?

Up in the house I sat Petra in her high chair, strapped her in, and checked the red binder in case it gave instructions for what to do if the children disappeared off the face of the earth. The whole thing must have been at least three inches thick and a cursory flick-through after breakfast had told me that it contained information on everything from how much Calpol to give and when, through to bedtime routines, favourite books, nappy rash protocol, homework schedules, and what washing capsules to use for the girls' ballet uniforms. Virtually every moment of the day was accounted for, with notes ranging from what snacks to serve, right through to which TV programmes to choose, and how much they were allowed to watch.

The one thing it didn't cover was total disappearance – or at least, if it did, I couldn't find the page where it was mentioned, but as I skimmed down the carefully annotated 'typical week-end day', I saw that Petra was overdue for lunch, which might explain her irritability. I didn't really want to start preparing food before I'd tracked down Maddie and Ellie, but at least I could give Petra a snack to tide her over and stop her grumbling.

6 a.m., the page began. *All the younger ones (but particularly Ellie) are prone to early wakings. To that end, we have installed the sleep-training 'Happy Bunny clock' app in the girls' room. It's a digital clock with a screen image of a sleeping bunny that soundlessly switches over to an image of a wide-awake 'Happy Bunny' at 6 a.m. If Ellie wakes before this please gently (!) encourage her to check the clock and get back into bed if the bunny is still asleep. Obviously use your judgement regarding nightmares and toilet accidents.*

Jesus. Was there nothing in this house that wasn't controlled by the bloody app? I scanned down the page, skipping past suggested outfits and wet-weather clothes, and acceptable breakfast menus, down to mid-morning.

10.30–11.15. Snack – eg some fruit (bananas, blueberries, grapes QUARTERED for Petra please), raisins (sparingly only – teeth!), breadsticks, rice cakes or cucumber sticks. No strawberries (Ellie is allergic), no whole nuts (nut butters are OK but we only buy the sugar/salt-free kind), and finally Petra is not allowed snacks containing refined sugar or excess salt (older girls are allowed sugar in moderation). This can be hard to police if you are out so in that scenario I suggest taking a snack box.

Well, at least the app didn't prepare the snacks. Still, I'd never encountered anything like this level of detail at any other nannying job – at Little Nippers the staff handbook was a slim pamphlet that concentrated mostly on how to report staff sickness. Rules, yes. Screen time, sanctions, red lines, allergies – all of that was normal. But this – did she think I had spent nearly ten years in childcare without knowing you had to cut up grapes?

As I closed the scarlet folder and pushed it away from me across the table, I wondered. Was it the unsettling changes of staff that had made Sandra so controlling? Or was she just a woman desperately trying to be there for her family, even when she couldn't be physically present? Bill, it was clear, felt no compunction about leaving his children alone with a comparative stranger, however well qualified. But Sandra's binder spoke of a very different type of parent – one very conflicted about the situation she was in. Which begged the question of why, in that case, she was so determined to be with Bill, rather than at home? Was it really just professional pride? Or was there something else going on?

There was a huge marble fruit bowl in the centre of the concrete table, freshly stocked with oranges, apples, satsumas and bananas, and with a sigh, I ripped a banana off the bunch, peeled it, and placed a few chunks on Petra's tray. Then I went into the playroom to see if Maddie had returned. She wasn't there, nor was she in the living room, or anywhere in the house as far as I could tell. At last I went to the utility-room door, the one she had left by, and called out into the woods.

'Maddie! Ellie! Petra and I are having ice cream.' I paused, listening for the sound of running feet, cracking branches. Nothing came. 'With sprinkles.' I had no actual idea if there were sprinkles but at this point I didn't care about false advertising, I just wanted to know where they both were.

More silence, just the sound of birds. The sun had gone in, leaving the air surprisingly chilly, and I shivered, feeling the goosebumps rise on my bare arms. Suddenly hot chocolate seemed more appropriate than ice cream, in spite of the fact that it was June.

'OK!' I called again, more loudly this time. 'More sprinkles for me!'

And I walked back into the house, leaving the side door open a crack.

In the kitchen I did a double take.

Petra was standing up in her high chair on the far side of the breakfast bar, triumphantly waving a chunk of banana at me.

'Fuck!'

For a moment all feeling drained out of me, and I stood, frozen to the spot, looking at her precarious stance, the unforgiving concrete beneath her, her small wobbly feet on the slippery wood.

And then, regaining my senses, I ran, stumbling over a stray teddy, staggering around the corner of the breakfast bar to snatch her up, my heart in my mouth.

'Oh my God, Petra, you bad, bad girl. You *mustn't* do that. Jesus. Oh Jesus Christ.'

She could have died – that was the long and short of it. If she'd fallen and struck her head on the concrete floor, she would have been concussed before I could reach her.

How could I have been so stupid?

I'd supervised toddlers a million times before – I'd done all the right things, pulled her chair away from the counter so she couldn't push herself backwards with her feet, and I was sure, *certain* in fact, that I'd done up those clips. They were far too stiff for little fingers.

So how had she got free?

Had she wriggled out?

I examined the clips. One side was still fastened. The other was open. Shit. I must have not pushed one home quite hard enough, and Petra had worked it loose, and then managed to squirm out of the other side of the restraint.

So it was my fault after all. The thought made my hands feel cold with fear, and my cheeks feel hot with shame. Thank *God* it hadn't happened when Sandra was here. That kind of safeguarding stuff was pretty much nannying 101. She would have been within her rights to sack me there and then.

Though of course ... she still could, if she was watching over the cameras. In spite of myself, my eyes flicked up to the ceiling, and sure enough there was one of those little white egg-shaped domes in the far corner of the room. I felt my face flush and looked away hastily, imagining Sandra seeing my guilty reaction.

Fuck. *Fuck*.

Well, there was nothing I could do, apart from hope that Sandra and Bill had better things to do than pore over the footage of their security cameras every hour of the day and night. I was pretty confident that Bill hadn't so much as glanced at the app since leaving, but Sandra ... somehow that binder spoke of a level of intensity that I had not quite anticipated, from her relaxed, cheerful manner at interview.

But with any luck they would be in a mobile black spot, or even in the air by now. Did the footage record? How long was it stored for? I didn't know, and somehow I doubted whether that information was in the binder.

The realisation was unsettling. I could be being watched, right now.

It was with a strange performative feeling that I hugged Petra tightly to my chest, and dropped a shaky kiss on the top of her head. Beneath my lips I felt the gentle flex of her fontanelle, the fragility of a baby-soft skull almost, but not quite, closed over.

'Don't do that again,' I told her firmly, feeling the adrenaline still pulsing through me, and then, with an effort at restoring normality, I lifted her up and took her over to the sink, where I wiped her face. Then I looked at my watch, trying to breathe slowly and normally, and remember what I had been doing before Petra scared the life out of me.

It was just gone one. The binder had said Petra ate lunch '12.30–1' and then went down for a nap at 2 p.m. But in spite of that, she was grousing and rubbing her eyes crossly, and I found myself mentally adding up timings and trying to figure out how to handle this. At the nursery they'd gone down straight after lunch more or less, around one.

I didn't want to mess with her routine so early in the day, but on the other hand, stretching out a tired, cranky baby until the specified time wasn't a great idea either, and would probably result in a bad night's sleep if she was the type of child who got more wired the more exhausted she became. I stared doubtfully down at the top of her head, trying to decide. Suddenly, the idea of a quiet hour or so to round up Maddie and Ellie was very appealing. It would definitely be easier without a fussy toddler in tow.

Fretfully, Petra scrubbed a balled-up fist at her eyes and gave a tired sob, and I made up my mind.

'Come on you,' I said aloud, and took her upstairs to her room.

Inside the blackout blinds were already drawn, and I switched on the illuminated mobile as the binder had instructed and put her gently down on her back. She rolled over onto her tummy and rubbed her face into the mattress, but I sat quietly beside her, one hand on her wriggling spine, while the soft light show played over the ceiling and walls. Petra was grumbling to herself, but her cries were getting farther apart, and I could tell she was ready to go under at any moment.

At last, she seemed to be completely asleep, and I stood carefully and laid her rabbit comforter gently over one hand, where she could find it if she woke. For a moment she stirred and I froze, but her fingers only tightened onto the material as she let out a soft little snore. With a sigh of relief, I picked up the monitor that was hooked over the end of the cot, tucked it into my belt, and tiptoed out of the room.

The house was completely silent, as I stood on the landing, listening for the sound of running feet or childish laughter.

Where the hell were they?

I hadn't been in Sandra and Bill's room, but I knew from the layout of the house that the window must overlook the drive, and holding my breath slightly, I turned the handle and opened the door.

The sight made my breath catch in my throat for a moment. The room was huge. They must have knocked together at least two other bedrooms to make it – maybe even three. There was an enormous bed piled high with plump cushions and white bedlinen, and facing it a huge carved stone fireplace. Three long windows overlooked the front of the house. One was open a few inches and muslin curtains fluttered a little in the breeze.

There were drawers left slightly open, and a closet ajar, and I felt a sharp tug of curiosity as I crossed the silver-grey carpet to the central window, but I pushed it down. For all I knew, Sandra and Bill could be watching me right now, and while I had an alibi for wanting to look out of the window over the drive, I certainly had no excuse for rummaging in their cupboards.

When I reached the window, Ellie was nowhere in sight, the curve of drive where she had been lying was empty. I was not sure whether that was a relief. At least Jack wouldn't run her over when he brought the Tesla back. But where on earth was she? Sandra had seemed remarkably relaxed about the children running off into the woods but every bone in my body was screeching discomfort with the situation – at the nursery we'd had to risk-assess everything from a trip to the park through to messy play with porridge oats, and there were a billion risks I had absolutely no way of knowing. What if there was a pond in the grounds? Or a steep fall? What if they climbed a tree and couldn't get down? What if the fencing wasn't secure and they wandered out into the road? What if a dog –

I broke off my mental litany of worst-case scenarios.

The dogs. I'd forgotten to ask Sandra whether their routine was down to me, but presumably an extra walk couldn't hurt, and surely they would be able to find the children? If nothing else, their presence would give me an excuse to go hunting in the woods without looking to the children like they were running rings around me. I had to establish myself as someone firmly in charge right from the outset, otherwise my authority was going to be shot to pieces, and I would never recover.

I pushed aside the unsettling thought of what would happen when Rhiannon returned and a teenager was added to the mix. Hopefully Sandra would be home by then to back me up.

Downstairs the dogs were lying in their baskets in the kitchen, though they both looked up hopefully as I walked in carrying their leads.

'Walkies!' I said brightly, and they bounded over. 'Good girl ... er ... Claude,' I said as I struggled to find the right attachment on the collar, though in truth I wasn't sure if I had the girl or the boy. Claude bounded around me excitedly as I wrestled with Hero, but at last I had them both on leads and a handful of dog biscuits in my pocket in case of problems, and I set off, out of the utility-room door, across the gravelled yard, past the stable block, and into the woods.

It was a beautiful day. In spite of my growing anxiety about the children, I couldn't help but notice that as I walked down a winding, faintly marked path through the trees, the dogs straining at their leashes. The sun filtered through the canopy above, and our movements sent golden dust motes spinning and whirling up from the rich loam underneath our feet, the sun gleaming off the tiny particles of pollen and old man's beard that floated in the still air beneath the trees.

The dogs seemed to have a definite idea of where they were going, and I let them lead, conscious of the fact that they were probably puzzled about being kept on leashes in their own garden. They'd have to put up with it, though. I had no idea if they'd come when I called, and I couldn't risk losing them as well.

We were heading downhill, towards the bottom of the drive, though I couldn't see it through the trees. Behind me I heard the crack of a twig and turned sharply, but there was no one there. It must have been an animal, a fox perhaps.

At last we broke out of the cover of the trees into a little clearing, and my stomach gave an uncomfortable lurch, for there it was – the thing I'd been fearing ever since the girls had disappeared – a pond. Not very deep, but plenty deep enough for a small child to drown. The water was peat-coloured and brackish, an oily scum floating on the surface from the decomposing pine needles. I poked it doubtfully with a stick and bubbles of stagnant air floated lazily to the surface, but to my relief the rest of the pond looked undisturbed, the water clear except for the swirls of mud my stick had stirred up. Or ... nearly undisturbed. Walking around the far side I saw the imprints of small shoes on the bank, skidding as if two little girls had been messing around by the water's edge. There was no way of knowing when they had been made, but they looked fairly fresh. The prints led down the bank, becoming deeper and deeper as the mud softened, and then turned and went away again, back into the forest. I followed them for a few metres until the ground became too hard to take a print, but there were two sets of shoes, and at least I knew now that they were probably together, and almost certainly safe.

The dogs were whining and straining against their leads, desperate to get into the muddy pond and splash about, but there was no way I was having that. I wasn't bathing a pair of filthy dogs on my first day on top of everything else.

There was no path up through the woods in the direction the footsteps had been leading, but I followed in as near an approximation as I could, when suddenly a crackling scream split the air. I stopped dead, my heart thumping erratically in my chest for the second time that day, the dogs barking hysterically and leaping at the end of their leashes.

For a second I didn't know what to do. I stood, looking wildly around. The scream had sounded close at hand, but I could see no one, and I couldn't hear any footsteps over the noise the dogs were making. Then it came again, long and almost unbearably high-pitched, and with a stomach-lurching realisation, I understood.

I pulled the baby monitor out of my pocket, and watched as the lights flared and dipped in time with the long, bubbling shriek of pure fear.

For a moment I just stood there paralysed, holding the monitor in my hand, the dogs' leads looped around my wrist. Should I try to access the cameras?

With shaking hands, I pulled out my phone and pressed the icon of the home management app.

Welcome to Happy, Rowan, the screen said, with agonising slowness. *Home is where the Happy is!* And then, to my despair, *Updating user permissions. Please be patient. Home is where the Happy is!*

I swore, stuffed both the phone and the receiver back into my pocket, and began to run.

I was a long way from the house, down a slope, and my breath was tearing in my throat by the time I left the cover of the trees and saw the house in front of me. The dogs had broken away from me some way back, tugging their leads out of my numb fingers, and now they were leaping and gambolling in front and behind me, barking joyfully, convinced that this was all some kind of game.

When I reached the front door, it was standing ajar, in spite of the fact that I knew it had been closed when I left – I had used the utility-room door, leaving it open for Maddie and Ellie in case they returned, and for a second I thought I might be sick. What had I done? What had happened to poor little Petra?

I was almost too frightened to stumble the last few steps up the flight of stairs to the nursery, but I forced myself, leaving the dogs in the hallway, tangled up in their own leads, and at last I was outside Petra's door, sick with fear about what I was about to find.

It was closed, just as I'd left it, and I pushed down a sob in my throat as I turned the knob – but what I found there made me stop short on the threshold, blinking and trying to fight down my gasping breath.

Petra was asleep, in her cot, arms flung out to either side, sooty lashes sweeping her pink cheeks. Her bunny was clutched in her left hand, and she had plainly not stirred since I had put her down.

It didn't make sense.

I had just enough self-control left to back out of the room, closing the door quietly behind me, before I sank to the floor in the hallway outside, my back hard against the knobbly ban- nisters, my face in my hands, trying not to sob with shock and relief, feeling the wheeze in my chest as my lungs laboured to take in enough oxygen to stabilise my pounding pulse.

With shaky hands, I pulled my inhaler out of my pocket and took a puff, then tried to make sense of it all. What had happened?

Had the sound *not* come from the monitor? But that was impossible – it was equipped with lights that illuminated to show
when the baby was crying, in case you had the volume turned
low for some reason. I had *seen* the lights. And the noise had
been coming from the speaker, I was certain of it.

Had Petra had a nightmare and cried out? But when I thought
back, that didn't make sense either. It was not a baby's cry. That
was part of what had frightened me so much. The sound I'd
heard was not the fretful wail I knew so well from the nursery,
but a long, throbbing shriek of terror, one made by a much older
child, or even an adult.

'Hello?'

The voice came from downstairs, making me jump again,
convulsively this time, and I stood, my pulse racing, and leaned
over the bannisters.

'Hello? Who is it?' My voice came out not sharp and author-
itative as I had intended, but quavering and squeaky with fear.
'Who's there?' It had been an adult voice, a woman, and now
I heard footsteps in the hall, and saw a face below, peering up
at me.

'You'll be the new nanny, I dare say?'

It was a woman, perhaps fifty or sixty years old, her face rud-
dy and her body foreshortened by my perspective. She looked
plump and motherly, but there was something in her voice and
her expression that I couldn't quite pin down. It wasn't welcome,
that was for sure. A sort of ... pinched disapproval?

There were leaves in my hair, and as I began to make my way
down the flight of steps towards the ground floor, I saw that I'd
left a trail of spattered mud on the thick carpet, in my headlong
flight to Petra.

Two buttons had come adrift on my blouse and I fastened
them and coughed, feeling my face still hot with exertion and
fright.

'Um, hello. Yes. Yes, I'm Rowan. And you must be ... '

'I'm Jean. Jean McKenzie.' She looked me up and down, not troubling to conceal her disapproval, and then shook her head. 'It's up to you, Miss, but I don't approve of keeping children locked out, and I dare say Mrs Elincourt wouldnae like it either.'

'Locked out?' I was puzzled for a moment. 'What do you mean?'

'I found the poor bairns shivering on the step in their sundresses when I came to clean.'

'But wait –' I put out a hand – 'hang on a second. I didn't lock anyone out. They ran away from *me*. I was out looking for them. I left the back door open for them.'

'It was locked when I arrived,' Jean said stiffly. I shook my head.

'It must have blown shut but I didn't lock it. I wouldn't.'

'It was *locked* when I arrived,' was all she said, with a touch of stubbornness this time. Anger flared inside me, replacing the fear I'd felt for Petra. Was she accusing me of lying?

'Well ... maybe it came off the latch or something,' I said at last. 'Are the girls OK?'

'Aye, they're having a bite in the kitchen wi' me.'

'Were you –' I stopped, trying to figure out how to phrase this without placing myself even lower in her estimation. Plainly, for whatever reason, this woman didn't like me, and I mustn't give her any ammunition to report to Sandra. 'I came back because I heard a sound from Petra on the baby monitor. Did you hear her?'

'She's not let out a peep,' Jean said firmly. 'I've been keeping my eye on them all –' unlike you, was the unspoken subtext – 'and I'd have heard her if she was greeting.'

'Greeting?'

'Crying,' Jean said impatiently.

'Maddie then? Or Ellie? Did either of them come up?'

'They've been down in the kitchen with me, Miss,' Jean said, a touch of real crossness in her voice. 'Now if you'll excuse me, I need to be getting back to them. They're too wee to be left alone wi' the stove.'

'Of course.' I felt my cheeks flush with the implied criticism. 'But please, that's my job. I'll give them lunch.'

'I've given it to them already. The poor wee mites were ravenous, they needed something hot in them.'

I felt my temper, already frayed by the stress of the morning, begin to break.

'Look, Mrs … ' I groped for the name, and then found it, 'McKenzie, I've already explained, the girls ran away from me, I didn't lock them out. Maybe if they got a bit cold and scared waiting for someone to let them in, that'll make them think twice about running off next time. Now if you don't mind me, I've got work to do.'

I pushed past her and stalked into the kitchen, feeling her eyes boring into my back.

In the kitchen Maddie and Ellie were sitting at the breakfast bar eating chocolate-chip cookies and drinking juice, with what looked like the remains of a pizza on a plate by the sink. I felt my jaw tighten. All of those foods were strictly on Sandra's 'occasional treat' list. I'd been planning to settle them down for a film in the afternoon with some cookies in the TV room. Now that was off the menu, Mrs McKenzie was in their good books and I would be the bitch nanny who locked them out and had to enforce a healthy supper.

I pushed down my irritation and made myself smile pleasantly.

'Hello, girls – were you playing hide-and-seek?'

'Yes,' Ellie said with a giggle, but then she remembered our earlier quarrel, and frowned. 'You hurt my wrist.'

She held it out, and there, to my chagrin, was a ring of bruises on the pale skin of her stick-thin wrist.

I felt my cheeks colour.

I thought about arguing with her but I didn't want to raise the issue in front of Mrs McKenzie, and besides, it seemed like I'd done enough to antagonise them both today. Better to swallow my pride.

'I'm ever so sorry, Ellie.' I bent down beside her at the breakfast bar so that our heads were on a level, speaking softly so that Mrs McKenzie wouldn't hear. 'I truly didn't mean to. I was just worried you'd hurt yourself on the drive, but I really apologise if I was holding your arm too hard. It was an accident, I promise, and I feel terrible about it. Can we be friends?'

For a second, I thought I saw Ellie wavering, then she jerked and gave a little whimper.

Beneath the breakfast bar I saw Maddie's hand whip back into her lap.

'Maddie,' I said quietly, 'what just happened?'

'Nothing,' Maddie said, almost inaudibly, speaking to her plate more than me.

'Ellie?'

'N-nothing,' Ellie said, but she was rubbing her arm, and there were tears in her bright blue eyes.

'I don't believe you. Let me see your arm.'

'Nothing!' Ellie said, more fiercely. She pulled down her cardigan and gave me a look of angry betrayal. 'I said nothing, go away!'

'OK.'

I stood up. Whatever chance I had had there with Ellie, I'd blown it for the moment. Or rather Maddie had.

Mrs McKenzie was standing against the counter, her arms crossed, watching us. Then she folded the tea towel and hung it over the stove rail.

'Well, I'll be away now, girls,' she said. Her voice, when she spoke to the children, was softer and far more friendly than the terse, clipped tone she'd used with me. She bent and dropped a kiss on top of each head, first Ellie's blonde curls, then Maddie's wispy dark locks. 'You give your wee sister a kiss from me, now, mind.'

'Yes, Mrs M,' Ellie said obediently. Maddie said nothing, but she squeezed Mrs McKenzie's waist with one arm, and I thought I saw a wistful look in her eye as her gaze followed the woman to the door.

'Goodbye now, girls,' Mrs McKenzie said, and then she was gone. Outside I heard a car start up, and bump down the drive to the road.

Alone in the kitchen with the two little girls I felt suddenly drained and I sank down on the armchair in the corner of the room, wanting nothing more than to put my face in my hands and bawl. What had I taken on with these two hostile little creatures? And yet, I couldn't blame them. I could only imagine how I would have reacted if I'd been left for a week with a total stranger.

The last thing I could cope with was losing the children in the grounds again, so while they finished up their cookies, I crossed into the hallway and examined the inside of the big front door. There was no key – no keyhole even, as I'd observed the very first time I had arrived. Instead the white panel I had noticed contained a thumb sensor – Sandra had programmed my thumbprint into her phone app earlier that morning, before she left, and shown me how to operate it.

There was a matching panel on the inside, and I gingerly touched it, watching as a series of illuminated icons sprang into life. One of them was a big key, and remembering Sandra's instructions, I tapped it cautiously, and heard a grinding click as the deadlocks inside the door slid home. There was something rather dramatic, even ominous about the sound, almost like a prison cell lock grinding into place. But at least the door was secure now. There was no way Maddie or Ellie could even reach the panel without a set of steps, let alone activate the lock, since I very much doubted Sandra would have programmed their fingerprints into the system.

Then I went into the utility room. The door here operated with just a regular lock and key – as if Sandra and Bill's budget had run out, or as if they didn't care about the servants' entrance. Or maybe there was some practical reason one door needed to be traditionally operated. Something to do with power cuts or building regulations, perhaps. Either way, it was a relief to be faced with technology an average person could figure out, and it was with a feeling of satisfaction that I twisted the key firmly in the lock and then tucked it away on the door frame above, just as the binder had instructed. *We keep all keys for the doors operated by traditional locks on the door frame above the corresponding door, so that they are handy in case of emergency, but out of reach of the children*, the paragraph had read. There was something comforting about seeing it up there, high up and far away from little fingers.

Mission accomplished, I went back into the kitchen, my best and brightest smile firmly plastered on.

'Right, girls, what do you say we go through to the TV room and watch a movie. *Frozen? Moana?*'

'Yay, *Frozen!*' Ellie said, but Maddie butted in.

'We hate *Frozen.*'

'Really?' I made my voice sceptical. '*Really?* Because do you know, I love *Frozen.* In fact I know a singalong version of *Frozen* where they have the words on the screen and I'm really good at joining in all the songs.'

Behind Maddie I could see Ellie looking desperate, but too scared to contradict her sister.

'We *hate Frozen*,' Maddie repeated stubbornly. 'Come on, Ellie, let's go play in our room.'

I watched as she slid down from her stool and stomped into the hallway, the dogs' eyes following her with puzzlement as she went. In the doorway she paused and jerked her head meaningfully at her sister. Ellie's bottom lip quivered.

'We can still watch it if you want, Ellie,' I said, keeping my voice as light as I could. 'We could watch it together, just you and me. I could make popcorn?'

For a minute I thought I saw Ellie hesitate. But then something in her face seemed to harden, and she shook her head, slid from her stool, and turned to follow her sister.

As the sound of their footsteps faded away up the stairs, I sighed, and then turned to put the kettle on, to make myself a pot of tea. At least I would have half an hour to myself, to try to figure out the situation.

But before I had even finished filling the kettle, the baby monitor in my pocket gave a crackle, and then broke into a fretful coughing cry, telling me that Petra had woken up, and I was back on duty.

No rest for the wicked, then.

What had I taken on?

I know I'm going on. And I know you must be wondering when the hell I'm going to get to the point – to the reason I'm here, in this prison cell, and the reason I shouldn't be.

And I promise you, it's coming. But I can't – I can't seem to explain the situation quickly. That was the problem with Mr Gates. He never let me explain properly – to show how it all built up, all the little things, all the sleepless nights and the loneliness and the isolation, and the craziness of the house and the cameras and everything else. To explain properly, I have to tell it how it happened. Day by day. Night by night. Piece by piece.

Only that sounds as if I'm building something – a house perhaps. Or a picture in a jigsaw. Piece by piece. And the truth is, it was the other way round. Piece by piece, I was being torn apart.

And the first piece was that night.

That first evening ... well, it wasn't the worst, but it wasn't the best either, not by a long stretch.

Petra woke up from her nap cranky and fretful, and Maddie and Ellie refused to come out of their room all afternoon, even for supper, no matter how much I pleaded, no matter what ultimatums I laid down. *No pudding unless you are downstairs by the time I count from five ... four ... three ...* no sound of feet on the stairs ... *two ... one and a half ...*

It was when I said one and a half that I knew I had lost.

They weren't coming.

For a moment I thought about dragging them out. Ellie was small enough for me to grab her round the waist and carry her forcibly downstairs – but I had just enough sanity left to know that if I started that way, I would never be able to dial it back, and besides, it wasn't Ellie who was the problem, it was Maddie, and she was eight and solidly built and there was no way I could carry a kicking, screaming, fighting child down that long, curving staircase all by myself, still less force her to sit down and eat something once I got her into the kitchen.

In the end I capitulated and, after checking Sandra's suggested menu plan in the binder, I took pasta and pesto up to their bedroom – though the memory of those meek little heads bent over Jean McKenzie's chocolate-chip cookies was bitter in the back of my head as I knocked on the door and heard Maddie's fierce *Go away!*

'It's me,' I said meekly. 'I've got your pasta. I'll leave it here outside the door. But me and Petra will be downstairs having ice cream if you want some pudding.'

And then I left. It was all I could do.

Downstairs in the kitchen, I tried to stop Petra throwing her pasta on the floor, and I watched Maddie and Ellie on the iPad. My personalised log-in gave me permission to view the cameras in the children's room, playroom, kitchen and outside, and to control the lights and the music in some of the other rooms, but there was a whole menu of settings on the left that was greyed out and unavailable. I guessed I would have needed Sandra's log-in to control those.

Although I still found it a little creepy to be able to spy on the children from afar like this, I began to appreciate how useful it was. I was able to watch from my seat by the breakfast bar as Maddie moved towards the bedroom door, and then came back into view of the cameras, dragging the tray of food across the carpet.

There was a little table in the middle of the room, and I watched as she directed Ellie to one seat and put out their bowls and cutlery, and sat opposite her sister. I didn't have the sound on, but it was plain from her actions that she was bossing Ellie around and telling her to eat up – probably making her try the peas I had mixed into the pesto, judging by Ellie's gestures as she protested. My heart gave a funny little clench, of angry pity mixed with a kind of affection. Oh, Maddie, I wanted to say. It doesn't have to be like this. We don't have to be enemies.

But for the moment at least, it seemed like we did.

After supper I bathed Petra, listening with half an ear to the sounds of some kind of audiobook coming from Maddie and Ellie's room, and then I put her to bed, or rather tried to.

I did exactly as the binder said, following the instructions to the letter just as I had at lunchtime, but this time it wasn't working. Petra groused and thrashed and ripped off her nappy, and then when I put her firmly back into it and poppered her sleepsuit up the back, so she couldn't take it off, she began to wail, loudly and persistently.

For more than an hour I followed the binder's instructions and sat there, with my hand patiently on her back, listening to the soothingly repetitive jingle of the mobile and watching the lights circle on the ceiling, but it wasn't helping. Petra was getting more and more upset, and her cries were raising in pitch from irritated to angry, and from there to borderline hysterical.

As I sat there, stroking and trying not to let the tension in my wrist and hand convey itself to Petra, I glanced nervously up at the camera in the corner of the room. Maybe I was being watched right now. I could imagine Sandra at some corporate event, tensely sipping champagne as she followed the nursery feed on her phone. Was I about to get a call asking me what the hell I was doing?

The binder said to avoid taking Petra out of her cot after the lights were out, but the alternative, just leaving her there, didn't seem to be working either. In the end I picked her up and put her over my shoulder, walking her up and down the room, but she wailed angrily in my arms, arching her back as though trying to tip herself out of my grasp. So I put her back in the cot and she hauled herself to her feet and stood, sobbing furiously, her little red face pressed against the bars.

It seemed like there was nothing I could do, and my presence was only making her more furious.

At last, with a final, guilty glance at the camera, I gave up.

'Goodnight, Petra,' I said aloud, and then stood and left the room, closing the door firmly behind me, and listening as the sound of her cries diminished as I walked down the corridor.

It was gone 9 p.m., and I felt wrung out, exhausted by the effort of battling with the children all evening. I thought about going straight downstairs for a glass of wine, but in reality I *had* to check on Maddie and Ellie.

I could hear nothing coming from behind their bedroom door, and when I peered through the keyhole, everything inside seemed to be dark. Had they turned off the lights? I thought about knocking, but decided against it. If they were falling asleep the sound of a knock would probably undo all that.

Instead, I turned the knob very quietly, and pushed. The door opened a crack, but then met resistance.

Puzzled, I pushed harder, and there was a toppling crash, as a pile of something – I wasn't sure what – stacked up against the inside of the door fell with a clatter to the floor. I held my breath, waiting for wails and cries, but none came – apparently the children had slept through it.

Gingerly now, I slid through the gap I had created and switched on the torch of my phone to survey the damage. I wasn't sure whether to laugh or cry. They had piled up nearly all their movable furniture – cushions, teddies, books, chairs, the little table from the centre of the room – into a barricade on the inside of the bedroom door. It was comic, and yet at the same time more than a little pathetic. What were they trying to protect themselves against? Me?

I swung the torch around the room, and saw one of the bedside lamps, which they had unplugged and stacked on top of the pile of stuff. It had fallen to the floor when I toppled the stack, and the shade was wonky, but fortunately the bulb was not broken. Carefully, I straightened the shade, and then plugged it back in and set it on Ellie's bedside table. As the soft pink glow suffused the room, I saw them, curled together in Maddie's bed, looking for all the world like two little cherubs. Maddie's arms were firmly around her sister, almost constrictively, and I thought about trying to loosen her grip, but then decided against it. I'd dodged a bullet once with that huge crash, no point in rocking the boat further.

In the end, I moved just enough stuff away from the door to make it possible to slip in and out without causing an avalanche, and then left them, turning on Happy's listening function on my phone so that I could hear if they woke up.

Petra was still sobbing as I tiptoed quietly past her room, but the volume had decreased, and I hardened my heart and didn't look in. I told myself she would settle faster if I left her to it. And besides, I'd had nothing to eat or drink since noon – too busy trying to feed and bathe the girls to make supper for myself. I was suddenly ravenous, light-headed and desperate for food.

Downstairs, in the kitchen, I walked over to the fridge. 'You are low on milk,' said the robot voice, as I touched the door, making me jump convulsively. 'Shall I add it to the shopping list?'

'Er ... yes,' I managed. Was I going insane, talking aloud to a household appliance?

'Adding milk to your shopping list,' said the voice brightly, and again the screen on the door lit up, showing a list of groceries. 'Eat happy, Rowan!'

I tried not to think about how it figured out who was standing in front of it. Face recognition? Proximity of my phone? Either way, it felt distinctly unsettling.

At first sight the fridge contents looked distressingly healthy – a huge drawer full of green veg, tubs of fresh pasta, various pots of things like kimchi and harissa, and a large jar of something that looked like pond water, but which I thought might be kombucha. However, right at the back, behind some organic yogurts, I saw a cardboard pizza box, and with some difficulty I inveigled it out, and opened it up. I was just sliding the baking tray into the oven, when there was a sharp rap from the glass wall on the other side of the kitchen table.

I jumped and swung round, scanning the room. It was getting dark, rain spattering the glass, and although the far side of the room was in shadow, I could see very little outside except the jewelled droplets running down the enormous glass pane. I was just beginning to think I might have imagined it, or that perhaps a bird had flown into the glass, when a dark shape moved against the gloaming, black against grey. Something – some*one* – was out there.

'Who is it?' I called out, a little more sharply than I had intended. There was no answer, and I marched past the breakfast bar, around the kitchen table, and towards the glass wall, shrouded in darkness.

There was no panel over here – or none that I could see – but then I remembered the voice commands.

'Lights on,' I said sharply, and somewhat to my surprise, it worked – the huge brutalist chandelier above my head illuminating suddenly into a blaze of LED bulbs. The blast of brilliance left me blinking and astonished. But as soon as my eyes adjusted,

I realised my mistake. With the lights on, I could see absolutely nothing outside now apart from my own reflection in the glass. Whereas whoever was out there could see me very plainly.

'Lights off,' I said. Every light in the entire room went out immediately, plunging the kitchen into inky darkness.

'Shit,' I said under my breath, and began to feel my way back across the kitchen towards the panel by the door, to try to restore the settings to something halfway between retina-burning brilliance and total darkness. My eyes were still dazzled and hurting from the blast of light from the chandelier, but as my fingers finally sought out the control panel, I looked back towards the window, and thought, though I could not be sure, that I saw something whisk away around the side of the house.

I spent the rest of the time while the pizza was cooking glancing nervously over my shoulder into the dark shadows at the far side of the room, and chewing my nails. I had turned the baby monitor off, the better to hear any more sounds from outside, but Petra's sobs still filtered faintly down the stairs, not helping my stress levels.

I was tempted to put on some music, but there was something unnerving about the idea of drowning out the sound of a potential intruder. As it was, I hadn't seen or heard anything definite enough to call the police. A shape in the darkness and a knock that could have been anything from an acorn to a bird . . . it wasn't exactly *Friday the 13th*.

It was maybe ten or fifteen minutes later – though it felt like much more – when I heard another sound, this time from the side of the house, a knock that set the dogs barking from their baskets in the utility room.

The noise made me jump, though there was something more homely and ordinary about it than the hollow bang of before, and when I went through to the utility room, I could see a dark shape silhouetted outside the rain-spattered glass panes in the door. The figure spoke, his voice almost drowned by the hiss of the rain.

'It's me. Jack.'

Relief flooded through me.

'Jack!' I wrenched the door open, and there he was, standing just under the threshold, hunched in a raincoat, hands in pockets. The water was streaming down his fringe and dripping from his nose.

'Jack, was that you, before?'

'Before when?' he asked, looking puzzled, and I opened my mouth to explain – and then thought better of it.

'Never mind, it doesn't matter. What can I help with?'

'I won't keep you,' he said, 'I just wanted to check you were all right, with it being your first day and all.'

'Thanks,' I said awkwardly, thinking of the awful afternoon, and the fact that Petra was probably still sobbing into the baby monitor. Then, on an impulse I added, 'Will you – I mean, do you want to come in? The kids are in bed. I was just getting myself some supper.'

'Are you sure?' He looked at his watch. 'It's pretty late.'

'I'm sure,' I said, standing back to let him inside the utility room. He stood, dripping into the mat, and then stepped gingerly out of his boots.

'I'm sorry it's so late,' he said, as he followed me into the kitchen. 'I was meaning to come over before, but I had to take that bloody mower over to Inverness to be serviced.'

'You couldn't fix it?'

'Oh, aye, I got it running. But it clapped out again yesterday. Whatever's the matter, I can't seem to get to the bottom of it. But never mind about that. I didn't come to moan at you about my troubles. How was it with the kids?'

'It was –' I stopped, feeling, with horror, my bottom lip quiver treacherously. I wanted to put on a brave face – what if he reported back to Sandra and Bill? But I just couldn't do it. And besides, if they looked at the security footage they would know the truth soon enough. As if to set the seal on it, Petra gave a long bubbling wail of grief from upstairs that was loud enough to make Jack's head turn towards the stairs.

'Oh God, who am I kidding,' I said wretchedly. 'It was awful. The girls ran away from me after Bill and Sandra left, and I went to look for them in the woods and then that woman – what's her name? Mrs McKinty?'

'Jean McKenzie,' Jack said. He pulled his raincoat off and sat at the long table, and I found myself sinking into a chair opposite. I wanted to put my head in my hands and cry, but I forced myself to give a shaky laugh.

'Well, she turned up to clean and found the girls sitting on the doorstep claiming I'd locked them out which I absolutely *didn't*, I'd deliberately left the door open for them. They hate me, Jack, and Petra's been screaming for like an hour and –'

The wail came again, and I felt my stress level rise in tandem with its pitch.

'Sit down,' Jack said firmly, as I made to rise. He pushed me back into my chair. 'I'll see if I can settle her. She's probably just not used to your face, it'll be better tomorrow.'

It was in defiance of every safeguarding rule I'd ever been taught, but I was too tired and desperate to care – and besides, I told myself, Sandra and Bill would hardly have kept him on the premises if they thought he was a danger to their kids.

As the sound of his steps receded up the stairs, I switched on the baby monitor and listened to the door of Petra's room swish gently open and her choking, gasping cries subside as her body was lifted from the crib.

'There, there, my little love,' I heard, a low, intimate croon that made my cheeks flush as if I were eavesdropping, though Jack must surely know the baby monitor was plugged in. 'There,

there, ma poor wee lassie.' Upstairs, away from me, his accent was somehow stronger. 'Shh ... shh now, Petra ... there, there ... what a fuss over nothing.'

Petra's cries were lower now, more hiccups and grumbling than real distress, and I could hear the creak of the boards as Jack paced softly up and down, holding her, soothing and gentling the fretful baby with a surprisingly practised touch.

At last she fell silent, and I heard his feet stop, and the rattle of the cot bars as he leaned over, lowering her gently to the mattress.

There was a long pause, and then the shush of the door against the carpet, and Jack's feet on the stairs again.

'Success?' I said, hardly daring to believe it, as he entered the kitchen, and he nodded, and gave a little wry smile.

'Aye, I think the poor wee thing was knackered, she was just looking for an excuse to put her head down. She fell asleep almost as soon as I picked her up.'

'God, Jack, you must think I'm a complete –' I stopped, not sure what to say. 'I mean, *I'm* the nanny. I'm supposed to be good at this kind of stuff.'

'Don't be silly.' He sat again at the table, opposite me. 'They'll be fine when they get to know you. You're a stranger to them, that's all. And they're testing you. They've had enough nannies this past year to make them a bit mistrustful of a new one waltzing in and taking over. You know what kids are like – once they see you're here to stay and won't be off abandoning them again, it'll get better.'

'Jack ... ' It was the opening I'd been waiting for, and yet now it was here, I wasn't sure how to phrase my question. 'Jack, what *did* happen with those other nannies? Sandra said they left because they thought the house was haunted, but I can't believe ... I don't know, it just seems preposterous. Have you ever seen anything?'

As I said it I thought of the shadow I'd seen outside, and pushed the image away. It was probably just a fox, or a tree moving in the wind.

'Well ... ' Jack said, rather slowly. He reached out one of his big, work-roughened hands, the nails still a little grey with oil in spite of what must have been repeated scrubbing, and picked up the baby monitor I had laid down on the table, turning it thoughtfully. 'Well ... I wouldn't say –'

But whatever he had been about to say was cut short by a loud, rather peremptory voice saying, 'Rowan?'

Jack broke off, but I jumped so hard I bit my tongue and swung round, looking wildly for the source of the voice. It was that of an adult female, not one of the children, and it was very human, quite distinct from the robotic drone of the Happy app. Was someone in the *house*?

'Rowan,' the voice repeated, 'are you there?'

'He-hello?' I managed.

'Ah, hi, Rowan! It's Sandra.'

With a rush of mingled relief and fury, I realised – the voice was coming out of the speakers. Sandra had somehow dialled into the house system, and was using the app to talk to us. The sense of intrusion was indescribable. Why the hell couldn't she have just phoned?

'Sandra.' I swallowed back my anger, trying to restore my voice to the cheerful, upbeat tone I'd mastered at interview. 'Hi. Gosh, how are you?'

'Good!' Her voice echoed around the kitchen, magnified by the surround sound system, bouncing off the high glass ceiling. 'Tired! But more to the point, how are *you*? How's everything on the home front?'

I felt my eyes flicker to Jack, sitting at the table, thinking of how he had been the one to get Petra down. Had Sandra seen? Should I say something? I willed him not to cut in, and he didn't.

'Well … calm, right now,' I said at last. 'They're all in bed and safely asleep. Though I have to admit, Petra was a bit of a struggle. She went down like a lamb at lunchtime, but maybe I let her sleep too long, I don't know. She was really hard to get down this evening.'

'But she's asleep now? Well done.'

'Yes, she's asleep now. And the other two went down quiet as mice.'

Scared, defensive, angry mice – but they had at least been quiet. And they were asleep.

'I let them have supper in their room as they seemed really tired. I hope that was OK?'

'Fine, fine,' Sandra said, as though dismissing the question. 'And they behaved OK the rest of the day?'

'They –' I pursed my lips, wondering how truthful to be. 'They were a bit upset after you left, to be honest, especially Ellie. But they calmed down in the afternoon. I offered to let them watch *Frozen*, but they didn't want to. They ended up playing in their room.' Well, that part was true enough. The problem was that they hadn't come *out* of their room. 'Listen, Sandra, are there rules about the grounds?'

'How do you mean?'

'I mean, are they really allowed to just roam around, or should I be keeping them in? I know you and Bill are relaxed about it, but there's that pond – I'm just – it's making me a bit nervous.'

'Oh, that,' Sandra said. She laughed, the sound echoing around the space in a way that made me wish I knew how to control the volume on the speakers. 'It's barely six inches deep. Honestly, it's the reason Bill and I bought a place with big grounds, to give the children a bit of freedom to run wild. You don't need to helicopter them every second. They know they're not allowed to do anything silly.'

'I – I'm –' I stopped, struggling with how to put my concerns without sounding like I was criticising her parenting. I was horribly conscious of Jack sitting across the table from me, his eyes politely averted, trying to pretend he wasn't listening. 'Look, you know them better than I do, of course, Sandra, and if you're happy they're OK with that I'll take your word on it, but I'm just – I'm used to a closer level of supervision, if you know what I mean. Particularly around water. I know the water isn't that deep, but the mud –'

'Well, look,' Sandra said. She sounded a little defensive now, and I cursed myself. I had tried so hard not to sound critical. 'Look, you must use your common sense, of course you must. If you see them doing something stupid, step in. It's your job to supervise them, that goes without saying. But I don't see the point of having children stuck in front of the TV all afternoon when there's a big beautiful sunny garden outside.'

I was taken aback. Was this a dig about the fact that I had tried to bribe them with a film?

There was a long, uncomfortable pause, while I tried to figure out what to say. I wanted to snap the truth – the fact that it was impossible for one person to adequately supervise a five-year-old, an eight-year-old and a baby who could barely toddle, when they were scattered across several acres of wooded grounds. But I had a feeling that doing so would get me fired. It was plain that Sandra didn't want to discuss the risks involved in letting the girls roam.

'Well,' I said at last, 'I totally take that point, Sandra, and obviously I'm very keen to take advantage of the beautiful grounds for myself as well. I'll –' I stopped, groping for what to say. 'I'll use my common sense, as you suggest. Anyway, we had a pretty good day, considering, and the girls seem – they seem to have settled well. Would you like me to check in with you tomorrow?'

'I'll be in meetings all day, but I'll call before bedtime,' Sandra said, her voice slightly softer now. 'I'm sorry I didn't manage to speak to the girls before bed, but we were having dinner with a client. And anyway, it probably would have unsettled them. I find it's better to be out of sight, out of mind at first.'

'Yes,' I said. 'Sure. I can appreciate that.'

'Well, goodnight, Rowan. Sleep tight, I'm sure you will, you'll have an early start tomorrow, I'm afraid!'

She gave another laugh. I made myself echo it, though in truth I was feeling anything but amused. The idea of starting all this all over again at 6 a.m. was giving me a kind of sick feeling. *How* had I ever thought I could do this?

Remember why you're here, I thought grimly.

'Yes, I'm sure I will,' I said, trying to infuse a smile into my voice. 'Goodnight, Sandra.'

I waited – but there was no click, or any sign that she had hung up, or closed the app.

'S-Sandra?' I said uncertainly, but she seemed to be gone. I slumped back in my chair, and ran my hand over my face. I felt exhausted.

'I should be going,' Jack said, awkward, evidently taking my gesture as a hint. He stood, pushing back his chair. 'It's late, and you've an early start, I'd imagine, with the girls tomorrow.'

'No, stay.' I looked up at him, suddenly desperate not to be left alone in this house of hidden eyes and ears and speakers. The company of a person – a real flesh-and-blood person, not a dis-embodied voice, was irresistible. 'Please. I'd rather have some-one to eat with.' A whiff of something burning came from the oven, and I suddenly remembered the pizza. 'Have you eaten?'

'No, but I won't take your supper.'

'Of course you will. I put a pizza in the oven just before you arrived. It's probably burnt by now, but it's huge. I won't manage it all myself. Please, give me a hand, honestly, I want you to.'

'Well ... ' He glanced at the utility-room door, towards the garage and, I assumed, his little flat above, its windows dark. 'Well ... if you insist.'

'I do.' I put on oven gloves and opened the door of the hot oven. The pizza was done. Overdone, in fact, the cheese crisping and charred around the edges, but I was too hungry to care. 'Sorry, it's a bit blackened. I completely forgot about it. Do you mind?'

'Not at all. I'm hungry enough to eat a horse, let alone a slightly burnt pizza.' He grinned, the tanned skin of his cheeks crinkling.

'And I don't know about you,' I said, 'but I need a glass of wine.'

'I wouldn't say no.'

He watched as I chopped the pizza into slices and found two glasses in the cupboard.

'Are you OK with eating off the board?' I asked, and he gave another of his wide grins.

'I'm more than OK. It's you that's taking the risk I'll gobble all your dinner if it's not safely ring-fenced, but if you're fine with that, it's not my lookout.'

'I'm more than OK too,' I said, and to my surprise, I found myself returning his grin with a slightly shy smile of my own, but a real one, not the forced, watery attempt of earlier tonight.

There was silence for a few minutes as we both worked our way through a greasy, delicious slice each, and then another. At last Jack picked up his third, and spoke, balancing it on his fingertips, angling the slice so that the grease dripped back onto the board.

'So ... about what you were asking earlier.'

'The ... the supernatural thing?'

'Aye. Well, the truth is, I've not seen anything myself, but Jean, she's ... well, not superstitious exactly. But she loves a good yarn.

She's always filling the kids' heads with folk tales – you know, selkies and kelpies, that sort of thing. And this house is very old, or parts of it are anyway. There's been the usual amount of deaths and violence, I suppose.'

'So ... you think Jean's been telling the girls stuff and they've been passing it on to the nannies?'

'Maybe. I wouldn't want to say for sure either way. But, look, those other nannies were very young, most of them at least. It's not everyone who's cut out to live in a place like this, miles away from a town or a bar or a pub. Au pairs, they don't want to be here, they want to be in Edinburgh or Glasgow, where there's nightclubs and other people who speak their own language, you ken?'

'Yeah.' I looked out of the window. It was too dark to see anything, but in my mind's eye I saw the road, stretching away into darkness, the miles and miles of rolling hills, the mountains in the distance. There was silence apart from the rain. Not a car, not a passer-by, nothing. 'Yeah, I can understand that.'

We sat in silence for a moment. I don't know what Jack was thinking, but I was filled with a mix of strange emotions – stress, tiredness, trepidation at the thought of the days stretched out ahead of me, and something else, even more unsettling. Something that was more about Jack, and his presence, and the scatter of freckles across his broad cheekbones, and the way his muscles moved beneath the skin of his forearm as he folded the final pizza slice into a neat parcel, and finished it off in two quick bites.

'Well, I'd best be away to my bed.' He stood, stretching so that I heard his joints click. 'Thanks for the meal, it was nice to have someone to talk to.'

'Same.'

I stood, suddenly self-conscious, as if he had been reading my thoughts.

'You'll be all right?' he asked.

I nodded.

'Well, I'm just over the garage, in the old stable block if you need anything. It's the door around the side, the one painted green with a swallow on the plate. If anything happens in the night –'

'What would happen?' I broke in, surprised, and he gave a laugh.

'That came out wrong. I just meant, if you need me for any-thing, you know where I am. Did Sandra give you my mobile?'

'No.'

He pulled a leaflet off the fridge and scribbled his number in the margin, then handed it to me.

'There you go. Just in case, like.'

Just in case, what? I wanted to ask again, but I knew he would only laugh it off.

His gesture had been meant as a reassuring one, I was sure of it. But somehow it had left me feeling anything but.

'Well, thanks, Jack,' I said, feeling a little awkward, and he grinned again, shrugged himself into his wet coat, and then opened the utility-room door and ducked out into the rain.

After he'd gone I made my way into the utility room myself to lock up. The house felt very still and quiet somehow without his presence, and I sighed as I reached above the top of the door frame for the key. But it wasn't there.

I patted my way along the frame, feeling with my fingertips among the dust and little crunching lumps of dead insect, but there was nothing there.

It wasn't on the floor either.

Could Jean have moved it? Or knocked it down while dusting?

Except, I had a crystal-clear memory of putting the key up there after Jean left, just as Sandra had instructed, to keep it handy in case of an emergency, but out of reach of the children. Could it have fallen down? But if so, what had happened to it? It was large, and brass. Too big to go unnoticed on the floor, or to fit up a Hoover pipe. Had it got kicked under something?

I got down on my hands and knees and shone my phone's torch under the washing machine and tumble dryer, but could see nothing under either, just flat white tiles and a few dust bunnies that quivered when I blew them aside. It wasn't behind the mop bucket either. Then, in spite of my doubts, I went to the cupboard where the downstairs Hoover lived – but the dust chamber had been emptied. There was nothing in there. It was the bagless kind with a clear plastic cylinder that you could see the dust circulating in – even setting aside the question of whether the key could have got inside, there was no way anyone could have tipped out a big brass key without noticing it.

After that I scoured the kitchen, and even checked the bin – but there was nothing there.

At last I opened the utility-room door and stared out into the rain towards the stable block, where a light had come on in the upstairs window. Should I call Jack? Would he have a spare key? But if he did, could I really bear for him to think me so disorganised and helpless that I had waited only ten minutes before taking up his offer of help?

As I was wavering, the light in his window went out, and I realised he had probably gone to bed.

It was too late. I wasn't going to drag him out in his night clothes.

After a last glance around at the yard directly outside the door, in case the key had got kicked outside somehow, I shut the door.

I'd ask Jack in the morning.

In the meantime, oh God, what would I do? I'd … I'd have to barricade the door with something. It was absurd – we were miles away from anywhere, behind locked gates, but I knew I wouldn't sleep well if I felt the place was insecure.

The handle was a knob, not the kind you could put a chair under to stop it from turning, and there was no bolt, but at last, after a lot of searching, I found a wedge-shaped doorstopper in the cupboard. I rammed it firmly into the gap beneath the door and then turned the doorknob to test it.

Somewhat to my surprise, it held. It wouldn't stop a determined burglar – but then very little would. If someone was really that set on breaking in they could just smash a window. But at the very least, it did give the impression that the door was locked, and I knew I would sleep more soundly because of it.

When I went back into the kitchen to clear away the pizza box and our plates, the clock above the stove read 11.36, and I could not suppress a groan. The girls would be up at six. I should have been in bed hours ago.

Well, it was too late to undo that. I'd just have to forgo a shower and get to sleep as quickly as possible. I was so tired, I was pretty sure that wouldn't be a problem anyway.

'Lights off,' I said aloud.

The room was instantly plunged into blackness, just the faint glow from the hallway illuminating the concrete floor. Smothering a yawn, I made my way up the stairs to bed, and was asleep almost before I had undressed.

When I woke, it was with a start, to complete darkness, and a sense of total disorientation. Where was I? What had woken me?

It took a minute for the memory to come back – Heatherbrae House. The Elincourts. The children. Jack.

My phone on the bedside table said it was 3.16 a.m. and I groaned, and let it fall back to the wood with a clunk. No wonder it was still dark, it was the middle of the fucking night.

Stupid brain.

But what the hell had woken me? Was it Petra? Had one of the girls cried out in their sleep?

I lay for a moment, listening. I could hear nothing, but I was a floor away, and there were two closed doors between me and the children.

At last, suppressing a sigh, I got up, wrapped my dressing gown around myself, and went out onto the landing.

The house was quiet. But something felt … wrong, though I couldn't put my finger on it. The rain had stopped, and I could hear nothing at all, not even the far-off roar of a car, or the whisper of wind in the trees.

When realisation came, it was in the shape of two things. The first was the shadow on the wall in front of me, the shadow cast by the wilting peonies on the table downstairs.

Someone had turned the hall lights on downstairs. Lights that I was sure I had *not* left on when I went to bed.

The second came as I began to tiptoe down the stairs, and it made my heart almost stop, and then begin beating hard enough to leap out of my chest.

It was the sound of footsteps on a wooden floor, slow and deliberate, exactly like the other night.

Creak. Creak. Creak.

My chest felt like it was constricted by an iron band. I froze, two steps down, looking at the light on the landing below, and then up at where the noise seemed to be coming from. Jesus Christ. Was someone in the house?

The light I could have understood. Perhaps Maddie or Ellie had got up to use the loo and left it on – there were dim little night lights plugged into the wall at intervals, but they would probably have switched on the main hallway light anyway.

But the footsteps … ?

I thought of Sandra's voice, suddenly coming without warning over the sound system in the kitchen. Could *that* be the answer? The bloody Happy app? But how? More importantly *why*? It didn't make sense. The only people with access to the app were Sandra and Bill, and they had no possible motivation to scare me like this. Quite the reverse in fact. They had just gone to enormous trouble and expense to recruit me.

Besides, it just didn't sound like it was coming from the speakers. There was no sense of a disembodied noise, the way there had been with Sandra's voice in the kitchen. There, I'd had no impression of someone standing behind me, talking to me. It had sounded exactly like what it was – someone being broadcast through speakers. This, though, was different. I could hear the footsteps start on one side of the ceiling and move slowly and implacably to the other. Then they paused, and reversed. It sounded … well … as if there was someone pacing in the room above my head. But that made no sense either. Because there *was* no room up there. There was not so much as a loft hatch.

An image suddenly flashed into my head – something I hadn't thought of since the day I arrived. The locked door in my room. Where did it lead to? *Was* there an attic? It seemed improbable that someone could have entered through my room, but I could *hear* the footsteps from above.

Shivering, I tiptoed back into my own room, and flicked the switch on the lamp by my bed. It didn't turn on.

I swore, Mr Wrexham. I'm not too proud to admit it. I swore, long and loud. I had turned that light off by the switch, so why the fuck wouldn't it turn back *on* by the switch? What kind of sense did this stupid lighting system make anyway?

Furiously, not caring about the music or the heating system or anything else, I mashed my hand against the featureless panel on the wall, bashing randomly at the squares and dials as they illuminated beneath my palm. Lights flickered on and off in closets, the bathroom fan came on, a brief burst of classical music filled the air and then fell silent as I jabbed at the panel again, and some unseen vent in the ceiling suddenly began to blow out cold air. But finally, the main overhead light came on.

I let my hand fall to my side, breathing heavily, but triumphant. Then I set about trying to open the locked door.

First I tried the key to my bedroom door, which Sandra had shown me, tucked away on the door frame like the others. It didn't fit.

Then, I tried the key to the wardrobe on the other side. It didn't fit either.

There was nothing above the door frame except a little dust.

Finally, I resorted to kneeling down and peering through the keyhole, my heart like a drum in my breast, beating so hard I thought I might be sick.

I could see nothing at all – just unending blackness. But I could *feel* something. A cool breeze that made me blink and draw back from the keyhole, my eye watering.

It was not just a cupboard inside that space. *Something* else was there. An attic, perhaps. At the very least, a space big enough to have a draught, and a source of air.

The footsteps had stopped, but I knew that I would not sleep again tonight, and at last I wrapped my duvet around myself and sat, my phone in my hand, the overhead light blazing down on me, watching the locked door.

I don't know what I was expecting. To see the handle turn? For someone – some*thing* – to emerge?

Whatever it was, it didn't happen. I just sat there, as the sky outside my window began to lighten and a thin lemon-yellow streak of dawn crept across the carpet, mixing with the artificial light from above.

I felt nauseous with a mix of fear and tiredness, and dread of the day ahead.

At last, when I heard a low fractious wail come from downstairs, I loosened my grip on my phone, flexed my stiff fingers, and saw that the display said 5.57.

It was morning. The children were waking up.

As I crawled from my bed, my hand went up involuntarily to touch my necklace – but my fingers grazed only my collarbone, and I remembered that I had taken it off that first night, spooling it on the bedside table, just as I had done before the interview.

Now, I turned to pick it up, and it wasn't there. I frowned, and looked down the back of the little nightstand. Nothing. Had Jean McKenzie tidied it away?

The wail from downstairs came again, louder this time, and I sighed and abandoned the hunt. I would look for it later.

But first I had to get through another day.

Coffee maker – preloaded with beans and connected to mains water. Operated via the app, select 'appliances' from the menu, then 'Baristo' and then choose from the preprogrammed selections or customise your own. If beans logo shows, the hopper needs to be refilled. If the ! error logo shows then there is either a Wi-Fi issue, or a problem with the water pressure. You can program it to dispense at a particular time every day, which is great for mornings, but of course you must not forget to put a cup underneath it the night before! The preprogrammed selections are as follows –

Jesus. I had confined myself mostly to tea since getting here, mainly because the coffee maker was so extremely intimidating – a chrome beast of a thing covered with buttons and knobs and dials. Sandra had explained when I arrived that it was Wi-Fi-enabled, and app-operated – but Happy was proving to be the least intuitive system I had ever encountered. However, after my sleepless night, I had decided that a cup of coffee was the only thing that was going to make me feel halfway normal, and while Petra chewed her way through a dish of mini rice cakes, I had resolved to try to figure it out.

I hadn't even switched it on, when a voice behind me said, 'Knock knock ... '

I jumped and swung round, my nerves still jangling with the traces of last night's stale fear.

It was Jack, standing in the open doorway to the utility room, jacket on and dog leashes in hand. I had not heard him come in and evidently my shock and ambivalence must have shown in my face.

'Sorry, I didn't mean to make you jump. I did knock, but you didn't hear, so I let myself in. I've come to collect the dogs for their walk.'

'No problem,' I said, as I turned to take away Petra's rice cakes. She had stopped eating them, and was mashing one into her ear. Jack's unexpected presence at least answered my question about whether I was also responsible for the dogs, and was one thing I could tick off my list. Claude and Hero were gambolling around, excited to get going, and Jack hushed them sharply. They fell silent at once, noticeably more quickly than they had obeyed Sandra, and he grabbed the collar of the largest one and began clipping on its lead.

'Sleep well?' he asked casually, as the lead slipped into place.

I turned, my hand frozen in the act of wiping Petra's face. *Sleep well?* What did that mean? Did he ... did he ... know?

For a minute I just stood there, gaping at him, while Petra took advantage of my momentary lapse of attention to grab a particularly soggy rice cake and mash it into my sleeve.

Then I shook myself. He was just asking in the way people do, to be polite.

'Not particularly well, actually,' I said rather shortly, wiping my sleeve on the dishcloth and taking Petra's rice cake away from her. 'I couldn't find the key to the back door last night, so I couldn't lock up properly. Do you know where it's gone?'

'This door?' He jerked his head towards the utility room, one eyebrow raised, and I nodded.

'There's no bolt on it either. In the end I wedged it with a bit of wood.' Though much good it had done. Presumably Jack had simply shoved the wedge aside without even noticing when he opened the door. 'I know we're in the middle of nowhere, but it didn't make for a very comfortable night.'

That and the sound of footsteps, I thought, but I couldn't quite bring myself to tell him about that. In the cold light of day it sounded crazy, and there were too many alternative explanations. Central heating pipes expanding. Joists shrinking as the roof cooled from the heat of the day. Old houses shifting. In my heart of hearts, I knew that none of those fully explained the sounds I had heard. But I didn't know how to convince Jack of that. The key, however, was different. It was something clear … and concrete.

Jack was frowning now.

'Sandra usually keeps the key on the door frame above. She doesn't like to keep it in the lock in case the kids mess around with it.'

'I know that.' There was an edge of impatience in my voice that I tried to dampen down. It was not Jack's fault that this had happened. 'I mean, she told me that. It was in the binder. And I put it up there yesterday, but it's not there now. Do you think Jean could have taken it?'

'Jean?' He looked surprised, and then gave a short laugh and shook his head. 'No, I don't think so. I mean, why would she? She has her own keys.'

'Someone else then?'

But he was shaking his head.

'No one comes up here without me knowing about it. They couldn't get through the gate for a start.'

I didn't remind him that Jean had found the door locked when I came back from looking for Maddie and Ellie. I hadn't locked it. So who had?

'Maybe it fell down somewhere,' he said, and went back through to the utility room to look, the dogs following like faithful shadows, sniffing around as he pushed aside the dryer and peered under the washing machine.

'I already looked,' I said, trying to keep irritation out of my tone. And then, when he didn't straighten up or deviate from his search, 'Jack? Did you hear me? I checked everywhere, even the bin.'

But he was shifting the washing machine aside, grunting a little with the effort, the castors screeching on the tiled floor.

'Jack? Did you hear me? I said I *already* –'

He ignored me, leaning over the counter, one long arm stretched down the back of unit.

'*Jack* –' There was real irritation in my voice now, but he interrupted me.

'Got it.'

He straightened, triumphantly, a dusty brass key in his fingers. I let my mouth snap shut.

I had looked. I had *looked*. I had a clear memory of peering under that washing machine and seeing nothing but dust.

'But ... '

He came across, dropped it into my palm.

'But ... I looked.'

'It was tucked behind the wheel. I expect you wouldn't have seen. Probably fell out when the door slammed shut and skidded under there. All's well that ends well – isn't that what they say?'

I let my hand close around the key, feeling the brass ridges bite into my palm. I had *looked*. I had looked *carefully*. Wheel or no wheel, how could I have missed a three-inch brass key, when that was exactly what I was looking for?

There was no way I could have missed seeing that key if it was there. Which meant that maybe ... it *wasn't* there. Until someone dropped it down there.

I looked up and met Jack's guileless hazel eyes, smiling down at me. But it couldn't be. He was so *nice*.

Maybe ... a bit too nice?

You went straight to the washing machine, I wanted to say. *How did you know?*

But I could not bring myself to voice my suspicions aloud.

What I actually said was, 'Thank you.' But my voice in my own ears sounded subdued.

Jack didn't reply, he was already dusting off his hands and turning for the door, the dogs wheeling and yelping around his feet.

'See you in an hour or so?' he said, but this time, when he smiled, it no longer made my heart leap a little. Instead I noticed the tendons in the back of his hands, the way he kept the dogs' leashes very short, pulled in against his heel, dominating them.

'Sure,' I said quietly.

'Oh, and I nearly forgot – today's Jean's day off. She won't be coming up, so no point in leaving the dishes for her.'

'No problem,' I said.

As he turned and made his way across the courtyard, dogs firmly at heel, I watched him go, turning the sequence of events over in my mind, trying to figure out what had happened.

Although I'd suggested Jean's name to Jack, I didn't honestly believe she was responsible. I remembered putting the key on the frame after she had gone. So unless she'd come back – which didn't seem likely – then she couldn't be to blame.

What had happened after that … Jack had come in by that door, I recalled, but had I unlocked it? No … I was pretty sure I'd just opened it – presumably Jack must have unlocked it with his own set of keys. Or had I unlocked it then? It was hard to remember.

Either way, it was technically possible that he had pocketed the key at some point during his visit, and dropped it down there just now. But why? To freak me out? It seemed unlikely. What could he possibly gain by engineering another nanny's departure?

Jean, I could have believed more easily. She had plainly disliked me. But even there – setting aside the likelihood of her creeping back to the house after she'd departed, which seemed more and more implausible the more I thought about it, she seemed to have a genuine affection for the children, and I couldn't believe she would deliberately leave the house unsafe and unsecured while they were asleep.

Because that was the final, unnerving possibility. That someone had taken it to ensure access to the house in the night. Not Jean or Jack, who had their own sets of keys but ... someone else.

But no – that was crazy, I was beginning to talk myself into hysteria. Maybe it *had* been there all along. Tucked behind the wheel, Jack had said. Was it possible I just hadn't looked hard enough?

I was still thinking myself round in circles, when there was an impatient noise from the kitchen, and I turned to see Petra kicking irritably against her high chair. I hurried back into the room, undid her straps and dumped her into the playpen in the corner of the kitchen. Then I pulled my ponytail tighter, plastered on my best smile, and began looking for Maddie and Ellie.

They were in the playroom, huddled in a corner, whispering something, but both heads turned when I clapped my hands.

'Right! Come on, girls, we're going to go for a picnic. We can have sandwiches, crisps, rice cakes ... '

I had more than half expected them to refuse, but to my surprise Maddie got up, dusting down her leggings.

'Where are we going?'

'Just the grounds. Will you show me around? I heard from Jack you have a secret den.' That was completely untrue – he hadn't said anything at all, but I'd never met a child who didn't have some kind of hidey-hole or cache.

'You can't see our den,' Ellie said instantly. 'It's secret. I mean –' She stopped at a glaring, furious look from Maddie. 'I mean, we don't have one,' she added miserably.

'Oh, what a shame,' I said breezily. 'Well, never mind, I'm sure there's lots of other interesting places. Put your wellies on. I'm going to put Petra in the pushchair so she doesn't wander off, but then let's set off. You can show me all the best picnic spots.'

'OK,' Maddie said. Her voice was calm and level, even a little triumphant, and I found myself glancing at her suspiciously.

Even with Maddie's co-operation, it took a surprisingly long time to make the picnic and get everyone out of the house, but at last we were done, and heading off round the back of the house, along a bumpy pebbled path that crested a small hill, and then led down the other side. The views from this side of the grounds were just as spectacular, but, if anything, even bleaker. Instead of the little crofts and small villages scattered between us and the distant mountains, here there was nothing but rolling forest. In the far distance some kind of bird of prey circled lazily over the trees, looking for its kill.

We wound our way through a rather overgrown vegetable garden, where Maddie helpfully showed me the raspberry canes and herb beds, and past a fountain, full of a slightly brackish scum. It was not working, and the statue on top was cracked and grey with lichen, and it occurred to me then what a strange contrast the house made with this rather wild, unkempt garden. I would have expected outdoor seating areas and decking and elaborate planting schemes, not this slightly sad, crumbling neglect. Perhaps Sandra wasn't an outdoor person? Or maybe they had spent so long working on the house, they hadn't had time to tend to the grounds yet.

There was a set of swings tucked behind a dilapidated kitchen greenhouse, and Ellie and Maddie leapt on them and began competing to go higher. For a moment I just stood and watched them, and then something in my pocket gave a buzzing, jangling leap, and I realised my phone was ringing.

When I pulled it out, my heart gave a funny little jolt as I read the caller ID. It was the last person I'd been expecting, and I had to take a deep breath before I swiped the screen to accept the call.

'Hello?'

'Heeeeey!' she shrieked, her familiar voice so loud I had to hold the phone away from my ear. 'It's me, Rowan! How are you? Oh my God, long time no speak!'

'I'm good! Where are you? This must be costing you a fortune.'

'It is. I'm in a commune in India. Mate, it's amazing here. And sooo cheap! You should totally resign and come and join me.'

'I – I did resign,' I said, with a slightly awkward laugh. 'Didn't I tell you?'

'WHAT?'

I held the phone away from my ear again. It had been so long since we'd had an actual phone conversation, I'd forgotten how loud she could be.

'Yup,' I said, still holding the phone a few inches from my ear. 'Handed my notice in at Little Nippers. I left a few days ago. The look on Janine's face when I told her she could stick her stupid job was almost worth all the hours there.'

'I bet. God, she was such a cow. I still can't believe Val didn't give you that job when I left.'

'Me too. Listen, I meant to call you, I wanted to tell you – I've moved out of the flat.'

'What?' The line was crackly, her voice echoing across the long miles from India. 'I didn't hear you. I thought you said you'd left the flat.'

'Yeah, I did. The post I've taken up, it's a residential one. But listen, don't worry, I'm still paying the rent, the pay here is really good. So your stuff is still there, and you'll have a place to come back to when you finish travelling.'

'You can afford that?' Her tinny, faraway voice was impressed. 'Wow! This post must pay *really* well. How did you swing that?'

I skated round that one.

'They really needed someone,' I said. It was the truth, at least. 'But anyway, how are you? Any plans to come back?'

I tried to keep my voice casual, not letting on how important her answer was to me.

'Yeah, of course.' Her laugh echoed. 'But not yet. I've still got seven months left on my ticket. But oh, mate, it's good to hear your voice. I miss you!'

'I miss you too.'

Ellie and Maddie had got down off the swing, and were walking away from me now, down a winding brick path between overgrown heathers. I tucked the phone under my ear and began pushing the buggy across the rough ground, following.

'Listen, I'm working right now actually, so … I should probably … '

'Yeah, sure. And I should go too, before this bankrupts me. But you're OK, yeah?'

'Yeah, I'm OK.'

There was an awkward pause.

'Well, bye, Rowan.'

'Bye, Rach.'

And then she hung up.

'Who was that?' said a little voice at my elbow, and I jumped, and looked down, to see Maddie scowling up at me.

'Oh … just a friend I used to work with. We were flatmates, back in London, but then she went travelling.'

'Did you like her?'

It was such a funny question I laughed.

'What? Yes, yes of course I liked her.'

'You sounded like you didn't want to talk to her.'

'I don't know where you got that idea.' We walked a bit further, the buggy bumping over a loose brick in the path, while I considered her remark. Was there a grain of truth in it? 'She was calling from abroad,' I said at last. 'It's very expensive. I just didn't want to cost her too much money.'

Maddie looked up at me for a moment, and I had the strangest feeling of her black button eyes boring into mine, and then she turned and scampered after Ellie, crying out 'Follow me! Follow me!'

The path led down and down, away from the house, growing more uneven by the second. Once it had been herringbone brick, but now the bricks had cracked in the frost and grown loose, some of them missing altogether. In the distance I could see a brick wall, about six foot high, with a wrought-iron metal gate, which seemed to be where the children were heading.

'Is that the edge of the grounds?' I called after them. 'Hold up, I don't want you going out onto the moors.'

They stopped and waited for me. Ellie had her hands on her hips and was panting, her little face flushed.

'It's a garden,' she said. 'It's got a wall around it, like a room but no roof.'

'That sounds exciting,' I said. 'Like the Secret Garden. Have you ever read that?'

'Of course she hasn't, she's not old enough to read chapter books,' Maddie said repressively. 'But we watched it on TV.'

We had drawn level with the wall now, and I could see what Ellie meant. It was a crumbling red-brick wall, slightly taller than I was, that seemed to be enclosing one corner of the grounds, forming a rectangular section quite separate from the rest of the landscaping. It was the kind of structure that might easily have enclosed a kitchen garden – protecting delicate herbs and fruit trees from frost – but the trees and creepers I could see emerging above the high walls didn't look at all edible.

I tried the handle of the gate.

'It's locked.' Through the twining metalwork I could see a wild, overgrown mass of bushes and creepers, some kind of statue partly obscured by greenery. 'What a shame, it looks very exciting in there.'

'It *looks* locked,' Ellie said eagerly, 'but Maddie and I know a secret way of getting inside.'

'I'm not sure –' I began, but before I could finish, she wound her little hand through the intricate metal fretwork, through a space far too narrow to admit even a fine-boned adult's hand, and did something I could not see to the far side of the lock. The gate sprang open.

'Wow!' I said, genuinely impressed. 'How did you do that?'

'It's not very hard.' Ellie was flushed with pride. 'There's a catch on the inside.'

Gently, I pushed the gate open, listening to the hinges squeal, and pushed Petra inside, thrusting aside the trailing fronds of some creeper that was hanging overhead. The leaves brushed my face, tickling my skin with an almost nettlish sensation. Maddie ducked in behind me, trying not to let the leaves trail in her face, and Ellie came in too. There was something mischievous about her expression, and I wondered why Bill and Sandra kept this place locked.

Inside, the walls protected the plants from the exposed position of the rest of the grounds, and the contrast to the muted heathers and trees outside, and the austerity of the moors beyond, was startling. There were lush evergreen bushes studded with berries of all types, overgrown tangled creepers, and a few flowers struggling to survive beneath the onslaught. I recognised a few – hellebores and snowberries springing up from between dark-leaved laurels, and what I thought might be a laburnum up ahead. As we turned a corner, we passed underneath an ancient-looking yew, so old it formed a tunnel over the path, its strange, tubular berries crunching under-foot. Its leaves had poisoned the ground, and nothing grew underneath its spread. There were more greenhouses in here, I saw, though they were smaller, still with enough glass in their broken frames to have built up an impressive amount of conden-sation. The inside of the glass was blotched with green lichen and mould, so thick that I could barely see the remains of the plants inside, though some struggled up through the broken panes of the roof.

Four brick paths quartered the garden, meeting in a small circle in the centre, where the statue stood. It was so covered in ivy and other creepers that it was hard to make out, but as I drew nearer, brushing aside some of the foliage, I saw that it was a woman, thin and emaciated and broken down, her clothes ragged, her face skull-like, her blank stone eyes fixing mine with an accusing stare. Her cheeks were scored with what looked like scratches, and when I peered closer I saw that the nails on her skeletal hands were long and pointed.

'God,' I said, taken back. 'What a horrible statue. Who on earth would put up something like that?' But there was no answer. The two little girls had disappeared into the thicket of greenery, and I could not see them. Peering closer I saw that there was a name on the pedestal she crouched on. *Achlys*. Was it some kind of memorial?

All of a sudden I felt a violent desire to get out of this over-grown nightmarish tangle of plants, out to the open air of the mountains and grounds.

'Maddie!' I called sharply. 'Ellie, where are you?'

No answer came, and I suppressed a momentary unease.

'Maddie! We're going to have lunch now. Let's go and find a spot.'

They waited, just long enough for me to start feeling serious panic, and then there was a burst of giggles and both children broke cover and pelted down the path in front of me, towards the gate, and the cool clean air outside.

'Come on,' Maddie shouted over her shoulder. 'We'll show you the burn.'

The rest of the morning passed without incident. We had a quiet – even a nice – lunch on the shores of the peat-dark burn that cut through the corner of the grounds, and then afterwards the girls took off their shoes and socks and paddled in the tea-coloured waters, screeching at the cold, and flicking me and Petra with ice-cold droplets that made me shriek, and Petra babble with excited glee. Only two things marred the general contentment – the first, Ellie's shoe falling in the burn. I managed to retrieve it, but she was tearful, and sobbed when we had to go and she had to put the soggy shoe back on.

The other was the prickling of my forehead, where the creeper had brushed me. From an initial tingle, it was now properly itching, like a nettle sting, but more painful. I splashed the cold water from the burn onto it, but the itching continued, hard to ignore. Was it some kind of allergic reaction? I'd never experienced a plant allergy before, but perhaps this was something native to Scotland I would not have encountered down south. Either way, the thought of the reaction getting worse while I was alone with the children was not comforting – nor was the realisation that I had left my inhaler back at the house.

All in all I was glad when the sky clouded over, and I could suggest packing up and starting home. Petra fell asleep on the way back to the house, and I parked her buggy in the utility room. To my surprise, both Maddie and Ellie fell in with my suggestion of a film, and we were cuddled up in the media room, me with a growing sense of superiority, when there was a crackle and Sandra's voice came over the speakers.

'Rowan? Is now a good time to chat?'

'Oh, hi, Sandra.' It was less unnerving second time around, but still unsettling. I found myself glancing up at the cameras, wondering how she knew which room I was in. The girls were both absorbed in the film, and didn't seem to have noticed their mother's voice coming over the speakers. 'Hang on, I'll go through to the kitchen, so we can chat without disturbing the girls.'

'You can divert the call to your phone if that's easier.' Sandra's disembodied voice followed me as I eased myself out from beneath Ellie and walked through to the kitchen. 'Just open the Happy app and click on the phone icon, then the divert arrow.'

I did as she said, ignoring the bloody *Home is where the Happy is!*, pressed the icons she had instructed, and then lifted the phone to my ear. To my relief, her voice sounded again, this time from the phone speaker.

'Done?'

'Yes, I'm on the phone now. Thanks for showing me how to do that.' If she could only have mentioned it last night rather than having that awkward conversation in front of Jack ... but never mind. The rash on my forehead prickled, and I tried to ignore the desire to scratch it.

'No problem,' Sandra was saying briskly. 'Happy is amazing when you get used to it, but I have to admit, it takes a while to figure out all the intricacies! How's today going, anyway?'

'Oh, really good.' I perched on the edge of a stool, resisting the urge to look up at the camera in the corner. 'It's going great, thanks. We had a really good morning exploring the grounds. Petra's asleep, and the girls are –' I hesitated, thinking of her remark yesterday, but then forged on. No point in second-guessing myself all the time, and besides, she would presumably know what the girls were up to, if she had checked the cameras before calling. 'The girls are watching a film. I thought you wouldn't mind as they were out in the fresh air this morning. I think they needed some down time.'

'Mind?' Sandra gave a little laugh. 'Heavens, no. I'm not one of those helicopter parents.'

'Would you like to speak to them?'

'Absolutely – it's why I called, really. Well, and to check you were coping of course. Do you want to put Ellie on first?'

I went back through to the den and handed Ellie the phone. 'It's Mummy.'

Her face was a little uncertain as she picked up the receiver, but she broke into smiles as she heard her mother's voice, and I went back into the kitchen, not wanting to hover too obviously, but listening with half an ear to Ellie's end of the conversation. At some point Sandra must have asked to be put across to Maddie, for there was a short whining complaint from Ellie, and then I heard Maddie's voice, and Ellie came padding disconsolately through to me.

'I miss Mummy.' Her bottom lip was wobbling.

'Of course you do.' I crouched down, not wanting to risk a hug that might be rejected, but trying to make myself available on her level if she wanted comforting. 'And she misses you too. But we'll have lots of –'

But my remark was cut off by Maddie, coming through with the phone held out and a strange expression in her black eyes. I was not sure what it was – a mix of trepidation and glee, it looked like.

'Mummy wants to talk to you,' she said. I took the phone.

'Rowan –' Sandra's voice was clipped and annoyed – 'what's this I hear about you taking them into the locked garden?'

'I – well –' I was taken aback. What the hell? Sandra hadn't said anything about the garden being out of bounds. 'Well, I did, but –'

'How dare you force your way into an area of the grounds that we expressly keep locked for the children's safety, I can't believe how irresponsible –'

'Hang on a minute. I'm very sorry if I've made a mistake, Sandra, but I had no idea the walled garden was out of bounds. And I didn't force my way in anywhere. Ellie and Maddie –'

Ellie and Maddie seemed to know how to open the gate, was what I had been going to say, but Sandra didn't let me finish. Instead she interrupted with an angry sigh of exasperation and I fell silent, reluctant to talk over her and increase her annoyance.

'I told you to use your common sense, Rowan. If breaking into a poison garden is your idea of common –'

'*What?*' I butted in, not caring about rudeness now. 'What did you say?'

'It is a *poison* garden,' Sandra spat. 'As you would know if you'd bothered to read the binder I provided. Which you clearly did not.'

'A poison –' I reached for the binder, beginning to frantically flick through the pages. The injustice stung. I *had* read the fucking thing, but it was 250 pages long. If there was critical information she should have put it up front, rather than burying it in pages and pages about acceptable types of crisps and the right type of shoes to wear for PE. 'Just – what even is that?'

'The previous owner of Heatherbrae was an analytical chemist with a speciality in biological toxins, and this was his personal –' She stopped, clearly too pissed off with the whole situation even to find words. 'His personal testing ground I suppose. Every single plant in that garden is toxic in some degree – some of them *extremely* toxic. And many of them you don't need to ingest, brushing past them or touching the leaves is enough.'

Oh. My hand went up to the blistering rash on my forehead, which made a sudden kind of sense.

'We're trying to find the best way to deal with it, but the bloody thing has heritage status or something. In the meantime we keep it firmly locked up, and I must say, it never occurred to me that you would take the children for a stroll –'

It was my turn to butt in now.

'Sandra –' I made my voice level, and calmer and more reasonable than I really felt – 'I apologise unreservedly for not paying sufficient attention to that page in the binder. That is 100 per cent on me and I'll rectify that immediately. But you should know, it wasn't my idea to go in there. Maddie and Ellie suggested it, and they know how to open the lock without a key – there's some kind of override on the inside, and Ellie can reach it. They've clearly been in there before.'

That shut Sandra up. There was silence on the other end of the phone while I waited for her response. I could hear her breathing, and I wondered for a minute if I had made a bad strategic mistake in bringing up the fact that she clearly had no idea where her children had been roaming. Then she coughed.

'Well. We'll say no more about it for the moment. Can you put me back on to Maddie please?'

And that was it. No 'thanks for bringing it to my attention'. No admission that she herself wasn't exactly winning parenting golds. But perhaps that would have been too much to hope for.

I passed the phone back to Maddie, who gave me a little smile as I handed it over, her dark eyes full of malice.

She took it back through to the media room, Ellie padding after her, hoping for another turn, and as Maddie's end of the conversation grew fainter, I picked up the tablet that was lying on the kitchen counter, and opened Google. Then I typed in 'Achlys'.

A series of terrifying images popped up across the top of the screen – a variety of white, skull-like female faces in different states of decomposition, some pale and beautiful, with ravaged cheeks, others rotting and putrefying, with a stench of death coming from their rictus mouths.

Beneath them were various search entries, and I clicked one at random.

Achlys (pronounced ACK-liss) – Greek goddess of death, misery and poison, it read.

I shut the screen down. Well, binder or no binder, I couldn't say I hadn't been warned. It had been right there, written on the base of the statue in the centre of the garden. I just hadn't understood the message.

'I'm done.' Maddie's voice came from the media room, and pushing down my irritation I walked back through to where the girls were crouched on the sofa, plainly waiting for me with some trepidation. I said nothing as Maddie handed back the phone, just unpaused the film and sat down on the far end of the sofa to continue watching, though their eyes kept flicking across to me, very different emotions on each face. Ellie's was anxious ... waiting to be told off. She had known that they were not supposed to go into that garden, and she had allowed herself to be tempted – to show her cleverness in opening the gate and letting us in. Maddie's expression was very different, and harder to read, but I thought I could tell what it was. Triumph.

She had wanted me to get into trouble, and I had.

It was much later, over supper, as I wiped tomato sauce from Petra's cheek, and swallowed my own mouthful of alphabetti spaghetti, that I said, casually, 'Girls, did you know that the plants in that garden were dangerous?'

Ellie's eyes flicked to Maddie who seemed to be wavering.

'What garden?' she said at last, though her tone didn't hold a question mark. She was buying herself more time, I thought. I gave her my sweetest smile, and shot her a look that said *don't fuck with me, dear.*

167

'The poison garden,' I said. 'The one with the statue. Your mum said we weren't supposed to go in there. Did you know?'

'We're not allowed in without a grown-up,' Maddie said evasively.

'Ellie, did you know?' I turned to her, but she refused to meet my eyes, and at last I took her chin, forcing her to look at me.

'Ow!'

'Ellie, look at me, did you know those plants were dangerous?'

She said nothing, just tried to twist her chin away.

'*Did you know?*'

'Yes,' she whispered at last. 'Another girl died.'

It was not the answer I had been expecting, and I stopped, letting her chin go in my surprise.

'What did you say?'

'There was another little girl,' Ellie repeated, still not meeting my eyes. 'She died. Jean told us.'

'Jesus!' The word slipped out without my realising, and I saw from Maddie's smirk that that too would be stored up to repeat to Sandra next time she called.

'What happened? When?'

'A long time ago,' Maddie said. It was plain that, unlike Ellie, she did not mind talking about the subject. In fact there was even a kind of relish in her tone. 'Before we were born. She was the little girl of the man who lived here before us. It's why he went saft.'

For a moment I didn't understand the last word, but then it came to me. She was saying the word 'soft' but with a Scottish accent, repeating whatever Jean McKenzie had said to her.

'He went soft? Soft in the head you mean?'

'Yes, he had to be put away. Not straight away, but after a while. Living here with her ghost,' Maddie said, matter-of-factly. 'She used to wake him in the middle of the night with her crying. After she was gone. Jean told us. So after a while he stopped sleeping.

He just used to pace backwards and forwards all night long. Then he went mad. People do go mad, you know, if you stop them from sleeping for long enough. They go mad, and then they *die*.'

Pacing. The word gave me a sharp jolt, and for a second I didn't know what to say. Then I remembered something else.

'Maddie –' I swallowed, trying to figure out how to phrase my question. 'Maddie ... is ... is that what you meant? Before? When you said, the ghosts wouldn't like it?'

'I don't know what you mean.' Her face was stiff and expressionless, and she had pushed her plate away.

'When you hugged me, that day I first came. You said *the ghosts wouldn't like it.*'

'No I didn't,' she said stonily. 'I didn't hug you. I don't hug people.' But she had overreached herself with that last remark. I might have believed that she hadn't said what I thought I'd heard, but there was no way I could forget that stiff, desperate little hug. She *had* hugged me. And the knowledge suddenly made me sure of what I'd heard too. I shook my head.

'You know there's no such thing as ghosts, right? No matter what Jean's told you – it's just rubbish, Maddie, it's just people who are sad about other people who have died, and wish they could see them again, so they make up stories, and they imagine they see them. But it's all nonsense.'

'I don't know what you're talking about,' Maddie said, and she shook her head so that her straight dark hair flapped against her cheeks.

'There *aren't* any ghosts, Maddie. I promise you that. They're just make-believe. They can't hurt you – or me – or any of us.'

'Can I get down now?' she asked flatly, and I sighed.

'Don't you want pudding?'

'I'm not hungry.'

'Go on then.' She slid from her chair, and Ellie followed, her obedient little shadow.

I put a yogurt in front of Petra and then went round to clear the girls' plates. Ellie's was just the usual mess of toast crusts and spaghetti sauce, with as many peas as possible hidden under her spoon. But Maddie's ... I was about to scrape it into the compost bin when I stopped, turning the plate.

She had eaten most of her supper, but a dozen or so alphabet letters had been left, and now I saw, just as I was about to throw them away, that the letters seemed to be arranged into words. The phrase was sliding diagonally across the plate where I had tipped it towards the compost bin, but it was still just readable.

W E   H
      A T
        E U

We hate you.

Somehow, seeing it there in the innocence of alphabetti spaghetti was more upsetting than almost anything else. I scraped the plate with a violence that made the spaghetti ricochet off the inside of the compost bin lid, and then threw it into the sink, where it hit a glass, and they both shattered, sending shards of glass and spatters of tomato sauce flying.

Fuck.

Fuck fuck fuck fuck *fuck.*

'I hate you too!' I wanted to scream after their retreating backs, as they padded quietly away into the media room to fire up Netflix. 'I hate you too, you vile, creepy little shits!'

But it wasn't true. Not completely.

I did hate them – in that moment. But I saw myself, too. A prickly little girl, full of emotions too big for her small frame, emotions she could not understand or contain.

'*I hate you,*' I remembered sobbing into my pillow, after my mother threw away my favourite teddy bear, too old, too shabby, too babyish for a big girl like me, according to her. 'I hate you so much!'

But it wasn't true then either. I loved my mother. I loved her so much that it suffocated her – or that was the impression she gave. All those years of small hands being disentangled from sleeves and skirts, and untwined from around necks. *That's enough now, you'll mess up my hair,* and *Oh for goodness' sake, your hands are filthy,* and *Stop being a baby now, a big girl like you.* All those years of being too needy, and too grabby, and too grubby-handed – of trying to be better and neater, and just more lovable.

She didn't want me. Or that's what it felt like, at times.

But she was all I had.

Maddie had so much more than me – a father, three sisters, a beautiful house, two dogs – but I recognised her sadness and her anger and her frustration – an angry little dark changeling among her blonde sisters.

We even looked alike.

When she looked at me, with that touch of triumph in her dark, boot-button eyes, I had recognised something else too, and now I knew what it was. It was a flash of myself in those eyes. A flicker of my own dark brown eyes, and my own determination. Maddie was a woman with a plan, just like I was. The question was, what was it?

I was so tired after my near-sleepless night the night before that I bundled the girls upstairs to bed ridiculously early. To my surprise they didn't protest, and I found myself wondering if they were as tired as I was.

Petra went down with no more than a token protest, and when I went to check on Maddie and Ellie they were both in their pyjamas – or almost there, in the case of Ellie. I helped her figure out which way her top went, and then shepherded them into the bathroom, where they did their teeth obediently as I stood over them.

'Do you want a story?' I asked as I tucked them into their little beds, and I saw Ellie's eyes flicker to Maddie, looking for permission to speak. But Maddie shook her head.

'No. We're too big for stories.'

'I know that's not true,' I said with a little laugh. 'Everyone likes bedtime stories.'

Any other night I might have sat myself down, cracked open a book and begun anyway, in defiance of Maddie's refusals. But I was tired. I was *so* tired. Being with the girls all day from sun up to sunset was exhausting in a completely different way to the nursery, a way I hadn't fully anticipated or understood until now. I thought of all the mums who had dropped their children off talking about how exhausted they were, and the slight contempt I'd felt for them when all they had to deal with was one or two at the most, but now I realised what they'd been talking about. It wasn't as physical as the work at the nursery, or as intense, but it was the way it stretched, endlessly, the way the needing never stopped, and there was never a moment when you could hand them over to your colleague and run away for a quick fag break to just be yourself.

I was never off duty here. Or at least, not for the foreseeable future.

'I tell you what,' I said at last, seeing Ellie's chin wobble, 'how about I put on an audiobook?'

Pulling out my phone, I managed to navigate to the Happy media system, and then to the audio files, where I scrolled through the list of titles. The organisation was confusing – there didn't seem to be any distinction between the different file types, and Mozart was listed alongside *Moana*, Thelonious Monk and L. M. Montgomery – but as I scrolled, I felt a little warm head thrust up under my arm, and Ellie's small hand took the phone.

'I can show you,' she said, and pressed an icon that looked like a stylised panda bear, and then another icon that looked like a flattened out V, but which I realised, as Ellie pressed it, must be supposed to indicate books.

A list of children's audiobooks flashed up.

'Do you know which one you want?' I asked, but she shook her head, and scanning the list, I selected one at random – *The Sheep-Pig* by Dick King-Smith which seemed perfect. Long, calming, and nice and wholesome. I pressed play, selected 'Girls' bedroom' from the list of speakers, and waited for the first notes of the introductory music. Then I tucked Ellie in.

'Do you want a kiss?' I said. She didn't reply, but I thought I saw a little nod, and I bent, and swiftly kissed her baby-soft cheek before she could change her mind.

Next, I went across to Maddie. She was lying there with her eyes tight shut, though I could see her pupils moving beneath the paper thinness of her lids, and I could tell from her breathing she was nowhere near asleep.

'Do you want a goodnight kiss, Maddie?' I asked, knowing what the answer would be, but wanting to be fair.

She said nothing. I stood for a moment, listening to her breathing, and then said, 'Goodnight, girls. Sweet dreams, and sleep well for school tomorrow,' and then I left, shutting the door behind me.

Out in the hallway I breathed a tremulous, almost incredulous sigh of relief.

Could it be true? Were they really all safely in bed, washed, brushed and no one screaming? It seemed, compared to last night, anyway, deceptively easy.

But perhaps ... perhaps I had turned a corner with them. Perhaps that first angry protest was just shock at being away from their mum, with a comparative stranger in charge. Maybe a nice day together and a phone call from Sandra was all it had taken.

My heart softened as I checked the lock on the utility-room door, did battle with the front-door panel and the lights in the hall, and then climbed the flights of stairs to my own room with a weariness I was having increasing trouble overcoming.

I was passing Bill and Sandra's room when I thought I heard something. Or perhaps saw it – it was hard to know. A little flicker of movement in the sliver of darkness between the door and the frame. Was it just my imagination? I was so tired. It could be my mind playing tricks on me.

Very, very quietly, not wanting to disturb the girls, I pushed the door with the flat of my hand, listening to it shushing across the thick silver carpet.

Inside, the room was quite empty and still. The curtains were undrawn, and though in London it would have been getting dark, here we were so far north that the sun was only just sliding behind the mountains. Livid squares of reddish light slanted obliquely across the floor, turning the carpet into a kind of fiery chessboard, though the corners of the room were in deep, impenetrable shadow. I let my hand slip over the thick, crisp cotton of their duvet cover as I passed their bed, glancing into the shadows, feeling my pulse quicken with the audacity of this intrusion. If Sandra were watching through the monitor now, what would she see? Someone prowling around her bedroom, fingering her bedlinen. *I thought I heard a noise ...* I practised the excuse in my head, but I knew it was no longer true. I had been looking for an excuse.

There was a pair of earrings on the bedside table closest to the door. This must be Sandra's side. Which meant that Bill slept ...

I tiptoed round the bed, keeping to the shadows as far as I could. I knew from peering at Maddie and Ellie's bedroom monitor that the resolution of the images in darkness was not good. It was very hard to make out anything beyond the little pool of warm light cast by the night light, and in here the contrast between the squares of sunset and the deep shadow in the rest of the room was even greater.

Very, very quietly, I slid open Bill's bedside-table drawer, and looked down at the tumble of personal possessions inside. A watch with a broken strap. A slew of loose change. A few tickets, a hay-fever spray, a comb. I'm not sure what I had been hoping for – but if it was to get a sense of the person who lived here, slept here, laid his head on the crisp white pillow, I was disappointed. It was strikingly impersonal.

I thought of that meeting in the kitchen, of his denimed leg slipping between my thighs with a confident intrusiveness born of long practice, and I felt sick. *Who are you?*

Suddenly, I had to get out, and I hurried across the chequered carpet, no longer caring about keeping to the shadows, or whether Sandra or Bill saw me. Let them see. Both of them.

Up in my room, I closed the door with a feeling of barricading myself away from the rest of the house. As the curtains drew themselves robotically over the windowpane, my last glimpse of the outside world was of the bloody streaks of sunset fading behind the far-off peaks of the Cairngorms, and of a light in Jack's window shining steadfastly across the darkening courtyard.

I thought of him, as I let my head sink into the goose-feather softness of the pillow. I thought of his hands that morning, the ease with which he restrained the two excited dogs, the way he dominated them, keeping them at heel. And I thought of the key, and how he had gone unerringly to the place where it had been hidden, a place I had already checked.

But then I remembered other things – his kindness that first night, in coming to check on me. And his voice over the baby monitor, putting Petra to sleep, crooning to her with a gentleness that made my stomach clench in a strange way I could not pin down. There had been no deception there. No pretence. That gentleness was real, I was certain of it.

And I wondered, if it had been him in the kitchen that night, instead of Bill, would I have lurched queasily from the room with panicked disgust? Or would I have reacted very differently? Opened my legs to his, perhaps. Leaned forward. Blushed.

But even as the thought came to me, making my cheeks flush in the darkness, I remembered again, kneeling on the floor of the utility room, sweeping my phone torch beneath the washing machine. That key had *not* been there. The intervening hours had not made me doubt that fact any more – quite the reverse. I was totally sure now.

Which meant . . .

I rubbed my hands over my face, resisting the urge to scratch the fading itch left by the creeper. I was being absurd. There was no earthly reason why he would steal that key simply to unnerve me. He had his own set, after all, and his thumbprint was authorised for use on the front door. (Though … there was probably a record every time someone used that lock, my subconscious whispered. A record that wouldn't exist with an old-fashioned lock and key.)

But no. *No.* It made no sense. Why would he go to the trouble of making a key disappear for a few hours? What would he gain from it? Nothing, except to put me on my guard. And there was my necklace too – my necklace which I had still not found, though I'd not had time to look properly. That could not have been Jack, surely. This was paranoia, all of it. Things get lost all the time. Keys fall down. Necklaces get tidied away into pockets and drawers, and unearthed days later. There would be a perfectly reasonable explanation for all of this – one that did not require a conspiracy theory.

I pushed the thought down as I rolled over and let sleep cover me like a heavy blanket.

My last thought, as sleep claimed me, was not of Jack, nor of the key, nor even of Bill. It was of the footsteps in the attic.

And the old man who had lost his daughter to his poison garden.

There was another little girl.

My hand went vainly to my throat, trying to hold a necklace that wasn't there. And then at last I slept.

I woke to the sound of screams and a confusion so loud that my first instinct was to clap my hands over my ears, even as I bolted upright in my bed, staring wildly around, shivering with cold.

The lights were on – all of them, turned up to their brightest, most eye-searing maximum. And the room was icy cold. But the noise – Jesus, the *noise*.

It was music, or at least I supposed so. But so loud and distorted that the tune was unrecognisable, the howling and squealing coming from the speakers in the ceiling turning it into a formless din.

For a minute I couldn't think what the hell to do. Then I ran to the panel on the wall and began pushing buttons, my pulse pounding in my ears, the screeching misshapen music like a howl in my head. Nothing happened except that the lights in the closets turned on to join the rest.

'Music off!' I shouted. 'Speakers off! Volume down!'

Nothing, nothing.

From downstairs I could hear furious barking, and terrified steam-train shrieks coming from Petra's room, and at last, abandoning my attempts with the panel, I grabbed my dressing gown and fled.

The music was just as loud outside the children's rooms – louder even, for the narrow walls of the hallway seemed to funnel it. And the lights were on down here too, showing me a glimpse of Petra through the nursery doorway, standing up in her cot, her hair tousled on end, screaming in fear.

I snatched her up and ran to the girls' room at the end of the corridor, shoving the door open to find Maddie curled in a foetal position in her bed, her hands over her ears, and Ellie nowhere to be seen.

'Where's Ellie?' I bellowed, above the noise of the music and Petra's fire-engine wails. Maddie looked up, her face blank with fear, her hands still clapped over her ears, and I grabbed her wrist and hauled her to her feet.

'*Where's Ellie?*' I yelled directly into her face, and she pulled away, and fled down the stairs, with me following.

In the entrance hall the noise was just as bad, and there, in the middle of the Persian rug at the foot of the stairs, was Ellie. She was crouched into a little ball, her arms wrapped around her head. All about her leapt the terrified dogs, released from their beds in the utility room, adding their frantic barks to the cacophony.

'Ellie,' I shouted, 'what happened? Did you press something?'

She looked up at me, blank and uncomprehending, and I shook my head and then ran over to the tablet sitting on the metal breakfast bar. I opened up the home management app, but when I tapped in my access code, nothing happened. Had I misremembered it? I tapped it in again, the dogs' furious woofs like a jackhammer of sound against my skull. Still nothing. *You are locked* – I had time to read, before the screen lit up momentarily and then died – a red battery warning flashing for an instant before it went black. *Fuck.*

I slammed my hand onto the wall panel and the lights above the cooker turned on and a screen on the fridge began blasting out YouTube, but the music volume didn't reduce. I could feel my heart thumping wildly in my chest, growing more and more panicked as I realised I had no way of turning this thing off.

What a stupid fucking idea – a smart house? This was the least smart thing I could imagine.

The children were shivering now, Petra still letting out ear-splitting shrieks of distress next to my ear as the dogs ran in circles around us, and I tried power button on the tablet, more helplessly, not expecting the thing to work, and it didn't. The screen was completely dark. My phone was upstairs – but could I leave the terrified children long enough to fetch it?

I was staring round, wondering what on earth I was going to do, when I felt a touch on my shoulder. I jumped so wildly I almost dropped Petra, and swung round accusingly to find Jack Grant, standing so close behind me that my shoulder touched his bare chest as I turned. We both took an involuntary step back, me nearly tripping over a stool.

He was naked from the waist up and had plainly been asleep, judging by his rumpled hair, and he bellowed something, pointing at the door, but I shook my head, and he came close, cupping his hands around my ear.

'What's happening? I could hear the din from the stables.'

'I have no idea!' I yelled back. 'I was asleep – maybe one of the girls touched something – I can't get it to turn off.'

'Can I try?' he shouted, and I felt like laughing in his face. Could he? I would kiss him if he succeeded. I shoved the tablet at him, almost aggressively.

'Be my guest!'

He tried to turn the tablet on and realised, as I had, that it was out of power. Then he went to the utility room and opened up a cupboard there, the one where the Wi-Fi router was kept, along with the electricity meter. I'm not completely sure what he did in there, I was too busy comforting an increasingly distraught Petra, but all of a sudden everything went pitch-black, and the sound stopped with an abruptness that was disorientating. I found my ears were ringing with the aftermath.

In the silence, I could hear Ellie's panicked gasping sobs, and Maddie rocking back and forth.

Petra, in my arms, stopped crying, and I felt her little body go stiff with surprise. Then she let out a gurgling laugh.

'Night night!' she said.

Then there was a click, and the lights came back on – less brightly this time, and fewer of them.

'There,' Jack said. He came back through, wiping his forehead, the dogs padding in his wake, suddenly calm again. 'It's gone back to default settings now. Bloody hell. OK.'

There was sweat on his forehead in spite of the chill in the air, and when he sat down at the kitchen counter, the tablet in his hands, I could see his hands were shaking.

Mine, as I set Petra beside Maddie, were trembling too.

Jack plugged the tablet in and now he put it down to wait until it had enough charge to turn on.

'Th-thank you,' I said weakly. Ellie was still sobbing in the hallway. 'Ellie, there's no need to cry, sweetie. It's OK now. Look … um … ' I crossed the kitchen and began rummaging in the cupboards. 'Look … here we are, have a Jammie Dodger. You too, Maddie.'

'We've brushed our teeth,' Maddie said blankly, and I suppressed a hysterical laugh. *Fuck teeth*, was what I wanted to say, but I managed to bite it back.

'I think just this once, it'll be OK. We've all had a shock. Sugar is good for shock.'

'Aye, it's true,' Jack said rather solemnly. 'Back in the old day they'd make you drink sweet tea, but since I don't really like sugar in my tea, I'll have a Jammie Dodger too, thanks, Rowan.'

'See?' I handed one to Jack and bit into one myself. 'It's fine.' I spoke around the crumbs. 'Here you go, Maddie.'

She took it, warily, and then shoved it in her own mouth as if I was about to take it away again.

Ellie ate hers more slowly.

'Mine!' Petra shouted, holding up her arms. I gave a mental shrug. I wasn't going to win any prizes for child nutrition, but I no longer gave a fuck about that. Breaking one in half, I gave her a piece of biscuit too, and then threw a chunk to each of the dogs for good measure.

'OK, we're up and running again,' Jack said, as Petra began joyfully stuffing the biscuit into her mouth. For a minute I didn't realise what he meant, and then I saw that he was holding the tablet, the screen casting a glow onto his face. 'I've got the app open. Try your pin number first.'

I took the tablet from him, selected my username from the little drop-down menu, and put in the pin number Sandra had given me for the home management app.

YOU ARE LOCKED OUT, flashed up on the screen, and then when I tapped the little 'i' button next to the message, Sorry, you have entered your Happy number incorrectly too many times and are now locked out. Please enter an admin password to override this, or wait 4 hours.

'Ah,' Jack said ruefully. 'Easy mistake to make in the circumstances.'

'But wait,' I said, annoyed. 'Hang on, that makes no sense. I only entered my passcode once. How can it lock me out for that?'

'It doesn't,' Jack said. 'You get three goes, and it warns you. But I suppose with all the noise –'

'I only entered it once,' I repeated, and then, when he didn't reply, I said, more forcefully, 'Once!'

'OK, OK,' Jack said mildly, but he looked at me sideways beneath his fringe, something a little appraising in his eyes. 'Let me try.' I handed him the tablet, feeling irrationally annoyed. It was clear that he didn't believe me. So what had happened then? Had someone been trying to log in under my username?

As I watched, Jack switched users and entered his own pin. The screen lit up briefly, and then he was inside the app.

His screen was laid out differently to mine, I saw. He had some permissions that I didn't – access to the cameras in the garage, and outside – but not to those in the children's bedroom and playroom, as I did. The icons for those rooms were greyed out and unavailable. But when he clicked on the kitchen, he was able to dim the lights by tapping on the controls on the app.

The realisation was like a little shock.

'Hang on –' the words blurted out before I had thought through how to phrase it. 'You can control the lights in here from the app?'

'Only if I'm here,' he said, clicking through to another screen. 'If you're a master user – that's Sandra and Bill, basically – you can control everything remotely, but the rest of us can only control the rooms we're in. It's some sort of geolocation thing. If you're close enough to the panel in the room, you get access to that system.'

It made sense, I supposed. If you were close enough to reach a light switch, why not give you access to the rest of the room's controls? But on the other hand … how close was close? We were directly beneath Maddie and Ellie's room here. Could he control the lights in there from his phone down here? What about outside in the yard?

But I caught myself. This was pointless. He didn't need to access the controls from the yard. He had a set of keys.

Except … what better way to make someone think you weren't involved … when really you were?

I shook my head. I had to stop this. It could have been Ellie, fiddling with the iPad in the middle of the night. Perhaps she had come down to play Candy Crush or watch a movie, and accidentally pressed something she shouldn't have. It could have been some kind of preprogrammed setting that I'd switched on without realising, the app version of a butt-dial. It could have been Bill and Sandra, if it came to that. If I was going to be paranoid, I might as well go the whole hog, after all. Why stop at random handymen? Why not extend the suspicion to everyone? The fact that they had only just recruited me and had least reason of anyone to drive me away was neither here nor there. Or, for that matter, there were other users. Who knew what permissions Rhiannon might have?

I became suddenly aware that Jack was watching me, his arms folded across his very naked chest. I caught a glimpse of myself reflected in the glass wall of the kitchen – braless in my skimpy top, with my face still pillow-crumpled, and my hair like I'd been dragged through a bush backwards – so far from the neat, buttoned-up professional image I tried to project during the day that the contrast was laughable. I felt my cheeks grow hot.

'God, I'm so sorry, Jack. You didn't have to –' I ground to a halt.

He looked down at himself in turn, seeming to realise his own state of half-dress, and gave an awkward laugh, a flush of red staining his cheekbones.

'I should have put something on. I thought you were all being murdered in your beds so I didn't really stop to dress … Listen, you get the girls to sleep, I'll put a shirt on, settle the dogs, and then I'll run some virus software on the app.'

'You don't have to do that tonight,' I protested, but he shook his head.

'No, I want to. I can't for the life of me see why it's playing up, and I'll not have you all out of your beds a second time in one night. But you don't need to wait up for me. I can lock up after myself. Or I can sleep here if you're worried.' He gestured to the couch. 'I can bring over a blanket.'

'No!' It came out sharper and more emphatic than I had meant, and I struggled to cover my overreaction. 'No, I mean … you don't have to do that. Honestly. I'll –'

Shut up, you stupid girl.

I swallowed.

'I'll get the girls to bed, and come back down. I won't be long.'

At least, I hoped I wouldn't. Petra was looking worryingly wide awake.

It was maybe an hour later, after I'd tucked the girls back into bed for the second time that night, and soothed Petra into a state of not quite sleeping, but at least almost there, that I made my way back down to the kitchen. I was half expecting Jack to have packed up and gone, but he was waiting for me, a checked flannel shirt on this time, and a cup of tea in his hand.

'Do you want one?' he asked. For a minute I wasn't sure what he was talking about, then he raised his cup, and I shook my head.

'No, thanks. I won't sleep if I have anything caffeinated now.'

'Fair enough. Are you OK?'

I don't know why it was that simple question that did it. Maybe it was the genuine concern in his voice, or the enormous relief of being with another adult after so many hours spent alone with the children. Maybe it was just the shock of what happened, finally setting in. But I burst into tears.

'Hey.' He stood awkwardly, shoving his hands in his pockets and then taking them out again, and then, as if making up his mind, he crossed the kitchen quickly and put an arm around me. I turned – I couldn't help it – and buried my face against his shoulder, feeling my whole body shake with the sobs. 'Hey, hey there … ' he said again, but this time his voice came to me through his chest wall, deeper and softer, and somehow slower. His hand hovered above my shoulder, and then settled, very gently, on my hair. 'Rowan, it's going to be OK.'

It was that one word, *Rowan*, that brought me back to my senses, reminded me of who I was, and who *he* was, and what

I was doing here. I gulped furiously and took a step back, wiping my eyes on my sleeve.

'Oh my God, Jack, I'm so s-sorry.'

My voice was still shaky, and rough from crying, and he put out his hand. For a minute I thought he was going to touch my cheek, and I wasn't sure whether I wanted to pull away, or lean into his caress. Then I realised – he was offering me a tissue. I took it, and blew my nose.

'God,' I managed at last, and then I moved across to the kitchen sofa and sat down, feeling my legs about to give way. 'Jack, you must think I'm a complete idiot.'

'I think you're a woman who's had a bad scare and was keeping it together for the bairns. And I also think –'

He stopped, biting his lip at that. I frowned.

'What?'

'No, it doesn't matter.'

'It does.' Suddenly I wanted him to say whatever it was he had been about to say very badly indeed, even though I was more than a little afraid of what it might be. 'Tell me,' I pressed, and he sighed.

'I shouldn't say it. I don't bad-mouth my employers.'

Oh. So not what I had been half fearing then. Now I was just plain curious.

'But?'

'But … ' He broke off, chewing his lip, and then seemed to make up his mind. 'Ah, fuck it. I've said too much already. I think that Sandra and Bill should never have put you in this position. It's not fair on you and it's not fair on the children if it comes to that.'

Oh.

Now it was my turn to feel awkward. What could I say to that?

'I knew what I signed up for,' I said at last.

'Aye, but did you?' He sat down beside me, making the sofa cushions squeak. 'I bet they weren't 100 per cent honest about yon one, eh?'

'Who, Maddie?'

He nodded, and I sighed.

'OK, no, you're right, they weren't. Or not totally. But I'm a childcare professional, Jack. It's nothing I haven't encountered before.'

'Really?'

'OK, I maybe haven't encountered anyone quite like Maddie, but she's just a little girl, Jack. We're getting to know each other, that's all. We had a good day today.'

It wasn't quite true though, was it? She had tried to get me sacked, first by luring me into that bloody poison garden, and second by tattling on me to her mother in a way designed to make me look as bad as possible.

'Jack, is there any way it could have been ... ' I stopped myself, and amended what I had been going to say – 'one of the kids who set all that stuff off? They were playing with the tablet earlier, is there any way they could have ... I don't know ... preprogrammed it by accident?'

Or deliberately, I thought, but did not say.

But he shook his head.

'I don't think so. There'd be a record of a log-in. And anyway, from what you said, it overrode every single speaker and lighting system in the house. None of the users on this tablet have access rights to do that. You'd need an admin password for that.'

'So ... you'd have to be Bill or Sandra, basically? Is that what you're saying?' The thought was very odd, and my doubts must have shown on my face. 'Could the kids have got hold of their pin somehow?'

'Maybe, but they're not even down as users on this tablet. Look.' He clicked the little drop-down menu on the home management app that listed the possible users for this device. Me, him, Jean and a final one marked 'Guest'. That was it.

'So what you're saying is … ' I spoke slowly, trying to think it through, 'to get an admin level of access, you wouldn't just need Sandra's pin, you'd need her phone?'

'Pretty much, yeah.' He pulled out his own phone, and showed me his access panel. 'See? I'm the only user set up on my phone. It's the way it's configured.'

'And to set up new users on a device … '

'You need a specific code. Sandra would have given you one when you came here, no?'

I nodded.

'And let me guess, the code can only be generated by … '

'By an admin user, yup. That's about the size of it.'

It made no sense. Had Sandra or Bill done this somehow? It wasn't beyond the bounds of possibility – I had read up on the app when Sandra had first told me about it, and from what I could make out, the whole point of the system was that you could control it from anywhere with Internet access – check the CCTV when you were on holiday in Verbier, turn on the lights when you were upstairs and wanted to come down, lower the heating when you were stuck in a traffic jam in Inverness. But why would they?

I remembered what Jack had said when I went to take the girls up to bed, and though I knew I was clutching at straws, I still had to ask the question.

'And the virus scans?'

He shook his head.

'Nothing on the tablet, at any rate. It's clean as a whistle.'

'Shit.' I ran my hands through my hair, and he put his hand on my shoulder, touching me again, lightly, but I felt a kind of static charge run between us, making the hairs on my arm prickle, and I shivered lightly.

Jack made a rueful face, misinterpreting my reaction.

'Look at me, blethering away. You must be cold and tired – I'll let you get to bed.'

It wasn't true. Not any more. I wasn't cold, and suddenly I was very far from tired too. What I wanted was a drink, with him – and preferably one as strong as possible. I didn't usually drink spirits, but it was on the tip of my tongue to mention the bottle of Scotch in the cupboard in the kitchen. But I knew that if I did, I would be starting something very stupid indeed, something I might not be able to stop.

'OK,' I said at last. 'That's probably good advice. Thank you, Jack.'

I stood up, and he did too, setting down his tea and stretching until I heard his joints crack, and a little sliver of flat stomach showed between the bottom of his shirt and his waistband.

And then, I did something that surprised even myself. Something I had not intended to do, until the instant I found myself doing it.

I stood on tiptoes, and pulling his shoulder down towards me, I kissed his cheek. I felt the leanness of his skin, the roughness of a day-old beard beneath my lips, and the warmth of him. And I felt something at the core of me clench with wanting.

When I stepped back, his expression was blank surprise, and for a moment I thought I had made a horrible mistake, and the butterflies in my stomach intensified to the point of queasiness. But then his mouth widened into a broad grin, and he bent, and kissed me back, very gently, his lips warm and very soft against my cheek.

'Goodnight, Rowan. You're sure you'll be all right now? You don't need me to … stay?'

There was an infinitesimal pause before the last word.

'I'm sure.'

He nodded. And then he turned and left by the utility-room door.

I locked it after him, the key turning with a reassuring clunk, and then I tucked the key back into its resting place and stood watching his silhouette against the light streaming from the stable windows as he walked back to his little flat. As he mounted the stairs to his front door he turned and lifted a hand in farewell, and even though I was not sure he would be able to see me in the darkness, I raised mine in return.

Then he was gone, the door closed behind him, and the outside light clicked off leaving a shocking, inky darkness in its wake. And I was left standing there, my skin shivering, and fighting the urge to touch the place on my cheek where his lips had been with the tips of my fingers.

I did not know what he had meant when he offered to stay. What he had been hoping, expecting.

But I knew what *I* had wanted. And I knew that I had come very close to saying yes.

I know what you're thinking, Mr Wrexham. None of this is helping my case. And that's what Mr Gates thought too.

Because we know where this leads, you and I, don't we?

To me slipping out of the house on a rainy summer night, baby monitor in one hand, running across the courtyard and up the stairs to the stableblock flat.

And to a child's body, lying – but no. I can't think about that, or I'll start crying again. And if you lose it in here, you really lose it, I know that now. I never knew there were so many ways to deal with pain so unbearable that it cannot be endured, but in here I have seen them all. The women who cut their skin, and tear out their hair, and smear their cells with blood and shit and piss. The ones who snort and shoot and smoke their way to oblivion. The ones who sleep and sleep and sleep and never get out of bed, not even for meals, until they're nothing but bones and greyish skin and despair.

But I *have* to be honest with you, that's what Mr Gates didn't – couldn't – understand. It was acting a part that got me here in the first place. Rowan the Perfect Nanny with her buttoned-up cardigans, her pasted-on smile and her perfect CV – she never existed, and you know it. Behind that neat, cheerful facade was someone very different – a woman who smoked and drank and swore, and whose hand itched to slap on more than one occasion. I tried to cover her up – to neatly fold my T-shirts, when my instinct was to throw them on the floor, to smile and nod when I wanted to tell the Elincourts to fuck off. And when the police took me in for questioning, Mr Gates wanted me to keep on pretending, keep on hiding the real me. But where did that pretence get me? Here.

I have to tell the truth, the whole truth, and nothing but the truth. Because to leave out these parts would be less than the whole truth. To tell you only the parts that exonerate me would make me slip back into the old, old trap. Because it was the lies that got me here in the first place. And I have to believe that it's the truth that will get me out.

I had forgotten what day it was when I awoke. When my alarm went off I listened blearily for the sound of childish voices, and then, when only silence greeted me, I hit snooze and went back to sleep. It recurred ten minutes later, and this time I thought I could hear a noise coming from downstairs. After lying there for another ten minutes, gearing myself up for the day, I swung my legs out of bed and stood uncertainly, dizzy with lack of sleep. Then I went down into the kitchen to find not Maddie and Ellie, but Jean McKenzie, scrubbing the dishes and looking disapproving.

'Are the bairns not up yet?' she said as I came into the room, rubbing my eyes and longing for a coffee. I shook my head.

'No, we had a –' What should I say? Suddenly I couldn't bring myself to go into the whole story. 'A bit of a disturbed night,' I finished at last. 'I thought I'd let them sleep in.'

'Well, that's all very well on a weekend, but it's 7.25 and they need to be washed, dressed and in that car by 8.15.

8.15? I did a mental double take, and then realised. Fuck.

'Oh God, it's Monday.'

'Aye, and you'll need to be getting a move on if you're to make it in time.'

*

'I'm not going.' Maddie was lying face down on her bed, with her hands over her ears. I began to feel desperate. It wasn't so much what I would tell Sandra if I couldn't get the girls to school, but the fact that I *needed* this break. I had had barely three hours' sleep last night. I could cope with a fractious baby. I couldn't cope with two primary-school age children as well, let alone one as stroppy and recalcitrant as Maddie.

'You're going and that's that.'

'I'm not, and you can't make me.'

What could I say to that? It was true after all.

'If you get dressed now there'll still be time for Coco Pops.'

It had come to that then. Basically bribing her with Sandra's list of forbidden foods at every single obstacle. But it had worked with Ellie who was, I assumed, downstairs now, more or less dressed (though not washed or brushed), and eating cereal with Jean.

'I don't want Coco Pops. I don't *like* Coco Pops. They're for babies.'

'Well, that seems about right, given you're behaving like a baby!' I snapped, and then regretted it when I heard her laugh.

Don't react, I thought. Don't give her that hold over you. You have to stay calm, or she'll know she's got the power to get to you.

I thought about counting to ten, then I remembered the painful 'one and a half' of a couple of nights before, and hastily revised my plans.

'Maddie, I'm getting very bored here. Unless you want me to take you to school in your nightie, then I suggest you get your uniform on.'

She said nothing, and at last I sighed.

'OK, well, if you want to behave like a baby, I'll have to treat you like one, and get you dressed the way I do with Petra.'

I picked up the clothes and advanced slowly towards the bed, hoping that a bit of warning might induce her to scramble up and get her clothes on, but she just lay there, making herself as limp and heavy as she possibly could, so that my back screamed in protest as I began manhandling her into her clothes. She was as floppy as a rag doll, but a hundred times as heavy, and I was breathing hard when at last I stepped back. Her skirt was askew, and her hair was rumpled from where I had dragged the T-shirt over her head, but she was more or less dressed within the meaning of the act.

Finally, figuring that I might as well take advantage of her passivity, I pulled a sock on each foot and then jammed her school shoes on.

'There,' I said, trying to keep the triumph out of my voice. 'You're dressed. Well done, Maddie. Now, I'll be downstairs eating Coco Pops with Ellie if you want to join us. Otherwise I'll see you in the car in fifteen minutes.'

'I haven't done my teeth,' she said woodenly, nothing moving apart from her mouth. I gave a laugh.

'I don't give a –' I stopped myself just in time, and then rephrased, 'a monkey's. But if you're bothered … '

I went through to the bathroom in the hallway and put some toothpaste on the tip of the brush, intending to leave it up to her whether she brushed her teeth, but when I came back, holding the brush, she was sitting up on her bed.

'Will you brush for me?' she said, her voice almost normal after the sulky malice of a few minutes ago. I frowned. Wasn't eight a bit old to be having her teeth brushed? What had the binder said? I couldn't remember.

'Um … OK,' I said at last.

She opened her mouth like an obedient little bird and I popped the toothbrush in, but I hadn't been brushing for more than a few seconds when she twisted her head away from the brush and spat full in my face, a gob of minty-white phlegm sliding down my cheek and lips and onto my top.

For a minute I couldn't speak, couldn't say anything, and then, before I had time to think what I was doing, my hand shot out to slap her face.

She flinched, and with what felt like a superhuman effort, I stopped myself, my hand inches from her face, feeling my breath fast and ragged in my chest.

Her eyes met mine, and she began to laugh, totally without mirth, a kind of joyless, cackling glee that made me want to shake her.

My whole body was shuddering with adrenaline, and I knew how close I had come to really letting go – slapping the smirk off her knowing little face. If she had been my own child I would have done it, no questions. My rage had been white hot and absolute.

But I had stopped myself. I *had* stopped.

Was that what it would look like on the monitor though, if Sandra had been watching?

I couldn't trust myself to speak. Instead I got up, leaving Maddie laughing that joyless, grinding laugh on the bed, and I walked shakily through to the bathroom, still holding the tooth-brush, and with hands that trembled I wiped the toothpaste from my face and chest, and rinsed the flecks of spit out of my mouth.

Then I stood over the basin, letting the tap run, one hand on either side of the ceramic rim, feeling my whole body shake with pent-up sobs.

'Rowan?' The call came from downstairs, faint over the sound of running water and my own weeping gasps. It was Jean Mc-Kenzie. 'Jack Grant's outside wi' the car.'

'I'm – I'm coming,' I managed back, hoping my voice didn't betray my tears. Then I splashed water over my face, dried my eyes, and walked back into the bedroom where Maddie was waiting.

'OK, Maddie,' I said, keeping my voice as level as I could. 'Time for school. Jack's outside with the car, let's not keep him waiting.'

And to my unending shock, she got up calmly, picked up her school bag, and headed for the stairs.

'Can I have a banana in the car?' she said over her shoulder, and I found myself nodding, as if nothing had happened.

'Yes,' I said, hearing my own voice in my ears, flat and emotionless. Then I thought, I have to say something, I can't let this go. 'Maddie, about what just happened – you *cannot* spit at people like that, it's disgusting.'

'What?' She turned to look at me, her face a picture of injured innocence. 'What? I sneezed. I couldn't help it.'

And then she ran down the rest of the flight of stairs and out to the waiting car, as if the bitter struggle of the last twenty minutes had been nothing but a figment of my own imagination.

I found myself wondering who had won in that encounter, as I checked Petra's car seat and buckled myself in the front beside Jack. And then it struck me what a fucked-up dynamic this really was – that my relationship with this damaged little girl was not about caring and caregiving, but about winning and dominance and war.

No. No matter what the outcome of that situation was, I hadn't won. I had lost the moment I let Maddie make it into a battle.

But I hadn't hit her. Which meant that, if nothing else, I had triumphed over my own worst instinct.

I hadn't let the demons win. Not this time.

As the school gate clanged shut, I felt a kind of weak relief come over me, so that I almost sank to the pavement, my back to the iron railings, my face in my hands.

I had done it. I had *done* it. And now my reward was five hours of something close to relaxation. I still had Petra of course – but five hours with her was nothing compared to Ellie's uncomfortable misery, and Maddie's bitter campaign of vengeance.

Somehow though I stayed upright and walked back round the corner to the side road where Jack was waiting in the car with Petra.

'Success?' he asked as I opened the car door and slid in beside him, and I felt a grin crack my face wide, unable to conceal my own relief.

'Yes. They're behind bars for the next few hours anyway.'

'See? You're doing a great job,' he said comfortably, pressing on the accelerator so that we slid away from the kerb with the unnervingly silent hum I had come to expect from the car.

'I don't know about that,' I said, a little bitterly. 'It was touch and go getting Maddie out to the car, to be honest. But I've survived another morning, which is probably the main thing.'

'Now, what do you want to do?' Jack asked practically, as we drove towards the centre of the little town where the girls' primary school was. 'We can go straight back to the house if you've stuff to be getting on with, or we can stop off for a coffee, if you like, and I can show you a wee bit of Carn Bridge.'

'A little bit of a tour would be lovely. I've not really had a chance to see anything much apart from Heatherbrae, and Carn Bridge looked really pretty as we were coming through.'

'Aye, it's a bonny little place. And it's got a good coffee shop too, the Parritch Pot. It's down at the other end of the village, but there's not much in the way of street parking there, so I'll park up by the kirk, and we can walk down along the high street and I'll show you what there is to see.'

Ten minutes later, I had wrestled Petra into her buggy and we were walking down the main street of Carn Bridge, with Jack pointing out shops and pubs, and nodding at the occasional passer-by. It was a quaint little place, somehow built on a smaller scale than you expected from afar, the granite buildings neater and narrower than they seemed from a distance. There were empty shops too, I saw – one that had once been a butcher's and another that looked like it might have been a bookshop or a stationer's. Jack nodded when I pointed them out.

'There's plenty of big houses round about, but the little shops still find it hard going. The tourist ones are all right, but the small places can't compete with the supermarkets for price.'

The Parritch Pot was a neat little Victorian tea shop right at the bottom of the high street, with a brass bell that jangled as Jack opened the door and held it for me to manoeuvre Petra across the threshold.

Inside, a motherly-looking woman came out from behind the counter to welcome us.

'Jackie Grant! Well, and it's a good while since you were in here for a piece of cake. How are you doing, my dear?'

'I'm well, Mrs Andrews, thank you. And how are you?'

'Och, well, I cannae complain. And who's your lady friend?' She gave me a look I couldn't quite decipher. There was something ... well, *arch* was the closest word I could find to describe it, as if there was something more she could have said, but was holding back. Perhaps it was just good old-fashioned curiosity. I wanted to roll my eyes. It wasn't the 1950s any more. Surely men and women were allowed to have a cup of tea without setting tongues wagging, even in a little place like Carn Bridge.

'Oh, this is Rowan,' Jack said easily. 'Rowan, this is Mrs Andrews who runs the tea shop. Rowan is the new nanny up at Heatherbrae, Mrs Andrews.'

'Oh, so you are, my dear,' Mrs Andrews said, her brow clearing, and she smiled. 'Jean McKenzie did tell me and it slipped clean out my head. Well, it's a pleasure to meet you. Let's hope you've more staying power than the other lassies.'

'I hear they didn't last long,' I ventured. Mrs Andrews laughed and shook her head.

'No, indeed. But you don't look like the type to be easily scared.'

I pondered her words as I unclipped Petra from her buggy and slid her into the high chair Jack had fetched from the back of the tea shop. Was it true? A few days ago I would have said so. But now, as I remembered myself lying there stiff and trembling in bed, listening to the *creak* ... *creak* ... of footsteps above me, I was not so sure.

'Jack,' I said at last, after we'd placed our order and were waiting for our drinks to appear, 'do you know what's above my bedroom?'

'Above your bedroom?' He looked surprised. 'No, I didn't know there was another floor up there. Is it a storage loft, or a proper attic?'

'I don't know. I've never been up there. But there's a locked door in my room which I'm assuming leads up there, and, well ...' I swallowed, unsure how to phrase this. 'I thought ... well, I heard some odd noises up there a couple of nights ago.'

'Rats?' he asked, one eyebrow cocked, and I shrugged, too embarrassed to tell the truth.

'I don't know. Maybe. Maybe not though. It sounded … ' I swallowed again, trying not to say the word that hovered on the tip of my tongue – *human*. 'Bigger.'

'They make an awful racket in the night, or at least they can do. I've a bunch of keys somewhere – do you want me to have a try this afternoon?'

'Thanks.' There was a kind of comfort in sharing my fear, however guardedly, though I felt like something of a fool now the words had left my lips. After all, what was I going to find up there, other than dust and old furniture? But it couldn't hurt, and maybe there was some simple explanation – a window left open, an old chair rocking in the draught, a lamp swinging in the breeze. 'That's really kind.'

'There you go, now.' The voice came from behind us, and I turned to see Mrs Andrews holding two coffees – proper cappuccinos, made by a human being, rather than a bloody app. I set mine to my lips and took a long, hot gulp, feeling it scald the inside of my throat, heating me from within, and for the first time in a few days, I felt my confidence return.

'This is great, thank you,' I said to Mrs Andrews, and she smiled comfortably.

'Och, you're welcome. I don't suppose it's a patch on Mr and Mrs Elincourt's fancy machine up at Heatherbrae, but we do our best.'

'Not at all,' I said with a laugh, thinking of my relief at dealing with a real person for once. 'Actually, their coffee maker is a bit *too* fancy for me, I can't get to grips with it.'

'From what Jean McKenzie says, the whole house is a bit like that, no? She says that you take your life in your hands trying to turn on the light.'

I smiled, exchanging a quick glance with Jack, but said nothing.

'Well, it wouldn't be my taste, what they've done to it, but it's nice that they took the place on at least,' Mrs Andrews said at last. She wiped her hands on her apron. 'There's not many round here that would have, with that history.'

'What history?' I looked up, startled, and she made a shooing motion with her hand.

'Och, don't listen to me. I'm just a gossipy auld woman. But there's something about that house, you know. It's claimed more than one child. The doctor's little girl wasn't the first, by all accounts.'

'What do you mean?' I took another gulp of coffee, trying to quell the unease rising inside me.

'Back when it was Struan House,' Mrs Andrews said. She lowered her voice. 'The Struans were a very old family and not quite –' She pursed her lips primly. 'Well, not quite right in the head, by the end. One of them killed his wife and child, drowned them both in the bath, and another came back from the war and shot himself with his own rifle.'

Jesus. I had a sudden flash of the luxuriously appointed family bathroom at Heatherbrae, with the outsize tub and Moroccan tiles. It couldn't be the same bathtub, but it might conceivably be the same room.

'I heard there was … a poisoning,' I said uncomfortably, and she nodded.

'Aye, that was the doctor, Dr Grant. He came to the house in the fifties, after the last Struan sold up and moved over the border. He poisoned his little girl, or so they say. Some'll tell you by accident, others –'

But she broke off. Another customer had come in, setting the bell above the door jangling, and Mrs Andrews smoothed her apron and turned away with a smile.

'But listen to me rattling on. It's just idle gossip and superstition. You shouldn't pay any heed. Well, hello, Caroline. And what can I get for you this morning?'

As she moved away to serve her other customer, I watched her go, wondering what she had meant. But then I shook myself.

She was right. It *was* just superstition. All houses above a certain age had experienced deaths and tragedies, and the fact that a child had died at Heatherbrae didn't mean anything.

Still though, Ellie's words rang in my head as I tied Petra's bib more firmly under her chin and dug out the pot of rice cakes.

There was another little girl.

We took the long way round back to Heatherbrae House, driving slowly along past peat-dark burns and through sun-dappled pine forests. Petra snoozed in the back as Jack pointed out local landmarks – a ruined castle, an abandoned fort, a Victorian station decommissioned by Beeching. In the distance the mountains loomed, and I tried to keep track of the peaks that Jack named.

'Do you like hill walking?' he asked, as we waited at a junction with the main road for a lorry to pass, and I realised that I didn't know the answer to his question.

'I – well, I'm not really sure. I've never done it. I like walking, I guess. Why?'

'Oh … well … ' There was a sudden hesitation in his voice, and when I looked sideways at him, there was a flush of red across his cheekbones. 'I just thought … you know … when Sandra and Bill are back and your weekends are your own again, perhaps we might … I could take you up one of the Munros. If you liked the idea.'

'I … do,' I said, and then it was my turn to blush. 'I do like the idea. I mean, if you don't mind me being slow … I suppose I'd have to get boots and stuff.'

'You'd need good shoes. And waterproofs. The weather can turn very fast up on the mountain. But –'

His phone gave a little chirrup and he glanced down at it, and then frowned, and handed it across to me.

'Sorry, Rowan, that's from Bill. D'you mind telling me what he says? I don't want to read it while I'm driving, but he doesn't normally text unless it's urgent.'

I pressed the text on the home screen and a preview flashed up, all I could see without unlocking the phone, but it was enough.

'*Jack, urgently need the hard copies of the Pemberton files by to-night. Please drop everything and bring them* – and that's where it cuts off.'

'Fuck,' Jack said, and then glanced guiltily in the rear-view mirror to where Petra was sleeping. 'Sorry, I didn't mean to swear, but that's my afternoon and evening gone, and most of tomorrow too. I had plans.'

I didn't ask what his plans were. I felt only a sudden swoop of … not quite loss … not quite fear either … but a sort of unease at the realisation that he would be gone, and I would be quite alone with the children for the best part of twenty-four hours, by the time Jack had driven down, rested, and then driven back.

It meant something else, too, I realised, as we came out of the dark tunnel of pine trees into the June sunlight: no possibility of trying the attic door until he got back.

Jack left almost as soon as we got back, and although I had grate-fully accepted his offer to take the dogs with him, and relieve me of the responsibility to feed and walk them on top of everything else, the house had an unfamiliar, quiet feeling to it after they had all gone. I fed Petra and put her down for her nap, and then I sat for a while in the cavernous kitchen, drumming my fingers on the concrete tabletop and watching the changing sky out of the tall windows. It really was an incredible view, and in daylight like this, I could see why Sandra and Bill had hewn the house in half the way they had, sacrificing Victorian architecture for this all-encompassing expanse of hill and moor.

Still, though, it left an odd sensation of vulnerability – the way the four-square front looked so neat and untouched, while at the back it had been ripped open, exposing all the house's insides. Like a patient who looked well enough above their clothes, but lift their shirt and you would find their wounds had been left unstitched, bleeding out. There was a strange feeling of split identity too – as though the house was trying hard to be one thing, while Sandra and Bill pulled it relentlessly in the other direction, chopping off limbs, performing open-heart surgery on its dignified old bones, trying to make it into something against its own will – something it was never meant to be, modern and stylish and slick, where it wanted to be solid and self-effacing.

The ghosts wouldn't like it ... I heard it again in Maddie's reedy little voice, and shook my head. Ghosts. How absurd. Just folk tales and rumours, and a sad old man, living here after the death of his child.

It was more for want of anything else to do that I opened up my phone, typed in 'Heatherbrae House, child's death, poison garden'.

Most of the early results were irrelevant, but as I scrolled down and down, I came at last to a local-interest blog, written by some sort of amateur historian.

STRUAN – Struan House (now renamed Heatherbrae) near Carn Bridge, in Scotland, is another curiosity for garden historians, being one of the few remaining poison gardens in the United Kingdom (another being the famous example at Alnwick Castle in Northumberland). Originally planted in the 1950s by the analytical chemist Kenwick Grant, it is thought to feature some of the rarest and most poisonous examples of domestic plants, with a particular focus on varieties native to Scotland. Sadly, the garden was allowed to fall into disrepair after the death of Grant's young daughter, Elspeth, who died in 1973, age 11, having, according to local legend, accidentally ingested one of the plants in the garden. Although in its day occasionally open to researchers and members of the public, Dr Grant closed the garden completely after his daughter's death, and after he himself passed away in 2009, the house was sold to a private buyer. Since the sale, Struan has been renamed Heatherbrae House, and it's believed that it has been the subject of extensive remodelling. It is unknown what remains of the poison garden, but it is to be hoped that the current owners appreciate the historical and botanical importance of this piece of Scottish history, and maintain Dr Grant's legacy with the respect it deserves.

There were no photographs, but I returned to Google and typed in 'Dr Kenwick Grant.' It was an unusual name, and there were few results, but most of the pictures that came up seemed to be of the same man. The first was a black-and-white picture of a man aged perhaps forty, with a neatly clipped goat-like beard and small wire-framed spectacles, standing in front of what looked like the wrought-iron gate of the walled garden where Maddie, Ellie and I had entered yesterday. He was not smiling, his face had the look of one that didn't smile easily, with an expression naturally serious in repose, but there was a kind of pride in his stance.

The next photograph made a sad contrast. It was another black-and-white shot, recognisably the same man, but this time Dr Grant was in his fifties. His expression was totally different, a distorted mask of emotion that could have been grief, or fear, or anger, or a mix of all three. He seemed to be running towards an unseen photographer, his hand outstretched, either to push the camera away or shield his own face, it was not clear which. Behind the goat-like beard his mouth was twisted into a snarling grimace that made me flinch, even through the tiny screen and the passage of decades.

The final photograph was in colour, and it was a shot that seemed to have been taken through the bars of a gate. It showed an elderly man, stooped and bent, wearing a buff overall and a wide-brimmed hat that shaded his face. He was extremely thin, to the point of emaciation, and leaning on a stick, and his glasses were thick and fogged, but he was staring fiercely at the person taking the photo, his free hand upraised in a bony fist, as though threatening the viewer. I clicked on the picture, trying to find out the context for the shot, but there was none. It was just a Pinterest page, with no information on where the picture had been found. *Dr Kenwick Grant*, the caption read, *2002*.

As I closed down the phone, my overwhelming emotion was a kind of desperate sadness – for Dr Grant, for his daughter, and for this house, where it had all happened.

Unable to sit in silence with my thoughts any longer, I got up, put the baby monitor in my pocket, and grabbing a ball of catering string from the drawer by the cooker, I left the house by the utility-room door, tracing the path the girls had shown me the day before.

The sun of the morning had gone in, and I was cold by the time I reached the cobbled path that led to the poison garden. It was strange to think it was June – down in London I would have been sweating in short skirts and sleeveless tops, and cursing the shitty air con at Little Nippers. Up here, almost halfway to the Arctic Circle, I was beginning to regret not taking my coat. The baby monitor was silent in my pocket as I reached the gate and slipped my hand through the metalwork to try to trip the catch, as Ellie had done.

It was more difficult than she had made it look. It was not just the fact that the hole in the wrought iron was too narrow for my hand to fit comfortably, it was also the angle. Even after I had forced my hand through, swearing as the rust ripped skin off my knuckles, I could not get my fingers to the catch.

I changed position, kneeling on the damp cobbles, feeling the chill strike up through the thin material of my sheer tights, and at last managed to get a fingertip to the tongue of the latch. I pressed, pressed harder ... and then the gate opened with a clang and I almost fell forward onto the worn bricks.

It was hard to believe that I had ever mistaken it for a regular garden. Now that I knew its history, the warning signs were everywhere. Fat, black laurel berries, the thin needles of yew, straggling patches of self-seeded foxglove, clumps of nettles, which I had taken to be weeds when I first entered the garden but which, I now saw, bore a rusted metal tag dug deep into the earth, labelled *Urtica dioica*. And others, too, that I did not recognise – a plant with flamboyant mauve flowers, another that brushed my leg with a sensation like tiny needles. A patch of something that looked like sage, but must have been something very different. And, as I pushed open the door of a tumbledown shed, a profusion of mushrooms and toadstools, still sprouting gamely in the dark.

I could not suppress a shudder as I drew the door quietly shut, feeling the damp wood grate on the flags. So many poisons – some tempting, some decidedly not. Some familiar, and some I was certain I had never seen before. Some so beautiful I wanted to break off a branch and stick it in a jug in the kitchen – except that I did not dare. Even the familiar plants in these surroundings looked strange and ominous – no longer grown for their lovely flowers and colours, but for their deadliness.

I hugged my arms around my body as I walked, partly to protect myself, but the garden was so overgrown that it was impossible to avoid brushing up against the plants completely. The touch of the leaves felt like prickles on my skin, and I was unable to tell any more which plants were toxic to touch, or whether it was pure paranoia on my part that sent my skin itching and tingling when I brushed past.

It was only when I turned to leave that I noticed something else – a set of pruning shears, sitting on the low brick wall holding back one of the beds. They were new and bright, not in the least rusted, and looking up, I saw that the bush above my head had been pruned – not much, but enough to clear the path. And further up, I saw that a piece of garden twine had been used to hold back a swag of creeper.

In fact, the more I looked, the more I was sure – this garden was not as neglected as it appeared. Someone had been tending to it – and not Maddie or Ellie. No child would have thought of neatly cutting back that hanging branch – they would have snapped it off, or just ducked under it, if they were even tall enough to notice.

So who then? Not Sandra. I was sure of that. Jean McKenzie? Jack Grant?

The name sounded in my head with a curious chime. Jack … Grant.

It wasn't an uncommon surname, particularly around here, but still. Dr Kenwick Grant. Could it really be coincidence?

As I stood, wondering, the baby monitor in my pocket gave a little grumbling squawk, recalling me to reality, and I remembered what I had come here to do.

Picking up the shears, I hurried back to the gate, and pulled it firmly shut behind myself. The *clang* as it closed set a flock of birds rising into the sky from pine trees up the slope, and seemed to echo back at me from the hills opposite, but I was in too much of a hurry now to care.

Taking the string out of my pocket, I clipped off a generous length and then I stood on tiptoe and began to wind it round and round the top of the gate, above the height of my own head, where no child could possibly reach, twining it in and out of the ornate fitting and round the brick lintel above, until at last the string was used up, and the gate was totally secure. Then I tied it in a granny knot, wrapping the ends around my fingers and pulling the string tight until my fingertips went white.

The baby monitor in my pocket wailed again, more determinedly this time, but I was sure now that the gate was secure, and that nothing short of a ladder would enable Maddie and Ellie to break in this time. Dropping the shears into my pocket, I picked up my phone and pressed the Happy app speaker icon.

'Coming, Petra, there, there, sweetheart, no need to cry, I'm coming.'

And I ran up the cobbled path to the house.

The next few hours were taken up with Petra, and then figuring out how to drive the Tesla to collect the girls from school. Jack had taken the Elincourts' second car, a Land Rover, with him to meet Bill, and had given me a quick crash course in driving the Tesla before he left, but it was an undeniably different style and it took me a few miles to get used to it – no clutch, no gears, and a strange slowing every time you took your foot off the accelerator.

The girls were both tired after their day at school. They said nothing as we drove home, and the afternoon and evening passed without incident. They ate supper, took turns playing on the tablet, and then got into their pyjamas and climbed into bed with barely a peep. When I went up at eight to turn out their lights and tuck them in, I heard an adult's voice, coming over the speakers.

At first I thought that they were listening to an audiobook, but then I heard Maddie say something, her small voice inaudible through the door, and the amplified voice on the speakers replied, 'Oh, darling, well done! Ten out of ten! I'm very proud of you. And what about you, Ellie? Have you been practising your spellings too?'

It was Sandra. She had dialled into the children's room and was talking to them before they fell asleep.

For a moment I stood, hovering outside the door, my hand on the doorknob, listening to their conversation, half hoping – half fearing – to hear something about myself.

But instead, I heard Sandra tell the girls to snuggle down, the lights dimmed, and she began to sing a lullaby.

There was something so loving, so personal about the simple act, Sandra's voice wavering over the high notes, and tripping over an awkward lyric, that I was left feeling like an eavesdropper. I wanted, more than anything, to open the door, tiptoe in, and cuddle Maddie and Ellie, kiss their hot little foreheads, tell them how lucky they were to have a mother who at least *wanted* to be there, even if she couldn't.

But I knew that would break the illusion that their mother was really present, and I backed away. If Sandra wanted to speak to me, no doubt she would dial down to the kitchen when she'd finished.

While I ate and tidied up, I waited, slightly nervously, for the sound of her voice, crackling over the intercom, but it didn't come. By 9 p.m. the house was silent and I locked up and went to bed with a feeling like walking on eggshells.

After I had done my teeth and turned out the lights, I lay down in bed, feeling my limbs ache with weariness. My phone was in my hand, but instead of plugging it in to charge and going straight to sleep, I found myself googling Dr Grant again.

I stared at his photo for a long time, thinking of Mrs Andrews's words in the cafe. There was something about the contrast between that first picture and the last that was almost shocking, something that spoke of long nights of grief and agony – perhaps even in this very room. What had it been like to live here all those years, with the local gossip swirling around him, and the memories of his daughter so stark and painful?

Returning to the search screen, I typed in 'Elspeth Grant death Carn Bridge' and waited as the links came up.

There was no photo – at least none that I could find. And she had not had much of an obituary, just a passage in the *Carn Bridge Observer* (now defunct) stating that Elspeth Grant, much loved daughter of Dr Kenwick Grant and the late Ailsa Grant, had died in St Vincent's Cottage Hospital on 21 October 1973, aged 11 years.

Another brief piece a few weeks later, this time in the *Inverness Gazette*, recorded the results of a post-mortem and inquest on Elspeth's death. It seemed she had died from eating *Prunus laurocerasus*, or cherry laurel berries, which had been accidentally made into jam. The berries were apparently easily mistaken for cherries or elderberries, by inexperienced foragers, and it was thought that the child had gathered them herself and brought them to the housekeeper, who had simply tipped them into the pan without checking. Dr Grant never ate jam himself, preferring porridge and salt, the housekeeper did not live in and took her meals at her own house in the village, and Elspeth's nanny had resigned her post almost two months before the incident, so Elspeth was the only person to ingest the poison. She had become unwell almost straight away, and had died of multiple organ failure, in spite of strenuous efforts to save her.

A verdict of misadventure was brought, and no charges were filed as a result of her death.

So. Elspeth had been the only person who was ever in danger of eating that jam. I could see why gossip had arisen – though quite why it had settled on Dr Grant, and not the unnamed housekeeper, was unclear. Perhaps it had been a case of local people looking after their own. And what of the nanny? She had resigned 'just two months before', according to the writer of the piece, managing to put the simple phrase in such a way as to make it sound both innocent and suggestive, but presumably she could have had nothing to do with the incident, or it would have been raised at the inquest. Her absence had been noted purely in connection with the fact that Elspeth had been unsupervised at the time of picking the berries, and therefore, by inference, more likely to make a slip concerning identification of the plants.

The more I pondered the idea, though, the more problems there seemed to be with the suggestion that Elspeth had gathered the berries by accident. I was a 1990s child of the suburbs, totally unused to fruit picking, and even I had a vague idea of what laurel looked like, compared to elderberry. Would the daughter of a poisons expert, with a locked garden explicitly dedicated to deadly plants really make such a slip?

Rereading the piece, I felt a sudden surge of sympathy for the nanny, the missing link in the case. She was not interviewed. Whatever had become of her was not stated. But she had missed, by just a few weeks, the possibility of being embroiled in scandal. What future was there for a nanny whose child had died in her care, after all? A very bleak one indeed.

I'm not sure when finally I drifted off, my phone still in my hand, but I know that it was very late when a sudden sound jerked me from sleep. It was a ding-dong noise, like a doorbell, not one of my usual alerts. I sat up, blinking and rubbing my eyes, and then realised the noise was coming from my phone. I stared at the screen. The Happy app was flashing. *Doorbell sounding*, said the screen. It came again, a low 'bing-bong' that seemed to be able to override all my do-not-disturb settings. When I pressed the icon a message flashed up. *Open door? Confirm / Cancel.*

I hastily pressed cancel, and clicked through to the camera icon. The screen showed me a view of the front door, but the outside light was not on, and inside the shelter of the porch I could see nothing but grainy pixelated darkness. Had Jack come back? Had he forgotten his keys? Either way, as the doorbell sounded for the third time, I could hear the chimes filtering up the stairwell as well as coming out of my phone, and I knew I had to answer it before the noise woke the girls.

The room was unnaturally cold, and I pulled on my dressing gown before padding quietly downstairs, my feet soft on the thick carpet runner, picking my way in the semi-darkness but not wanting to turn on the lights and risk waking the children. In the hallway I had a moment's struggle with the thumb panel, and then the door swung silently open to reveal ... nothing.

It was quite dark. The Land Rover's parking space was still empty, and none of the motion-sensitive security lights around the yard were on, though the porch light flicked on as soon as I stepped over the threshold, detecting my presence. I shaded my eyes against its harsh glare and peered across the yard and down the drive, shivering slightly in the cool night air. Nothing. There were no lights on in Jack's flat either. Had something triggered it by mistake?

Closing the door, I climbed slowly back up towards my bedroom, but I was barely halfway up the second flight when the bell sounded again.

Damn it.

With a sigh, I belted my dressing gown tighter and made my way back downstairs, hurrying this time.

But when I wrenched open the door, again, there was no one there.

I slammed the door harder than I meant to this time, the tiredness making my frustration boil over for a second, and I stood in the dark of the hallway, holding my breath and listening for a sound from upstairs, the rising siren of Petra's wail perhaps. But none came.

Nevertheless, this time, instead of setting back upstairs to my own room, I stopped and peered in at Petra, sleeping peacefully, and then into Maddie and Ellie's room. In the soft glow of their night light I could see both of them lying fast asleep, sweaty hair strewn across the pillow, their cherubic little mouths open, their soft snores barely disturbing the quiet. They looked so small and vulnerable in sleep, both of them, and my heart clenched at my anger towards Maddie that morning. I told myself that tomorrow I would do better – that I would remember how young she was, how disorientating it must be to be left with a woman she barely knew. Either way, it was clearly not one of them playing with the doorbell, and I shut the door softly, and made my way back upstairs to my room.

It was still very cold, and as I closed the door behind me, the curtains billowed out, and I realised why. The window was open.

I frowned as I walked across to it.

It was open, and not just slightly, as if someone had wanted to air the room, but completely open, the bottom sash pushed up as high as it would go. Almost – the thought came unbidden – as if someone had been leaning out to smoke a cigarette, though that was absurd.

No wonder the room was cold. Well, it was easily solvable at least – easier than battling with the control panel at any rate. The curtains, doors, lights, gates and even the coffee machine in this place might be automated, but the windows at least were still Victorian originals, blessedly operated by hand. Thank God.

I yanked the sash down, drew the brass catch across, and then scampered back into the still-warm sanctuary of the feather duvet, shivering pleasurably as I snuggled back into its folds.

I was drifting back off to sleep when I heard it ... not the doorbell this time, but a single, solitary *creeeeak*.

I sat up in bed, my phone clutched to my breast. Shit. Shit shit *shit*.

But the next sound did not come. Had I misheard? Was it not the footsteps that had woken me the night before, but something else? Just a branch in the wind, perhaps, or an expanding floorboard?

I could hear nothing apart from the whoosh of my own blood in my own ears, and at last I lay slowly back down, still clutching my phone in my hand, and shut my eyes against the darkness.

But my senses were on high alert, and sleep seemed impossible. For more than forty minutes I lay there, feeling my pulse thumping, feeling my thoughts race with a mixture of paranoia and wild superstitions.

And then, half as I'd feared, half as I'd been waiting for, it came again.

Creeeeak …

And then, after the smallest of pauses, *creak … creak … creak …*

This time there was no doubt – it was pacing.

My heart leapt into my throat with a kind of nauseating lurch, and my pulse sped up so fast that for a moment I thought I would faint, but then anger took over. I jumped out of bed and ran to the locked door in the corner of the room, where I knelt, peering through the keyhole, my heart like a drum in my chest.

I felt absurdly vulnerable, kneeling there in my night clothes with one eye wide open and pressed to a dark hole, and for a moment I had a sick, jolting fantasy of someone shoving something through the hole, a toothpick perhaps, or a sharpened pencil, roughly piercing my cornea, and I fell back, blinking, my eye watering with the dusty draught.

But there was nothing there. No toothpick, maliciously blinding me. Nothing to see either. Just the unending blackness, and the cool, dust-laden breeze of stale attic air. Even if there was a turn in the stair, or a closed door at the top, with a light on in the attic itself, *some* light would have escaped to pollute the inky dark of the stairs. But there was nothing. Not even the smallest glimmer. If there was someone up there, whatever they were doing, they were doing it in the dark.

Creak … creak … creak … it came again, unbearable in its regularity. Then a pause, and then again, *creak … creak … creak …*

'I can hear you!' I shouted at last, unable to sit there listening in silence and fear any longer. I put my mouth to the keyhole, my voice shaking with a mix of angry terror. 'I can hear you! What the fuck are you doing up there, you sicko? How dare you? I'm calling the police so you'd better get the fuck out of there!'

But the steps didn't even falter. My voice died away as if I had shouted into an empty void. *Creak … creak … creak …* and then, just as before, a little pause, and they resumed without the slightest loss of rhythm. *Creak … creak … creak …* And I knew in truth that of course I wouldn't call the police. What the fuck could I say? 'Oh, please, Constable, there's a creaking sound coming from my attic'? There was no police station closer than Inverness, and they would hardly be taking routine calls in the middle of the night. My only option was 999 – and even in my shaking state of fear, I had a pretty good idea what the operator would say if a hysterical woman rang the emergency number in the middle of the night claiming spooky sounds were coming from her attic.

If only Jack were here, if only *someone* were here, apart from three little girls I was paid to protect, not scare even further.

Oh God. Suddenly I could not bear it any longer, and I understood what dark terrors had driven those four previous nannies out of their post and away. To lie here, night after night, listening, waiting, staring into the darkness at that locked door, that open keyhole gaping into blackness …

There was nothing I could do. I could go and sleep in the living room, but if the noises started down there as well, I thought I might lose it completely, and there was something almost worse about the idea of those sounds continuing up in the attic while I, ignorant, slept down below. At least if I was here, watching, listening, whatever was up there could not ...

I swallowed in the darkness, my throat dry.

My palms were sweating, and I could not finish the thought.

I would not sleep again tonight, I knew that now.

Instead I wrapped myself in the duvet, shivering hard, turned on the light, and sat, with my phone in my hand, listening to the steady, rhythmic sound of the feet pacing above me. And I thought of Dr Grant, the old man who had lived here before, the man Sandra and Bill had done their very best to get rid of, painting and scouring and remodelling until there was barely a trace of him left, except for that horrible poison garden, behind its locked gate.

And except, perhaps, whatever paced that attic in the night.

I heard the words again, in Maddie's cold little matter-of-fact voice, as if she were beside me, whispering in my ear. *After a while he stopped sleeping. He just used to pace backwards and forwards all night long. Then he went mad. People do go mad, you know, if you stop them from sleeping for long enough ...*

Was I going mad? Was that what this was?

Jesus. This was ridiculous. People didn't go mad from two nights' lack of sleep. I was being completely melodramatic.

And yet, as the footsteps passed above me again, slow and relentless, I felt a kind of panic rise up inside me, possessing me, and I could not stop my eyes turning towards the locked door, imagining it opening, the slow tread, tread of old feet on the stairs inside, and then that cadaverous, hollow face coming towards me in the darkness, the bony arm outstretched.

Elspeth ...

It was a sound not coming from above, but in my own mind – a death-rattle cry of a grief-stricken father for his lost child. *Elspeth ...*

But the door did not open. No one came. And yet still above me, hour after hour, those steps continued. *Creak … creak … creak …* the ceaseless pacing of someone unable to rest.

I could not bring myself to turn out the light. Not this time. Not with those ceaseless, restless footsteps above me.

Instead I lay there, on my side, facing the locked door, my phone in my hand, watching, waiting, until the floor beneath the window opposite my bed began to lighten with the coming of dawn, and at last I got up, stiff-limbed and nauseous with tiredness, and made my way down to the warmth of the kitchen to make myself the strongest cup of coffee I could bear to drink, and try to face the day.

The ground floor was empty and echoing, eerily quiet without the snuffling, huffing presence of the dogs. I was surprised to find that a part of me missed the distraction of their questing noses and constant begging for treats.

As I made my way across the hall to the kitchen, I found I was picking up a treasure trail of the girls' possessions – a scatter of crayons on the hall rug, a My Little Pony abandoned beneath the breakfast bar and then – oddly – a single purple flower, wilting, in the middle of the kitchen floor. I bent down, puzzled, wondering where it had come from. It was just a single bloom, and it looked as if it had fallen from a bouquet or dropped from a house plant, but there were no flowers in this room. Had one of the girls picked it? But if so, when?

It seemed a shame to let it die, so I filled a coffee mug with water and stuck the stem into it, and then put it on the kitchen table. Perhaps it would revive.

I was quietly nursing my second cup of coffee and watching the sun rise above the hills to the east of the house, when the voice came, seemingly from nowhere.

'Rowan ... '

It was a reedy quaver, barely audible, and yet somehow loud enough to echo around the silent kitchen, and it made me jump so that scalding coffee slopped over my wrist and the sleeve of my dressing gown.

'Shit.' I began mopping up, twisting at the same time to see the source of the voice. There was no one there, at least no one visible.

'Who's there?' I called, and this time I heard a creak from the direction of the stairs, a single creak, so eerily like those of the night before that my heart skipped a beat. 'Who *is* it?' I called again, more aggressively than I had intended, and strode angrily out into the hallway.

Above me a small figure hesitated at the top of the stairs. Ellie. Her face was worried, her lip trembling.

'Oh, sweetheart ... ' I felt instantly contrite. 'I'm sorry, you scared me. I didn't mean to snap. Come down.'

'I'm not allowed,' she said. She had a blanket in her hands, twisting the silky trim between her fingers, and with her bottom lip stuck out and wobbling dangerously close to tears, she looked suddenly much younger than her five years.

'Of course you are. Who says you're not allowed?'

'Mummy. We're not allowed out of our rooms until the bunny clock's ears go up.'

Oh. Suddenly I remembered the paragraph in the binder about Ellie's early rising, and the rule about the Happy Bunny clock, which clicked over to the wide-awake bunny at 6 a.m. I looked back through the arch to the kitchen clock. 5.47.

Well, I couldn't exactly contradict Sandra's rule ... but here we were, and there was a large part of me that was relieved to see another human being. Somehow with Ellie around, the ghosts of the night before seemed to retreat back into absurdity.

'Well ... ' I said slowly, trying to pick my way between backing up my employer, and compassion to a small child hovering on the verge of crying. 'Well, you're up now. Just this once, I think we can pretend the bunny woke up early.'

'But what will Mummy say?'

'I won't tell anyone if you don't,' I said, and then bit my lip. It's one of the cardinal rules of childcare – don't ask a child to keep secrets from a parent. That's the path to all kinds of risky behaviour and misunderstandings. But I'd said it now, and hopefully Ellie had read it as a light-hearted remark rather than an invitation to conspire against her mother. I couldn't help but glance up at the camera in the corner – but surely Sandra wouldn't be awake at 6 a.m. unless she had to be. 'Come on down and we'll have a hot chocolate together and then when the bunny wakes up you can go up and get dressed.'

Down in the kitchen, Ellie sat on one of the high stools, kicking her heels against the legs of the chair, while I heated up milk on the induction hob and stirred in chocolate powder. As Ellie drank, and I sipped my now-cooling coffee, we talked, about school, about her best friend Carrie, about missing the dogs, and at last I ventured to ask about whether she missed her parents. Her face crumpled a little at that.

'Can we phone Mummy again tonight?'

'Yes, of course. We can try, anyway. She's been very busy you know that.'

Ellie nodded. Then, looking out of the window, she said, 'He's gone, hasn't he?'

'Who?' I was confused. Was she talking about her father, or Jack? Or perhaps … perhaps someone else? 'Who's gone?'

She didn't answer, only kicked her legs against the stool.

'I like it better when he's gone. He makes them do things they don't want to do.'

I don't know why, but the words gave me a sharp flashback to something I had barely thought about since my very first night here – that crumpled, unfinished note from Katya. The words sounded inside my head, as though someone had whispered them urgently into my ear. *I wanted to tell you to please be –*

Suddenly it felt more like a warning than ever.

'Who?' I said, more urgently this time. 'Who are you talking about, Ellie?'

But she misunderstood my question, or perhaps deliberately chose to misinterpret it.

'The girls.' Her voice was matter-of-fact. And then she put down her hot chocolate and slid from the stool. 'Can I go and watch some TV?'

'Ellie, wait,' I said, standing too, feeling my heart suddenly pounding in my chest. 'Who are you talking about? Who's gone? Who makes the girls do things?'

But I was too urgent, and as my hand closed on her wrist, she pulled away, suddenly frightened by my intensity.

'Nothing. I don't remember. I made it up. Maddie told me to say it. I didn't say it anyway.' The excuses tumbled out, one after another, each as silly as the one before, and she twisted her small hand out of my grip. I had no idea what to say. I thought about following her as she slipped from the room, and the sound of the *Peppa Pig* theme tune filtered back into the play-room, but I knew it wouldn't work. I had scared her, and missed my chance. I should have asked more casually. Now she had closed down in that way small children do when they realise they have said something more momentous than they meant to. It was the same panic I had seen in little children when they repeated an inappropriate word without understanding the re-action it would elicit – a startled attempt to pedal back from a response they had not anticipated, followed by total shutdown, and a denial that they ever said it. If I pushed Ellie now, I would only be shooting myself in the foot, and preventing any further confidences.

The girls ... He makes them do things they don't want to do ...

My stomach turned over. It was the kind of thing every safe-guarding manual warned about – the nightmare scenario you hoped never to encounter. But … was it? What girls was Ellie talking about? Herself and Maddie? Or some completely different girls? And who was the 'he'? Bill? Jack? Or someone else entirely – a teacher or … ?

But no. I pushed away the image of the wild grief-stricken face staring out of my phone screen at me. That was pure fantasy. If I went to Sandra with something like that, she'd be entitled to laugh in my face.

But *could* I go to Sandra with something like this? When Ellie would deny what she said, and when it might be nothing at all? There was nothing that I could pinpoint, after all, to say 'this is definitely worrying'.

I was still staring after Ellie, biting at the edge of my nail, when a noise from the hallway made me jump, and I turned to see the door opening and Jean McKenzie standing on the door-step, taking off her coat.

'Mrs McKenzie,' I said. She was neatly dressed in a woollen skirt and a white cotton blouse and I suddenly felt very conscious of my own state of undress, in a dressing gown, with not a great deal beneath.

'You're up early,' was all she said, and I felt the prickle of her disapproval. Maybe it was the lack of sleep, or the leftover anxiety from Ellie's words, but my temper suddenly boiled up.

'Why don't you like me?' I demanded.

She turned to look back at me from stashing her coat in the hall cupboard.

'I beg your pardon?'

'You heard me. You've been completely off with me ever since I arrived. Why?'

'I think you're imagining things, Miss.'

'You know full well I'm not. If it's about that business on the first day, I didn't shut the damn door, and I *didn't* lock the children out. Why would I?'

'Kindness is as kindness does,' Jean McKenzie said cryptically, and she turned to go into the utility room, but I ran after her, grabbing her arm.

'What the hell does that even mean?'

She pulled herself out of my grip, and suddenly her eyes blazed at me with what I could only call hatred.

'I'll thank you not to handle me like that, Miss, and not to swear in front of the bairns, either.'

'I was asking you a perfectly reasonable question,' I retorted, but she ignored me, stalking away to the utility room, rubbing her arm with exaggerated care as if I'd given her a friction burn. 'And stop calling me *Miss*,' I called after her. 'We're not in bloody Downton Abbey.'

'What would you prefer me to call you then?' she snapped over her shoulder.

I had turned on my heel, preparing to wake up Maddie, but her words stopped me in my tracks, and I swung round to stare at her expressionless back, bent over the utility-room sink.

'Wh-what did you say?'

But she did not answer, only turned on the taps, drowning out my voice.

'Goodbye, girls!' I called, watching them through the school gate as they traipsed into their classrooms. Maddie said nothing, she just trudged onwards, head down, ignoring the chatter of the other little girls. But Ellie looked up from her conversation with a little red-headed girl, and waved. Her smile was sweet and cheerful, and I felt myself smile back, and then down at Petra, jiggling and gurgling on my hip. The sun was shining, the birds were singing, and the warmth of a beautiful June day was filtering through the leaves of the trees. The fears and fantasies of last night – the memory of that twisted, grief-racked face peering out from the screen of my phone – all of that seemed suddenly preposterous in the light of day.

I was just strapping Petra back into her car seat when my phone pinged, and I glanced at it, wondering if it was something important. It was an email. From Sandra.

Oh shit.

Paranoid thoughts flitted through my mind – had she seen the camera footage of me almost hitting Maddie, or the endless stream of treats I had been bribing the girls with? Or was it something else? Something Jean McKenzie had said?

My stomach was fluttering butterflies as I clicked to open, but the subject header was matter-of-fact enough – 'Update'. Whatever that meant.

Hi Rowan,

Sorry to email but I'm in a meeting and can't talk, and I wanted to send you a quick update with how things are going here. The trade fair has gone super well, but Bill has been called away to Dubai to do some troubleshooting out there, which means I'm going to have to take over on the Kensington project – not ideal as it means I will be away for a little longer than I had hoped, but it can't be helped. I should be back by next Tuesday (i.e. a week today). Are you managing OK? Does that sound doable?

In terms of the children, Rhiannon finishes school today. Elise's mum has kindly volunteered to collect both girls (they live down near Pitlochry so have to drive past anyway) and Rhi will be back at Heatherbrae any time from about 12 onwards. I have texted her so she knows what's going on, and she's excited to meet you.

Jack spoke to Bill yesterday and mentioned that you are getting on very well with the girls, I'm very glad to hear it's all going OK. Do call if you have any concerns – I will try to ring tonight before the girls' bedtimes.

Sandra x

I shut down the email, unsure whether my overriding emotion was one of relief, or trepidation. I most definitely *was* relieved – not least about the fact that Jack had apparently put in a good word for me. But another week ... I had not realised until I read Sandra's words how much I had been counting on her arrival back this Friday, ticking off the days in my head like a prison sentence.

And now ... four more days added onto my term. And not just with the little ones, but with Rhiannon too. How did I feel about that?

The idea of having someone else in the house was undeniably comforting. There *was* something absurd about the memory of those slow, measured footsteps, but even in daylight, I could feel the hairs beginning to rise up on my arms as I recalled lying there, listening to them pacing back and forth. Having *someone*, even a stroppy fourteen-year-old, in the next bedroom would definitely take the edge off.

But as I started up the Tesla, the image that flashed through my head was a different one – that scarlet scrawl across the bedroom door, *FUCK OFF, KEEP OUT OR YOU DIE*. There was something there. Something very close to Maddie's furious, wordless anger.

Perhaps, whatever it was, I would be able to get to the bottom of it with Rhiannon.

The school run back to Heatherbrae took longer than the previous morning because there was a van on the road ahead of me. I followed it slowly from Carn Bridge, tapping gingerly at the accelerator, sure that it would turn off at every junction we came to, but inexplicably it seemed to be going the same way, even as the road narrowed and grew more rural. It was with some relief that I realised we were nearly at the turn-off to Heatherbrae House, and I was just about to signal left, when the van signalled too, and drew up over the drive, forcing me to stamp on the brakes.

As I waited, the Tesla silently idling, the passenger door opened and a girl jumped out, a rucksack on her shoulder. She said something to the driver and the back door of the van popped open. She dragged a huge case out, thumping it carelessly onto the gravel, and then slammed the door and stepped back as the driver pulled away from the kerb. I was just about to lean out and ask her who she was, and what she was doing in the middle of nowhere, when she pulled her phone out of her pocket and held it up to the proximity sensor of the gates, and they swung open.

It couldn't be Rhiannon, surely – she wasn't due back until the afternoon, and that disreputable van certainly didn't look like it belonged to anyone's mother. Was it someone who worked here? But in that case, why the huge trunk?

I waited a few minutes for her to clear the gates, and then pressed on the accelerator. The Tesla slid smoothly up the drive behind the girl who turned, with a look of surprise on her face. However, instead of moving out of the way she stood her ground, hands on her hips, and the huge case at her feet. I braked again, feeling the gravel scrunch beneath the tyres, and wound down the window.

'Can I help you?'

'I should be the one asking you that,' the girl said. She had long blonde hair, and a clipped expensive accent, without a trace of Scots in it. 'Who the hell are you and what are you doing in my parents' car?'

So it *was* Rhiannon.

'Oh, hello, you must be Rhiannon. Sorry, I wasn't expecting you back for another few hours. I'm Rowan.'

The girl was still looking at me blankly, and I added, beginning to feel a little impatient, 'The new nanny? I thought your mum told you.'

It seemed stupid to be carrying on this conversation through a car window, so I put the car into park and got out, holding out my hand.

'Nice to meet you. Sorry not to be expecting you, your mum said you wouldn't be here until 12.'

'Rowan? But you're –' the girl began, a furrow between her narrow brows, then something cleared and she shook her head. There was a smile on her lips, and it was not a very nice one. 'Never mind.'

'I'm what?' I dropped my hand.

'I said, never mind,' Rhiannon said. 'And don't pay any attention to what my mum told you, she hasn't got a fucking clue which way is up. As you may have already realised.' She looked me up and down, and then said, 'Well, what are you waiting for?'

'What?'

'Give me a hand with my case.'

I was getting more and more irritated but there was no point in starting off on the wrong foot, so I swallowed my anger and wheeled the case around to the back of the Tesla. It was even heavier than it looked. Rhiannon didn't wait for me to load it up, but climbed into the back seat, beside Petra.

'Hello, brat,' she said, though there was an undertone of affection in her voice that had been notably absent when she spoke to me. And then, to me, as I slid into the driver's seat, 'Well, let's not sit here all day admiring the view.'

I gritted my teeth, swallowed my pride, and pressed down so hard on the accelerator that gravel spat from behind the wheels as we began to move up the drive towards Heatherbrae House.

Inside the house Rhiannon stalked into the kitchen, leaving me to unload both Petra and the huge heavy trunk. When I finally made it inside, Petra in tow, I saw that Rhiannon had already installed herself at the metal breakfast bar, and was eating a giant sandwich she had clearly just put together.

'Sooooo.' Her voice came out like a drawl. 'You're Rowan, are you? I must say, you don't look anything like what I was expecting.'

I frowned. There was something a little malicious in her voice, and I wondered what exactly she meant.

'What were you expecting?'

'Oh … I don't know. Just someone … different. You don't look like a Rowan, somehow.' She grinned, and then before I could react, took another bite of sandwich and said, thickly, through the mouthful, 'You need to put more mayonnaise on the fridge order. Oh, and where the hell are the dogs?'

I blinked. I felt like it should be me asking the questions, grilling her. Why did I always seem to be on the wrong end of a power struggle? But it was a perfectly reasonable question, so I tried to keep my voice even as I answered it.

'Jack was called away to take some paperwork to your dad. He took the dogs with him – he thought they'd enjoy the trip.'

That hadn't been what he'd said at all, but somehow I didn't want to admit to this haughty teenager that I hadn't felt equal to the task of wrangling three small children and two Labradors.

'When's he back?'

'Jack? I don't know. Today, I imagine.'

Rhiannon nodded, chewing thoughtfully, and then said, around a mouthful of food, 'By the way, it's Elise's birthday to-night and her mum's invited me over for a sleepover. Is that OK?'

There was something in her tone that made it clear that I was being asked only as a formality, but I nodded.

'I'd better text your mum and check, but of course, that's fine by me. Where does she live?'

'Pitlochry. It's about an hour's drive, but Elise's brother will give me a lift.'

I nodded, pulled out my phone, and texted a quick message to Sandra. *Rhiannon safely back – wants to go to a sleepover with Elise tonight. Assume that's OK but please confirm.*

The message pinged back almost straight away. *No problem. Will call 6pm. Give my love to Rhi.*

'Your mum sends love and says it's fine,' I reported back to Rhiannon, who rolled her eyes as if to say *well, duh.* 'What time are you getting picked up?'

'After lunch,' Rhiannon said. She swung her legs over the side of the stool and shoved the dirty plate across the counter towards me. 'Laters.'

I watched her as she made her way up the stairs, long legs in school uniform stalking up the graceful curve of the staircase and then disappearing around the bend.

She did not come down for lunch. I wasn't particularly sur-prised, given the sandwich she'd eaten a couple of hours before, but since I was making lunch for me and Petra, I felt like I should at least ask if she wanted to join us. I tried to speak to her using the intercom function, but it refused to connect. Instead a message pinged back via the app. *NOT HUNGRY*. Huh. I hadn't even known it could do that.

OK, I messaged back. As I was putting my phone away, another thought occurred to me, and I pulled it back out of my pocket and reopened the Happy app. Feeling a little queasy, I clicked on the menu that showed the list of cameras available for me to access. As I scrolled down the list to *R*, I told myself I wouldn't look, but at least that way I would know ... but when I got down there 'Rhiannon's room' was greyed out and unavailable, which was mostly a relief. There would have been something inexpressibly inappropriate about cameras in a fourteen-year-old girl's bedroom.

It was as I was spooning yogurt into Petra's eager mouth, dodging her 'helping' fingers as she tried to grab the spoon, that I heard footsteps on the stairs and peered into the hallway to see Rhiannon, holding a small bag in one hand and her phone in the other.

'Elise's brother's here,' she said abruptly.

'At the door?' I glanced automatically at my phone, puzzled. 'I didn't hear the bell.'

'Duh. At the gates.'

'OK.' I resisted the urge to bite back a sarcastic retort. 'I'll buzz him in.'

My phone was on the counter, but I'd barely even opened up the app, let alone navigated the menu of the various gates, doors and garages I had access too, before Rhiannon was already halfway to the door.

'No need.' She pressed her thumb to the panel and then swung open the front door. 'He's waiting for me down by the road.'

'Wait.' I moved the yogurt out of Petra's reach, and then ran hastily after Rhiannon. 'Hang on a sec, I need a number for Elise's mum.'

'Uh . . . why?' Rhiannon said, heavy with sarcasm, and I shook my head, refusing to get drawn into her defiance.

'Because you're fourteen years old, and I've never met the woman and I just do. Do you have it? If not I'll ask your mum.'

'Yeah, I've got it.' She rolled her eyes, but pulled out her phone, and then cast around for a bit of paper. One of Maddie's drawings was lying on the stairs, and she picked it up and scribbled a number on the back. 'There. Happy?'

'Yes,' I said, though it was not entirely true. She slammed the door behind her, and I watched through the window as she disappeared around the curve in the drive, and then looked down at the piece of paper. The number was scribbled across one corner along with the name Cass and I tapped it into the messenger app on my phone.

Hi Cass, it's Rowan here, I'm the Elincourts' new nanny. I just wanted to say thank you for having Rhiannon tonight and if there's any problems, please call or text this number. If you could let me know what time you'll be dropping her off, that would be great. Thanks. Rowan.

The reply came back reassuringly quickly, while I was spooning the last of the yogurt into Petra.

Hi! Nice to 'meet' you. Pleasure, it's always nice to have Rhi over. I imagine we'll have her back by lunchtime tomorrow but let's play it by ear. Cass.

It was only when I went to put Maddie's drawing back on the stairs that I finally looked at it. It reminded me of the drawing I'd found on the first night, of the house, and the pale little face staring out. But there was something distinctly darker and more disturbing about this one.

At the centre of the page was a crude figure – a little girl, with curly hair and a sticking-out skirt – and she seemed to be locked inside some kind of prison cell. But when I peered at it more closely, I realised it must be meant to represent the poison garden. The thick black bars of the iron gate were scored across her figure, and she was clutching at them with one hand, and holding something in the other – a branch, I thought, covered in green leaves and red berries. Tears were streaming down her face, her mouth was open in a despairing wail, and there were red scribbles of blood on her face and on her dress. The whole image was encircled in thick black spiralling lines, as if I were staring down the wrong end of a telescope, into some kind of nightmarish tunnel into the past.

On the one hand, it was just a little girl's drawing, no different from the sometimes violent scribbles I had seen at the nursery – superheroes gunning down baddies, policemen fighting robbers. But on the other ... I don't know. It was hard to put my finger on what made me recoil, but there was something so indescribably nasty about it, so chilling and so full of satisfaction and glee in the macabre subject matter, that I let the paper drop from my fingers to the floor as if it had burned me.

I stood there, ignoring Petra's increasingly irritable cries of 'Down. Down! Peta down NOW!' behind me, and stared at the picture. I wanted to screw it up and throw it away, but I knew what the child protection advice at Little Nippers would have been. Put the drawing on file. Flag concerns with the safeguarding officer at the nursery. Discuss the issues raised in the drawing with parents/guardians if deemed appropriate.

Well, there was no safeguarding officer here except me. But if I were Sandra, I was pretty sure that I would want to know about this. Where Maddie was getting this stuff from, I wasn't sure, but it needed to be stopped.

Feeling more disturbed than I wanted to admit, I picked the drawing up, and slid it carefully into one of the drawers in the study. Then I returned to the kitchen and set about cleaning Petra up, and putting her down for her nap.

I hadn't meant to fall asleep in Petra's room, but I woke with a start, the armchair's gingham cover wet with drool beneath my cheek, and my heart pounding for reasons I could not put my finger on. Petra was still slumbering in her cot as I struggled upright, trying to figure out what had happened, and what had woken me so abruptly.

I must have drifted off while waiting for her to fall asleep. Had I – *shit*, the thought came like a sudden punch to the solar plexus – had I slept through school pickup? But no. When I checked my phone it was only 1.30.

Then it came again, the noise that had woken me from sleep. The doorbell. *Doorbell sounding* flashed my phone. And then *Open door? Confirm / Cancel.*

A Pavlovian jolt of dread flooded through me, and for a moment I sat there, paralysed, half dreading, half expecting the *creak … creak …* to commence as it had last night, but it didn't, and at last I forced myself to move. I swung my feet to the floor and stood up, waiting for my blood pressure to settle and my heart to stop drumming with panic in my ears.

As I did so, I wiped the corner of my mouth, and looked down at myself. It was only a few days since I'd turned up – note-perfect in my rendition of Rowan the Perfect Nanny, in her tweed skirt and neatly buttoned cardigan. I looked far from perfect now. I was wearing crumpled jeans, and my sweatshirt was stained with Petra's breakfast. I looked much closer to the person I really was, as if the real me was leaking out of the cracks in the facade, taking over.

Well, it was too late to change now. Instead I left Petra sleeping peacefully in her cot, and made my way down the stairs to the hallway, where I pressed my thumb to the panel, and watched as the door swung silently open.

For a second it seemed like a continuation of last night – there was no one there. But then I saw the Land Rover parked across the driveway, heard the retreating crunch of gravel, and peering round the side of the house, I saw a tall, broad figure, disappearing towards the stables, two dogs bounding at his heels.

'Jack?' I called, my voice croaky with sleep. I cleared my throat and tried again. 'Hey, Jack, was that you?'

'Rowan!' He turned at the sound of my voice and came striding back across the yard, grinning widely. 'Yes, I rang the bell, I was going to ask if you fancied a cup of tea. But I thought you must have gone out.'

'No ... no, I was ... ' I paused, unsure what to say, then, in view of my sleep-crumpled face and draggled clothes, decided maybe the truth was best. 'I'd fallen asleep actually. Petra's down for her nap and I must have drifted off. I – well, I didn't get a very good night's rest.'

'Oh ... were the girls playing up?'

'No, no, it's not that. It's ... ' I paused again, and then screwed up my courage. 'It's those noises I was talking about. From the attic. I got woken up again. Jack, you know those keys you mentioned ... '

He was nodding.

'Aye, sure, no problem. Want to try it now?'

Why not? The girls were at school, Petra would probably nap for at least an hour longer. It was as good a time as any.

'Yes please.'

'I'll have to hunt them out, give me ten minutes and I'll be with you.'

'OK,' I said. I felt better already. The chances were, there was a simple explanation for the noise, and we were going to discover it. 'I'll put the kettle on. See you in ten minutes.'

In the event, he was back sooner than ten, a tangle of rusty keys in one hand and a toolkit in the other, a big bottle of WD40 sticking out the top. The dogs followed him in, panting excitedly, and I found myself smiling as I watched them sniffing diligently around the kitchen, hoovering up all the scraps the children had dropped. Then they flopped down on their beds in the utility room as though the whole trip had exhausted them beyond measure.

The kettle had just boiled, and I poured out two mugs and held one out to Jack. He shoved the keys in his back pocket, took it and grinned.

'Just what I needed. D'you want to finish the teas down here or take them up?'

'Well, Petra's still asleep actually, so it might be a good idea to crack on before she wakes up.'

'Suits me,' he said. 'I've been sitting in the car all morning. I'd rather drink on the go.'

We carried everything carefully upstairs, tiptoeing past Petra's room, although when I peered in she looked like she was out for the count, sprawled like someone dropped from a great height onto a soft mattress.

Up in my bedroom, the curtains were still drawn, the bed rumpled, and my worn clothes were still scattered across the soft wheat-coloured carpet. I felt my cheeks flush, and putting down my cup I hastily picked up my bra and knickers from the night before, along with a blouse, and shoved them into the laundry basket in the bathroom, before opening the curtains.

'Sorry,' I said. 'I'm not normally such a slob.'

That was totally untrue. Back at my flat in London the majority of my underwear lived in a pile in the corner of the room, washed only when the clean pairs in my drawer ran out. But here, I'd been trying hard to keep up the image of meticulous neatness. Apparently it was slipping.

Jack, however, didn't seem bothered, and was already trying the door in the corner of the room.

'It's this one, is it?'

'Yes, that's right.'

'And you've tried all the other cupboard keys?'

'Yes – all the ones I could find.'

'Well, let's see if any of these match.'

The ring he was holding held maybe twenty or thirty keys of varying sizes, from a huge black iron one which I guessed must be the original key to the gate, before the electric lock had been installed, through to small brass ones which looked like they might be for desks or safes.

Jack tried a medium-sized one which fitted through the hole but rattled around loosely inside, plainly too small for the lock, and then a slightly larger one, which fitted, but did not turn all the way.

He squirted the can of lubricant inside the lock and tried again, but it still turned only a quarter of the way, and then stopped.

'Hmm ... it could be jammed, but if it's the wrong key I don't want to risk forcing it and breaking the shank in the lock. I'll try a few more.'

I watched as he tried maybe four or five others of the same size, but they were worse, either not fitting in at all, or jamming before he'd managed even a quarter-turn. At last he seemed to make up his mind and returned to the second key he'd picked out.

'This is the only key on the bunch that has any give at all, so I'll try it again with a bit more force, and if it breaks, well, we'll just have to get the locksmith in. Wish me luck.'

'Good luck,' I said, and he began to force the key.

I found I was wincing pre-emptively as I watched him apply pressure, first gently, and then harder, and at last so hard that I could see the shaft of the key bending slightly, the round bow at the top twisting, twisting ...

'Stop!' I cried, just as Jack gave an exclamation of satisfaction and there was a noisy scrape and click, and the key completed the full turn.

'Got it!' He stood, wiping the lubricant off his hands, and then turned to me with a mock courtly bow. 'D'you wish to do the honours, milady?'

'No!' The word was out before I could think better of it, and then I forced a laugh. 'I mean ... I don't mind. It's up to you. But I warn you, if there's rats, I'll scream.'

It was a lie. I'm not afraid of rats. I'm not afraid of very much, normally. And I felt like the worst kind of female cliché sheltering behind the big strong man. But Jack had not lain there, night after night, listening to that slow, stealthy *creak ... creak ...* above his head.

'I'll take one for the team, then,' he said with a very small wink. And he twisted the handle, and the door opened.

I don't know what I expected. A staircase disappearing into the darkness. A corridor hung with cobwebs. I found I was holding my breath as the door swung back, peering over Jack's shoulder.

Whatever I expected, it wasn't what was there. It was just another closet. Very dusty, and badly finished so that you could see the gaps in the plasterboard, and much smaller and shallower than the one where I'd hung my clothes, but a closet nonetheless. An empty bar hung, slightly lopsided, about six inches down from the ceiling as if awaiting hangers and clothes.

'Huh,' Jack said. He tossed the keys on the bed, looking thoughtful. 'Well, that's weird.'

'Weird? You mean, why lock up a perfectly usable closet?'

'Well, I suppose so, but what I really meant is, the draught.'

'The draught?' I echoed stupidly, and he nodded.

'Look at the floor.'

I looked where he pointed. Across the floorboards were streaks, where a breeze had plainly forced dust through the narrow gaps, and looking more closely at the stained and dusty plasterboard I could see the same thing. When I put my hand to the gap, there was a faint cool breeze, and the same dank smell that I had noticed coming from the keyhole last night when I had peered through, into the darkness.

'You mean ... '

'There *is* something back there. But someone boarded it up.'

He moved past me, and began rummaging in his toolkit, and suddenly, I was not at all sure that I wanted to do this.

'Jack, I don't think – I mean, Sandra might –'

'Ah, she won't mind. I'll board it back up more neatly if it comes to it, and she'll have a working closet instead of a locked door.'

He took out a small crowbar. I opened my mouth to say something else – something about it being my bedroom, about the mess, about –

But it was too late. There was a crunching noise, and a slab of plasterboard toppled forward into the room, so that Jack only just got out of the way. He picked it up, carefully avoiding the rusty nails that were sticking out of the edges, and propped it against the side of the closet, and I heard his voice, echoing now, as he let out a long, satisfied, 'Ah ... '

'Ah, what?' I said anxiously, trying to peer past him, but his big frame filled the doorway, and all I could see was darkness.

'Have a look,' he said, stepping back. 'See for yourself. You were right.'

And there it was. Just as I had imagined. The wooden treads. The swags of cobwebs. The staircase winding up into darkness.

I found my mouth was dry, and my throat clicked as I swallowed.

'Do you have a torch?' Jack asked, and I shook my head, feeling suddenly unable to speak. He shrugged.

'Nor me, we'll have to make do with phones. Mind your feet on those nails.' And he stepped forward into the blackness.

For a moment I was completely frozen, watching him disappear up the narrow stairs, the beam of his phone a thin glimmer in the black, his footsteps echoing ... *creak* ... *creak* ...

The sound was so close to the noise of last night, and yet, there was something different about it too. It was more ... solid. More real, faster, and mixed with the crunch of plasterboard.

'Holy shit,' I heard from above, and then, 'Rowan, get up here, you've got to see this.'

There was a lump in my throat as if I was about to cry, though I knew that I wasn't, it was pure fear that had lodged there, silencing me, making me unable to ask Jack what was up there, what he had found, what he needed me to see so urgently.

Instead, I switched on my phone torch with fingers that shook, and followed him into the darkness.

Jack was standing in the middle of the attic, staring open-mouthed at his surroundings. He had switched his phone off, and there was light coming from somewhere, a thin, grey light, that I couldn't immediately locate. There must be a window somewhere, but that wasn't what I was looking at. What I was looking at were the walls, the furniture, the *feathers*.

They were everywhere.

Strewn across the broken rocking chair in the corner, in the dusty, cobwebbed crib, over the rickety doll's house and the dusty chalkboard, across the pile of smashed china dolls piled up against the wall. Feathers, feathers, and not down from a burst pillow either. These were thick and black – flight feathers from a crow, or a raven I thought. And there was a stench of death too.

But that wasn't all of it. It wasn't even the worst of it.

The strangest thing was the walls – or rather, what was written on them.

Scribbled on all of them, in childish crayon letters, some small, some huge and scrawled, were words. It took me a minute or two to make them out, for the letters were misshapen and the words badly spelled. But the one right in front of me, the one staring me in the face over the small fireplace in the centre of the room, was unmistakable. *WE HATE YOU.*

It was exactly the same as the phrase Maddie had spelled out in her alphabetti spaghetti, and seeing it here, in a locked, boarded-up room she could not possibly have entered, gave me a jolt to the stomach as if I'd been punched. It was with a kind of sick dread that I held up my phone torch to some of the other phrases.

The goasts donet like you.

They hate yu.

We want you too go awa.

The gosts are angrie.

They haite you.

Get out.

There angry

Wee hate you.

We hite u.

GO AWAY.

We hate you.

Again and again, small and large, from tiny letters etched with concentrated hate in a corner by the door, to the giant sprawling scrawl above the fireplace that I had seen when I first entered.

We hate you. The words had been bad enough, sliding in slimy orange juice across a plate. But here, scrawled in a demented hand across every inch of plaster, they were nothing short of malevolent. And in my head I heard Maddie's little sobbing voice again, as though she had gasped the words in my ear – *the ghosts wouldn't like it.*

It was too close to be coincidence. But at the same time, it was totally impossible. This room was not just locked, it was boarded up, and the only entrance was through my own bedroom. And without question, *someone* else had been up here, and it had not been Maddie. I had heard those relentless, pacing footsteps just moments after staring down at Maddie's sleeping form.

Maddie had not written those words. But she had repeated them to me. Which meant … was she repeating what someone had whispered to *her* … ?

'Rowan.' The voice seemed to be coming from a great distance, hard to hear beneath a shrill buzzing coming from inside my own skull. Through the ringing I felt a hand on my arm. 'Rowan. *Rowan*, are you OK? You look a bit strange.'

'I'm – I'm OK –' I managed, though my voice was strange in my ears. 'I'm all right. It's just – oh God, who *wrote* that?'

'Kids messing about, don't you think? And, well, there's your explanation for the noise.'

He nudged with his foot at something in the corner, and I looked to see a pile of mouldering feathers and bones, held together by little more than dust.

'Poor wee bastard must have got in through that window and couldn't get out, battered himself half to death trying to escape.'

He pointed to the opposite wall, to a minute window, only a little bigger than a sheet of paper. It was grey with dirt, and partway open. Letting go of my arm Jack strode over and slammed it shut.

'Oh – oh my God.' I found I couldn't catch my breath. The ringing in my ears intensified. Was I having some kind of panic attack? I groped for something to hold on to, and my fingers crunched against dead insects, and I let out a strangled sob.

'Look,' Jack said practically, seeming to make up his mind, 'let's get out of here, get you a drink. I'll come back in a bit, clear up the bird.'

Taking my hand, he led me firmly towards the stairs. The feel of his large, warm hand in mine was unspeakably reassuring, and for a moment I let myself be pulled towards the door and the stairs, back towards the main house. But then something inside me rebelled. Whatever the truth of this attic, Jack was not my white knight. And I was not some terrified child who needed protecting from the reality of what lay behind this locked door.

As Jack turned sideways to edge between a pile of teetering chairs and a dried-up paintbox, I took the opportunity to pull my hand out of his.

Part of me felt I was being ungrateful. He was only trying to be reassuring, after all. But the other part of me knew that if I fell into this role, I might never escape it, and I could *not* allow Jack to see me that way – as yet another hysterical, superstitious woman, hyperventilating over a pile of feathers and some childish scribbles.

And so, as Jack disappeared down the stairs towards the floor below, I made myself stop and turn, taking a last, long look back at that dust-shrouded room, filled with smashed dolls and toys, broken furniture and the spoiled debris of a lost childhood.

'Rowan?' Jack's voice came from down the stairs, hollow and echoing up the narrow corridor. 'Are you coming?'

'Yes!' I said. My voice was cracked and I coughed, feeling my chest tighten. 'I'm coming!'

I moved quickly to follow him, filled with a sudden dread of the door shutting, being trapped up here with the dust and the dolls and the stench of death. But my foot must have caught on something for as I reached the top of the stairs, there was a sudden rushing clatter and the pile of dolls shifted and collapsed in on itself, china limbs cracking against each other with ominous chinks, dust rising up from threadbare, moth-eaten dresses.

'Shit,' I said, and watched, horrified, as the little avalanche subsided.

At last all was quiet, except for one single decapitated china head rolling slowly towards the centre of the room. It was the way the warped floorboards bowed, I knew, but for a crazy second I had the illusion that it was pursuing me, and would chase me down the stairs, its cherubic smile and empty eyes hunting me down.

It was just that though, an illusion, and a few seconds later it came to a rocking halt facing the door.

One eye had been punched out, and there was a crack across one pink cheek that gave its smile a curiously mocking appearance.

We hate you, I heard in the corner of my mind, as if someone had whispered it in my ear.

And then I heard Jack's voice again, calling me from the bottom of the stairs, and I turned, and followed him down the wooden steps.

Stepping out into the warmth and light of the rest of the house felt like returning from another world – after a trip into a particularly dark and nightmarish Narnia perhaps. Jack stood aside to let me out, and then shut the door behind us both and locked it. The key screeched in protest as he did so, then we both turned and made our way down to the bright, homely comfort of the kitchen.

I found my hands were shaking as I tried to rinse out the tea-cups and put the kettle on to boil, and at last, after a few minutes of watching me, Jack stood up and walked over to me.

'Sit down, and let me make you a cup for a change. Or would you prefer something a wee bit stronger? A dram, maybe?'

'Whisky you mean?' I said, slightly startled, and he grinned, and nodded. I gave a shaky laugh. 'Bloody hell, Jack. It's barely lunch.'

'All right then, just tea. But you sit there while I make it. You're always running around after those kids. Have a sit down for a change.'

But I shook my head, stubborn. I would not be that woman. I would not be one of those other four nannies ...

'No, I'll make the tea. But it would be great if you could –' I paused, trying to think of a job he could do, to soften the refusal of help. 'If you could find some biscuits.'

I remembered giving Maddie and Ellie Jammie Dodgers after the shock of the speakers going off in the middle of the night. *Sugar is good for shock*, I heard my own voice saying, as if I were a frightened child, able to be jollied back to cheerfulness with a forbidden treat.

I'm not normally like this, I wanted to say, and it was true. I wasn't superstitious, I wasn't nervy, I wasn't the kind of person who saw signs and portents around every corner and crossed themselves when they saw a black cat on Friday the 13th. That *wasn't* me.

But for three nights now I'd had little or no sleep, and no matter what I tried to tell myself I *had* heard those noises, loud and clear, and they were not a bird, whatever Jack thought. The senseless, panicked crashing of a trapped bird – that would have been scary enough, but it was nothing like the slow, measured *creak … creak …* that had kept me awake, night after night. And besides, that bird was dead – long dead. There was no way it could have been making noises last night, or any night for a while. In fact judging by the smell and the state of decomposition, it had probably been up there for several weeks.

The smell …

It had stayed with me, fusty and choking in my nostrils, and as I carried the tea across to the sofa, I found I could still smell it, even though I'd washed my hands. It clung to my clothes, and my hair, and glancing down I saw a long streak of grey on the sleeve of my jumper.

The sun had gone in, and in spite of the underfloor heating, the room was not particularly warm, but I shrugged the sweat-shirt off and put it aside. I felt that I'd have frozen rather than put it back on.

'Here you go.' Jack sat beside me, making the springs of the sofa squeak, and handed me a rich tea biscuit. I dipped it automatically into my tea then took a bite, and shivered, I couldn't help myself. 'Are you cold?'

'A bit. Not really. I mean, I have a jumper, it's just I didn't – I couldn't –'

I swallowed, then, feeling like a fool, I nodded at the streak of attic dust I'd noticed on the sleeve.

'I can't get the smell of that place out of my head. I thought maybe it was in my sweater.'

'I understand,' he said quietly, and then, as if reading my thoughts, he stripped off his own jacket, streaked with cobwebs, and laid it aside. He was only wearing a T-shirt underneath, but in contrast to my chill, his arms were warm, so warm that I could feel the heat from his skin as we sat, not quite touching, but uncomfortably close on the small two-seater sofa.

'You've goose pimples all up your arms,' he said, and then, slowly, as if giving me time to move away, he put out a hand and rubbed the skin of my upper arm gently. I shivered again, but it was not with cold, and for a long moment I had an almost overwhelming urge to close my eyes and lean into him.

'Jack,' I said, at the same time as he cleared his throat, and the baby monitor on the counter let out a crackling wail.

Petra.

'I'd better go and get her.' I stood, setting the tea down on the counter, and then staggered as a sudden wash of dizziness came over me, from standing up too fast.

'Hey.' Jack stood too, putting a hand on my arm, steadying me. 'Hey, are you all right?'

'I'm fine.' It was true, the moment of faintness had passed. 'It's nothing. I get low blood pressure sometimes. And I'm just – I didn't sleep well last night.'

Ugh. I had already told him that. He was going to think I was coming apart, adding amnesia to my list of frailties. I was better than this. Stronger than this. I had to be.

I badly wanted a cigarette, but the CV I had handed in to Sandra had said 'non-smoker' and I couldn't risk unpicking that particular thread. I might discover everything unravelled.

I found myself glancing up, towards the ever-watching egg-shaped eye in the corner of the room.

'Jack, what are we going to tell Sandra?' I asked, and then the baby monitor crackled into life again, this time a more determined cry that I could hear both through the speaker, and coming down the stairs. 'Hold that thought,' I said, and sprinted hastily for the stairs.

Ten minutes later I was back down with a freshly changed Petra, grumpy and blinking, and looking as tousled and confused as I felt. She glowered at Jack as I came back into the kitchen, her little hands gripping my top like a small marsupial, but when he chucked her under the chin she gave a little, reluctant smile, and then a proper one as he pulled a funny expression, laughing and then twisting her face away in that funny way children do when they know they're being charmed into good spirits in spite of themselves.

She let herself be settled in her high chair with some segments of satsuma, and then I turned back to Jack.

'I was just saying – Sandra and Bill. We have to tell them about the attic – right? Or do you think they know?'

'I'm not sure,' Jack said thoughtfully. He rubbed his chin, his fingers rasping over dark auburn stubble. 'They're sort of perfectionists, the way that cupboard was boarded up inside didn't look like their work. And I can't imagine they'd leave all that crap up there. Sorry, excuse my French, Petra,' he said formally, giving her a little mock bow. 'All that rubbish, is what I meant to say. They cleared the house when they moved in from what I understand – I didn't start work until a couple of years after they bought it, so I didn't see the renovations, but Bill'll bore the hind leg off a donkey if you give him an excuse to talk about the work. I can't imagine them just ignoring something like that. No, my best bet is that they'd never opened the cupboard and didn't know the attic was there. The key was pretty stiff, you'd be forgiven for thinking you had the wrong one. It's only because I'm a stubborn bastard I forced it.'

'But ... the poison garden,' I said slowly. 'They did just ignore that, right?'

'The poison garden?' He looked at me, startled. 'How do you know about that?'

'The girls took me in,' I said shortly. 'I didn't know what it was at the time. But my point is they've done the same thing there, haven't they? Shut the door, forgotten about it?'

'Well,' Jack said slowly, 'I ... well, I think that's a bit different. They've never been as hands-on in the grounds. There's nothing up there to harm anyone, though.'

'What about the writing?'

'Aye, that's a bit weird, I'll give you that.' He took a long gulp of tea, and frowned. 'It looked like a child, didn't you think? But according to Jean, there'd been no kids in the house for more than forty years when the Elincourts moved in.'

'It did look like a child.' My thoughts flickered to Maddie, then Elspeth, and then to the heavy man-like tread I'd heard, night after night. That had not been the step of a child. 'Or ... like someone pretending to be a child,' I added slowly, and he nodded.

'Could be vandals, I suppose, trying to creep people out. It's true the house was empty for a long time. But then ... no, that doesn't make sense. Vandals would hardly have boarded up behind themselves. It must have been the previous owners did that.'

'Dr Grant ... ' I paused, trying to think how to phrase the question that had been hovering at the edge of my mind ever since I had read the newspaper article. ' Did you ... I mean, are you ... ?'

'Related?' Jack said. He gave a laugh, and shook his head. 'God, no. Grants are ten a penny up here. I mean, I suppose we'd have all been part of the same clan back in the day, but there's no connection between our families nowadays. I'd never even heard of the man until I began working here. Poor bastard killed his daughter, isn't that the story?'

'I don't know.' I looked down at Petra, at the soft vulnerable curve of her skull beneath the thistledown hair. 'I don't know what happened to her. She ate poison berries according to the inquest.'

'I heard he fed her some experiment from his dabblings. That's what the folk in Carn Bridge'll tell you if you ask.'

'Jesus.' I shook my head, though whether in denial or disgust, I wasn't sure. There was something inexpressibly upsetting about hearing the suggestion in Jack's cheerful, matter-of-fact voice, and I wasn't sure what bothered me most – the idea that Dr Grant might have killed his own child and got away with it, or the fact that local gossip had apparently tried and condemned him as a murderer in the absence of any concrete proof.

It seemed impossible, though, that anyone would poison their own child, and it hardly fitted with the wild, grief-stricken face I'd seen on the web. He looked like a man destroyed by his own pain and despair, and all of a sudden, I felt a fierce urge to defend him.

'The article I read said that Elspeth accidentally picked cherry laurel berries thinking they were elderberries or something, and the cook made them into jam, not realising what they were. I can't see how that could be anything more than an accident.'

'Well, the folks round here would have you believe that he was –' He stopped, looking at Petra, and seemed to think better of whatever he had been about to say, even though she was too little to understand any of it. I knew how he felt. There was something obscene about discussing such horrible things in front of her. 'Well, never mind. Not a pretty story, either way.' He drained his cup and put it neatly in the dishwasher, and then gave a little wry smile, very different from the warmth of his usual broad, expansive grin. 'There's a reason the house was empty for a decade before Sandra and Bill bought it. There's not many from round here would have lived at Struan, even if they had the money to renovate it.'

Struan. The name from the article gave me a little prickle, a reminder that whatever Sandra and Bill had done to erase it, this house had a past, and people in Carn Bridge remembered it. But Jack was continuing on, untroubled.

'What d'you want me to do about it, then?'

'Me?' I asked, startled. 'Why do I need to decide?'

'Well, it's your bedroom it opens onto. I'm not a superstitious man, but I wouldn't fancy sleeping next to that lot myself.'

I shuddered, unable to help myself.

'Yup, me neither. So ... what are my options?'

'Well, I suppose I can board it up, leave it for Sandra and Bill to decide when they get back. Or I could try to ... tidy the attic up a wee bit.'

'Tidy it up?'

'Paint over some of that writing,' he said. 'But that would mean leaving it open. I mean, I could lock the door, but it wouldn't be worth boarding over the inside again, if we were planning to go back in. I don't know how you feel about that.'

I nodded, biting my lip. Truth be told, I didn't want to sleep in the room again, and in fact I wasn't sure if I could. The thought of lying in that bed, listening to the *creak* ... *creak* ... of the boards, with that demented writing just feet away from me behind nothing more sturdy than a locked cupboard door ... well, it creeped me out. But the idea of boarding the room back up didn't seem much better either.

'I think we should paint it,' I said at last. 'If Sandra and Bill agree, of course. We can't – we can't just *leave* it. It's too horrible.'

Jack nodded. Then he pulled the bunch of keys out of his back pocket, where he had stashed them, and began winkling the long black attic key off the bunch.

'What are you doing?' I asked, just as it came clear with a little click. He held it out.

'Take it.'

'Me? But I don't want –' I swallowed, trying not to show the depth of revulsion I felt. 'I don't want to *go* up there.'

'I know that. But if it were me, I'd feel better knowing that I had the key in my own hands.'

I pressed my lips together, then took the key from him. It was heavy, and very cold, but to my surprise, he was right. There was something … not quite powerful, but at least an illusion of control in holding the key in my own hands. That door was locked. And only I had the power to unlock it.

I pushed it into my jeans pocket. I was just trying to work out what to say, when Jack nodded again, but this time at his watch.

'Have you seen the time?'

I looked down at my phone.

'Shit.'

I was late to pick up the girls.

'I'd better go, but – but thank you, Jack.'

'What for?' He looked genuinely surprised. 'The key?'

'Not that. Just – I don't know. Taking me seriously. Not making me feel like an idiot for being freaked out.'

'Listen.' His face softened. 'That writing freaked me out too, and I'm all the way across the courtyard. But it's over, OK? No more mysterious noises, no more writing, no more wondering what's behind that door. We know now, and it's creepy and a little bit sad, but it's done, OK?'

'OK,' I said, and I nodded. I should have known it was too good to be true.

I have been scared a lot in prison, Mr Wrexham. The first night as I lay there, listening to the laughs and shouts and shrieks of the other women, trying to get used to the feeling of the narrow concrete walls closing around me, and many, many nights following that. And later, after one of the other girls beat me up in the cafeteria and I was moved to another wing for my own protection, as I lay there trembling in a strange cell, remembering the hate on her face, and the way the guards had waited just that slight instant too long before intervening, counting down the hours until the next day when I'd have to face them all again. And the nights when the dreams come, and I see her face again, and I wake with the stench of blood in my nostrils, shaking and shaking.

Oh God, I've been scared.

But I have never been quite as scared as I was that night in Heatherbrae House.

The girls flaked out early, thankfully, and all three of them were out for the count by half past eight.

And so, at quarter to nine, I climbed the stairs to the bedroom – I could no longer think of it as *my* bedroom – on the top floor.

I found I was holding my breath as I touched the door handle. I could not help imagining something horrible flying out and ambushing me – a bird, clawing at my face, or perhaps for the writing to have spread like a cancer out from behind the locked door and across the walls of the bedroom. But when at last I forced myself to turn the knob, shoving the door open with a violence that sent it banging against the wall, there was nothing there. The closet door was closed, and the room looked just as it had that first night I had seen it, apart from a few flecks of dust that Jack and I had trodden across the carpet in our haste to get out of the attic.

Still though, I knew I couldn't possibly sleep here, so I slid my hand under my pillow and grabbed my pyjamas, quickly, as if I were expecting to find something nasty there, waiting. I changed into my pyjamas in the bathroom, did my teeth, and then I rolled up my duvet and carried it downstairs to the media room.

I knew if I just lay down and waited for sleep I would be waiting a long time, maybe all night, while the images of the attic intruded and the words on the wall whispered themselves again and again in my ears. Drugging myself into oblivion with a familiar film seemed like a better option. At least if I had a loud laugh track ringing in my ears, I would not be wincing at every warped floorboard and sigh from the dogs. I was not sure if I could bear to lie there in silence, waiting for the *creak ... creak ...* to start up again.

Friends seemed about the right level of intensity, and I put it on the huge wide-screen TV, pulled the duvet up to my chin ... and slept.

When I woke, it was with a sense of complete disorientation. The TV had gone onto standby in the night, and there was daylight streaming underneath the blackout blinds in the media room.

There was a hot heavy weight on my legs ... no ... *two* heavy weights, and my chest was tight and wheezing. Hauling myself into a sitting position and pushing my hair out of my eyes I looked down, expecting to see the two dogs, but there was only one black hairy monster sprawled across the foot of the sofa. The other hot little body was Ellie.

'Ellie?' I said huskily, and then felt in the pocket of my dressing gown. My inhaler was in there, as always, but it knocked against something unfamiliar as I drew it out, and with an odd rush I remembered the key, and all the crazy events of yesterday. Then I wiped the mouthpiece of the inhaler on my dressing gown, put it to my lips and took a long hissing puff. The relief was instant, and I took a deeper breath, feeling the release in my chest, and then said again, more loudly, 'Ellie. Sweetheart, what are you doing here?'

She woke up, blinking and confused, and then realised where she was and smiled up at me.

'Good morning, Rowan.'

'Good morning to you too, but what are you doing down here?'

'I couldn't sleep. I had a bad dream.'

'Well, OK, but –'

But … what? I wasn't sure what to say. Her presence had shaken me. How long had she been padding around the house last night by herself without me hearing her? She had evidently been able to get out of bed and come all the way downstairs and tuck herself in beside me without me hearing a thing.

There didn't seem much I could say at this point though, so I just rubbed the sleep out of my eyes and then pulled my legs out from under the dog and stood up.

As I did, something fell out of the folds of the duvet and hit the floor with a dull ceramic-sounding crack.

The sound made me jump. Had I knocked over a forgotten coffee mug or something? I'd had hot milk last night, but I could have sworn I'd left the cup safely on the coffee table. In fact, yes, there was the mug still sitting on its coaster. So what had made the noise?

It was only when I pulled up the blind and folded the duvet that I saw it. It had rolled halfway under the sofa before coming to a halt, facing me, so that its wicked little eyes and cracked grin seemed to be laughing at me.

It was the doll's head from the attic.

The feeling that washed over me was – it was like someone had poured a bucket of ice water over my head and shoulders, a drenching, paralysing deluge of pure fear that left me unable to do anything but stand there, shaking and gasping and shivering.

I heard, as if from a long way away, Ellie's reedy little voice saying, 'Rowan, are you all right? Are you OK, Rowan? You look funny.'

It took a huge effort for me to drag myself back from the brink of panic and realise that she was talking to me, and that I needed to answer.

'Rowan!' There was a frightened whine in her voice now, and she tugged at my nightshirt, her little fingers cold against the skin of my waist. '*Rowan!*'

'I – I'm OK, honey,' I managed. My voice was strange and croaky in my ears, and I wanted to grope my way to the couch and sit down, but I couldn't bring myself to go anywhere near that ... that *thing*, with its mocking little grin.

But I had to. I couldn't leave it under there, like an obscene little grenade, waiting to explode.

How? How had it got there? Jack had locked the door, I had *seen* him do it. And he had preceded me down the stairs. And I had the key in my pocket. I could feel it, warm against my thigh with my own body heat. Had *I* ... could I have possibly ... ?

But no. That was absurd. Impossible.

And yet, there it was.

It was while I was standing there, trying to get a hold of myself, that Ellie bent down to see what I was staring at, and gave a little squeal.

'A dolly!'

She crouched, bum jutting in the air like the toddler she still half was, and reached, and I heard a sudden roar in my ears, my own voice shouting, 'Ellie, for God's sake, don't touch it!' and felt myself snatching her up, almost before I realised what I was going to do.

There was a long moment of silence, Ellie hanging limp and heavy in my arms, my own breath panting in my ears, and then her whole body stiffened and she let out a wail of indignant shock and began to cry, with all the desolate surprise of a child told off for something they had not realised was wrong.

'Ellie,' I began, but she was struggling in my arms, her face red and contorted with upset and anger. 'Ellie, wait, I didn't mean –'

'Let me go!' she howled. My instinct was to tighten my arms around her, but she was thrashing like a cat, digging her nails into my arms.

'Ellie – Ellie, calm *down*, you're hurting me.'

'I don't care! Let me go!'

Kneeling, painfully, trying to keep my face away from her thrashing hands, I let her slide to the floor, where she collapsed with a wail onto the rug.

'You're mean! You shouted!'

'Ellie, I didn't mean to scare you, but that doll –'

'Go away!' she wailed. 'I hate you!'

And then she scrambled to her feet, and ran from the room, leaving me ruefully rubbing the scratches on my arms. I heard her feet on the stairs, and then the slam of the door of her room.

Sighing, I went through to the kitchen and tapped on the tablet. When I clicked through to the camera, it was to see Ellie face down in bed, plainly bawling, with Maddie sleepily rubbing her eyes in puzzled surprise at being woken up like this.

Shit. She had come to me last night for reassurance – and for a moment there I had thought we were making a breakthrough. And now I had screwed it up. Again.

And it was all because of that vile little doll's head.

I had to get rid of it, but somehow I could not bring myself to touch it, and in the end I went through to the utility room and got a plastic bin liner. I slid it over my hand, inside out, like a makeshift glove, and then knelt and reached under the sofa.

I found I was holding my breath, absurdly, as I reached into the dark, slightly dusty space, my fingers groping for the hard little head. I touched hair first, just a few straggling strands, for the little porcelain skull was almost bald, and I used it to tug the head itself closer, and then closed my hand over it in one firm, swift movement, like scooping up a dead rat, or some insect you fear may still sting you, even dead.

I was gripping it hard – as if the force of my grip could stop it exploding or escaping from my grasp. It did neither. But as I stood, gingerly, I felt something twinge in my index finger, a shard of glass, so sharp I had barely felt it go in. It had pierced the bag itself and driven into my finger, drawing blood, which now dripped with a steady rhythm onto the wooden floor. The head was not china, I realised, but painted glass.

At the sink I pulled the glass out of my finger and then wound my hand in a piece of kitchen paper, before wrapping the head in a tea towel, and then another bin bag. I tied the top and stuffed it deep, deep into the rubbish bin, feeling like I was burying a corpse. My finger throbbed as I pressed down on it, making me wince.

'What happened to Ellie?'

The voice made me jump, as if I'd been caught hiding the evidence of something guilty, and swinging round I saw Maddie standing in the doorway. Her expression was slightly less truculent than usual, and with her hair standing on end she looked like what she was – just a little girl with a comical case of bed head, woken up too early.

'Oh ... it's my fault,' I said ruefully. 'I'm afraid I shouted at her. She was about to touch some broken glass and I scared her, trying to stop her. I think she thought I was angry ... I just didn't want her to hurt herself.'

'She said you found a doll and you wouldn't let her play with it?'

'Just a head.' I didn't want to go into the whys and wherefores with Maddie. 'But it was made of glass, and sharp where it had got cracked. I cut myself clearing it up.'

I held out my hand like evidence, and she nodded sombrely, seemingly satisfied with my incomplete explanation.

'OK. Can I have Coco Pops for breakfast?'

'Maybe. But, Maddie –' I stopped, not quite sure how to phrase what I wanted to ask. Our rapprochement felt so fragile that I was scared of endangering it, but there were too many questions buzzing in my head to abandon the topic completely. 'Maddie, have you ever ... do you know where the doll came from?'

'What do you mean?' Her face was puzzled, guileless. 'We've got lots of dolls.'

'I know, but this is a special, old-fashioned doll.'

I couldn't bring myself to fish the nightmarish broken head out of the bin, so instead I pulled out my phone and searched on Google Images for 'Victorian doll', scrolling down until I found one that was a slightly less malevolent version of the doll from the attic. Maddie stared at it, frowning.

'There was one like that on TV one time. It was a programme about selling ankeets.'

'Ankeets?' I blinked.

'Yes, old things that are worth a lot of money. A lady wanted to sell an old doll for money but the person in charge of the show told her it wasn't worth anything.'

'Oh ... antiques. I know the show you mean. But you've never seen one in real life?'

'I don't think so,' Maddie said. She turned away, and I tried to read her expression. Was she being *too* casual? Wouldn't a normal child ask more questions than this? But then I shook myself. This second-guessing of everything was starting to border on paranoia. Children were self-absorbed. I knew that well enough from the nursery. Hell, there were plenty of *adults* who were incurious enough not to question something like this.

I was just trying to formulate a way of bringing the conversation back to the writing on the wall and Maddie's alphabetti spaghetti, when she changed the subject abruptly, bringing it back to her original question with the single-mindedness typical of young children.

'So, *can* I have Coco Pops for breakfast?'

'Well ... ' I bit my lip. Sandra's list of 'occasional' foods were being consumed more and more frequently by the day. But then again, she shouldn't have it in the house if she didn't want the children to eat it, should she? 'Yes, I guess so, just for today. But it's the last time this week, OK? Back to Weetabix tomorrow. Go up and get your school uniform on, and I'll have it ready by the time you get down. Oh, and will you tell Ellie there's a bowl for her too, if she wants it?'

She nodded, and as she disappeared upstairs I reached for the kettle.

I was spooning some porridge into Petra's mouth with my uninjured hand, when a little face appeared at the kitchen door and then just as quickly slipped away, leaving a piece of paper scudding across the floor.

'Ellie?' I called, but there was no answer, only the sound of feet disappearing. Sighing, I made sure that Petra's straps were secure and went to pick up the piece of paper.

To my surprise it was a typed letter, formatted like an email, though with no subject, and nothing in the 'to' field. Under the Gmail header was a single line of text with no punctuation.

Dave Owen I am very sorry for scratching and waning away from you and saying that I hate you please don't be angry and don't go away like the others I am sorry love Ellie p. S. I got dressed by myself

Dave Owen? The words made my brow furrow, but there was no mistaking the intent of the rest of the message, and I un-clipped Petra, put her in the playpen in the corner, and picked up the letter again.

'Ellie?'

Silence.

'Ellie, I got your letter, I'm really sorry for shouting. Can I say sorry to you too?'

There was a long pause, then a little voice said, 'I'm in here.'

I made my way through the media room to the living room. At first sight it looked empty, but then a movement caught my eye, and I walked slowly to the far corner of the room, filled with shadow where the morning sun had not yet come round. She was wedged in between the end of the sofa and the wall, almost invisible apart from her blonde hair and the tips of her shoes peeping out.

'Ellie.' I crouched down, holding out the letter. 'Did you write this?'

She nodded.

'It's really good. How did you know all the spellings? Did Maddie help you?'

'I did it myself. Only … the acorn helped me.'

'The acorn?' I was puzzled, and she nodded.

'You push the acorn and you tell it what you want to write and it writes it down for you.'

261

'What acorn?' I was bewildered now. 'Can you show me?' Ellie flushed with shy pleasure at demonstrating her own cleverness, and squeezed out of the little corner. There was dust on her school skirt, and her shoes were on the wrong feet, but I ignored both, and followed her through to the kitchen where she picked up the tablet, opened up Gmail and pressed the microphone symbol above the keyboard. Light dawned. It did look a little bit like a stylised acorn – particularly if you had no idea what an old-fashioned microphone looked like.

Now she spoke into the tablet.

'Dear Rowan, this is a letter to say I am very sorry, love Ellie,' she said slowly, saying the words as distinctly as her childish palate would allow.

Dave Owen – the letters unfurled on the screen, as if by magic – *this is a letter to say I am fairy* –

there was an infinitesimal pause and the app self-corrected – *very sorry love Ellie.*

'And then you press the dots here and it prints on the printer in Daddy's study,' she said proudly.

'I see.' I wasn't sure whether I wanted to laugh or cry. I compromised by crouching down, and hugging her. 'Well, you're very clever, and it's a lovely letter. And I'm very sorry too. I shouldn't have shouted, and I promise I'm not going anywhere.'

She hung on to me, breathing heavily on my neck, her chubby cheek warm against mine.

'Ellie,' I said softly, unsure if I was about to wreck our hard-won confidence, but unable not to ask. 'Ellie, can I ask you something?'

She didn't say anything, but I felt her nod, her little pointy chin digging into the tendon that ran from my collarbone to my shoulder.

'Did you … did you put that dolly head on my lap?'

'No!' She pulled back, looking at me, a little upset, but not as much as I'd feared. She shook her head vehemently, her hair flying like thistledown. Her eyes were wide, and I could see in them a kind of desperation to be believed. But why? Because she was telling the truth? Or because she was lying?

'Are you sure? I promise I won't be angry. I just … I wondered how it got there, that's all.'

'It wasn't *me*,' she said, stamping her foot.

'It's OK, it's OK,' I back pedalled a little, not wanting to lose what ground I'd gained. 'I believe you.' There was a pause, and she slipped her hand in mine. 'So … ' I was treading carefully now, but this was too important not to press a little further. 'Do you … do you know who did?'

She looked away at that, not meeting my eyes.

'Ellie?'

'It was another little girl,' she said. And somehow I knew that was all I would ever get out of her.

'Maddie, Ellie, come on!' I was standing in the hallway, keys in hand as Maddie came flying down the stairs with her coat and shoes already on. 'Oh, well done, sweetie. You did your shoes yourself!' She slipped past, avoiding my outstretched arms, but Ellie, coming out of the downstairs toilet, was less quick and I caught her up, growling like a bear, kissed her squashy little tummy, then set her squealing and laughing back onto the floor, and watched as she scampered out of the front door after her sister to clamber into the car.

I turned back, to pick up their school bags, and as I did, I almost collided with Mrs McKenzie, standing with her arms folded in the archway that led to the kitchen.

'Shit!' The word slipped out without meaning to, and I flushed, annoyed with myself for giving her more ammunition for her dislike of me. 'I mean, gosh, I didn't hear you come in, Mrs McKenzie. Sorry, you startled me.'

'I came in the back way, I had mucky shoes,' was all she said, but there was something a little bit softer than usual in her face, as her eyes followed the girls out to the car. 'You're ... ' She stopped, and then shook her head. 'Never mind.'

'No, what?' I said, feeling annoyed. 'Come on, if you've got something to say ... '

She pursed her lips, and I folded my arms, waiting. Then, quite unexpectedly, she smiled, transforming her rather grim face, making her look years younger.

'I was just going to say, you're doing very well with those girls. Now, you'd best be getting a move on, or you'll be late.'

As I drove back from Carn Bridge Primary School, Petra strapped into the car seat behind me, pointing out of the window and babbling her half-talk, half-nonsense syllables to herself, I found myself remembering that first drive back from the station with Jack – the evening sunset gilding the hills, the quiet hum of the Tesla as we wound through the close-cropped fields, filled with grazing sheep and Highland cows, and over stone bridges. It was grey and drizzling today, and the landscape felt very different – bleak and raw and entirely unsummer-like. Even the cows in the fields looked depressed, their heads lowered, rain dripping off the tips of their horns.

When the gate swung inwards and we began to climb the winding drive up to the house, I had a sharp flash of déjà vu back to that first evening – the way I had sat there beside Jack, scarcely able to breathe with hope and wanting.

We swung round the final curve of the drive, and the squat grey facade of the house came into view, and I remembered, too, the rush of emotion I had felt on seeing it for the first time, golden and warm and full of possibilities.

It looked very different today. Not full of the potential for a new life, new opportunities, but grey and forbidding as a Victorian prison – only I knew that was a kind of a lie as well, that the Victorian facade presented to the driveway was only half the story, and that if I walked round to the back, I would see a house that had been ripped apart and patched back together with glass and steel.

Last of all, my gaze went to the roof, the stone tiles wet and slick with rain. The window Jack had shut was not visible from here, it opened onto the inner slope of the roof, but I knew that it was there, and the thought made me shiver.

There was no sign of Jean McKenzie's car in the drive – she must have already left for the day – and both Jack and the dogs were nowhere to be seen, and somehow, what with everything that had happened, I could not bring myself to enter the house alone. It had come to something, I thought, as I parked the car and unclipped Petra from her seat, that even fending off the dogs from trying to put their noses up my skirt would have been a welcome distraction from the silent watchfulness of that house, with its glassy egg-shaped eyes observing me from every corner.

At least out here I could think and feel and speak without watching my every word, my every expression, my every mood.

I could be *me*, without fearing that I would slip up.

'Come on,' I said to Petra. Her buggy was in the boot of the car, and I opened it up and slid her in, clipping the rain cover over her. 'Let's go for a walk.'

'Me walk!' Petra shouted, pushing her hands against the plastic, but I shook my head.

'No, honey, it's too wet, and you've not got your waterproofs on. You stay snug and dry in there.'

'Puggle!' Petra said, pointing through the plastic. 'Jumpin muggy puggle!' It took me a minute to realise what she was saying, but then I followed her gaze to the huge pool of water that had collected on the gravel in the old stable yard, and understanding clicked.

Muddy puddles. She wanted to jump in muddy puddles.

'Oh! Like Peppa Pig, you mean?' She nodded vigorously. 'You haven't got your wellies on, but look –'

I began to walk faster, and then jog, and then with an enormous splash, I ran, buggy and all, through the puddle, feeling the water spray up all around us and patter down on my anorak and the buggy's rain cover.

Petra screamed with laughter.

'Again! More puggle!'

There was another puddle further round the side of the house and obligingly I ran through that too, and then another on the gravelled path down towards the shrubbery.

By the time we reached the kitchen garden, I was soaked and laughing, but also getting surprisingly cold, and the house was beginning to seem a little bit more welcoming. Full of cameras and malfunctioning tech it might be, but at least it was warm and dry, and out here my fears of the night before seemed not just silly, but laughable.

'Puggle!' Petra shouted, bouncing up and down underneath her clips. 'More puggle!'

But I shook my head, laughing too.

'No, that's enough, sweetie, I'm wet! Look!' I came round to stand in front of her, showing her my soaked jeans and she laughed again, her little face scrunched up and distorted through the crumpled plastic.

'Woan wet!'

Woan. It was the first time she had made an attempt at my name, and I felt my heart contract with love, and a kind of sadness too – for everything I could not tell her.

'Yes!' I said, and there was a lump in my throat, but my smile was real. 'Yes, Rowan is wet!'

It was as I was turning the buggy round to start the climb back up to the house that I realised how far we had come – almost all the way down the path that led to the poison garden. I glanced over my shoulder at the garden as I began to push the buggy up the steep brick path – and then stopped.

For something had changed since my last visit.

Something was missing.

It took me a minute to put my finger on it – and then I realised. The string tying up the gate had gone.

'Just a second, Petra,' I said, and ignoring her protests of 'more puggles!' I put the brake on the buggy and ran back down

the path to the iron gate, the gate where Dr Grant had been pho-
tographed, standing proudly before his research playground, so
many years ago, the gate I had tied up securely, in a knot too
high for little hands to reach.

The thick white catering string had gone. Not just untied, or
snipped and thrown aside, but gone completely.

Someone had undone my careful precautions.

But who? And why?

The thought nagged at me as I walked slowly back up the hill
to where Petra was still sitting, growing increasingly fretful, and
it continued to nag as I pushed the buggy laboriously back up
the hill, to where the house was waiting.

By the time I reached the front door, Petra was cross and griz-
zling, and looking at my watch I saw that it was long gone her
snack time, and in fact getting on for lunch. The buggy's wheels
were caked with mud, but since I had left the key to the utility
room on the inside, I had no option other than the front door, so
at last I got her out of the buggy, folded it awkwardly with one
hand, holding Petra against my hip with the other to stop her
running off in search of more puddles, and left it in the porch.
Then I pressed my thumb to the white glowing panel, and stood
back as the door swung silently open.

The smell of frying bacon hit me instantly.

'Hello?'

I put Petra down cautiously on the bottom stair, shut the door,
and prised off my muddy boots.

'Hello? Who's there?'

'Oh, it's you.' The voice was Rhiannon's, and as I picked up
Petra and began to make my way through to the kitchen, she
came out of the doorway, holding a dripping bacon sandwich in
one hand. She looked terrible, green around the gills and with
dark shadows under her eyes as if she'd slept even less than me.

'Oh, you're back,' I said unnecessarily, and she rolled her eyes and stalked past me to the stairs, taking a great bite of sandwich as she did.

'Hey,' I called after her as a blob of brown sauce hit the tiled floor with a splat. 'Hey! Take a plate, can't you?'

But she was already gone, loping up the stairs towards her room.

As she passed, though, I caught a whiff of something else – low and masked by the scent of bacon, but so odd and out of place, and yet so familiar, that it stopped me in my tracks.

It was a sweet, slightly rotten smell that jerked me sharply back to my own teenage years, though it still took me a minute to pin down. When the association finally clicked into place, though, I was certain – it was the cherry-ripe reek of cheap alcohol, leaching out of someone's skin the morning after it's been drunk.

Shit.

Shit.

Part of me wanted to mutter that it was none of my business – that I was a nanny and had been hired for my expertise with younger children, that I had no experience with teenagers and no idea of what Sandra and Bill would consider appropriate. Did fourteen-year-olds drink now? Was that considered OK?

But the other part of me knew that I was *in loco parentis* here. Whether or not Sandra would be concerned, *I* had seen enough to worry me. And there were plenty of red flags about Rhiannon's behaviour. But the question was, what should I do about it? What *could* I do about it?

The questions nagged at me as I made myself and Petra a sandwich, and then put her down for her nap. I could go and question Rhiannon – but I was pretty sure she'd have a ready excuse, assuming she deigned to talk to me.

Then I remembered. Cass. If nothing else, she would be able to explain the exact sequence of the night's events to me, and maybe give me an idea of whether I was ascribing more to this than I should. A bunch of fourteen-year-old girls at a birthday party ... it wasn't impossible Cass had supplied some alcopops herself, and Rhiannon had just drunk more than her fair share.

Cass's return text was still in my list of messages, and I scrolled down until I found it, and pulled out the number. Then I waited while it rang.

'Yup?' The voice was rough, and Scottish, and very male.

I blinked, looked at the phone to check I had dialled the right number, and then put it back to my ear.

'Hello?' I said cautiously. 'Who is this?'

'I'm Craig,' said the voice. It didn't sound like a kid – the voice had to be someone at least twenty, maybe older. And it definitely didn't sound like anyone's mum, or dad for that matter. 'More to the fucking point, who the fuck are you?'

I was too shocked to reply. For a second I simply sat there, mouth open, trying to figure out what to say.

'Hello?' Craig said irritably. 'Hellooo?' And then, beneath his breath, 'Stupid cunts wi' their fucking wrong numbers.'

And then he hung up.

I shut my mouth, and walked slowly through to the kitchen, still trying to figure out what had just happened.

Plainly, whoever that number belonged to, it wasn't Elise's mum. Which meant ... well, it could have meant that Rhiannon had written it down wrong, except that I had texted that number and got back a confirmation, supposedly from 'Cass'.

Which meant that Rhiannon had been lying to me.

Which also meant that, very probably, she hadn't been out with Elise at all. Instead she had very likely been with Craig.

Fuck.

The tablet was lying on the kitchen island, and I picked it up and tried to compose an email to Sandra and Bill.

The problem was, I didn't know what to begin with. There was too much to say. Should I start with Rhiannon? Or Maddie's behaviour? Or should I lead with my concerns about the attic? The noises, and the way Jack and I had broken in, and the crazy writing?

What I wanted to tell them was everything – from the dead, rotten smell that still hung in my nostrils, and the broken shards of the doll's head in the rubbish bin at the foot of the drive, right through to Maddie's scribbled prison-cell drawing, and my conversation with Craig.

Something is wrong, I wanted to write. *No, scrap that, everything is wrong*. But ... how could I tell them about Rhiannon and Maddie without seeming like I was criticising their parenting? How could I say what I had seen and heard in this house without being dismissed as just another superstitious nanny? How could I expect to persuade someone who hadn't even seen the inside of that creepy, demented room?

The subject line first then. Anything I could think of seemed either hopelessly inadequate or ridiculously dramatic, and in the end I settled on *An update from Heatherbrae*.

OK. OK. Calm and factual. That was good. Now for the body of the email.

Dear Sandra and Bill, I wrote, and then sat back and nibbled at the fraying edge of the plaster on my finger, trying to think what to put next.

First of all, I should tell you that Rhiannon arrived back this morning safe and sound, but I have a few concerns about her account of her trip to Elise's.

OK, that was good. That was clear and factual and non-accusatory. But then how to segue from that into

Stupid cunts wi' their fucking wrong numbers.

Let alone from that to

We hate you

There angry

GO AWAY

We hite you

Most of all, how to explain that I would not – could not – sleep in that room again, listen to those footsteps pacing above, breathe the same air as those rotted, dusty feathers.

In the end I just sat there, staring at the screen, remembering the slow *creak ... creak ...* on the boards above me, and it was only when I heard Petra's cranky wail coming over the intercom and looked at the clock that I realised it was time to pick up Maddie and Ellie from school.

Gone to get the girls, I tapped out on the messaging screen to Rhiannon, *we need to talk when I get back*. And then, leaving the email unsent on the tablet, I ran upstairs to change Petra and bundle her into the car.

I didn't think of the email again until nearly 9 p.m. The afternoon had been a good one. Maddie and Ellie had both been delighted to see Rhiannon, and she'd been touchingly sweet with them – a far cry from the glossy, entitled private-school brat she played with me. She was visibly hung-over, but she played Barbies with them in the playroom for a couple of hours, ate some pizza, and then disappeared upstairs while I did battle with baths and bed and then tucked the girls in with a kiss and turned out the lights.

When I came downstairs I was gearing myself up for the promised discussion, trying to imagine what Rowan the Perfect Nanny would have done. Firm but clear. Don't lead with sanctions and accusations, get her to talk.

But Rhiannon was waiting in the kitchen, tapping her nails on the counter, and I did a double take at what she was wearing. Full make-up, heels, miniskirt and a midriff-baring top that showed off a pierced navel.

Oh shit.

'Um,' I began, but Rhiannon forestalled me.

'I'm going out.'

For a second I had no idea what to say. Then I pulled myself together.

'I don't think so.'

'Well, I do.'

I smiled. I could afford to smile. It was growing dark. I had the keys to the Tesla in my pocket and the nearest station was the best part of ten miles.

'Are you planning to walk in those heels?' I asked. But Rhiannon smiled back.

'No, I've got a lift coming.'

Double shit.

'OK, look, Rhiannon, this is very funny and everything, but you do know there's absolutely no way I can let you do that? I'll have to call your parents. I have to tell them –' Oh fuck this, fuck *accusations*, I had to say something to make her realise she'd been rumbled. 'I have to tell them you came home stinking of alcohol.'

I expected the words to act like a punch to the gut, but she barely reacted.

'I don't think you should do that,' was all she said.

But I had already picked up my phone.

I hadn't checked it since before supper, and to my surprise, there was an email icon flashing. It was from Sandra.

I pressed it, in case it was something I should know about before I spoke to her, and then blinked in puzzlement as the subject header came up.

Re: An update from Heatherbrae

What? Had I sent the email without meaning to? I had logged into my personal Gmail on the children's tablet, the one they used for playing games, and had a horrible feeling that I had forgotten to log out. Could Petra or one of the girls have accidentally pressed send?

Panic-stricken, I opened up Sandra's reply, expecting something along the lines of '?? What's going on?' but it was totally different.

> Thanks for the update, Rowan, sounds good. Glad Rhiannon had a fun time with Elise. Bill is off to Dubai tonight and I'm at a client dinner, but do text if anything urgent and I'll try to FaceTime the girls tomorrow. X

It didn't make sense. At least, it didn't until I scrolled down a little further and looked at the email I had supposedly sent, at 2.48 p.m., a good twenty minutes after I'd left to collect Maddie and Ellie.

> Dear Bill and Sandra,
>
> Just an update from home. All is good, Rhiannon is back safe and sound from Elise's house, and she seems to have had a great time.
>
> We've had a very nice afternoon and she's a credit to you both. Maddie and Ellie both send love.
>
> Rowan

There was total silence and then I turned to Rhiannon.

'You little shit.'

'Charming,' she drawled. 'Is that the kind of language they expected at Little Nippers?'

'Little – what?' How did she know where I'd worked? But then I pulled myself together, refusing to be derailed. 'Look, don't try to change the subject. This is utterly unacceptable, and stupid to boot. First of all, I know about Craig.' A look of shock flickered across Rhiannon's face at that. She recovered herself quickly, her expression back to bored indifference almost instantly. However, I had seen it and I couldn't stop a triumphant smile from spreading across my own face. 'Oh yes, didn't he tell you that? I rang "Cass". Obviously the first thing I'm going to do is call your mum and explain that you sent that email, and the second thing I'm going to do is tell her about this Craig person, and explain that you propose waltzing out with this guy I've never met, in a top that barely comes to your navel and see what she has to say on that subject.'

I don't know what I had expected – perhaps a show of temper, or even for Rhiannon to start crying and begging to be let off.

But her reaction was neither of those things. Instead, she smiled, rather sweetly, in a way that was totally unnerving, and said, 'Oh, I don't think you'll do that.'

'Give me one good reason why not!'

'I'll do better than that,' she said. 'I'll give you two. Rachel. Gerhardt.'

Oh fuck.

The silence in the kitchen was absolute.

For a second, I thought my knees were about to give way and I groped my way for a bar stool, and slumped down on it, feeling my breath catch in my throat.

I was cornered. I realised that now. I just didn't know quite how tight that corner was going to get.

Because this is where it gets very, very bad for me, doesn't it, Mr Wrexham?

This is where the police case on me shifted from being some-one in the wrong place at the wrong time, to someone with a motive.

Because she was right. I couldn't ring Sandra and Bill.

I couldn't do that, because Rhiannon knew the truth.

It will be no surprise to you, Mr Wrexham, not if you've read the newspaper pieces.

Because you will have known right from the outset that the nanny arrested in the Elincourt case was not Rowan Caine, but Rachel Gerhardt.

But to the police, it was like a bombshell. Or no, not a bombshell. More like one of those exploding piñatas that showers you with gifts.

Because I had handed them their case on a plate.

Afterwards they focused very hard on how I managed to do it, as if I were some kind of criminal mastermind, who had plotted all this in exhaustive detail. But what they couldn't seem to understand was how temptingly, laughably simple it had been. There had been no forgery, no elaborate identity theft or manufactured papers. *How did you obtain the fake identity papers, Rachel?* they kept asking, but the truth was, there had been no fake papers. All I had done was pick up my friend Rowan's nannying paperwork from her bedroom in our shared flat, and show it to Sandra. DBS check, Ofsted registration, first-aid certificate, CV, none of it had any photographs. There was absolutely no need for me to fake anything, and no way of Sandra knowing that the woman standing in front of her was not the person named on the certificates she was holding out.

And, I tried to tell myself, it wasn't much of a deception. After all I really did have those credentials – most of them, anyway. I had a DBS check and a first-aid certificate. Like Rowan, I had worked in the baby room at Little Nippers, albeit not quite as long as she had, and not as supervisor. And I had done nannying beforehand, though not as much, and I wasn't sure that my references would have been quite as gushing. But the basics were all there. The name thing was just a ... technicality. I even had a clean driving licence, just as I had told Sandra. The only problem was that I couldn't show it to her because of the photo. But everything I had told her – every qualification I had claimed – it was all true.

Everything except for my name.

There was luck involved of course too. It had been lucky that Sandra had agreed to my request and hadn't contacted Little Nippers themselves for a reference. If she had, they would have told her that Rowan Caine had left a couple of months back. Lucky that she never pushed me on the driving licence.

And it had been lucky, too, that she used a remote payroll service, so that I never had to present Rowan's passport in person and could simply forward the scan she had left on her computer desktop along with our shared bills.

The biggest piece of good fortune was that banks, slightly incredibly, didn't seem to care whose name was on a BACS transfer, as long as the account number and sort code matched up. That had been something I'd never expected. I had lain awake wondering how to figure that part out. Claim that my account was in a different name? Ask for cash, or cheques made out to R. Gerhardt and cross my fingers Sandra didn't ask why? I'd practically laughed when I found out that none of that mattered, that if you paid by transfer you could put Donald Duck in the payee box and it would go through. It seemed unbelievably careless.

But the truth was, to begin with, I hadn't even looked past that first stage. All I had focused on was getting that interview, standing in Heatherbrae House, looking Sandra and Bill in the eye. That was all I had wanted. That was the only reason I had answered the ad. And yet somehow, the opportunities had kept presenting themselves, like temptingly wrapped gifts on a plate, begging me to pick them up and make them mine.

I shouldn't have done it, I know that now, Mr Wrexham. But can't you see – can't you see what it must have been like?

Now, standing in the kitchen with Rhiannon laughing in my face, I felt a great wave of panic break over me, followed by a strange sense of something else – almost of relief, as if I had known this moment was coming, and was relieved to have it over and done with.

For a moment I thought about bluffing, asking her what she meant, pretending I had never heard the name Rachel Gerhardt. But only for a moment. If she had got far enough to discover my real name, she was not going to be thrown off the scent by an indignant denial.

'How did you find out?' I asked instead.

'Because, unlike my dear parents, I bother to do a little digging when a new girl turns up out of the blue. You'd be surprised what you can find out online. They teach it in school now, you know, managing your digital footprint. I guess they didn't do that in your day?'

The barb was palpable, but I didn't bother to respond. It scarcely seemed important. What mattered was how far she had dug, and why – and what exactly she had found out.

'It didn't take me long to track down Rowan Caine,' Rhiannon was saying. 'She's pretty boring, isn't she? Not much ammunition.'

Ammunition. So that was what this was about. Rhiannon had been digging around online for any little indiscretion she could use as leverage. Only she had stumbled on something much, much bigger.

'I couldn't understand it,' she said, a little smile tugging at the corner of her mouth. 'It all matched up – the name, the date of birth, the time at that nursery with the stupid twee name – *Little Nippers*,' she said mockingly. 'Ugh. But then suddenly there were all these pictures from Thailand and Vietnam. And when I saw you on the driveway, I began to think I'd fucked up, that maybe I *did* have the wrong person. It took me a few hours to track down the real you. Must be losing my touch. Shame for you she doesn't keep her friend-list private. Or that you didn't bother to delete your Facebook profile.'

Fuck. So it had been as simple as that. As simple as scrolling down a list of Rowan's Facebook friends and picking out the face I had so obligingly posted up for all the world to see. How could I have been so stupid? But truthfully, it had never occurred to me that anyone would join the dots so assiduously. And I hadn't been setting out to deceive, that's the thing. That's what I tried to explain to the police. If I had really been setting up a fraudulent second life, wouldn't I have bothered to cover my tracks?

Because this *wasn't* fraud, not really. Not in the way the police meant. It was ... it was just an accident, really. The equivalent of borrowing your friend's car while they're away. I never meant for all this to happen.

The problem was, the thing I couldn't tell the police, was *why* I had come to Heatherbrae under an assumed name. They kept asking me and asking me and digging and digging, and I kept floundering, and trying to come up with reasons – things like, Rowan's references were better than mine (which was true) and she had more experience than me (true again). I think at first they thought I must have some deep dark professional secret – a lapsed registration, or a conviction as a sex offender or something. And of course none of that was the case, and as hard as they tried to find something, there was nothing wrong with my own papers.

It looked very, very bad for me, I knew that, even at the time. But I kept telling myself, if Rhiannon hadn't discovered why I had come here, then perhaps the police wouldn't either.

But that was stupid, of course. They are the police. It's their job to dig.

It took them some time. Days, maybe even weeks, I can't totally remember. The interrogation starts to run together after a while, the days blurring into each other, as they picked and picked and prodded and probed. But eventually they came into the room holding a piece of paper and they were smiling like Cheshire cats, while simultaneously somehow trying to look grave and professional.

And I knew. I knew that they knew.

And I knew that I was sunk.

But that was afterwards. And I'm getting ahead of myself.

I have to tell the other part. The hardest part. The part I can't quite believe even now.

And the part I can't fully explain, even to myself.

I have to tell you about that night.

After Rhiannon walked out, I stood for a long moment in the hallway, watching the lights of the van disappear down the drive, and trying to figure out what I should do. Should I phone Sandra? And say what? Confess? Brazen it out?

I looked at my watch. It was just gone half nine. The line from Sandra's email floated into my head – *Bill is off to Dubai tonight and I'm at a client dinner, but do text if anything urgent.*

There was no way I could ambush her with all this in the middle of a client dinner, still less text it through.

Oh hi, Sandra, hope all is good. FYI, Rhiannon has gone out with a strange bloke, and I applied for this job under a fake name. Speak soon!

The idea would have been laughable if the whole situation hadn't been so serious. Shit. *Shit.* Could I email her and explain the situation properly? Maybe. Though if I were going to do that, I should really have done it earlier, before Rhiannon sent that fake update. It would be even harder to explain myself now.

But as I pulled the tablet towards myself, I realised I couldn't really email. That was the coward's way out. I owed her a call – to explain myself, if not face-to-face, then at least in person. But what the hell could I say?

Shit.

The bottle of wine was there on the kitchen counter, like an invitation, and I poured out a glass, trying to steady my nerves, and then another, this time with a glance at the camera squatting in the corner. But I no longer cared. The shit was about to hit the fan, and soon whatever footage Sandra and Bill had on me would be the least of my worries.

It was deliberate self-sabotage, I knew that really, in my heart of hearts as I filled the glass for the third time. By the time there was only one glass left in the bottle I realised the truth – I was too drunk to call Sandra now, too drunk to do anything sensible at all, except go to bed.

Up on the top landing, I stood for a long time, my hand on the rounded knob to my bedroom, summoning up the courage to enter. But I could not do it. There was a dark crack at the bottom of the door, and I had a sudden, unsettling image of something loathsome and shadowy slithering out from beneath it, following me down the stairs, enveloping me in its darkness . . .

Instead, I found myself letting my hand drop, and then backing away, almost as if that dark something might indeed come after me if I turned my back. Then, at the top of the stairs, I turned resolutely and all but ran back downstairs to the warmth of the kitchen, ashamed of myself, of my own cowardice, of everything.

The kitchen was cosy and bright, but when I shut my eyes I could still smell the chilly breath of the attic air coursing out beneath my bedroom door – and as I stood, irresolute, wondering whether to make up a bed on the sofa or try to stay awake for Rhiannon's return, I could feel the throb of my finger where I had sliced it on that vile broken doll's head. I had put a plaster over it, but the skin beneath felt fat and swollen, as if infection was setting in.

Walking over to the sink, I pulled off the dressing, and then jumped, convulsively, as there was a thud at the back door.

'Wh-who is it?' I called out, trying not to let my voice shake.

'It's me, Jack.' The voice came from outside, muffled by the wind. 'I've got the dogs.'

'Come in, I'm just –'

The door opened, letting in a gust of cold air, and I heard his footsteps in the utility room, and the thud of his boots as he pulled them off and let them drop onto the mat, and the barking of the dogs as they capered around him, and he tried to hush them. At last they settled into their baskets, and he came into the kitchen.

'I don't normally walk them so late, but I got caught up. I'm surprised you're still awake. Good day?'

'Not really,' I said. My head was swimming, and I realised afresh how drunk I was. Would Jack notice?

'No?' Jack raised an eyebrow. 'What happened?'

'I had a –' Jesus, where to start. 'I had a bit of a run-in with Rhiannon.'

'What kind of a run-in?'

'She came back and we –' I stopped, unsure how to put this. It felt completely wrong to put the full picture to Jack before I confessed to Sandra, and I was pretty sure I would be breaking all sorts of confidentiality guidelines if I discussed Rhiannon's problems with someone who was not her parent. But on the other hand, I felt that I might go crazy if I didn't confide at least some of this in another adult. And perhaps there was history here, for it was becoming clearer and clearer that not everything had been included in that big red binder. 'We argued,' I said at last. 'And I threatened to call Sandra and she – she just –' But I couldn't finish.

'What happened?' Jack pulled out a chair, and I sank into it, feeling despair wash over me again.

'She's gone. She's gone out by herself – with some awful un-suitable friend. I told her not to, but she went anyway, and I don't know what to do – what to tell Sandra.'

'Look, don't worry about Rhiannon. She's a canny wee thing, pretty independent, and I highly doubt she'll come to any harm, much as Sandra and Bill might disapprove.'

'But what if she does? What if something happens to her and it's on my watch?'

'You're a nanny, not a jailer. What were you supposed to do – chain her to her bed?'

'You're right,' I said at last. 'I know you're right, it's just – oh God,' the words burst out of me of their own accord. 'I'm so *tired*, Jack. I can't think, and it doesn't help that my hand hurts like a bastard every time I touch anything.'

'What happened to your hand?'

I looked down at it, cradled in my lap, feeling it throb in time with my pulse.

'I cut it.' I didn't want to go into the hows and whys now, but the thought of that grinning, evil little face made me shudder, involuntarily.

Jack frowned.

'Can I take a look?'

I said nothing, just nodded, and held out my hand, and he took it very gently, angling it towards the light. Very lightly, he pressed the puffy skin either side of the cut, and made a face.

'It doesn't look too good, if you don't mind me saying. Did you put anything on it when you cut it?'

'Just a plaster.'

'I didn't mean that, I meant antiseptic. Anything like that?'

'Do you think it really needs it?'

He nodded.

'It's deep, and I don't like the way it's puffed up like that, looks like it could be getting infected. Let me go and see what Sandra's got in.'

He stood, pushing back his chair with a screech and walked through to the utility room where there was a small medicine cabinet on the wall. I had found the plasters in there earlier, and hadn't noticed anything like TCP or surgical spirit, just a jumble of Peppa Pig plasters and bottles of children's liquid paracetamol.

'Nothing,' Jack said, coming back through into the kitchen. 'Or at least nothing except six different flavours of Calpol. Come back to mine, I've got a proper first-aid kit in the flat.'

'I – I can't.' I straightened up, pulled my hand away, curled my injured finger to my palm, feeling it throb with pain. 'I can't leave the kids.'

'You're not leaving anyone,' Jack said patiently. 'You're right across the courtyard, you can take the baby monitor. Sandra and Bill sit out in the garden all the time in the summer. It's no different. If you hear a peep you can be back there before they even wake up.'

'Well … ' I said slowly. Thoughts flickered through the back of my head, their edges softened and blurred by the amount of wine I'd drunk earlier. I could ask him to bring the first-aid supplies back here, couldn't I? But a little part of me – OK, no, a big part of me – that part was curious. I wanted to go with Jack. I wanted to see inside his flat.

And, to be completely truthful, Mr Wrexham, I wanted to get out of this house.

If you really thought there was a threat, how could you leave the kids to deal with it? It was the woman police officer who asked me that, barely trying to conceal her disgust as she asked the question.

And I tried to explain. I tried to tell her how the kids had seen nothing, heard nothing. How every little bit of malevolence had seemed to be directed solely at *me*. *I* had heard the footsteps. *I* was the one who had read those messages. *I* had been kept awake, night after night, by the noises and the doorbells and the cold.

None of the others, even Jack, had seen or heard what I had.

If there was something in that house, and even now I only half believed that there could be, in spite of everything that had happened, *if* there was, then it was out to get me. Me and the other four nannies who had packed up and left in a hurry.

And I just wanted five minutes out from its influence. Just five minutes, with the baby monitor in my pocket and the tablet with its surveillance cameras under my arm. Was that too much to ask?

The police officer didn't seem to buy it. She just stood, shaking her head in disbelief, her lip curled with contempt for the stupid, selfish, careless bitch sitting opposite her.

But do *you* buy it, Mr Wrexham? Do you understand, how hard it was, shut up there, night after night with nothing but the sound of pacing footsteps? Do you understand why just those few yards across the courtyard seemed like both nothing at all and everything?

I don't know. I'm not sure if I've managed to convince you, to explain what it was like, what it was *really* like.

All I can tell you is that I picked up the monitor and the tablet, and I followed Jack as he crossed the kitchen, and held open the back door for me, shutting it behind us both. I felt the warmth of his skin, as he shepherded me across the dark, uneven cobble-stoned courtyard to the stairs up to his flat. And I mounted the stairs after him, watching the flex and shift of his muscles under his T-shirt as he climbed.

At the top he pulled a key out of his pocket, twisted it in the lock, and then stood back to let me pass inside.

Inside, I expected Jack to fumble for a panel or pull out his phone, but instead he reached out, flicked something, and as the lights came on, I saw a perfectly ordinary light switch made of white plastic. The relief was so absurd, and so great, that I almost laughed.

'Don't you have a control panel?'

'No, thank God! These were designed as staff accommodation. No point in wasting technology on the likes of us.'

'I suppose so.'

He flicked on another light, and I saw a small, bright sitting room, furnished with good basics and a faded cotton sofa. The remains of a log fire smouldered in the little stove in the corner, and I could see a kitchenette on the far side. Beyond was another door that I supposed was his bedroom, but it didn't seem polite to ask.

'Right, sit here,' he said, pointing at the sofa, 'and I'll be back with a proper dressing for that cut.'

I nodded, grateful for the sense of being taken care of, but mostly just content to sit there, feeling the warmth of the fire on my face and the reassuringly cheap and cheerful Ikea cushions at my back while Jack rummaged in the kitchen cupboards behind me. The sofa was exactly like the one Rowan and I had back in our flat in London. Ektorp, it was called, or something like that. It had been Rowan's mum's before she handed it down to us. Guaranteed to last for ten years, with a washable cotton cover that had once been red, in Jack's case, but had faded to a slightly streaky dark pink with sun and repeated launderings.

Sitting on it was like coming home.

After the luxurious split personality of Heatherbrae, there was something not just refreshing, but endearing about this place. It was solidly built, and all of a piece – no sudden disorientating switches from Victorian opulence to sleek futuristic technology. Everything was reassuringly homey, from the mug stains on the coffee table to the medley of photos propped on the mantelpiece – friends and their kids, or maybe nieces and nephews. One little boy cropped up more than once, clearly a relative from the family resemblance.

I felt my eyes closing, two sleep-deprived nights catching up with me ... and then I heard a cough and Jack was standing in front of me, a dressing and some disinfectant in one hand, and two glasses in the other.

'D'you want a drink?' he asked and I looked up puzzled.

'A drink? No, I'm fine thanks.'

'Are you sure? You might need something to take the edge off when I put this stuff on. It's going to sting. And I think there's a wee bit of glass or something still in there.'

I shook my head, but he was right. It did sting like fuck, first when he dabbed it with TCP, and then again when he pushed a pair of tweezers deep inside the cut, and I felt the sickening grind of metal against glass, and the sting of a forgotten shard sliding deeper into my finger.

'Fuck!' The groan slipped out without me meaning to voice it, but Jack was grinning, holding something bloodstained up at the end of his tweezers.

'Got it. Well done. That must have hurt like a bastard.'

My hand was shaking as he sat down beside me.

'You know, you've stuck it out longer than the last few.'

'What do you mean?'

'The last couple of nannies. Actually, I tell a lie, Katya made it to three weeks, I think. But since Holly, they've come and gone like butterflies.'

'Who was Holly?'

'She was the first one, the one who stayed the longest. Looked after Maddie and Ellie when they were wee, and she stayed for nearly three years, until –' He stopped, seeming to think better of what he had been about to say. 'Well, never mind that. And number two, Lauren, she stayed nearly eight months. But the one after her didn't last a week. And the one before Katya, Maja her name was, she left the first night.'

'The first *night*? What happened?'

'She called a taxi, left in the middle of the night. Left half her things too – Sandra had to send them on.'

'I don't mean that, I mean what happened to make her leave?'

'Oh, well ... that I don't really know. I always thought –' He flushed, the back of his neck staining red as he looked down at his empty glass.

'Go on,' I prompted, and he shook his head, as if angry at himself.

'Fuck it, I said I wouldnae do this.'

'Do what?'

'I don't bad-mouth my employers, Rowan, I told you that on the first day.'

The name gave me a guilty jolt, a reminder of all that I was concealing from him, but I pushed the thought aside, too intent on what he had been about to say to worry about my own secrets. Suddenly I had to know what had driven them away, those other girls, my predecessors. What had set them running?

'Jack, listen,' I said. I hesitated, then put a hand on his arm. 'It's not disloyalty. I'm their employee too, remember? We're colleagues. You're not shooting your mouth off to an outsider.

You're allowed to talk about work stuff to a colleague. It's what keeps you sane.'

'Aye?' He looked up from his contemplation of the whisky glass, and gave me a little wry smile, rather bitter. 'Is that so? Well … I've said half of it already, so I might as well tell you the whole lot. You've maybe a right to know anyway. I always thought what scared them off –' He took a breath, as if steeling himself to do something unpleasant. 'I thought it was maybe … Bill.'

'*Bill?*' It was not the answer I had been expecting. 'In – in what way?'

But the words were no sooner out of my mouth than I knew. I remembered his behaviour on my own first night, the spread thighs, the persistent offerings of wine, his knee insinuating itself, unwanted, between my own …

'Shit,' I said. 'No, you don't need to say. I can imagine.'

'Maja … she was on the young side,' Jack said reluctantly. 'And very pretty. And it crossed my mind that maybe he'd … well … come on to her, and she'd not known what to do. I'd wondered before – Bill had a black eye one time, when Lauren was here, and I did think maybe she'd … you know … .'

'Belted him one?'

'Aye. And if she did, he must have deserved it or she'd have been sacked, you know?'

'I guess. Jesus. Why didn't you tell me?'

'Bit hard to say *oh aye, by the by, ma boss is a wee bit o' a perve,* you know? Difficult to bring it up on a first day.'

'I can see that. Fuck.' My cheeks felt as flushed as Jack's, though in my case it was more than half wine. 'God. Ugh. Oh *yuck.*'

The sense of betrayal was out of all proportion, I knew that. It wasn't like I hadn't known. He'd tried it on with me, after all. But somehow the idea that he'd been systematically preying on his daughters' carers, time after time, careless of the fact that he was helping to drive them away ... I suddenly felt a desperate urge to wash myself, scrub all traces of him off my skin, even though I'd not seen him for days, and when I had, he'd barely touched me.

Ellie's voice filtered through my head, her reedy little treble. *I like it better when he's gone. He makes them do things they don't want to do.*

Was it possible she had been talking about her own father, predating the young women and girls his wife had picked out to look after his children?

'Jesus.' I put my face in my hands. 'The absolute fucker.'

'Listen –' Jack sounded uncomfortable – 'I could be wrong, I don't have any proof of this, it's just –'

'You don't need proof,' I said wretchedly. 'He tried it on with me the first night.'

'*What?*'

'Yup. Nothing –' I swallowed, gritting my teeth. 'Nothing I'd get very far with at an employment tribunal. All vague remarks and "accidentally" blocking my way. But I know when I'm being harassed.'

'Jesus, God, Rowan, I'm so – I'm so sorry – I'm just –'

'It's not your fault, don't apologise.'

'I should have bloody said something! No wonder you've been a bag of nerves, hearing blokes creeping about in –'

'No,' I said forcefully. 'That's nothing to do with it. Jack, I'm a grown woman, I've been hit on before, it's nothing I couldn't handle. The attic stuff is completely unrelated. This is – it's something else.'

'It's fucking disgusting, is what it is.' His cheeks were flushed, and he stood, as if unable to contain his anger while sitting still. He paced to the window, then back, his fists clenched. 'I'd like to –'

'Jack, leave it,' I said urgently. I stood up too, and put my hand on his arm, pulling him round to face me, and then – God, I don't even know how it happened.

I don't have the words for it, without writing it like a trashy novel. Melting into each other's arms. Lips coming together like a crash of waves. All those stupid clichés.

Except there was no melting. No softness. It was hard, and fast, and urgent, and more than a little painful in its intensity. I was kissing and being kissed, and then I was biting, my own skin between his teeth too, and then my fingers were in his hair, and his hands were fumbling my buttons, and then it was skin against skin and lips against lips and – I can't write this to you. I can't write this but I can't stop remembering it. I don't know how to stop.

Afterwards, we lay in each other's arms in front of the wood fire, our skin slicked with sweat and stickiness, and he fell asleep, his head on my breast, rising and falling gently with every breath I took. For a while, I just watched him, the way his skin paled to milk white below his hips, the brush of freckles on the bridge of his nose, the dark sweep of his lashes on his cheeks, the curl of his hand around my shoulder. And then I looked up, to the mantelpiece above us both, where the baby monitor sat, silently waiting.

I could not go back. And yet I had to.

At last, when I could feel I was beginning to slip into sleep myself, I knew that I had to get up, or risk lying here all night, and waking to find the girls making their own breakfast, while I conducted a chilly walk of shame back to the main house in the dawn light.

And there was Rhiannon too. I couldn't take the chance of her finding me here when she did come back from wherever she was. I had enough explaining to Sandra to do already, without adding night-time walks to the agenda.

Because I had to fess up to her. That was the only possibility, I had realised that as I lay in Jack's arms ... maybe I had even known before. I had to fess up to everything, and risk losing the job. If she sacked me – well, I couldn't blame her. And in spite of everything, in spite of the financial hole I would find myself in, with no job, and no money, and no references, in spite of all that, I would just have to suck it up, because I deserved it.

But if I explained, if I really explained *why* I had done what I'd done, then maybe, just maybe ...

I had my jeans almost on when I heard the noise. It was not over the baby monitor, but it came from somewhere outside the house, a noise halfway between a crack and a thud, as if a branch had fallen from a tree. I stopped, holding my breath, listening, but there were no more sounds, and no squawking wail from the baby monitor to indicate that whatever it was had woken Petra and the others.

Still, I pulled out my phone and checked the app. The camera icon marked 'Petra's room' showed her flung on her back with her usual abandon, the picture pixelated and ill-defined in the soft glow from the night light, but the shape was clear. As I watched, she sighed and stuck her thumb in her mouth.

The camera in the girls' room showed nothing at all, I'd forgotten to switch their night light on when I tucked them in, and the resolution was too poor to show anything except grainy black, punctuated by the occasional grey speckle of interference. But if they'd woken up they would have switched on the bedside light, so the absence was good news.

Shaking my head, I buttoned up my jeans, pulled my T-shirt over my head, and then bent, and very softly kissed Jack on the cheek. He said nothing, just rolled over and murmured something indistinct, that might have been 'Night, Lynn'.

For a moment my heart stilled, but then I shook myself. It could have been anything. *Night, love. Night then.* And even if it was 'Night, Lynn' or Liz, or any other name, so what? I had a past. Maybe Jack did too. And God only knew, I had too many secrets of my own to hold someone else's up to the light to condemn them.

I should have just left.

I should have picked up the baby monitor, walked to the door, and let myself out.

But before I returned to the house, I could not resist one final look back at Jack, lying there, his skin golden in the firelight, his eyes closed, his lips parted in a way that made me want to kiss him one last time.

And as I glanced back, I saw something else.

It was a purple flower, lying on the countertop. For a minute I couldn't work out why it looked familiar, nor why my gaze had snagged on it. And then I realised – it was the same as the flower I had found the other morning in the kitchen, and put into the coffee cup to revive. Had *Jack* left the flower on the kitchen floor? But no – he had been away that night, running errands for Bill ... hadn't he? Or was that a different night? Lack of sleep was making the days blur, run into each other, and it was becoming hard to remember which of the long, nightmarish stretches of darkness belonged to which morning.

As I stood there, frowning, trying to remember, I noticed something else. Something even more mundane. But something that made me stop in my tracks, my stomach lurching with unease. It was a little coil of string. Totally innocuous – so why had it unnerved me so?

I walked back across the room, and picked it up.

It was a hank of white catering string, doubled and tripled up, and tied with a granny knot that was suddenly horribly familiar. And it had been cleanly severed – snipped in half by a very sharp knife, or perhaps the very pair of pruning shears I had rescued from the poison garden.

Whichever it was, it didn't really matter now.

What mattered was that it was the hank of string I had wound around the poison garden gate, too high for little hands to reach – the string I had put there to keep the girls safe. But what was it doing in Jack's kitchen? And why was it lying next to that innocent-looking flower?

As I pulled out my phone and opened up Google, there was a sick fluttering feeling in my chest, as if I already knew what I was going to find. 'Purple flower poisonous' I typed into the search bar, and then clicked on Google Images, and there it was, the second image, its strange drooping shape and bright purple colour totally unmistakable. *Aconitum napellus (monkshood)* I read, the feeling of sickness growing inside me with every line. *One of the most toxic flowers native to the UK. Aconitine is a potent heart and nerve toxin, and any part of the plant, including stems, leaves, petals or roots, can be deadly. Most deaths result from ingesting A. napellus, but gardeners are advised to use extreme caution in handling cuttings, as even skin contact can cause symptoms.*

Underneath it was a list of deaths and murders associated with the plant.

I shut down the phone, and turned to look at Jack, unable to believe it. Had it really been him, all along?

Him in the locked garden, pruning the poisonous plants, keeping that horrible place alive.

Him undoing the safety measures I had set up, to try to protect the children.

Him carefully selecting the most poisonous blossom he could find, and leaving it lying in the middle of the kitchen floor. All I had done was handle it – but it could so easily have been found by the children, or even one of the dogs.

And I had just fucked him.

But why? Why would he do it? And what else was he responsible for?

Had he been the person who hacked into the system to jolt us all out of our beds in the middle of the night with deafening music and terrified screams?

Was he the one who had been setting off the doorbell, jerking me from sleep, and keeping me awake with the terrifying *creak, creak* of stealthy footsteps?

And worst of all, had he been the one who wrote those horrible things in the locked attic room, and then boarded up after himself, only to 'rediscover' it when the time was right?

I found that my breath was coming quick and short, my hands shaking as I shoved the phone back into my pocket, and suddenly I had to get out, get away from him at all costs.

Not troubling now to be silent, I flung open the door to the flat, and stepped out into the night, slamming it behind me. It had started to rain again, and I ran, feeling the rain on my cheeks, the tightness in my throat, and the blurring of my eyes.

The utility-room door was still unlocked, and I let myself in, leaning back against the door and using my T-shirt to wipe my eyes, trying to get a hold of myself.

Fuck. *Fuck.* What was it about me and the men in my life? Why were they such shits, all of them?

As I stood there, trying to calm my gulping breath, I remembered the faint sound I'd heard before, as I was dressing. The house was just as I'd left it, no sign of Rhiannon's high heels kicked off in the hallway, or handbag abandoned on the bottom step of the stairs. But I hadn't really expected that. I would have heard a car pulling up. It had probably been one of the dogs.

I wiped my eyes again, peeled off my shoes, and walked slowly through to the kitchen, feeling the faint warmth of the underfloor heating striking up through the concrete. Hero and Claude were curled sleepily in their baskets, snoring quietly. They looked up as I came in, and then laid their heads wearily back down as I sat at the breakfast bar, put my head in my hands, and tried to decide what to do.

I could not go to bed. No matter what Jack had said, Rhiannon was still missing, and I couldn't just forget that fact. What I should do – what I *needed* to do, in fact – was write an email to Sandra. A proper one, explaining everything that had happened.

But there was something else I had to do first.

For the more I thought about it, the more Jack's behaviour did not add up. It wasn't just the poison garden – it was everything. The way he was always hanging around when things went wrong. The fact that he seemed to have keys to every room in the house, and access to parts of the home management system that he shouldn't. How had he known how to override the app that night when the music came screaming out of the speakers? How had he just happened to have a key to the locked attic door?

And whatever he said, he was, after all, a Grant. What if there was some connection I was missing? Could he be some long-lost relative of Dr Kenwick Grant, come back to drive the Elincourts out from his ancestral home?

But no – that last *what if* was too much. This wasn't some nineteenth-century peasant's revenge drama. What would Jack gain from driving the Elincourts out of their own home? Nothing. All he'd get would be another English couple in their place. And besides, it wasn't the Elincourts who seemed to be targeted. It was me.

Because the fact was that four nannies – five if you counted Holly – had left the Elincourts. No, not left, they had been systematically driven away, one by one. And I might have believed that Bill's roving hands were responsible, if it hadn't been for my own experiences in Heatherbrae House. Someone in this house, someone or some*thing*, was driving the nannies away, in a deliberate and sustained campaign of persecution.

I just didn't know who.

Somewhere behind my eyes, a dull throbbing ache had begun, echoing the pain in my hand – the light-headedness from the wine I'd drunk earlier was already morphing into the beginnings of a shocking hangover. But I couldn't give way to that now. Slowly, unsteadily, I slid from the breakfast bar stool, walked over to the sink, and splashed my face, trying to wake myself up, clear my head for what I was about to do.

But as I stood, water dripping from my loose hair, hands braced either side of the sink, I saw something. Something that had not been there when I left, I was sure of it – or at least as sure as I could be, for now nothing seemed certain any more.

To the right of the sink was my almost empty wine bottle. Only now it was totally empty. What should have had a glass left in it, was now completely drained. And in the groove around the edge of the waste-disposal unit was a single crushed berry.

It could have been the remnants of a blueberry or a raspberry, mashed out of all recognition, but, somehow, I knew it was not.

My heart was thumping as I reached, very slowly, into the waste-disposal unit.

Deep, deep into the metal mouth I reached, until my fingers touched something at the bottom. Something soft and hard by turns, into which my fingers sank as I clawed up the mass.

It was a mush of berries. Yew. Holly. Cherry laurel.

And in spite of the water I'd sluiced down the drain, I could smell, quite clearly, the dregs of wine still clinging to them.

It didn't make sense. *None* of it made sense. Those berries had not been in the wine when I left – how could they have been? I had opened the bottle myself.

Which meant, someone had put them in there when I was not looking. Someone who had been in this kitchen tonight, after the children were in bed.

But then ... but then someone else had tipped them out.

It was like there were two forces in the house, one fighting to drive me away, another to protect me. But who – *who* was doing this?

I didn't know. But if there were answers to be found, I knew where I had to look.

My chest was tight as I straightened up, and I groped in my jeans pocket for my inhaler and took a puff, but the tension didn't loosen, and I found my breath was coming quick and shallow as I made my way to the stairs, and began to climb into the darkness.

As I got closer and closer to the top landing, I couldn't help remembering the last time I had stood there, hand on the rounded knob, simply unable to go any further – unable to face whatever watchful darkness lay behind that door.

Now, though, I was beginning to suspect that whatever haunted Heatherbrae was very human. And I was determined that this time, I would turn the knob, open the door, and find evidence to that effect – evidence that I could show Sandra when I told her about tonight's events.

But when I got to the landing, I found I didn't need to open it at all. For my door ... the door to my room, was open. And I had left it closed.

I had a clear, a crystal-clear memory, of standing in front of it, looking at the crack beneath it, totally unable to turn the handle.

And now it stood open.

It was very cold again, even colder than it had been that time I woke in the night, shivering, to find the thermostat turned down and the air conditioning blasting out. But this time I could feel it was more than just the chill of the room, it was an actual breeze.

For a moment I felt every part of that firm resolution shrivel down like plastic in a flame, disappearing down into the core of me, melting and curling into a hard blackened core.

Where was the breeze coming from? Was it the attic door? If it was open again – in spite of the lock and the key in my pocket, and in spite of Jack lying asleep in his flat across the courtyard – I thought I would scream.

Then I got a hold of myself.

This was insane. There was no such thing as ghosts. No such thing as haunting. There was nothing in that attic but dust and the relics of bored children, fifty years dead.

I walked into the room and pressed the button on the panel.

Nothing happened. I tried a different square, one I was sure had made the lamps come on last night. Still nothing, though an unseen fan began to hum. For a long moment I stood in the dark, trying to figure out what to do. I could smell the cold dusty air that blew through the attic keyhole, and I could hear something too – not the *creak, creak* of before, but a low, mechanical buzzing that puzzled me.

And then, out of nowhere, a sudden wave of anger washed over me.

Whatever it was, whatever was up there, I would *not* let myself be scared like this. Someone, some*thing*, was trying to drive me away from Heatherbrae, and I was not giving into it.

I don't know if it was the remnants of the wine in my veins that gave me courage, or the knowledge that when I rang Sandra the next day, very likely I would be going home anyway, but I took my phone out of my pocket, switched on the torch, and strode across the bedroom to the attic door.

As I did so, the buzzing sounded again. It was coming from above my head. The sound was familiar, but I couldn't put my finger on why. It sounded like a furiously angry wasp, but there was something ... something robotic about it, a quality that did not make me think it was a living thing.

I felt in my jeans pocket for the key, which was still there from yesterday, hard and unyielding against my leg, and I drew it out.

Softly, very softly, I put the key into the closet door, and turned it. It was stiff – but not as stiff as last time. The WD40 had done its work, and although I felt resistance, it turned quietly, without the screech of metal on metal it had given when Jack forced the lock.

Then I set my hand to the door, and opened it.

The smell was just as I remembered from last time – dank, musty, the smell of death and abandonment.

But there *was* something up there, I could see that now, something casting a low white glow that illuminated the cobwebs the spiders had woven across the attic steps. Yet, no one had been up here since Jack and me, that was plain. It was not just the key in my pocket that told me that – but the thick unbroken webs across my path, painstakingly respun since my last passage. There was no way someone could have passed this way without disturbing them. As it was, I was forced to step cautiously, sweeping my hand in front of my face to try to keep the clinging strands out of my eyes and mouth.

What *was* the light? The moon, shining through that tiny window? Perhaps, though it was so covered with grot, I would have been surprised.

At the top of the stairs I drew a silent breath, steeling myself, and then I stepped into the attic.

I saw two things straight away.

The first was that the attic was just as I had last seen it when I took a final glance back at the place before following Jack down the steps the day before. The only thing that was missing was the doll's head that had rolled out from the pile to rest in the centre of the room. That was gone.

The second was that the moon *was* shining into the attic, and surprisingly brightly, for the window – the window that Jack had shut – was open again. He had evidently not latched it properly and it had blown open in the night. Striding angrily across the creaking boards I slammed it, harder than he had, and fumbled in the darkness for a catch. At length I found one – a long tongue drilled with holes. It was covered in thick cobwebs, and I was forced to brush them aside with my hands, feeling the crunch of long-dead prey in the webs, as I wiggled it back into place, ensuring that there was no way the window could work itself open again.

At last it was secure, and I stepped back into the room, wiping my hands. The light had dimmed instantly as I shut the window, the mildewed glass shutting out everything but a thin trickle. But as I turned back to the stairs, the thin beam from my torch illuminating a narrow path across the floorboards, I noticed something else. There was another light. A fainter, bluer one this time, and it was coming from a corner of the attic opposite the window, a corner totally in shadow, a corner where no light had a right to be.

My heart was thudding as I crossed the floor. Was it an opening to one of the rooms downstairs? Something else? Whatever the source of the light was, it was hidden behind a trunk, and I pulled it roughly aside, no longer trying to be quiet, for I no longer cared who found me up here, I had only one instinct – to find out what was really going on.

What I saw made me draw back, astonished, and kneel down in the dust to look closer.

Hidden behind the old trunk, was a small pile of belongings. A book. Some chocolate bar wrappers. A bracelet. A necklace.

A handful of twigs and berries – wilting, yes, but by no means desiccated.

And a mobile phone.

It was the light from the phone that I had seen from across the attic, and as I picked it up, it buzzed again, and I realised that was the source of the odd noise I had heard earlier. It had evidently updated, and was stuck in a loop of trying to turn itself back on, failing, and restarting, buzzing each time.

It was an old model, similar to one I'd had myself a few years ago, and I tried a trick that had sometimes worked when my own phone was dying, holding the volume up and power buttons simultaneously for a long press. It hung for a moment, the screen whirling, and then went black, and I pressed restart.

But as I waited for it to reload, something caught my eye. A silvery glint, coming from the little pile of rubbish I had pushed aside to pick up the phone.

And there it was, strewn innocently across the floorboards among the rest of that pathetic pile of detritus, the light from my phone torch glinting from one of its curves.

My necklace.

My heart was beating fast in my throat as I picked it up, unable to believe it. My necklace. *My* necklace. What was it doing here, in the darkness?

I don't know how long I sat in the kitchen, my fingers wrapped around a mug of tea, letting the thin links of my necklace chain trickle through my fingers, and trying to make sense of it all.

I had brought the phone down too, but without a pin code I couldn't open it to see who it belonged to. All I could tell was that it was old, and that it appeared to be connected to the Wi-Fi but didn't seem to have a SIM card in.

It wasn't the phone that bothered me though. That was strange, yes, but there was something personal about finding my necklace hidden up there, amid the darkness and the rotting feathers. I should have been thinking about Rhiannon, worrying about where she was, and the argument we were bound to have when she walked through the door. I should have been thinking about Sandra, considering my options and trying to work out what to say – how to tell her the truth.

I was thinking about both things. But above and below and around those thoughts were twined the links of my necklace, as I tried to figure out chronologies and timings and work out how my necklace could have disappeared inside a locked room, behind a door to which the only key lay in my pocket, up a corridor sealed by a hundred unbroken spiderwebs. Had it been up there before, when Jack and I first broke in? But that explained nothing. That cupboard had been boarded up for months, *years*. The dust traces, the thick swags of cobwebs, no one had entered via the stairs for a long, long time. And the window was barely large enough for me to get my head and shoulders through, and it looked out onto sheer slates.

After I found the necklace I had scoured every inch of the room looking for trapdoors, loft hatches, hidden doors – but there was nothing. The Victorian floorboards ran from side to side in an unbroken line, the walls gave onto nothing except for the roof tiles, and I had moved every stick of furniture, looked at every inch of the ceiling from below. Whatever else I was unsure of, I was absolutely certain that there was no way in or out apart from the flight of stairs leading up from my room.

The moon was still high in the sky, but the clock above the stove had ticked through 3 and 4 a.m., when I at last heard tyres on the gravel of the drive, whispered laughter outside the porch, and the sound of the front door swinging automatically open as someone activated the thumb-pad lock. The door closed stealthily as the van drove off, and I heard cautious footsteps, and then a stumble.

My stomach flipped, but I forced myself to stay calm.

'Hello, Rhiannon.' I kept my voice level, and I heard the footsteps on the hallway flags freeze, and then an exclamation of disgust as Rhiannon realised she had been busted.

'Fuck.'

She walked unsteadily through to the kitchen. Her make-up was half-way down her face, and her tights were laddered, and she smelled strongly of some mix of sweet alcohol – there was Drambuie in there I thought, and Malibu too, along with something else, Red Bull perhaps?

'You're drunk,' I said, and she gave a nasty laugh.

'Kettle black. I can see the wine bottles in the recycling from here.'

I shrugged.

'Fair point, but you know I can't let you get away with this, Rhiannon. I have to tell your parents. You can't just walk out like that. You're fourteen. What if something happened and I didn't know where you were or who you were with?'

'OK,' she said, slumping down at the kitchen island and pulling the biscuit tin towards her. 'You do that, *Rachel*. And good luck with the fallout.'

'It doesn't matter,' I said. As she picked out a biscuit and pushed the tin away, I took a digestive too, dunking it calmly in my tea, though my hands were shaking a little beneath my careful control. 'I've made up my mind. I'm going to tell your mum. If I lose my job, so be it.'

'*If* you lose your job?' She snorted derisively. '*If*? You're delusional. You're here under a fake name, probably with fake qualifications for all I know. You'll be lucky if you don't end up getting sued.'

'Maybe,' I said, 'but I'll take that risk. Now get upstairs and wipe that stuff off your face.'

'Fuck you,' she said, through a mouthful of digestive, her words accompanied by an explosion of biscuit crumbs that spattered across my face, making me recoil, blinking and brushing fragments out of my eyes.

'You little bitch!' My temper, so carefully held, was suddenly fraying fast. 'What is wrong with you?'

'What's wrong with *me*?'

'Yes, you. All of you, actually. Why do you hate me so much? What have I ever done to any of you? Do you actually want to be left here alone? Because that's what's going to happen if you keep being such a fucking bitch to the staff.'

'What the fuck do you know about it?' she spat, and suddenly she was as angry as me, pushing back her metal stool so that it toppled and fell with a ringing clang onto the concrete floor. 'You can fuck off as far as I'm concerned, we don't want you, we don't *need* you.'

There was a biting retort on the tip of my tongue, but somehow, as she stood there, the kitchen spotlights making her tousled, tangled blonde hair glow like fire, her face twisted into a grimace of rage and pain, she looked so like Maddie, so like *me*, that my heart gave a little skip.

I remembered myself, aged fifteen, coming in after curfew, standing in the kitchen with my hands on my hips shouting at my mum, 'I don't care if you were worried, I never asked you to stay up, I don't need you looking out for me!'

It was a lie, of course. A total lie.

Because everything I did, every test I aced, every curfew I broke, every time I tidied my room and every time I didn't – all of it was aimed at one thing. Making my mother notice me. Making her *care*.

For fourteen years, I had tried so hard to be the perfect daughter, but it was never enough. No matter how neat my handwriting, no matter how high I scored in the spelling test, or how good my art project was, it was never enough. I could spend a whole afternoon colouring a picture for her, and she would notice the one place I had sneezed and jerked my pen across the line.

I could spend my Saturday tidying my room to perfection – and she would grumble that I had left my shoes in the hall.

Whatever I did was wrong. I grew too fast, my clothes were too expensive, my friends were too noisy. I was too chubby, or, conversely, I picked at my food. My hair was too messy – too thick, too hard to tame into the neat plaits and ponytails she favoured.

And so as I crossed the line from child to teenager, I began to do the opposite. I had tried being perfect – now I tried being imperfect. I stayed out. I drank. I let my grades slip. I went from total compliance to serial defiance.

It made no difference. No matter what I did, I was not the daughter I should have been. All I was doing now was confirming that fact to both of us.

I had ruined her life. That was always the unspoken message – the thing that hung between us, making me clutch at her even harder as she pulled away. And at last, I couldn't deal with seeing that truth in her face any more.

I left home at eighteen, with nothing but a handful of mediocre A levels and the offer of an au pair job in Clapham. By that time I was old enough not to have a curfew, or someone sitting up for me past their bedtime, reproach in their eyes when I came home.

But I was very, very far from not needing anyone to look out for me.

Maybe Rhiannon was too.

'Rhiannon –' I stepped forward, trying to keep the pity out of my voice – 'Rhiannon, I know that since Holly –'

'Don't you dare say her name,' she growled. She took a step backwards, stumbling on her high heels, and suddenly she looked like what she was – a little girl, teetering in clothes too old for her that she had barely learned how to wear. Her lips were curled in a way that could have been anger, but I suspected meant she was trying not to cry. 'Don't you *dare* talk about that slut-faced hell witch here.'

'Who – Holly?' I was taken aback. There was something here, something different from the generalised world-hating hostility I had felt emanating from Rhiannon up until now. This was pointed, vicious, *personal*, and Rhiannon's voice shook with it.

'What – what happened?' I asked. 'Is this because she abandoned you?'

'Abandoned us?' Rhiannon gave a kind of derisive, hooting laughing. 'Fuck no. She didn't abandon us.'

'Then what?'

'*Then what?*' she imitated, cruelly mocking my south London accent, blurring her cut-glass consonants, swallowing the final t into an Estuary drawl. 'She stole my fucking father, if you must know.'

'What?'

'Yes, my dear darling daddy. Shagged him for the best part of two years, and had Maddie and Ellie wound round her little finger covering up for them both, telling my mother lies. And do you know what the worst part of it was? I didn't even realise what was going on until my friend came to stay and pointed it out. I didn't believe her at first – so I set them up to find out the truth. My dad doesn't have cameras in his study – did you ever notice that?' She gave a bitter, staccato laugh. 'Funny that. He can spy on the rest of us – but *his* privacy is sacrosanct. I got Petra's baby monitor, and I plugged it in under his desk and I *heard* them – I heard him telling Holly that he loved her, that he was going to leave my mum, that she just had to be patient, that they were going to be together in London, just like he'd promised.'

Oh fuck. I wanted to put my arms around her, hug her, tell it was OK, that it was not her fault, but I couldn't move.

'And I heard her too, begging, wheedling, telling him she just couldn't wait, that she wanted them to be together – I *heard* it, all the stuff that she wanted to do to him – it was –' She stopped, choking with disgust for a moment, and then seemed to pull herself together, folding her arms, her face set in a mask of grief too old for her. 'So, I framed the bitch.'

'What –' But I couldn't finish. I could barely even form the word.

Rhiannon smiled, but her face was twisted like she was holding back tears.

'I got her in front of the cameras, and I wound her up until she hit me.'

Oh God. So this was where Maddie had learned it.

'And then I told her to get out, or I'd put the footage on You-Tube and ensure she never worked in this country again, and ever since then –'

She stopped, gulping, and then tried again.

'And ever since –'

But she couldn't finish. She didn't need to. I knew the truth, what she was trying to say.

'Rhiannon –' I stepped towards her, my hand outstretched like I was trying to tame and gentle a wild animal, my own voice shaking now. 'Rhiannon, I swear to you, there is no way in a thousand – no, a *million* years, I'd ever have sex with your father.'

'You can't promise that.' Her face was swollen, there were tears running down her cheeks now. 'That's what they all think, when they come here. But he keeps on, and on, and on, and they can't afford to lose their jobs, and he's got money, and he can even be kind of charming, when he wants to be, you know?'

'No.' I was shaking my head. 'No, no, no. Rhiannon, listen, I – I can't explain, but just – no. There's no way. There's just no way I'd ever do that.'

'I don't believe you,' she said. The words came out like sobs. 'He's done it before, you know. Before Holly. And that time he *did* leave. He had another family. Another child, a *baby*. I heard my m-mother t-t-talking one day. And he l-*left* them – it's who he is and if I hadn't stopped him – he j-just –'

But she couldn't finish. Her voice dissolved into sobs. I felt an awful kind of realisation wash over me, and I put my hands on her arms, trying to steady us both, linking us both, trying to communicate everything I could not say with the certainty of my voice.

'Rhiannon, listen, I can promise you this – this is absolutely cast iron. I swear on – on my *grave*, I am never, ever going to sleep with your father.'

Because.

It was on the tip of my tongue.

I am never, never going to sleep with your father because –

I wish I had finished the sentence, Mr Wrexham. I wish I had just said it, told her, explained. But I was still clinging on to the idea of explaining the reason for my deception to Sandra the next day, and I couldn't tell Rhiannon the truth before I confessed to her mother. I had to confess that I wasn't Rowan, and Sandra's pity and understanding about why I had come to her house under a false name was my only chance of making it out of the situation without being at minimum sacked, and very possibly sued.

But you don't need me to finish the sentence, do you, Mr Wrexham? You know why. At least, I imagine you do, if you've read the papers. You know, because the police know. Because they found out. Because they put two and two together, as you are very possibly doing, even now.

You know that the reason I would never sleep with Bill Elincourt was because he was my father too.

I told you, Mr Wrexham, didn't I, that I wasn't even looking for a job when I stumbled across the advert. In fact I was doing something totally different, something I'd done many times before.

I was googling my father's name.

I'd always known who he was, and for a while I'd even known *where* he was – a fancy semi-detached house in Crouch End, with electric gates that slid automatically across the driveway, and a shiny BMW on the forecourt. I had been there once in my mid-teens, under cover of a pretended shopping trip to Oxford Street with a friend. I remember the taste in my mouth, the way my hands shook when I showed the bus driver my travel card, every step of the walk from Crouch End Broadway.

I stood outside that gate for a long time, consumed with a strange mix of fear and anger, too afraid to ring the bell and face up to the man I'd never met, the man who had walked out when my mother was nine months pregnant.

He sent cheques for a while, but he wasn't on my birth certificate, and I suppose my mother was too proud to pursue him and force him to pay.

Instead she picked herself up, got a job in an insurers firm, and met the man she eventually married. The man – the message was very clear – that she *should* have been with all along.

And so, when I was six, we moved into his boxy little house.

It was their home. Hers and his. It was never mine. Not from the day I moved into the little room above the stairs, and was told sharply not to scuff my suitcase on the hall skirting boards. Not until the day I packed a different, larger suitcase, and moved out, twelve long years later.

It was their home, but I – I was always there to spoil it for them. This living, breathing, constant reminder of my mother's past. Of the man who had left her. And every day, she had to look at me staring at her over the breakfast cereal with *his* eyes. When she brushed my thick, wiry hair into a ponytail, it was *his* hair she brushed, not her own fine, flyaway stuff.

For that was all I had from him. That, and the necklace he had sent me on my first birthday, the last contact I had from him. A necklace with my initial on it – R for Rachel.

Cheap, nasty tat, my mother had called it, but that didn't stop me from wearing it all the hours I was allowed. At weekends, at first, and every day in the holidays, and then when I began work as an au pair, tucking it beneath my T-shirts and plastic aprons, so that it was always there, the worn metal warm between my breasts.

I was working as a nanny in Highgate when she rang me up and told me. She and my stepfather were selling the house and retiring to Spain. Just like that. It wasn't that I had any particular affection for that house – I had never been happy there.

But it had been … well, if not my home, at any rate, the only place I could call home. 'Of course you're welcome to come and visit,' she said, her voice high and slightly defensive, as if she knew what she was doing, and I think it was that, more than anything, that made me lose it. *You're welcome to come and visit.* It was the kind of thing you say to a distant relative, or a friend you don't particularly like, hoping they won't take you up on the offer.

I told her to fuck off. I'm not proud of that. I told her that I hated her, that I'd had four years of therapy to try to deal with my upbringing, and that I never wanted to hear from her again.

It wasn't true. Of course it wasn't true. Even now, even here, at Charnworth, she was the first person I put on my prison call list. But she's never called.

It was two days after her announcement that I went back to Crouch End.

I was twenty-two. And I wasn't angry this time. I was just … I was terribly, terribly sad. I had lost the only parent I'd ever known – and my need to replace her with *something*, however poor and inadequate, was consuming me.

'Hello … Bill.' I had practised the words in my bedroom the night before, standing in front of the mirror. My face was scrubbed clean of make-up, making me look younger and even more vulnerable, though that hadn't been my intention, and I found that my voice was unnaturally high, as if I wanted to make an appeal to his pity. I didn't know what kind of daughter he'd want – but I was prepared to try and be that person. 'Hello, Bill. You don't know me but I'm Rachel. I'm Catherine's daughter.'

My heart was thudding in my chest as I walked up to the gate and rang the bell, waiting for the gate to slide back, or perhaps the crackle of voices to come over the intercom. But nothing happened.

I tried again, holding the buzzer long and hard, and eventually the front door opened and a small woman in an overall, holding a duster, came out across the shingled drive.

'Hello?' She was in her forties or fifties, and her voice was heavily accented, Polish I thought, or perhaps Russian. Eastern Europe. 'I can help you?'

'Oh … hello.' My pulse rate had sped up, until I thought I might possibly faint from nerves. 'Hello. I'm looking for Mr –' I swallowed. 'Mr Elincourt. Bill Elincourt. Is he here?'

'He is not here.'

'Oh, well, will he be back later?'

'He gone. New family now.'

'Wh-what do you mean?'

'He and him wife moved last year. Different country. Scotland. New family is here now. Mr and Mrs Cartwright.'

Oh. Fuck.

It was like a punch to the gut.

'Do you … do you have an address?' I asked, my voice faltering, and she shook her head. There was pity in her eyes.

'Sorry, I do not have, I am just cleaning.'

'You –' I swallowed hard. 'You mentioned a wife. Mrs Elincourt. Can I ask – what's her name?'

I don't know why that was suddenly important to me. Only that I knew the trail had gone cold, and any scraps of information seemed better than nothing. The cleaner looked at me sadly. Who did she think I was? A spurned girlfriend? A former employee? Or maybe she had guessed the truth.

'She called Sandra,' she said at last, very quietly. 'I must go now.' And then she turned and made her way back into the house.

I turned too and began the long walk back to Highgate, saving the bus fare. There was a hole in my shoe, and as I started up the hill, it began to rain, and I knew I had lost my chance.

After that I didn't try looking again in earnest for a few years. And then, one day, when I was idly typing 'Bill Elincourt' into Google, there it was. The advert. With a house in Scotland. And a wife called Sandra.

And a family.

And suddenly, I couldn't *not*.

It was like the universe had set this up for me – to give me a chance.

I didn't want him to be my dad, not now, not after all these years. I just wanted to … well, just to *see*, I suppose. But obviously, I couldn't travel up to Scotland under my own name without telling him who I was, and setting up a whole weight of expectation and potential rejection. Even with nearly thirty years of water under the bridge, it was unlikely that Bill would have forgotten the name of his first-born daughter, and Gerhardt was unusual enough as a surname for him to do a double take, and register it as that of the mother of his child.

But I didn't need to go under my own name. In fact, I had a better name, a better identity, just ready and waiting for me. One that would get me through the front door without any strings attached, at which point I could do whatever I wanted. And so I picked up the papers that Rowan had left so temptingly lying around in her bedroom – the papers that were, almost, going to waste. The papers so very, very close to my own that, really, it didn't seem like much of a deception at all.

And I applied.

I didn't expect to get the job. I didn't even want it. I just wanted to meet the man who had abandoned me all those years before. But when I saw Heatherbrae, I knew, Mr Wrexham. I knew that one visit was never going to be enough for me. I wanted to be a part of all this, to sleep in the softness of those feather beds, to sink into the velvet sofas, to bask under the rainwater showers – to be a part of this family, in short.

And I wanted, very, *very* badly, to meet Bill.

And when he didn't appear at the interview, I could see only one way to make that happen.

I had to get the job.

But when I did … and when I met Bill that first night, realised the kind of man he was, God, it's like a metaphor for this whole thing, Mr Wrexham. It's all connected. The beauty and luxury of the house, and the seeping poison underneath the high tech facade. The solid Victorian wood of a closet door, with its polished brass escutcheon – and the cold, rank smell of death that breathes out of the hole.

There was something sick in that house, Mr Wrexham. And whether Bill had been sick when he went there and brought it with him, or whether he had caught its sickness and become the man I met on that first night, that predatory, abusive man, I don't know.

All I know is that the two run hand in hand, and that if you scratched the walls of Heatherbrae House, scoring the hand-blocked peacock wallpaper with your nails, or gouging the polished granite tiles, that same darkness would seep out, the darkness that lay very close beneath Bill Elincourt's skin.

'*Don't look for him.*' That was one of the few things my mother had said to me about him, before she shut off the subject completely. '*Don't look for him, Rachel. Nothing good will come of it.*'

She was right. God, she was so right. And how I wish I'd listened to her.

'Come on,' I said at last. 'Up to bed, Rhiannon. You're tired, I'm tired, we've both had too much to drink … We'll talk about all this in the morning.'

I'd ring Sandra and explain. Somehow. With my head aching from the beginnings of a hangover, and tiredness scratching at the back of my eyes I could not quite think of the words, but they would come. They would have to. I couldn't carry on like this, being blackmailed by Rhiannon.

For a moment, as I climbed the stairs, Rhiannon in front of me, I had an absurd mental picture of Sandra welcoming me with open arms, telling me I completed their family, telling me – but no. That was ridiculous, and I knew it. Even the most generous of women would take time to adjust to a long-lost stepchild turning up, and to find out this way, in these circumstances … I had no illusions how the conversation was likely to pan out. Difficult would be the best-case scenario.

Well, I had made my bed, and I would have to lie on it. I would almost certainly be sacked – I couldn't really see any way around that. But I was fairly sure that Bill would not want to sue his estranged daughter, to whose mother he had paid just pennies in child support, before disappearing for good. It would not be a good look for Elincourt and Elincourt. No, it would be swept under the rug, and I'd be free to carry on. Alone.

And far away from Heatherbrae.

I hadn't really thought about my room and where I was going to sleep until we got to the second floor landing, and Rhiannon turned the handle on her graffitied bedroom door and flung her shoes in, with total unconcern.

'Goodnight,' she said, as if nothing had happened, as if the events of the night had been just another family row.

'Goodnight,' I said, and I took a deep breath, and opened the door to the bedroom. The strange phone was hard in my pocket and my necklace – the necklace I had feared Bill Elincourt might recognise – lay warm around my neck.

Inside, the door to the attic was shut and locked, as I had left it. I was about to grab my night things and take them downstairs to the sofa to try to catch a few hours before dawn, when there was a sudden gust of wind, making the trees outside groan. The curtains flapped suddenly and wildly in the breeze, and the fresh pine-laden scent of a Scottish night filled the room.

The room was still painfully cold, just as it had been earlier that night, and suddenly I realised. The cold had never come from the attic – it must have been the window, open all along. Only before I had been so fixated on finding out the truth of what was behind the locked door that I hadn't even glanced towards the curtains.

At least the chill was explained then. Nothing supernatural – just the cold night air.

But the problem was, I had not opened that window. I hadn't even touched it since I slammed it shut a few nights before. And now, suddenly, my stomach was turning over and over in a way that made me feel very, very sick.

Turning, I ran out of the room and down the stairs, ignoring Rhiannon's sleepy 'What the fuck?' as I slammed the door behind me. Down on the first floor, my heart hammering in my chest, I opened Petra's bedroom door, the wood shushing on the thick carpet, and waited for my eyes to get adjusted to the dim light.

She was there, quite asleep, her arms and legs flung out, and I felt my pulse rate calm, just a little, but I had to check on the others before I could relax.

Down the corridor then, to the door marked *Princess Ellie* and *Queen Maddie*.

It was shut, and I turned the handle very softly, pushing gently. It was pitch-black inside without the night light, the blackout curtains shutting out even the moonlight, and I cursed myself for forgetting to switch it on, but when my eyes got used to the darkness, I could hear the faint sound of snores, and I felt my breath coming a little more easily. Thank God. Thank God they were OK.

I tiptoed across the thick carpet and felt along the wall for the lead to the night light, followed it back to the switch, and then I switched it on. And there they were, Ellie scrunched into a tight little ball as though trying to hide from something, Maddie scooched down under the duvet so that I could see nothing except her shape beneath the covers.

My panic calmed as I turned back to the door, laughing at myself for my paranoia.

And then ... I stopped.

It was ridiculous, I knew that, but I just had to check, I had to *see* ...

I tiptoed across the carpet and drew back the cover. To find ...

... a pillow, pushed into the curved shape of a sleeping child.

My heart began to race sickeningly hard.

The first thing I did was check under the bed. Then all the cupboards in the room.

'Maddie,' I whispered, as loud as I dared, not wanting to wake Ellie, but hearing the panicked urgency in my own voice. 'Maddie?'

But there was no answering sound, not even a stifled giggle. Just nothing. Nothing.

I ran out of the room.

'Maddie?' I called louder this time. I rattled the handle of the bathroom, but it was unlocked, and when the door swung open I saw its emptiness, the moonlight streaming across the bare tiles.

'Maddie?'

Nothing in Sandra and Bill's bedroom either, just the unruffled smoothness of the bed, the moonlit expanse of carpet, the white columns of the open curtains standing sentinel either side of the tall windows. I flung open the closets, but the faint illumination of the automatic lights showed nothing but neat rows of suits and racks of high heels.

'What is it?' Rhiannon's sleepy voice came from upstairs. 'What the fuck's going on?'

'It's Maddie,' I called up, trying to keep the panic out of my voice. 'She's not in bed. Can you look upstairs? Maddie!'

Petra was stirring now, woken by my increasingly loud calls, and I heard her crotchety grumble, preparatory to a full-on wail, but I didn't stop to comfort her. I *had* to find Maddie. Had she come downstairs to find me when I was with Jack? The thought gave me an unpleasant lurch, followed by another, even more unpleasant.

Had she – oh God. Had she possibly *followed* me? I had left the back door unlocked. Could she have gone looking for me in the grounds?

Horrible visions ran through my mind. The pond. The beck. Even the road.

Ignoring Petra, I ran down the stairs, shoved my feet into the first pair of wellingtons I found at the back door, and ran out into the moonlight.

The cobbled yard was empty.

'Maddie!' I called, full-throated, desperate now, hearing my voice echo from the stone walls of the stables and back to the house. 'Maaaddie? Where are you?'

There was no answer, and I had a sudden, even more horrible thought, worse than the forest clearing, with the treacherously muddy pond.

The poison garden.

The poison garden left unlocked and unguarded by Jack Grant.

It had already killed one little girl.

Dear God, I prayed, as I began to sprint towards the back of the house, towards the path down through the shrubbery, my feet slipping in the too-big wellingtons. Please let it not claim another.

But as I rounded the corner of the house, I found her.

She was lying crumpled face down below my bedroom window, sprawled across the cobblestones in her nightdress, the white cotton soaked through and through with blood, so much blood I would never have imagined her small body could hold it all.

It ran across the cobbles like treacle, thick and sticky, slicking my knees as I knelt in it, clinging to my fingers as I picked her up, cradling her, feeling the bird-like fragility of her little bones, begging her, pleading with her to be OK.

But of course it was impossible.

She would never be OK again. Nothing would.

She was quite, quite dead.

The next few hours are the ones that the police have made me go over again and again, like nails scratching and scratching at a wound, making it bleed afresh every time. And yet, even after all their questions, the memories only come in snatches, like a night illuminated by flashes of lightning, with darkness in between.

I remember screaming, holding Maddie's body for what felt like the longest time, until first Jack came, and then Rhiannon, holding a wailing Petra in her arms, almost dropping her when she saw the horror of what had happened.

I remember her wail, that awful sound, as she saw her sister's body. I don't think I will ever forget that.

I remember Jack taking Rhiannon inside, and then trying to pull me away, saying she's dead, she's dead, we can't disturb the body, Rowan, we have to leave her for the police, and I couldn't let her go, I could only weep and cry.

I remember the flashing blue lights of the police at the gate, and Rhiannon's face, white and stricken as she tried to comprehend.

And I remember sitting there, covered in blood on the velvet sofa, as they asked me what happened, what happened, what happened.

And I still don't know.

I still don't know, Mr Wrexham, and that's the truth.

I know what the police think, from the questions they asked, and the scenarios they put to me.

They think that Maddie went up to my room to find me missing, and that she saw something incriminating up there – perhaps she went to the window, and saw me creeping back from Jack's flat. Or perhaps they think she found something in my belongings, something to do with my real name, my true identity.

I don't know. I had so much to hide, after all.

And they think that I came back to find her there, and realised what she had seen, and that I opened the window and that –

I can't say it. It's hard even to write it. But I have to.

They think that I threw her out. They think that I stood there, with the curtains blowing wide, and watched her bleed to death on the cobblestones, and then went back downstairs to drink tea, and wait calmly for Rhiannon to come home.

They think that I left the window open deliberately, to try to make it seem like she could have fallen. But they are sure that she didn't. I am not certain why. I think it's something to do with the position of where she landed – too far away from the building to be a slip, with an arc that could only have been caused by a push, or a jump.

Would Maddie have jumped? That's a question I have asked myself a thousand, maybe a million times.

And the truth is, I just don't know.

We may never know. Because the irony is, Mr Wrexham, in a house filled with a dozen cameras, there are none that show what happened to Maddie that night. The camera in her room shows nothing but darkness. It points away from the door, at the girls' beds, so there is not even a silhouette in the doorway to show what time Maddie left.

And as for my room ... oh God ... as for my room, that is one of the bricks in the edifice of evidence the police built against me.

'Why did you cover the security camera in your room if you had nothing to hide?' they kept asking me again, and again, and again.

And I tried to tell them – to explain what it's like to be a young woman, alone, in a strange house, with strangers watching you. I tried to tell them how I was OK with a camera in the kitchen, the den, the living room, the corridors, even with cameras in the girls' rooms. But that I needed somewhere, just one place, where I could be myself, unwatched, unmonitored. Where I could be not Rowan, but Rachel – just for a few hours.

'Would you want a camera in your bedroom?' I asked the detective, point-blank, but he just shrugged as if to say, it's not me on trial, love.

But the truth is, I did cover that camera up. And if I hadn't, we might know what happened to Maddie.

Because, I *didn't* kill her, Mr Wrexham. I know I've said that already. I told you in the very first letter I sent you. I didn't kill her, and you have to believe me, because it's the truth. But I don't know, writing these words in my cramped cell, with the Scottish rain drizzling down the window outside ... have I convinced you? How I wish I could persuade you to come here. I've put you on my list of visitors. You could come tomorrow, even. And I could look into your eyes and tell you – I didn't kill her.

But I didn't convince the police of that. I didn't convince Mr Gates either.

In the end, I'm not sure I even convince myself.

For if I hadn't left her that night, if I hadn't spent those hours with Jack, in his flat, in his arms, none of this would have happened.

I didn't kill her, but her death is on my hands. My little sister.

If you didn't kill her, who did? Help us out here, Rachel. Tell us what you think happened, the police asked, again and again, and I could only shake my head. Because the truth is, Mr Wrexham, I don't know. I have constructed a thousand theories – each wilder than the other. Maddie leaping like a bird into the night, Rhiannon coming back early from her night out somehow, Jean McKenzie hiding in the attic, Jack Grant creeping past me while I was waiting downstairs for Rhiannon.

Because Jack turned out to have secrets too – did you know that? Nothing as grand or melodramatic as what I had imagined – he wasn't related to Dr Kenwick Grant, or at least if he was, neither he nor the police managed to trace the link. And when I told the police about the hank of string in his kitchen and the *Aconitum napellus* blossom, he, unlike me, had a quick and reasonable explanation. Because Jack, it seemed, had recognised the purple flower sitting in the coffee cup on the kitchen table – or thought he had. And so he had taken it with him to compare it to the plants in the poison garden. When he discovered that what he had suspected was correct, that the flower in the kitchen was not just poisonous, but deadly, he had removed my makeshift string barrier, and replaced it with a padlock and chain.

No, Jack's deep, dark secret was much more mundane than that. And instead of exonerating me, it only piled up the evidence against me – adding to the weight of reasons I might have wanted to cover up my liaison with him.

Jack was married.

When they realised I didn't know, the police took great delight in ramming the fact home, reminding me at every possible opportunity, as if they wanted to see me wince with pain afresh each time. But the truth was, I was beyond caring. What did it matter, if Jack already had a wife and a two-year-old back in Edinburgh? He had promised me nothing. And in the face of Maddie's death, none of it seemed important.

I would be lying, though, if I said that in the days and weeks and months since I've been in here I hadn't thought of him, and wondered why. Why hadn't he told me about her? About his little boy? Why were they living apart? Was it financial – was he sending money back to them? If the Elincourts were paying him half as much as they'd offered me, it was more than plausible that he'd taken the job for money reasons.

But maybe not. Perhaps they were separated, estranged. Perhaps she'd thrown him out, and this offer of a job, with a flat attached, had been the perfect way to move on.

I don't know, because I never had the chance to ask him. I never saw him again, after I was taken down to the station for questioning, and then cautioned, and then remanded in custody. He never wrote. He never phoned. He never visited.

The last time I saw him was as I stumbled into the back of a police car, still covered in Maddie's blood, feeling his hands gripping mine, strong and steady.

'It'll be all right, Rowan.' It was the last thing he said to me, the last words I heard as the car door slammed shut behind me and the engine started up.

It was a lie. A lie, from first to last. I was not Rowan. And nothing was ever going to be all right again.

But the thing I keep coming back to is what Maddie said to me that very first time I met her, her arms wrapped hard around me, her face buried in my top.

Don't come here, she had said. *It's not safe.*

And then, those last words, sobbed in parting, and later denied, words that I am still certain I heard, months later.

The ghosts wouldn't like it.

I don't believe in ghosts, Mr Wrexham. I never have. I'm not a superstitious person.

But it was not superstition that I heard pacing the attic above me, night after night. It was not superstition that made me wake in the night, shivering, my breath white clouds in the moonlight, my room cold as an icebox. That doll's head, rolling across the Persian rug, that was real, Mr Wrexham. Real as you and me. Real as the writing on the walls of the attic, real as my writing to you now.

Because I know, I know that's when I really sealed my fate with the police. It wasn't just the fake name, and the stolen documents. It wasn't just the fact that I was Bill's estranged daughter, come back to exact some sort of twisted revenge on his new family. It wasn't any of that.

It was what I told them on that first awful night, sitting there in my bloodstained clothes, shaking with shock and grief and terror. Because that first night, I broke down and told them everything that had happened. From the footsteps in the night, to the deep, seeping sense of evil I felt when I opened the attic door and stepped inside.

That, more than anything that came after, was the moment the key turned in the lock.

That was when they *knew*.

I've had a lot of time to think in here, Mr Wrexham. A lot of time to think, and ponder, and figure things out since I started this letter to you. I told the police the truth, and the truth undid me. I know what they saw – a crazed woman, with a backstory more full of holes than a bullet-pocked signpost. They saw a woman with a motive. A woman so estranged from her family that she had come to their house under false pretences, to enact some terrible, unhinged revenge.

I know what I think happened. I have had a long time to put pieces together – the open window, the footsteps in the attic, the father who loved his daughter so much that it killed her, and the father who walked away from his children again and again and again.

And most of all, two pieces I never connected right up until the very end – the phone, and Maddie's white, pleading little face, that very first day as I drove away, and her whispered, anguished *the ghosts wouldn't like it.* And those two things were what did for me with the police. My fingerprints on the phone, and my account of what Maddie had said to me, and the domino of effects her words began.

But at the end of the day, it doesn't matter what I think, or what my theories are. It's what the jury thinks that matters. Listen, Mr Wrexham, I don't need you to believe everything that I've told you. And I know that presenting even half of what I've said here would get you laughed out of court, and risk alienating the jury forever. That's not why I told you all this.

But I tried to give just part of the story before – and it's what got me locked up here.

I believe that the truth is what will save me, Mr Wrexham, and the truth is that I didn't, that I *couldn't* kill my sister.

I picked you, Mr Wrexham, because when I asked the other women in here who I should get to represent me, your name came up more than any other lawyer. Apparently you've got a reputation for getting even no-hopers off the hook.

And I know that's what I am, Mr Wrexham. I have no hope any more.

A child is dead, and the police, and the public, and the press, they all want someone to pay. And that someone must be me.

But I didn't kill that little girl, Mr Wrexham. I didn't kill Maddie.

I loved her. And I don't want to rot in jail for something I didn't do.

Please, *please* believe me.

Yours truly,
Rachel Gerhardt

8 July 2019

Richard McAdams

Ashdown Construction Services, internal post

Rich, bit of a funny one, one of the guys working on the Charnworth redevelopment found this pile of old papers when he was ripping out a wall. Looks like one of the prisoners hid them. He didn't know what to do with them so he passed them to me and I said I'd ask around. I've only glanced at the top few, but looks to be a bunch of letters from an inmate to her solicitor before her trial – don't know why they were never posted. The guy who found them leafed through, and says it was quite a well-known case, he's a local from round here, and he remembered the headlines.

Anyway, he felt a bit awkward chucking them in the skip in case they were evidence or legally privileged or something, and he ended up on the wrong side of the law by destroying them. TBH I don't imagine it matters now – but to put his mind at rest, I said I'd see it was properly dealt with. Is there anyone in management you could sound out about it? Or do you think just ignore and bin? Don't want to get tied up in a load of paperwork.

The top part is her letters to the lawyer, but she'd also hidden a few letters written to her in the same place. They seem to be just family stuff, but I'm sticking them in the packet as well, just in case.

Anyway, be very grateful if I could leave it with you to decide what to do, if anything.

Cheers,
Phil

1 November 2017

Dear Rachel,

Well. It feels very strange addressing you by that name, but here we are.

I must start by saying how sorry I am about what happened. I imagine that's not what you expected me to say, but I am, and I'm not ashamed to say it.

What you must understand is that I have watched over those children for the best part of five years now – and I've watched more nannies come and go than I've had hot dinners. I was the one who had to sit and watch while that baggage Holly carried on with Mr Elincourt under his wife's nose, and I was the one who patched everything up when she walked out and left the girls in bits. And since then, I've had to sit there and watch as nanny after nanny came and went, and broke those poor bairns' hearts a bit more every time.

And every time they came, and they were another pretty young lass, I felt it like a cold hand around my heart and I lay awake at night and I wondered – should I tell Mrs Elincourt what kind of a man her husband was, and what kind of a woman that Holly was, and why she really left? And every time I found I couldn't do it, and I swallowed my anger, and I told myself it would be different next time.

So I confess, when I met you, and found out that Mrs Elincourt had hired yet another pretty young girl, my heart sank. Because I knew what he would be up to, and whatever kind of girl you were, whether you were one to make the most of your opportunities, like Holly, or one who shrank from him, I knew either way those poor children would be the ones to suffer again when you upped and left, maybe taking him with you this time. And that made me very angry. Yes it did. I'm not ashamed to say that. But I am ashamed of how I treated you – I should not have taken my anger out on you like that, and I feel heart sorry when I think back on some of the things I said to you. Because whatever the police say, I know that you would have walked a mile over glass before you hurt one of those little lassies, and I told the officer who interviewed me so, I wanted you to know that. I said, I did not like that girl, and I made no secret of it, but she would not have hurt wee Maddie, and you are barking up the wrong tree, young man.

So anyway, that is partly why I am writing. To say all of that to you, and get it off my chest.

But the other reason is because Ellie has written you a letter. She put it in an envelope and sealed it up before she gave it to me, and she made me promise not to read it, and I said I would not. I have kept that promise, because I think you should keep your word, even to children, but I must ask you, if there is anything in that letter you think I should know, or anything that you think her mother should know, you must tell us.

There is no point in writing to the house, for it is shut up, and God knows Mrs Elincourt has enough on her plate to worry about, poor woman. She has left her husband – did the police tell you that? She has taken the children and moved back down south to her own family. And Mr Elincourt has moved away too – there is some sort of lawsuit against him connected with an intern at his firm, or so they are saying in the village, and the rumour is that the house will have to be sold to pay for the legal fees.

But I am putting my address at the bottom of this letter, and I ask that if you have any concerns, you write to me there, and I will do whatever needs to be done. I have faith that you will do that, for I believe that you loved those children, as I did and do. I don't believe you will let any harm come to Ellie, will you? I have prayed to God, and tried to listen to His answer, and I am trusting you on this, Rachel. I pray that you won't let me down.

Yours very sincerely,
Jean McKenzie
15a High Street,
Carn Bridge

To:

From:

Subject:

Dave Owen only they said that your name is Rachel is that true
   I miss you a lot and I am fairy very sorry about what happened
especially because it's all my fault but I can't tell anyone especially not mummy or Daddy because they will be so angry and then
daddy will go away like he tried to before like Maddie always said
he would
   it was me Rowan I pushed mad he because she was going to
make you go away like the others she made all the others go
away by playing tricks with Mummy's old phone she took their
things and she kind into the Attic window up the roof from your
room the Attic was her secret den where she always went but
she said I was too little to climb up and the she made the happy
wake them up in the night and she took a YouTube video and
played it on the speakers on the happy to make it sound like
there was people in the Attic walking around but it wasn't it was
just the video and she took the dollies head out of the attic and
she made me put the doggies head on your lap and I am so sorry
because I said it wasn't true and it was it was me who did that
   she woke up and you weren't there and mad he was going
to poison you with you berries but I ran after her and I poured
the wine down the sink and then Maddie was fairy angry and

339

she said she said she was going to climb into the attic window again and get you into trouble with Mummy by setting off all the alarms because you had gone and I ran after her an eye asked not to do it and she said no I will do it or she will take Daddy away and I said no don't Rowan with nice and I don't want her to go she wouldn't do that and mad he said I'm going to a new can't stop me and she kind up and I pushed her I didn't mean for 2 happen and I am so sorry

please please please don't tell the police Rowan I don't want to go to prison and I am so sorry but it isn't fair for you to get told off for a thing I did so can you just say that it wasn't you and that you know who did it but you can't say who because it's a secret but it wasn't you

we are going away tomorrow to a new house daddy can't come right now but I hope you can I love you please come back soon love Ellie elancourt age 5 goodbye

ACKNOWLEDGEMENTS

Thank you so much to the tireless team of editors, publicists, marketeers, designers, sales reps, rights people, production editors, and everyone who works behind the scenes. That the book you hold in your hands is beautiful, readable and exists at all is largely down to their efforts.

To Alison, Liz, Jade, Sara, Jen, Brita, Noor, Meagan, Bethan, Catherine, Nita, Kevin, Richard, Faye, Rachel, Sophie, Mackenzie, Christian, Chloe, Anabel, Abby, Mikaela, Tom, Sarah, Monique, Jane, Jennifer, Chelsea, Kathy, Carolyn and everyone at Simon & Schuster and PRH, my heartfelt thanks.

Thanks also to Mason, Susi and Stephanie for being the very best readers.

To Eve and Ludo, guardian ninjas, thank you for always having my back.

To my fabulous writer friends – online and off – thank you for keeping me sane and laughing.

And of course to my family – thank you for being there, and for not making me live in a smart house.